END OF WAR

END OF WAR

METAL LEGION™ BOOK EIGHT

CH GIDEON

DISRUPTIVE IMAGINATION

LMBPN Publishing
PMB 196, 2540 South Maryland Pkwy
Las Vegas, NV 89109

First US edition, March 2020
Version 1.01, March 2020
eBook ISBN: 978-1-64202-780-8
Print ISBN: 978-1-64202-781-5

DEDICATION

We can't write without those who support us. On the home front, we thank you for being there for us.

We wouldn't be able to do this for a living if it weren't for our readers. We thank you for reading our books.

THE END OF WAR TEAM

Thanks to our Beta Readers

Micky Cocker, James Caplan, Kelly O'Donnell, and John Ashmore

Thanks to the JIT Readers

Dave Hicks
James Caplan
Kelly O'Donnell
Peter Manis
Diane L. Smith
Debi Sateren
John Ashmore
Micky Cocker
Misty Roa
Jeff Goode
Jeff Eaton
Paul Westman
Rachel Beckford

If we've missed anyone, please let us know!

Editor
Lynne Stiegler

ACRONYMS

- AP = Armor Piercing
- APC = Advanced Personnel Carrier or Armored Personnel Carrier
- CAC = Command And Control center
- CIG = Commander Intercept Group
- CIP = Combat Interceptor Patrol
- DIE = Durgan Industrial Enterprises
- ER = Extended Range
- FGF = Fleet Ground Force
- FOB = Forward Operating Base
- HE = High Explosive
- HQ = Headquarters
- HUD = Heads Up Display
- HPC = Heavy Plasma Cannon
- HVM = hyper-velocity missile
- HWP = Heavy Weapons Platform
- ILPF = Illumination League Peacekeeping Force
- KPH = kilometers per hour
- LRM = Long-Range Missile

- LZ = Landing Zone
- MIRV = Multiple Independently-targetable Reentry Vehicles
- MRM = Mid-Range Missile
- P2P = Point to Point
- PD = Point Defense
- PDF = Planetary Defense Force
- POI = Point of Interest
- RAP = Rocket Assisted Projectile
- SAM = Surface-to-Air Missile
- SOM = Surface-to-Orbit Missile
- SOP = Standard Operating Procedure
- SRM = Short-Range Missile
- TAC = Terran Armor Corps
- TFMC = Terran Fleet Marine Corps
- THCG = Terra Han Colonial Guard
- TRMC = Terran Republic Marine Corps
- ZOC = Zone of Control

GATEKEEPER

"Fuck yeah!" Major Trapper howled. "Bring it, girlfriend."

"Who are you talking to?" Colonel Lee "Roy" Jenkins asked over the point-to-point communication channel.

"Relax, Colonel. I got this. One *'Keeper* ready to tie up in a nice neat bow for you Metalheads."

"I like my bows tied tightly. Patching Jem to you. Looks like he's got the front door unlocked. Good hunting, Major."

"Roger." The major looked left and right. Twenty Marines, a full platoon, filled the dropship, but there was no drop coming. They would grapple the hull of the *GateKeeper* and enter through the massive cantilevered door protecting a suspected hangar bay. The Marines would enter using suit propulsion. They counted on a hangar bay having a pressure lock to allow access to the interior of the ship.

That was their hope. The plan would go FUBAR in a hurry if there wasn't.

"Opening the doors now," Jem reported.

Major Trapper could feel the adrenaline surge through his body the closer they came to entering the ancient ship. Helmets bobbed and boots tapped as the Marines sought to control their energy before being allowed to unleash it on a potential enemy.

"Don't blow up anything you shouldn't," Trapper told them over the open channel.

"Taking the fun out of it," someone replied, earning a bunch of snickers.

"Secure the ship. There probably isn't anyone on board. Just automated systems. First jarhead to kill a cleaning bot cooks the rest of us dinner."

"Pretty harsh, don't you think, sir?" Sergeant Traya Wu asked. As the platoon sergeant for the Solarian Marines, he didn't want any of his people getting shamed.

"Better than hacking off a hand," the major shot back before finishing on a better note. "There's only fifty of us. It won't be that bad. The easy answer is, don't be blowing away maintenance or cleaning bots. Shouldn't be hard, unless you've had too many crayons for lunch."

"How long is that joke gonna continue?" Wu wondered.

"Probably a couple hundred more years. I don't even know what a crayon is, but it's supposed to be funny." The major stood in the middle of the troop bay, anchoring his boots to the deck using the magnetic locks. "Enough bullshit. We need this ship. We need every asset we go after, and we need to get them without taking any losses. In a war of attrition, we lose. If we lose, humanity loses. Don't fuck this ship up. We need it. Bad."

"Aye, aye, Major," the Marines replied in unison.

Major Trapper studied the immensity of the ship on his suit's heads up display, the HUD, where the dropship projected a tactical display tracking the approach to target. The other Marines looked on with interest.

"We're going to be like fleas on a whale's ass," Private Ayala suggested.

"Have you ever slept in a tent with a mosquito?" Trapper

countered. "It'll be just like that. Prepare to disembark, on my command."

The dropship closed on the hull, traveling along its length like a bird soaring close to the ground. It slowed and entered the open hangar bay, to find it wasn't a place for ships. It opened up, wide and rounded.

"Do you think this is where they store the gates they seed throughout the universe?" Wu asked.

The answer appeared when they continued farther into the ship—a gate, ready for deployment, with another stored behind it as if they could be spun into space like flying discs.

"They don't just move the gates around in this thing. I think this is where they're built." Trapper looked for a landing area.

"Two o'clock high," the sergeant noted. The dropship's cameras rotated and zoomed to display a landing platform. "Looks narrow."

Sergeant Wu did a quick headcount. He was 1st Squad leader. Rast, Lindt, and Bing were in charge of 2nd, 3rd, and 4th Squads. The major filled the role of platoon sergeant as well as platoon commander, chief morale officer, and master bottle washer. The last one he delegated when he could, but the Marines operated independently. They all washed their own dishes at one point or another during an op. With the losses incurred by the Metal Legion during recent operations, they all made do. Every unit was now task-organized, a euphemism for kludged together from whoever was left.

They all had combat experience. They could speak freely with the major because he knew they'd earned their chops.

Trapper saw Wu counting heads. "Squad leaders, report." The major could have used his HUD to verify, which he did. The unit was green, but sometimes, one had to do things the old way. Reinforce the chain of command and show the Marines you trust them to do their jobs.

"One is green," Wu replied.

"Two is cool," Rast noted.

"Three is green," Lindt reported.

"Four to score," Bing added. All twenty Marines gave the thumbs-up simultaneously. Ayala turned his hand upright to give the finger to a Marine opposite, earning the bird in return.

"Cut the bullshit," Trapper said softly. "Mark the platform. 1st Squad to the door. 2nd, 3rd, and 4th, provide security at three, six, and nine o'clock. Dropship dust-off after delivery. Launch a relay drone into whatever the hell this cavern is called. Time to clear the ship, five seconds. Prepare to move out."

One of 4th Squad's Marines sent a drone skipping away into the vast gate launch bay of the immense ship.

Major Trapper watched the display and simultaneously counted down, his gloved fingers held high for all to see. The Marines unbuckled their harnesses and magnetically sealed their boots to the deck. The dropship swooped up, then jerked to a halt mid-maneuver, and the rear deck dropped. The Marines unlatched and ran. Trapper was first out, accelerating away from the ship. Squads separated when they hit the ramp, forming a security perimeter as the dropship headed for a corner away from anything that looked important.

Trapper stopped at a wide door that looked to open vertically. He wondered what kind of vehicles or personnel used it. He didn't waste more than a few nanoseconds contemplating it, though. The only use for it that mattered at this moment was for his Marines to get inside the ship.

Wu held up explosives, but Trapper shook his head.

The major activated his point to point, P2P, comm channel. "Trapper to Jem. Tell me you can get this door where we are open. Otherwise, things are going to get sticky. Blowing shit up is not my idea of ingratiating ourselves with our hosts."

"There is no information that anyone is alive aboard the

'*Keeper*. I have access and will activate it, but only after the main door is closed, at which point we will lose contact. Rest assured you won't be abandoned on the platform."

Trapper activated his rear-facing camera, and with growing trepidation, watched the great hangar bay door close. He looked for an access panel in case Jem didn't come through but trusted the explosives to do the job if needed. Blowing holes in airlocks wasn't optimal when it came to maintaining ship integrity. His orders had been clear: Capture the '*Keeper* intact and secure for further exploitation.

That's an easy order for the pencil pushers to give, Trapper thought. But then again, the order had come from Colonel Jenkins. If any commander had been deeper in the shit with his troops than Jenkins, Trapper didn't know who, besides the venerable former leader of the TAC, General Benjamin Akinouye. *Do or die. There is no try.*

Without a sound, the great door closed and sealed. Major Trapper held his breath for the few heartbeats it took before the door in front of him started retracting into the overhead.

"Stay frosty. Eyes front, Marines," Trapper ordered. The outward-facing security squads turned about to face the door. Wu's squad spread out evenly in front of the opening, prepared to engage. The door opened slower than he was comfortable with.

"On your faces," he barked through the 1st Squad comm channel. Instantly, the Marines dropped prone and aimed their railguns into the space beyond the door. Wu stayed on his knee, ready to assault forward if needed to neutralize an enemy. As the door continued to rise, the lights came on within, offering a welcoming environment of tables and chairs. Two bots trundled forward, but nothing like they'd ever seen before.

"Hold fire," Wu said before tactically moving forward, eyes over the barrel of his weapon, staring at the bots. Two Marines joined him without having to be told, while the final two maneuvered to a kneeling firing position.

Trapper strode past the front rank and waved 1ˢᵗ Squad's last two Marines to both flanks. He delivered the hand signal ordering 3ʳᵈ and 4ᵗʰ Squads to follow in trace. 2ⁿᵈ Squad was to provide rear security, but from within the space.

He moved past the bots he surmised to be for serving guests since he thought the space was a first-class lounge of some sort. It was immaculate, but it could have been thousands of years or maybe even thousands of generations since it last served a customer.

"I'm sorry. We'll have to pass on the tapas, but maybe next time. Please make sure you have some whiskey for my people when we return. They're a thirsty lot," he said using the suit's external speakers.

A Marine snickered at the jibe.

Sergeant Rast activated the platoon-wide channel. "Door is closing behind us. Secured. Looks like we're in."

"That's what she said," Private Ayala quipped.

"Stow it," Trapper shot back. The hairs on the back of his neck were standing up.

The bot started speaking, but the language was unintelligible. It kept repeating the phrases but started inserting English. "*Bega'luWa obran De'*is'to service. *Bega'luWa whiskey De'*is'to service. We are whiskey De'is'to service. We are whiskey at your service."

"I think I love this ship, Major," Wu said, keeping his eyes on the bots. "Tell them to bring the whiskey to us."

"Your atmosphere for maximum comfort while resting," the bot said in unaccented English.

"Confirm," Trapper reported. "Oxygen, nitrogen atmosphere has been established, with an Earth-normal gravity of one-point-zero gees. Damn. That was fast."

1st Squad moved into the massive lounge, leaving the bots behind. Wu gestured for 3rd Squad to branch right and 4th to go left. The space was as large as a cricket pitch. His five Marines couldn't cover the numerous exits.

"Jem?" Trapper tried on his P2P. The channel was dead, cut off cleaner than a cigar cutter snipping off the end of a nice smoke.

The Marines covered the front, flanks, and rear, freezing in place to await further orders. "Checking the doors, Major, one at a time. Cover me," Wu stated.

He eased forward, stowing his railgun to free his hands. He ran the sensor-heavy gloves along the seams of what he assumed was a doorway. He verified the data, unable to penetrate beyond a couple of centimeters, but it was enough. He found the mechanism to release the door embedded in the wall at chest height to his suit.

"The builders must have been a bit taller than the average Joe," Wu remarked before tapping the wall at the mechanism. Nothing happened. "Trying it with a bare hand."

He popped his glove free and held it in his off-hand as he tapped the right side of the doorway. It started to cycle. He rushed to put his glove back on, but the door receded upward with a swish before he could reestablish his suit's integrity. A laser lanced the opening, delivering a beam directly to the chest of Wu's Gamera-class combat armor.

2

THE ZEEN WORLDSHIP

The insectoid-like Zeen approached the single-seat Viper. "Despite the fineness of it, you have a bony ass, Major," Commander Knighton told Xi Bao as the metalhead balanced on the pilot's lap in one of the most uncomfortable travel configurations ever devised. Both women intently watched the Zeen.

"There's no way this would pass safety protocols," Xi replied, ignoring the flirtatious comment.

"It's the benefit of being a bunch of brigands. We get to make our own rules in order to save the galaxy from itself."

"Is the atmosphere established enough to pop the lid on this can?" Xi asked.

"How would I know? I can't see the dash or the HUD, or much of anything."

Xi looked for the digital gauge until she found out. "Shows an even twenty-one percent. Go ahead and pop us. I've had as much Viper fun as I can stomach."

"Is that O_2 reading inside or outside?"

"How the fuck would I know?" Xi wanted to glare at the woman, but there was no room to move in the small cockpit.

Had the major been any larger than she was, they would not have been able to pull off the transfer to the Zeen worldship.

"Did you flip the switch to external?" Knighton waited until she thought she could hear Xi grinding her teeth in anger. "It's right below the O2 gauge. It should be depressed for external."

Xi punched the button in. "Fifteen percent and climbing," the major reported with a huff. She steadied her breathing as the Zeen reached an articulated arm over the stubby wing of the space fighter and tapped the cockpit screen. "Nineteen percent. Good enough. Pop it."

The commander fumbled around Xi's nether regions until she roughly yanked a lever into Xi's right butt cheek.

"Damn, Commander! Your foreplay sucks something fierce. Maybe you should practice on a CPR dummy or something."

The Zeen looked oddly at Xi. "Asymmetry," it said through its translator, but unlike the last time she was on a worldship, she couldn't determine if the voice was masculine or feminine.

"The Zeen-Vorr-Terran Alliance retains its symmetry," Xi replied.

"Symmetry."

Xi climbed out, balancing on the wing for a moment before jumping to the landing deck of the worldship.

The cockpit closed, and Knighton powered up her Viper. "Got my orders, Major. Returning to the *Mencken*. It's been real, and it's been fun, but it hasn't been real fun."

"No shit," Xi agreed. "I'll call for my ride when I need it."

"I think you're already inside it. Enjoy your liaison duties, Major." Commander Knighton lifted off, rotated slowly to face the energy screen keeping the atmosphere in, and launched into the open area, bursting through to the void of space.

Bao faced her escort. "It's my honor to be on *Zeen Home Three*. The Terrans have a favor to ask," she started, but she stopped when the insectoid began to walk away. She hurried after it. "What is your name, or designation, or way I can address you besides, 'Hey you?'"

"Zeen understand human need for designations. Individual asymmetry allows symmetry for your species."

"Symmetry," Xi agreed. "So, what do I call you?"

"Hive has no designations. For purpose of human ambassador to Zeen, you are to call this Zeen Bob."

Xi snorted. "Bob? If that's how you want it. I was thinking more like Augustus the Fourth, Conqueror of the Unknown Worlds."

"Asymmetry. Bob. Symmetry."

"Spelled the same forward and backward. I understand." Xi cut to the purpose of her visit. "The Terrans need Zeen help to take the fight to Jemmin."

"Zeen have predicted this. Worldship plus *GateKeeper*. Symmetry."

"We have Marines aboard the *'Keeper* right now, securing it for us, or preventing Jemmin from securing it. Both achieve a similar goal, but I'm a fan of keeping it for our sole use."

"Vorr will be hostile to Terran efforts," the Zeen stated with surprising clarity. The insectoid towered over her as they walked at a good clip toward the center of the worldship. There they would descend past multitudes of Zeen in hibernation and thousands of ships—mainly space fighters, but some larger vessels, all contained neatly within the worldship.

"If things go as planned, Vorr and Jemmin will both become lesser powers by the end of this. We call this operation 'End of War.'"

"Galactic peace will create a void that must be filled to reestablish symmetry."

"Not if the humans are already there." Xi had to jog to keep up with the long-legged insectoid.

"Terran hierarchies poorly suited."

"The Zeen will help us, of course," Xi replied. "But it must be done. A galaxy under Jemmin or the Vorr is unacceptable. Asymmetry exists now. Time for the humans, the predators to take the reins."

"Zeen-Terran alliance. Not food. Symmetry."

"Every other jackwagon out there is food. Jemmin. Vorr. Finjou. Arh'kel. Brek. It's time to slap the shit out of them, if you get my drift."

"Asymmetry." The Zeen insectoid reached a precipice beyond which an empty tube descended into the depths of the worldship.

Xi peeked over. The hole appeared bottomless.

"Step." Bob didn't hesitate. The insectoid stepped into the abyss.

"Not food," Xi said. "Just until I turn myself into road pizza when I hit the bottom." She looked once more. The Zeen descended at an easy rate, not falling out of control. "Where's a dropship when you need one?"

She closed her eyes and launched herself over the edge.

Bridge of *H.L. Mencken*

Chief Petty Officer Malkovich had transferred to the *Mencken* with Captain Podsednik to take over the tactical position. He scanned space in front of the heavily armored and modified assault carrier parked outside the New America 2 gate at a respectable stand-off distance from the Zeen worldship, called *Zeen Home Three*. The 'Keeper remained at an equal distance on the far side of the worldship.

"Space is clear," Malkovich reported to break the monotony.

The dimensions were identical, but many of the visible systems were upgraded versions of *Dietrich Bonhoeffer's*. Kinetic dampers, air cyclers, and even power conduits were all of designs fifty years newer than those of the destroyed assault carrier. It was an improved version of TAC's longtime flagship, and the time was fast approaching to determine if the upgrades would make enough of a difference in the upcoming op.

Dangerous on its own, but even better in the middle of the two-hundred ship fleet that was on its way, the *Mencken* stood ready to lead the convoy to the Jemmin homeworld, assuming Jem could find it. Jem remained uncertain.

Podsy worried about Jem. The effort to find the 'Keeper had depleted him significantly. The more they asked of Jem, the more it cost it. Jem was killing itself to support the humans in their war against Jemmin.

"I'll be in my quarters," Podsy told the bridge crew and strode briskly from the bridge, his fleet uniform covering his artificial legs. He had learned to drive the legs almost without thought, but it took tremendous effort for him to walk lightly. He didn't give it the thought required and clumped down the wide and modern corridors of his ship. The captain's quarters weren't far from the bridge, just in case he was needed. The captain was in charge of the ship. Sleep was neither guaranteed nor frequent.

Being tired was part of the job, but the time for stims was not yet. That would happen when they were asked for more, even all they had. Podsy ran his hand along the corridor's wall, which was covered with utility paneling that provided one more barrier to the cold of space. It could be pulled off to patch other holes. Everything on board the *Mencken* served multiple purposes.

Even Podsy. He entered his quarters, securing the door behind him.

"Jem. Resume synchronization test four seven."

"Resuming," Jem replied, its voice hollow in the spacious

quarters. Podsy threw himself on the couch and pulled an auxiliary terminal from the tabletop in front of him.

"We have to find an alternative to help your processing systems." Jem knew exactly what they were doing and why, yet Podsy felt obligated to reiterate it if for no other reason than to kill time. He felt useless during the processing tests, besides monitoring the progress.

Test four seven was headed toward catastrophic failure. The processing errors had piled up—twenty-four thousand, thirty, thirty-six thousand.

"Stop the test," Podsy ordered, exasperated. "Recalibrate number four eight. Offset sigma three."

"Captain Podsednik," Jem said. "These tests are impacting my ability to run other processes."

Podsy leaned forward on his couch and hung his head until he stared at the floor. "I don't want you to die, Jem."

"One assumes that I am alive. I am a gestalt intelligence made up of four hundred ninety-two forebears, some of the sharpest minds of the Jem'un. I am a finite resource for this device."

"If it's not more computing power, what is it?" Podsy was ready to give Jem the entire One Mind system if he asked, but his friend would not do that.

"It is life energy. I am using what has been allocated to this device. If you are able to defeat Jemmin, then the Jem'un's final act in creating me will not have been in vain. Is it not better to go out fighting, according to the Metal Legion?"

"Damn, Jem. Don't pull that on me. We're doing everything we can to protect you. You have helped the Terrans more than any other single entity in the history of humanity. You drop the bomb that the Vorr are also in possession of a gestalt intelligence and then leave us hanging. How can we outsmart the other Jem'un and the Vorr lackeys if you've gone out like a supernova?

We need you on our side, Jem." Podsy stood and started to pace, clumping back and forth across his quarters.

Jem waited while Podsy worked through his concerns.

"As you wish, Jem. Stop testing my parameters, but you gotta help me to help you. There has to be something we can do."

"If you can recover the other gestalt intelligence, we may be able to merge, prolonging both our lives by becoming a single entity."

"I'll add that to my to-do list. You have any idea where they might be hiding their Jem'un?"

"Someplace extremely secure, I suspect."

"So, just like us," Podsy quipped, gesturing to his quarters and the greater ship beyond. "I bring you the assault carrier *Mencken*, carrying the most dedicated and committed fighting force ever assembled."

Podsy was only half-kidding.

"If Terran forces take the battle to the Vorr as well as Jemmin, my continued existence will be the least of our worries. The survival of the human race should be of greater concern. The die is cast, as you might say. I don't believe in fate, because there are always variables within one's control while being interdependent with other variables. One must account for what can be accounted for and influence that which can be influenced. I promised to be open with you. This mission to Jemmin has a low probability of success because the variables that cannot be controlled far outweigh those that can. The calculations show that a great deal of what you call 'luck' is called for."

"When we throw the dice, we're never looking for snake eyes or boxcars, but sometimes they come up anyway." Podsy stopped walking around. "Something is percolating. I need to talk to Colonel Jenkins."

Captain Podsednik hurried from the room, leaving Jem to wonder what the revelation was.

General Pushkin scowled darkly at the main screen in the conference room he'd taken over as his main Tactical Armor Corps (TAC) command post. "Where are they?" he growled, not directing his demand at Colonel Cao from the Solarian Marines, even though it was Solar forces they were waiting for. "Two hundred ships. The Zeen worldship is right there, along with the 'Keeper, and we have the *Mencken* and a few cats and dogs to protect them."

"I suspect they can protect themselves," Colonel Jenkins interjected. The air in the room grew heavy as the three men sat in uncomfortable silence. When no answers were forthcoming, General Pushkin helped himself to a cup of water, drinking slowly.

"Ideas?" Pushkin requested.

The colonel leaned forward, steepling his fingers over the conference table. "Do we have to have warships? What about freighters? We can increase our throw weight out there. Every platform is a good platform."

"Cannon fodder, Colonel. We condemn those crews to death."

Jenkins clenched his teeth. They'd had this argument before. It was the fight for the continuing existence of the human race. Pushkin saw it as another battle in a greater war.

"It's the end of the war, General. This is the final push."

Pushkin's demeanor changed. He tapped the computer screen on the table before him. "Comm, get me Admiral Corbyn."

After a short delay, Comm replied, "Patching him through now."

"General, what can I do you out of?"

Pushkin hadn't been ready for the quip. "We are thinking out loud and need your opinion. I'm here with Colonels Jenkins and Cao. Without word of the inbound military fleet, we were thinking to load up on freighters to bolster our numbers."

Jenkins appreciated that the general had said "we" instead of making it sound like Lee's plan. Good leaders did those kinds of things.

"We are working on just such a plan over here, General." The admiral was currently riding the *Sima Yi*, a Republican-class dreadnought. The massive ship gave the humans the combat capability necessary to stand toe to toe with the technologically superior Vorr and Jemmin, even if only for a short while. The ship's throw weight and offensive punch still needed escorts, of which the TAC's small conglomeration was significantly short. "We're taking the fight to the enemy, so we need logistics forward. We won't have any train back here. Not to Terra, not to Sol. We need to take it all with us."

"That's not how we were thinking," Pushkin said, shifting in his chair as the weight of their actions continued to increase. "We need support from the home front."

"We *want* support from the home front, but you know how that's going to be. Just asking is going to be dangerous for whoever answers the call." Corbyn's voice sounded tired, despite his attempts at being upbeat. "Alice can be convincing to the private sector, which is where any freighters would come from."

Leeroy choked back his feelings. "She hasn't been heard from since the media was taken off the air."

The small fleet of TAC ships had escaped, thanks to General Pushkin's relationship with Commodore Xin, whose mispositioned fleet had given TAC the opening they needed to get to the New America 1 gate. It was the last broadcast the team saw before transitioning across the event horizon.

The admiral quickly backtracked. "I'm sorry, Colonel. Anyone have an idea who we can tap to rally the militia, as it may be?"

"I think you would have been the best choice," Pushkin remarked, "at one time, but not right now. Someone has to keep the fleets intact."

"After Xi Bao," Jenkins muttered.

General Pushkin stiffened. He wasn't a fan of leading what had turned into a band of renegades and refugees, even though the TAC and the fleet carried most of the firepower available to humanity. He'd seen it before in the movies—a ragtag band running from an advanced enemy.

But the TAC wasn't so ragtag. They had teeth. He smiled inwardly.

"Xi isn't here. We need her working with the Zeen. They respect her, even though they determine everyone as either food or not food. She has earned all of humanity the designation of 'not food.' We owe her a debt of gratitude. I think you're our man, Lee. Rally the troops. As in, bring as many civilians on board to support the war effort as you can, something their governments are denying. In other words, business as usual, Lee. We'll break loose the destroyer *Blencathra* to take you to New America."

Lee contemplated the destroyer escort. An agile weapons platform, it reminded him of the torpedo boats of old—quick and hard to hit, carrying a heavy punch. Easy to destroy by nearly any modern weapon, especially those of the Vorr or Jemmin. What if New America started shooting before his message could be heard?

"I'm ready to go, General. I have one request. Please don't start the battle without me."

"*Powerslave* will be right where you left it. Don't be gone too long, Lee. This fight's all around us. It'll be best if we're not here when humanity arrives to stop us from saving them."

"Ain't that some shit?" Jenkins muttered as he stood to attention before hurrying from the conference room. When he hit the corridor beyond, he started running for the docking bay.

War waited for no man.

3

THE PRICE OF FREIGHT

The helm control officer aboard the *Blencathra* reported their imminent transit of the New America 1 gate. At their six o'clock and across the star system from the New America 2 gate waited three dreadnoughts, ready to repel any invaders coming from Nexus space. A Zeen worldship and the *'Keeper* appeared as pinpoints of light beyond.

"New America 2 is the most interesting place, don't you think?" Captain Van Dorn stated, hands behind his back. He always stood that way when transiting systems, despite the gees exerted on his body. He seemed to revel in the physical challenge to remain upright. His acceleration couch remained nearby, just in case. He would be the last one in and the first out when things got dicey. That wasn't now.

"It is the heart of our defense, it appears," Jenkins replied. "Aliens and humans alike. We stand ready to defend what's ours."

"We won't shoot Terran ships," the captain stated bluntly. "Or any human ship, for that matter. I don't want to be the one who instigates an intramural firefight. We have plenty of enemies out there, don't we?"

Van Dorn nodded toward the inky blackness of deep space.

"We do. More than we can handle, even if all humans were united in a singular purpose." The colonel hesitated. "But we're not, so we need to break out some trick plays. Are you ready to mark up the playbook, Captain?"

Van Dorn smiled. "I am." Captain Van Dorn of the Destroyer *Blencathra* hatcheted his arm toward the gate's image on the screen. "Take us through to New America."

The ship rotated with the gate, aligning while conducting intricate system checks to ensure the ship would be protected against the horrific forces pressing in from the event horizon. An unprotected ship would be crushed to its base atoms by not being prepared. They took no chances. Primary and secondary systems confirmed all was well. A tertiary redundancy also showed a green light. The ship slipped into the gate, and moments later, materialized in the New America star system.

Light traveled faster than the rockets fired at the destroyer. Engine plumes flared in the distance. Lights reflected off hulls in a line of ships, suggesting a blockade was in place.

"Evasive Maneuver Delta Four," Van Dorn ordered without hesitation. He gestured for Colonel Jenkins to take an acceleration couch while the stalwart captain took his position, adjusting his systems where he could see them. "I suggest you start transmitting your message, Colonel. I don't think we're going to be here for long."

The ship started twisting in space, accelerating smoothly through twelve gees while maintaining a nose-on orientation with the incoming missiles. "Prepare point-defense systems."

"Counterbattery?" the weapons officer inquired.

"No." The captain had just said he wouldn't kill humans. He wasn't so sure he would be able to keep that promise. His capital-grade railguns and ship-to-ship high-speed missiles could clear a path, but to where? Getting beyond the blockade would gain them nothing if they couldn't get back to the TAC fleet. "Point defense only. Helm, prepare to take us back through the gate."

Jenkins' mind raced. He strapped on his comm headset, fighting the g-forces to keep his hands moving. Wavelengths twisted like music across his eyepiece as he sought the right frequency. *I could use your help, Jem,* Jenkins thought. But the Jem'un wasn't there, so Jenkins would have to do it himself. A quick scan of the civilian frequencies and then a link-up, unencrypted. Freighters in a human-controlled system talking to each other. It was like a sunny day in the park for their captains.

"Attention, civilian space fleet. This is Colonel Jenkins of the Terran Armor Corps. You've seen what the Metalheads have done for humanity, on the newsfeeds and on the big screen. We're now fighting a war far away from home, far away from here. A war to save all of humanity. This isn't a battle on a distant planet. This is the end of it. This is our champion standing against their champion. Our David against their Goliath, but we need your help because it's not just one Goliath, but many. The battles before us string out like pearls on a necklace. We need everything you've got just to have a chance of winning, finally fighting our enemies at their house and not ours.

"That takes logistics. It takes numbers. And it takes willpower, which is the strength of all humans and something none of the aliens can understand. Join us at New America 2 in one day's time. Please, join the Metal Legion's fight for all humanity."

The *Blencathra* executed its loop and raced toward the gate, continuing a series of barrel rolls to stymie incoming projectiles from the blockade.

"You will stand down and prepare to be boarded," a voice ordered over the ship's main speakers. A new threat emerged from behind the gate. A heavy cruiser maneuvered slowly, seemingly lacking a sense of urgency.

Jenkins opened a private channel to Captain Van Dorn. "Is he giving us an opening to the gate?"

"We can get by, but we would expose our flank to his mains at point-blank range. One shot, and we'd be done." The captain chewed his lip before gritting his teeth and issuing the order. "Come about ninety degrees, pitch forty-five percent, flank speed. All hands, hold on."

The ship's engines redlined as Helm executed the maneuver, thrusters sending the nose up and over while the main engines added forward momentum. The destroyer creaked under the immense stresses put upon it. The acceleration couches gripped and squeezed the crew to keep most of them from passing out. Then the g-forces hit twenty-five, and even the most stalwart lost consciousness. The ship accelerated up and away from the blockade and the cruiser's efforts to put their target in a crossfire.

At fifteen gees, the crew started coming back to the present, even though the pressure held them immobile.

"Private channel to the cruiser's captain," Jenkins requested by grunting his words one at a time. Acceleration dropped to ten gees. The colonel still couldn't move but was able to flex his jaw enough to speak thanks to the couch's technology.

"Captain Xuwei. How can I help you?" The voice at the other end seemed calm and collected. Jenkins checked the board. The cruiser had stopped in front of the gate. The blockade ships were adjusting orientation but not pursuing the *Blencathra*. Colonel Jenkins mulled his response.

"Helm, slow us to a spiraling racetrack. Maintain forward momentum on the bow," Van Dorn ordered.

"Captain Xuwei, *ni-hao*. This is Colonel Lee Jenkins of the Terran Armor Corps. I'd love to deliver some witty banter, but we have no time. We have limited resources, and we're out here to drum up support for a ghost war that is all too real."

"That's why I answered your comm. You'll need to convince me this threat is real. I don't enjoy picket duty at New America. My family has grown up and moved away, but I'm a patriot, loyal to Terra. I've been told you're the enemy."

"We weren't the ones who fired," Jenkins said coldly.

"Following orders, Colonel. Unlike you, who seem to make up your own rules."

Jenkins struggled to find the words. Seven gees. When acceleration dropped below four, he could finally relax his jaw. "Sorry about the delay, Captain. Those gee forces put a real crimp in the brain bucket. I hear you on the orders, but you have to have received wildly conflicting orders that seem to defy reality. Life really is as simple as it seems, while also having complex elements that require further exploration. I expect you're not launching at us because there is doubt in your mind."

"Very perceptive. This is an encrypted private channel. If you ever share anything of this conversation, I will deny it. Do you understand?"

Jenkins relaxed but checked the board to make sure that no one was powering up to come after the *Blencathra*. He was pleased to see that three of the eight ships in the blockade had gone cold, cycling their engines for basic systems only.

"I understand." Jenkins wanted to remain noncommittal, even though he wasn't going to have to defend his actions before any more boards of inquiry. He was no longer playing that game.

"You are correct in orders we've received and their countermands. I believe we are on the verge of civil war, and I have no intention of joining the wrong side. The only problem is, I don't know who's wrong. It appears you are a third side, sure to irk the winner, no matter who that winner is. I go from a fifty percent chance of being right to zero. Those aren't the kinds of odds a warfighter prefers."

"If we remove the means for one side to overpower another, then no matter who wins, they'll still be toothless. We can talk about it after we've saved humanity. If we don't go out there right now and meet the enemy before he comes here, there will be no Terra and no Sol to fight over. For the record, Captain Xuwei, I'm a patriot too, loyal to all humanity."

The cruiser's captain clicked his tongue. Jenkins visualized him wanting to believe. He also wanted him out of the way so the *Blencathra* could fly through the gate and escape.

Freighter captains were pummeling the civilian channel, talking over each other as they argued both in support of TAC's request for help and against. Jenkins hesitated, but in the end, he couldn't let it go.

"Freighter captains. I don't know if any of you served in the military, but we need you. We can put you in the middle of a formation of heavies to protect you while you give us the means to continue fighting. In the end, all I can promise is the glory of saving humanity. If we don't win, none of it will matter. We'll die that much sooner than the others, but at least we will have tried."

"I was on New Australia when the Arh'kel arrived. I'm with you. I'm a hundred-megaton hauler running food-grade biomass. I'm accelerating toward you right now. Count me in, boss. This is the *Billy Spires*, over and out."

Before the colonel could reply, other freight drivers jumped into the mix, for and against. It degenerated into name-calling, with the word "traitor" being bandied about.

Captain Xuwei finally replied, "I see we have a number of freighters accelerating into the gate funnel, requesting permission for immediate passage through with a follow-on to the New America 2 gate. I expect that's your doing, Colonel."

"I requested assistance, but these civilian jocks make their own decisions."

"Cruiser is on the move," the weapons officer reported.

"Tactical!" Captain Van Dorn shouted. The main screen morphed into a tactical view of the situation. Five of the blockade ships showed flares as they kicked their engines into high gear and started moving. The cruiser accelerated away from the gate toward a flanking position opposite the *Blencathra*.

"What do you say we provide a cordon of honor for our brothers who will feed and clothe us, care for our wounded, and restock our armories?" Xuwei asked.

"I don't think we could do them any greater honor. Will you follow us through?" Jenkins asked, piping Van Dorn into the conversation.

"Yes. I shan't go first because they need to know that I'm coming. You've already seen the blockade break apart. It seems only three of those ships will be coming with us. Transmitting the identifiers of the other five to you. My wish is that they be allowed to retreat."

Three ships formed an inverted V and sailed toward the cruiser. Two broke away from the blockade, banking above and below the current orientation of the *Blencathra*. The final three ships started to slowly bring their engines to life. They turned their prows toward the system and started moving, well before their power plants reached max potential.

"Weapons, fire warning shots across the bow of the target designated Alpha Two," Van Dorn ordered.

The railguns spit hypervelocity tungsten through the void, drawing a curtain across the ship's line of flight.

"Send a postcard to Beta Four to let them know we're watching."

The weapons station targeted two long-range missiles,

sending them on a mission to flank the upper ship. Alpha Two immediately adjusted its flight profile, assuming a perpendicular pattern. The cruiser caught his attention with additional railgun fire. The small blockade frigate turned away and started accelerating to the greatest distance possible from both the TAC destroyer and the Terran cruiser.

Leaving only Beta Four, who maneuvered between the inbound missiles on a heading directly toward the *Blencathra*.

"Stand down, or you will be destroyed. Go your own way, Pilar. This isn't a fight you can win," Captain Xuwei stated over an open channel.

Jenkins climbed out of his acceleration couch and stumbled across the bridge to where Van Dorn was already on his feet. "How can we warn him off without hurting him?" Jenkins asked.

"How much damage are you willing to take to my ship?" the captain countered before turning to his weapons station. "Full spread. Railguns and missiles. Let him know he's not welcome to come any closer. Ready the pulse beam."

Weapons control tapped buttons and sent volley after volley of projectiles at the ship.

"Execute maneuver Alpha One," the captain ordered.

Helm tapped away, still in his couch.

"Incoming. PD systems hot. Launching countermeasures." Four missiles jumped from their canisters and drifted away from the destroyer, sounding bigger and louder than the actual ship. Active radars projected false sensor images of *Blencathra*.

Two inbounds attacked one of the decoy missiles. Another attacked the second. The third and fourth were ignored. Three missiles continued. Coil and chain guns unleashed a barrage of depleted uranium, enough to fill space with an invisible curtain. Two more missiles exploded in flight. The last clawed its way through the defensive fire, bouncing as no projectile penetrated the outer skin, only glancing and skipping away. The chain guns recycled and fired again. The missile exploded dangerously close. Blencathra rocked under the concussion.

"Distance to explosion?" Van Dorn asked.

"A hundred meters." Weapons Control checked the systems. "All green, cosmetic damage only."

"I'm done fucking around with this guy," Van Dorn stated.

"Missiles inbound." Helm pointed at the main screen.

All heads turned, eyes fixed on the plot. Missiles from the cruiser ripped across the void on a deadly intersect course with the Terran frigate.

The captain's fixation on attacking the *Blencathra* was his undoing. He never had a chance to respond. After the first missile penetrated the hull and exploded, scrambling the reactor, there was nothing left for the second missile to hit. The mini-supernova of the explosion shut down *Blencathra's* screens for a few moments.

"Board's clear," Weapons Control announced.

Van Dorn nodded to Jenkins. "What do you say we rally some freighters, Colonel? I think our point has been made. Comm, send our gratitude to Captain Xuwei and inform him we'll be preparing to transit the gate as soon as we have a count of the ships coming with us."

4

THE MARINES HAVE LANDED

Energies surged to accelerate the tungsten bolts to a hypervelocity, making the railguns bark as each projectile passed the speed of sound. In the enclosed space of the massive lounge, the weapons would have been ear-splitting for those not wearing armor.

"Cease fire!" Wu ordered, gesturing to his squad. Major Trapper moved close, weapon ready as he peered into the space beyond the door. A bot lay shattered, its pieces spread across the plush floor.

"What the hell is that?" Trapper asked, easing forward. "Cover me."

The Marines quickly selected their positions beside the door frame, holding firm to keep the major out of their lines of fire. Sergeant Wu directed the first two to hold and the second two to be ready to dive through the opening.

Major Trapper took a knee to better scan the remaining pieces. After studying them, he reached a conclusion. "Sergeant Wu," the major started. He checked the front plate of the Gamera combat armor. "That laser wasn't a weapon, was it?"

Wu shook his head inside his suit. "I don't believe so, sir. The suit did not register the hit or mark the bot as a threat."

"Ladies and gentlemen, our first kill on board the 'Keeper was a protocol bot measuring our very own Sergeant Wu for new clothes."

One of his squadmates slapped him on the back. "Where do I get mine?"

"Fuck off. You're wearing your dress uniform," the sergeant shot back.

Major Trapper checked the corridor visually and with the suit's short-range sensors. It was a dead-end, more of a fitting room than a passageway. "Looks like we're going to have to check them all. We need to find a way out of here and into the ship," Trapper remarked.

The Marines piled back into the main area.

Trapper pointed to Sergeant Bing. "Get me comm."

"Aye, aye, Major." The sergeant waved for his squad to follow. They ran toward the roll-up door that led to the landing platform, and once they reached it, they broke out a welding torch, tools, and the standard comm package of drones and transceivers.

"Wu, Rast, and Lindt. Check these doors to see if there is any way to tell them apart. I expect most are like the one we just went into. Find me the ones that are different."

With three suited salutes, the sergeants returned to their squads to issue the orders. Trapper knew the best way to guide Marines was to tell them the result he wanted and let them figure out how to get there. Trapper watched them get to work, splitting the room into three parts and sending their people to study the doors, both with their systems and the Mark One eyeball. There was nothing like seeing it for yourself to make a final determination. It was the human way.

"Personal memo, Major Trapper, Terran Marines. Belay

that. Delete and restart. Personal Memo. Major Trapper, Marine. The 'Keeper is an immense ship that at one time hosted aliens like an old-time cruise ship that plied the seas of Earth. Fancy dress and accommodations. Our entry into the 'Keeper was through the gate-launch bay, where we found at least three gates, seemingly ready for deployment. If we can figure out how to deploy them, we can change the odds. My mission is to secure the 'Keeper for further exploitation. I am adjusting the mission's parameters. I need to secure this ship for TAC use, to help us against an enemy who is closer to 'Keeper technology than Terran. We need this ship. We just have to figure out where the nerve center is and how to access it. One problem. This thing is as big as a planet, and we're trapped in a conference-sized room with bots that want to make clothes for us."

Trapper stopped dictating his log to watch the Marines of 2nd Squad as they seemed to find something interesting. It took Rast two seconds to figure it wasn't before signaling for the Marines to keep moving.

"Contact with Jem is important, even critical. Once we're into the guts of the ship, my order will be to split up two by two, with squad leaders in reserve. We have to cover more ground, unless Jem can direct us." Trapper thought he needed to say more but couldn't come up with anything that didn't sound like more whining. The Marines had a job to do.

"Where's my comm?!" Trapper barked.

The Zeen Worldship

The initial plunge twisted Xi's stomach in a knot right before flipping it over and slapping it hard. The fall slowed as she reached the mainstream of the shaft. Her guide spread himself to slow down, allowing her to catch up.

"I do not understand your fear," Bob said, gaining eloquence with each new phrase.

"I'm not a big fan of falling to my death. I like to have a lot of metal wrapped around me, with rockets to slow my descent. Once I'm on the ground, I like keeping my feet there."

"Not the descent, but the unknown regarding the speed of the fall. I understand. This is not like your usual planetfall. It is more like an elevator." The Zeen fell casually, limiting external movements to avoid rolling and twisting.

"I see that now." Xi tried to point and started to spin. She stopped her movements by lying spread-eagled across the wind and leveled out, wondering what mind had conceived that this was the best mode of moving individuals within the worldship. "How do you get back up?"

"Watch," the insectoid directed. He slipped his arms backward, creating small wings. He flew away from the center of the shaft. Before reaching the outer wall, the Zeen started upward.

Xi headed that way too, having no desire to land without her escort. She joined Bob by the wall before he reversed the maneuver and renewed his descent.

"I'll be damned." Xi relaxed during the seemingly endless fall. She guessed she could have made herself a torpedo to increase speed, but that seemed like it would have been an affront to the Zeen. She slowed her breathing and briefly closed her eyes.

"Symmetry," Bob said. "We find peace during transit. We join and descend as one."

It's not the destination, it's the journey, Xi thought.

Bob waved for Xi to follow as he maneuvered out of the main shaft, slowing his descent. When they reached a level that was not the bottom, he slid onto a platform, landing easily. Fearing she'd miss it, Xi torpedoed in, rolling to hit the platform shoulder first. She tumbled past the insectoid, breathing heavily when she finally came to rest. Bob looked at her oddly.

She stood and straightened her uniform. "Shall we?" she asked, looking at a nondescript corridor.

"You will get better over time." Xi thought Bob was trying to sound encouraging. Over time. How long was she going to be there? She settled for nodding, not caring whether Bob understood it.

She was still contemplating the time commitment when they entered a spherical chamber on a small trestle that led to the middle. Nothing represented the hive image more than what she saw. Individual hex-shaped compartments made up the walls. Zeen filled each of them, forearms on the ledges as they peered at her. From above to below, the Zeen remained still as Xi looked from one to the next, trying to tell them apart but failing miserably to find individual differences.

"Greetings to the Zeen hive," Xi stated softly, with her hands together. She bowed out of respect to the group.

Bob waved his arms. "Not food!" he declared, worried that her gesture would be taken as one of submission.

Xi quickly straightened. "Thanks, Bob. In human, that's being polite. Don't make me kill everyone here to show that I'm not food."

The insectoid called Bob stared at the small woman without blinking.

"That's called humor. Damn. This is going to be a long stay. In any case," Xi turned back to the inner part of the sphere and spread her arms wide to make herself look bigger, "I'm here to request your assistance in the fight against Jemmin."

"We agree," Bob translated after a series of clicks and arm-sawing gestures from the insectoids inside the honeycomb.

"That's it?" Xi wondered. Not being able to read the body

language or anticipate the countermoves of the Zeen created a rising anxiety within. She had not expected it to be that easy.

"There will be conditions to achieve symmetry."

There it is, Xi thought. "Let us discuss your conditions."

The Zeen shifted in their honeycombs, finally becoming animated. Xi watched with great interest but could discern nothing from their actions, only logging the movements for later study in case she could correlate them to actions. She needed more data points, as Lieutenant Styles would have said. How long ago would he have said that?

A lifetime and a half, or in TAC terms, a year.

"The human known as Xi Bao will remain with *Zeen Home Three.*"

"Can we rotate liaisons? I feel naked without my mech wrapped around me," Xi tried.

"Asymmetrical. Only Xi Bao."

Xi stood calmly while her mind launched a tirade of expletives. "What other conditions?"

"Terran fleet protects *Zeen Home Three.*"

Xi clasped her hands behind her back and paced two steps forward and two back on the narrow walkway through the middle of the spherical space. "Most ships will be responsible for their own defense, but *Zeen Home Three* will be at the back of any formations when we fly into enemy territory."

"Define enemy," Bob requested.

Moment of truth. Lying to the Zeen would get her nothing.

"Food is the enemy. Jemmin." Xi hesitated. Time to go all-in. "And the Vorr. And their lackeys the Arh'kel, even though we believe the Arh'kel are nothing more than a Jemmin bio-engineered weapon."

"Zeen-Terran Alliance. Symmetry." Bob was satisfied, as far as Xi could tell.

"No more Zeen-Vorr-Terran Alliance?"

"Asymmetry."

"Now you're speaking my language." Xi smacked her fist into her palm. The observers hanging out of the beehives clicked and beat their forelegs against the walls. "Yeah. Feel the power!" Xi slowly turned to take in the gathering—high, low, left to right.

Bob nudged her and spoke softly. "You are motivating the Zeen. We are ready to begin our journey to enemy space. Symmetry with Xi Bao and Terrans. Not food."

Xi smiled. "Not food, Bob. Let's go kick some ass, but I need to tell you one more thing." The insectoid waited for the revelation. "We're taking the *GateKeeper* with us."

5

PENETRATION

"No go on comm, Major," Sergeant Rast reported. "We've got relays set up between here and there, but we need that outer door open because it's made of something that's blocking our signal."

"Roger," Trapper confirmed. He didn't have to like it. He only had to accept that it was the truth. "Secure the comm and join 1st Squad. Sergeant Wu, tell me something good."

"'Something good,'" Wu repeated. "Still working it, Major."

Trapper gritted his teeth. He saw every minute as a waste of time, but his father, the infamous Sergeant Major Trapper, had told him to never be in a hurry to his own funeral. Slow and steady will win the race. The major tried to think what his father would do.

Kick over some rocks and see what was underneath. "4th Squad, check the floor and overhead," Trapper ordered.

Sergeant Bing immediately turned his Marines to scan the overhead areas and the flooring, kicking couches out of the way to see what was hidden beneath.

"I'll be damned, Major. You're like a hound dog." Bing

pointed at a space beneath one of the lounges, where an outline indicated an oversized maintenance access hatch.

"That's our way in. Bing, you found it, you take lead. Wu in reserve. 2nd and 3rd Squads, reinforce the breach."

The Marines moved into their tactical positions, looking more than ludicrous as their Gamera combat suits quickly filled the space around the hatch. Even Trapper couldn't see. Four railguns pointed at the hatch as Bing popped it and it slid into a recess into the floor. Wide steps led downward. Bing jammed his fist through the opening and scanned the space below. "Signal's bouncing. Looks like a passageway connecting to other major passageways. No activity as far as I can see, but conduits bordering the corridors are live with energy."

Trapper tapped one of the Marines on the shoulder, urging him to step aside. The major started to step into the opening, but Bing held out his arm.

"Please, sir. My squad will take the lead."

"Carry on, Sergeant," Trapper confirmed, pleased by his initiative. The major thought anyone was expendable because another Marine could take his place, but the least expendable was him. He wanted to lead from the front, and would when the time was right. For now, 4th Squad was on point. "Make us proud."

"Roger, 4th on point," Sergeant Bing confirmed.

Trapper tapped the feed from Bing's active scans. The passageway went straight as far as the pings reached, well over a kilometer before being blocked by corners. Various side passageways offered opportunities to split up.

"At the cross section half a klick down, 2nd Squad go left and 3rd Squad go right. Deploy a comm relay at the corner and keep going. Anywhere you take a turn, deploy a relay and send a report. I'll consolidate mapping data and disseminate," Major Trapper stated.

The corridor down which they traveled was easily large enough for the Marines in their oversized combat suits. It wasn't clear whether the originators had been giants or they used machinery that required the massive passages and spaces. Or maybe their technology wasn't concerned with efficiencies required for interior atmospherics and limitations on propulsion.

Clearly. The *'Keeper* was the most massive ship ever conceived, at least as far as the humans knew, and it seemed immune to the physics that constrained humanity. Trapper realized he was walking on a level surface and had been since they'd landed on the platform.

Artificial gravity.

"Captain Podsednik to Major Trapper. Come in, please." The voice was loud and clear on the Marines' squad channel. Instantly, Trapper held up his armored fist as the signal to freeze in place. The Marines stopped and held their weapons ready. They'd all heard the call.

"Trapper here. Good to hear your voice, Skipper." Trapper used the traditional Marine title for a boat captain or Marine captain.

"We had to open the gate hatch, but just a squeak. I figured you had placed repeaters, so we put a booster right outside the opening."

"I suggest you maintain this comm channel exactly as it is now. You think this ship is big from the outside, you should see it from in here." Trapper activated his system to link his data and mapping process with the *Mencken's* main computers. "Transmitting our data. We have penetrated the maintenance corridors, which seems to give us between-deck access throughout the ship, but it would be a tremendous help if you could tell us which way to go. We could spend the rest of our lives exploring this ship and not find what we're looking for."

"Processing your data now. Stand by."

Trapper wasn't a patient man, and being forced to wait chafed like cast iron underwear. He fidgeted within his suit.

"You shot up a protocol bot?" a new voice with a heavy Russian accent asked.

"General Pushkin. Thank you for that. Yes. We suspected it would dress us a million years out of fashion, and that simply will not do. Turns out, lacking fashion is a death sentence. If you're a protocol bot, anyway." Trapper chuckled to himself. *Wu owes us all a good steak.*

"I probably would have done the same thing, Major. It is hard keeping up with the fast-paced world of high-fashion," the general quipped.

"I have analyzed your data, Major," Jem interrupted. "I have partial access, but I'm going to need a physical link to one of the main data conduits. I need this to decrypt the *'Keeper's* processes."

"No sweat, Jem. What's it look like, and how do we tap it?" As he said it, he knew what the answer would be.

"I will know it when I see it."

"I was afraid you were going to say that. Just when I thought we might be saved from a blind pub crawl, we're back on it."

"I do not know what you reference," Jem admitted. "I will maintain access to the visual feeds from your platoon members, Major. The best chance of success is splitting up by individual to cover as much territory as possible."

"Two by two, Jem. We need to be able to cover each other in case the situation goes south."

A stream of unintelligible clicks sounded before Jem returned in its normal voice. "South is a relative direction. Have you encountered any hostility?"

"We have not," Trapper replied. "But it would be folly to think we're safe enough to scatter. Marines cover each other, and that is non-negotiable. We'll split into teams of two to cover as much ground as possible. I'll remain with Ayala and Jonas because someone has to keep an eye on them."

No one could see the major's wink, but the Marines snickered into their microphones before the sergeants started issuing orders. Major Trapper had randomly selected two Marines for no reason whatsoever except that he couldn't order everyone to buddy up and then defy his own order by stepping out solo.

"Pick up the pace. We're burning daylight. Split off and haul ass starting at this next intersection." Trapper watched the pair designations pop up on his HUD. Two by two.

4th Squad stepped off quickly, continuing their advance down the long corridor. 2nd and 3rd Squads split off right and left, leaving their squad leaders as the final pair. They debated for a moment before picking the corridor to the right because of a more extensive series of intersections nearby.

The suits took up most of the space in the corridor, and they traveled in a staggered configuration like a zipper since they couldn't move side by side.

"Problem up ahead, Major," Bing reported. Trapper saw it as one of many data streams crossing before his eyes. The corridor got shorter.

"Looks like crouch formation," Trapper replied.

"Crouching tiger, aye," Bing confirmed the unofficial posture for moving through interior passageways. The combat suit increased the Marines' combat capability, enhanced strength, provided protection, and increased speed, but one thing it couldn't do was make the wearer smaller. Size was its strength and weakness. Crawling in the suit was difficult and tiring, so they moved on all fours, dog-style. The view was exactly as one would expect.

The Marines kept their heads down, using their suits' systems to feed the visuals and tactical to their HUDs.

"Opens up not far ahead," Bing said. Two meters later, his suit lost power and collapsed, blocking the low-ceilinged corridor.

"Sergeant Bing?" Trapper blew out his breath as he stopped in place, happy his systems were still functional. "Jem, any ideas?"

Blencathra, New America 2 Space

The cruiser had not yet come through the gate, since a steady stream of freighters and other private craft were parading into NA2 space. Three of the blockade frigates had already transited and had been directed to hold station near *Blencathra*. They kept their power plants warm but weapons systems offline.

"Total count," Van Dorn requested.

"One hundred seventeen private ships and three Terran frigates have come through the gate after us," Helm reported.

Comm stood up. "Fleet Log is in touch, collecting inventory data and directing the freighters to a variety of staging areas. Some of the captains are complaining they'll spend all their time protecting flying junk carrying garbage no one needs when they should be fighting fleet battles."

Jenkins looked at Van Dorn, earning a nod before stepping front and center. "Comm, connect me with Admiral Corbyn."

"Roger that. Connecting now." With a few deft taps on her panel, the line was opened and the admiral confirmed to be on the other end.

"You brought us a few presents, Colonel. Thank you. Not sure we want all of them, but we'll decide that once the inventories are final." Admiral Corbyn's image filled the destroyer's main screen.

"Good morning, Admiral. If I may be so bold—"

"Nothing has stopped you yet," the admiral inserted before Jenkins could continue. He gestured for the colonel to keep speaking.

"I know. I'll work on that. But for now, these freighter captains joined us to contribute in any way they could. Even a less-than-optimal ship could be used for evacuation or search and recovery."

"We have a hundred-year-old baby-sized freighter filled with stem bolts, and not even the self-sealing kind. What do you suggest we do with him?" The admiral's tone was acerbic. He saw the problems of dealing with a hundred different ship designs, breakdowns, and needy ship captains making demands of his maintenance capabilities. And worse, ships falling behind, holding the fleet back. Freighters insisting they be protected so Jemmin didn't make a rear area attack, slaughtering the freighters and wasting the efforts and lives of the volunteers.

"Stem bolts would make a great shrapnel pattern. Many of these ships will have utility on suicide runs. The only mainte-nance we should do on them is ensuring the remote piloting is active. We can never go wrong with extra ships and supplies, no matter what those supplies are. Food is food. Metal is metal. And any weapons are good weapons, even if it's the ship itself."

"That's one attitude. All I see is our fleet scattered to kingdom come, with no ability to protect anyone because we'll be spread too thin." Admiral Corbyn's lip curled in distaste.

Colonel Jenkins nodded. "I think the Zeen worldship and 'Keeper' will draw all the attention. If we protect those, we protect everything. Some sacrifices might have to be made."

"I've sided with TAC for this, but it doesn't mean I like the armor tactics. I don't believe in cannon fodder, Colonel."

"I was cannon fodder forever ago at Durgan's Folly, but we proved them wrong. I never send people in just to get killed and punish the enemy by making them run out of ammunition. I think human life is far too precious for that, but this fight is for all of humanity. As long as we win, it doesn't matter if a single one of us staggers home to tell Terra or Sol about it. They'll figure it out when the enemy doesn't stop by for a visit."

Jenkins clenched his jaw. He preferred to be more upbeat, but the dark cloud hung over the Mercury Regression, their name for this campaign since the Terran government had ordered the Terran Armor Corps to surrender their assets and stand down.

"I understand the gravity of the situation, Lee. I'm sorry if I came across as harsh. I don't want to waste any energy looking in when we should be looking out."

"I get you, Admiral. I don't want to have nothing but the void behind us when we're engaged in an all-out dogfight."

Corbyn looked off-screen before turning back. "Gotta run, Colonel. How many more are coming?"

"No idea, Admiral. We were more effective than we expected. It was a bit surprising."

"Cruiser transiting," Helm reported.

"That's it, Admiral. The cruiser was bringing up the rear. We were able to add at least four warships, one with some horsepower. Their weaponry is greatly appreciated."

"Every missile, projectile, and plasma bolt." Corbyn executed a quick salute. "Carry on, Colonel. Something is happening with the Zeen worldship. Make no moves that could be misconstrued until we sort things out."

6

FILLING THE VOID WITH SPACE JUNK

"What is going on over there?" Podsy asked no one in particular. "Can you get Major Bao on the hook?"

"Unable to establish contact," Comm reported after a few attempts.

The Zeen worldship started to spin and flash like a Christmas ornament. "Anybody ever see anything like that before? Jem, any ideas?"

There was a long delay while the worldship began moving toward the 'Keeper. A parade of Zeen short-range space fighters launched from the opposite side of the artificial planetoid.

"Shields up, weapons hot. Follow those fighters and get us between wherever they're going and the worldship," Podsy ordered. "And get me some answers! Where the hell are they going?"

"They are heading toward the NA2 gate to establish a superior firing position to counter the enemy who is on their way," Jem finally announced.

"What enemy?" Podsy asked, his heart sinking as he thought about it. They couldn't be caught with their pants down—the whole invasion fleet, right here, including the 'Keeper and the worldship. "All hands to battle stations. Prepare to launch everything we have. Commander Knighton, report to the Vipers for an immediate combat launch. Comm, warn the *Sima Yi*, *Mencius*, and *Henry VIII* that the enemy is inbound through the Nexus gate."

The NA2 gate led to Nexus space, where the former Illumination League could travel back and forth to their home systems as well as to those of humanity. The gateway to the universe opened right on their front doorstep.

"Viper status?"

"Cold. Five minutes before they can scramble," the ground control officer reported.

"That's about four minutes too long," Podsy remarked, watching the tactical plots appear on the main viewscreen. The *Mencken* was finally overtaking the worldship, but *Zeen Home Three* wasn't heading for the gate. It was on an intercept course with the '*Keeper*.

Just like Podsy was trying to put the *Mencken* between the Zeen and the enemy, the Zeen were putting themselves between the '*Keeper* and the enemy. "If you had any doubt about the value of the '*Keeper*, that should erase it. The Zeen are down to two worldships, yet they're willing to sacrifice one to save the originators' ship."

"The '*Keeper* is irreplaceable," Jem noted. "The worldship's creators still exist. Whether they chose to rebuild or not would depend on need."

"Too hypothetical!" Podsy declared. "Let's make sure they don't have to make that decision. Raise Admiral Corbyn, please."

Podsy started tapping his foot and glaring at the comm station while trying to wait patiently.

"Getting busy over here, Captain," Admiral Corbyn started. "All hell's breaking loose and there isn't a single enemy in sight, but you know what *is* in sight? Every damn freighter in the galaxy is filling the void like space junk orbiting Earth."

"We have reason to believe Jemmin are on their way through the gate," Podsy said without preamble.

"Judging by the Zeen's actions, that's what I'm thinking, too."

Podsy refused to smile at the confirmation he'd received from the admiral. It wasn't about his ego. They had no idea what Jemmin were bringing, and it was all happening too quickly.

"Recommend a preemptive missile barrage," Podsy said.

The admiral gave him a withering glare. Podsy backed down. "We'll be in position. As soon as we can identify the targets as hostile, we'll unload on them."

"Aye, aye, sir." Andy Podsednik wanted to litter the area in front of the gate with ordnance and blow to hell anything coming through before they could see what hit them. He wished he knew what the Zeen knew. "Get me the Zeen. What is coming through the gate?"

Comm tapped frantically as Corbyn cut his comm channel with a tense wave. The front screen returned with a full tactical display. Terran and Solar ships maneuvered toward optimal firing positions, two dreadnoughts headed behind the gate and one jockeying to get in place out front. The *Mencken* poured on the speed to get into position.

"No response," Comm reported.

"Add that to the list of liaison duties for Major Bao," Podsy said to himself as a reminder. "Information-sharing." Podsy watched the screen. "Prepare to fire six ship-to-ship missiles. Make sure we can abort them in flight if needed. Target is the center of the gate."

"Target programmed," the weapons control officer confirmed.

"Fire."

Six missiles leapt into space on the wings of pneumatic discharge, a breath of fresh air to launch them away from the ship. The motors kicked in, and the missiles accelerated across the void.

"Board is lighting up with inquiries," Comm noted.

"Ignore them." Podsy crossed his arms in defiance.

"Gate is active, and a ship is coming through," Helm reported.

"Confirm ship class and origin," Captain Podsednik ordered, stepping closer to the main screen as if that would help him discern the truth more quickly.

"Jemmin cruiser!" Weapons noted. "*Sima Yi* is firing."

"Time to impact?" Podsy asked.

"Eight...seven..." Weapons counted down.

The screen lit up with activity as the dreadnoughts fired a mix of railguns and missiles. Once the Jemmin cruiser cleared the event horizon, its point defense systems lit up like a sun's corona flaring in anger. Two of the Terran missiles were vaporized in the first milliseconds, then two more. One unleashed its fury danger-close to the cruiser, and the last made it through the onslaught to deliver its deadly penetrator warhead into a gap between the heavily armored prow and the heavily defended midship.

The Jemmin cruiser's weapons went dark as the warhead nearly cut the ship in half, separating the brain from the body. Gases jetted from all sides as the fifty-kiloton nuke delivered its full wrath. Missiles from the dreadnoughts started hitting home. Railgun bolts stitched their way across the dying ship.

The Zeen fighters never fired a shot. They waited at a point in space between the worldship and the gate.

The Jemmin cruiser exploded with one final gasp, having never fired an offensive weapon.

"Time in NA2 space?" Podsy asked.

Weapons wore a broad grin. "Fourteen seconds. No transmissions detected."

Podsy didn't consider that an important piece of information. He expected Jemmin communicated in ways that the humans couldn't detect, in addition to the usual means.

"Good work, people, but stay frosty. That's not the end of it. Helm, get us into position behind the Zeen fighters."

The ship banked five degrees from its current course. The fighters were where Podsy wanted to be, but if they were willing to stay in the middle of the battle, who was he to argue?

"New contact," Helm reported.

"Shit. Fire! Fire a full spread."

From the first sighting of the Gatecrasher's prow, Podsy knew they were in trouble. Its weapon systems were directed backward, past the gate toward ships waiting to attack from behind. And it was clearing the decks, firing as it crossed the event horizon, before its targeting systems could return to full functionality.

"Firing railguns. Missiles away. Point defense systems active and ready to engage."

Eighteen missiles screamed toward the Gatecrasher dreadnought from the *Mencken*. The assault carrier rolled to present its most heavily armored side to the enemy while unleashing its railguns for as long as they could lead the target.

In unison, three Republican-class dreadnoughts sent everything they had downrange. Before the massive Jemmin Gatecrasher could clear into NA2 space, a barrage of over four hundred missiles and tens of thousands of tungsten railgun bolts accelerated to a hundredth the speed of light. Nowhere in the space before the gate was safe.

The Zeen fighters accelerated toward their enemy, firing as they approached.

Mencius and *Henry VIII* started evasive maneuvers against the blind barrage launched by Jemmin. They weren't trying to foil targeting systems, but present the lowest profile to the inbound ordnance. PD weapons started to fire well before the inbound was in effective range.

The premise of little bullet, big sky, didn't apply when the sheer volume of fire created clouds of projectiles.

The Gatecrasher cleared the gate and stopped firing for a moment as it tallied a full screen of Terran warships focused solely upon it. Then the fire began anew, with fifty missiles directed toward *Sima Yi*. Plasma balls started appearing on their way through space, bracketing the dreadnought to limit its evasive maneuvers, but Admiral Corbyn and the ship's captain, Commodore Meng, had no intention of getting channeled into a stream of deadly missile fire.

Sima Yi banked and accelerated to ten gees on its way out of the fire trap heading its way. It countered with hundreds of noisemakers and clouds of chaff to give the missiles something else to consider.

The first barrage to land went to the Terrans. Their attack on the Gatecrasher was nothing less than a concerted effort to kill one of the most powerful ships in the galaxy in the least amount of time possible. Massive rents appeared across the Gatecrasher's hull as missile after missile impacted. Up to ten meters deep, and they still hadn't penetrated deep enough to reach the ship's contained atmosphere.

The double-hulled design created a dead space that increased the ship's survivability.

The Zeen space fighters directed their fire toward the new rents in the Gatecrasher's hull, digging deeper and deeper, but not quickly enough. The Jemmin behemoth sniped two fighters in the first seconds of the engagement from the blanket defensive fire, but as soon as its systems came online, it focused its wrath, sending the greatest volume of PD fire in the direction of the Zeen.

Two strategic missiles lumbered from the Gatecrasher's aft section. They accelerated and kept accelerating well past one hundred and fifty gees on their way toward the Zeen worldship.

"Commander Knighton, please tell me you're ready to launch," Podsy said in almost prayer-like tones.

"She is, Captain," Tactical reported. "Squadron away."

"Kill those two missiles," Podsy ordered.

"Message received and understood," Comm replied, speaking for the intercept squadron. The main screen lit up with a single blip that represented all twelve Vipers. They burned toward an intercept with the ship-killer missiles, massive beasts with their own point defense weapons. They only had one purpose –destroy strategic enemy ships like the worldship or the *'Keeper*.

The Gatecrasher slewed around, turning away from the fleet occupying NA2 space.

Its target was clear; Jemmin wanted the *'Keeper*. Two dreadnoughts moved to intercept, still corkscrewing through space to minimize exposure to a single side of the ship.

A new cloud of missiles, plasma, and railgun bolts erupted from the Gatecrasher. The weapons painted a grim picture for the two dreadnoughts in their path.

Mencius and *Henry VIII* had no intention of making it easy for the massive Jemmin ship. They launched volley after volley of missiles to intercept the Gatecrasher. If the Terran ships were going to die, they would go out with empty launch tubes and depleted magazines. The dreadnoughts heated up with the fury of their response.

On the board, both ships started to glow.

"That's some serious shit right there," Tactical muttered while his hands danced across his panel, sending missile after missile into the fray while enjoying the anonymity of not being in the Gatecrasher's targets.

Not yet, anyway. "Parallel course," Podsy ordered, abandoning the intercept course, choosing not to close the distance. The *Mencken* was still in position to stand between the worldship and the Gatecrasher. Podsy knew that inevitably, Jemmin would turn their attention to him and every ship protecting the Zeen.

Commander Knighton's Vipers launched their first wave of short-range tactical missiles to destroy the strategic weapons streaking toward the worldship.

The Vipers' missiles unleashed a blinding laser defense system that exploded the incoming missiles' fuel tanks. One by one, they cleared the space. Not even shrapnel reached the ship-killers. They accelerated to two hundred gees.

On *Mencken*'s bridge, Comm piped in the squadron's tactical communications.

"Railguns," Commander Knighton ordered. "Laze that, you metal piece of shit."

"Right up your ass," another pilot replied, drifting in behind the missiles as they increased their distance. The Vipers had no chance of catching the ship-killers once they passed. "Firing."

"Everything you got, Suckerpunch," Knighton said. The other Vipers followed suit, gaining better firing angles before depressing their railgun triggers and holding them as they sent tungsten bolts at .01c.

Despite the missiles' speed, the railgun bolts were faster. They closed the distance and penetrated the exhaust ports.

"Can you feel me now?" Suckerpunch cried out.

"Easy to be bold when you aren't getting shot at," Knighton countered. One missile slowed to a ballistic trajectory. The other continued unerringly toward *Zeen Home Three* at two hundred gees. "Fire!"

The Vipers finished off the first missile, which went out with a whimper, dying without exploding. The Vipers shot past it and continued to draw a bead on the escaped weapon.

"Get me Chief Rimmer. I want that missile. We can turn that big bastard loose on Jemmin if we can figure it out."

"What if it blows?" Weapons Control replied.

"Then we'll have to make sure we don't crack it on this ship." Podsy pointed to the hundreds of ships dotting space between the gates to the Nexus on one side of the system and to New America 1 on the other. In between, New America 2 orbited the system's star. The residents would not have picked their planet for a major fight, but here it was, beating down their doors. First stop from Nexus space wasn't optimal, as it turned out. Instead of being a hub to the universe, it was the open doorway that let the monsters through.

The sight of the Gatecrasher launching missiles by the hundreds made Podsy's breath catch. A Terran cruiser took too long to get out of the way and was vaporized by missiles that probably weren't even aimed at it.

Mencius was already flying inverted to the rest of the formation to present a less battered profile to Jemmin. Damage control parties had sealed the breaches, but the mighty ship was battered and bruised, having suffered mightily for the sole fault of being the closest ship to the Gatecrasher when it turned toward the Originators' ship.

But the *Mencius* fought on fearlessly. Railguns continued to spew streams of deadly projectiles, counting on the cold of space to cool them between engagements. But there was no downtime. They fired, and continued to fire, filling the void with tungsten bolts.

Henry VIII had turned and run from the Gatecrasher to stay in front of it. The main focus of the ship was to fire backward past a gate it had just transited. Following one put the trailing ship in the danger zone of the ship's primary weapon systems.

Commodore Sosunova, captain of *Henry VIII* turned the ship and accelerated nose-on with the Gatecrasher in a high-stakes game of chicken. Neither had any intention of dying, but both were willing if it helped them achieve their objectives.

Podsy watched critically, taking in the data that threatened to overwhelm his senses. "Commander Knighton?" he asked.

"Wait one," came her reply.

Podsy stood next to the captain's chair and tapped his controls to manipulate the main viewscreen. The engagement between the Vipers and the missile was reaching a crescendo. Railgun fire poured from the twelve intact fighters. Podsy nodded slowly, appreciating the gift of life during combat. It could be snuffed out in a heartbeat, but for now, his people were alive and fighting for all they were worth.

The second missile lost directional control and started to spin while maintaining a general course toward the worldship. Its momentum slowed when its forward thrust ended.

"Get out of there, Commander," Podsy shouted at the comm station.

"Are we giving up?" the commander shot back, ending her question with a snarl.

"You don't want to be in the impact area..." Podsy started to explain while watching the Vipers execute a sharp bank, the missile well in front of them.

The Zeen worldship's mid-range defensives poured focused firepower using lasers and plasma weapons to rip the missile to shreds. The plasma tore through an opening and into the warhead, igniting a supernova that the Vipers saw from the blast wave that tore past them from behind. The space fighters bucked against the tear in the very fabric of space. Viper Five lost power.

"Thanks for saving my retinas," Knighton said softly. "Dispatch Recovery for Viper Five."

"On the way," Ground Control confirmed. In space battles, the GCO was relegated to search and rescue. "The recovery shuttle for the first missile has made contact. That thing is a little bigger than our recovery vessel."

"Commander, see if you can provide a tactical assist in towing that weapon to a safe haven. Comm, find me a freighter jock who isn't afraid of a little missile."

Comm looked sideways at the captain before confirming and broadcasting to the civilian fleet his request for a cargo hauler who wouldn't mind a catastrophic death if things didn't work out right.

"Tactical, send our condolences to Jemmin," Podsy said casually.

"Seventh salvo away," the weapons control officer stated. Tactical reached past his station to give Weapons a hearty clap on the back.

"We never stop sending greeting cards, because we care to send the very best," Tactical proclaimed.

"Well done." Podsy made eye contact with his people, pointing at them and nodding.

"New contact," Helm called. Podsy's head snapped toward the main screen. "Jemmin cruiser coming through the gate.

Sima Yi was close to the gate since it was racing to catch the Gatecrasher. The dreadnought didn't hesitate. From time of fire to impact was less than two seconds. Railgun bolts shredded the front half of the cruiser, and missiles took care of the rest. The Jemmin ship that cleared the event horizon was a dead hulk, drifting through space with gas jets for its death cries.

"Assume position beside the gate. I don't think we've seen the last ship through." Captain Podsednik marked a spot on the tactical grid.

The Gatecrasher was faltering under the withering fire from two dreadnoughts and two squadrons of Zeen Interceptors, along with as many random missiles as other Fleet ships could deliver. The Gatecrasher streamed debris, plasma, and gases.

Henry VIII continued to bear down, taking bow shot after bow shot, delivering one hundred percent of its capacity on target. The dreadnought accelerated as the Gatecrasher slowed. More explosions.

The Zeen dove in, finding the deepest rents in the formidable ship's armor and firing, missiles and bolts cut through the hardened shell into the soft underbelly. An explosion followed, sending a volcanic eruption of liquid metal into space. It froze quickly into a bizarre parody of an ice waterfall.

Henry VIII fired one final salvo as it pulled up, thrusters assisting vector control to force the dreadnought away from the dying Gatecrasher. Another explosion shook the massive Jemmin ship. In slow motion, the ship started to break in half, the two sections seemingly independent, but each just as dead without the other.

The Republican-class dreadnought skipped off the scattering debris, firing close-in weapons like coil guns and PD missiles to make sure the Gatecrasher was dead. *Henry VIII* continued to accelerate, expecting the fusion generators to lose containment and go supernova.

They weren't disappointed. The aft section sparked, vented, and blew.

Henry VIII was shaken to its core but emerged from the fireball intact, on its way back toward the gate.

The Zeen Interceptors took a casual turn and headed home. The 'Keeper stood in the distance, little more than a massive star in the night sky.

"Looks like the Zeen are satisfied the hardest part of this

fight is over," Podsy noted. "Still, take us to the gate. We'll hold down the fort until the others can get their ships back in order."

The external cameras captured images of *Sima Yi*, the dreadnought least engaged with the Gatecrasher. The ship was dented and battered, scarred horribly from missile impacts and explosions. But she flew proudly on, turning slowly to catch up with *Mencius*, to render aid to its limping comrade.

"GCO, status of Viper Five?"

"Recovery is thirty seconds from contact with the Viper. The missile recovery shuttle is using the remote arm to cargo-net the thing for towing. It's too big for anything else. They need Viper One's assistance.

Commander Knighton. Of course, she stayed behind.

"Viper recovery?"

"Ten recovered Vipers already being refueled and rearmed," Tactical reported.

Podsy acknowledged the report.

"I don't believe it," Comm stated. "We have not one, but two civvies with a death wish."

"Pick the one with the biggest bay and the least number of crew," Podsy directed. "And tell them to meet the missile recovery team somewhere off the beaten path. Shuttle pilot can select the coordinates. And give him my personal thanks. I'll send Lieutenant Styles to meet them and give it the once over to see what we can recover. I want that weapon."

"New contact!" Helm shouted.

7

A FRAGILE MIND

"Sorry about that, but I couldn't maintain this link during the battle, but I'm back now," Jem explained.

"What battle?" Major Trapper wondered while lying perfectly still to keep his systems online.

"Jemmin arrived, and they brought a Gatecrasher. My analysis of their attack suggests they know the 'Keeper is here, and they desire to take control of it. The Jemmin force has been destroyed. The small size of the effort is interesting. A Gatecrasher should have been accompanied by forty or fifty ships, but there were only two escorts."

"Where does that leave us?"

"Exactly the same place we were before. They knew the 'Keeper was here then. They know it's here now."

"You make it sound matter-of-fact, so let's talk about my favorite subject, which is me. How in the hell do I get my people out of the neuralyzer ray?"

"I've never heard of a neuralyzer beam. Can you share the details so that I may formulate an appropriate countermeasure?"

"I made it up. These are the times that try men's souls,

grating their patience like a fine Romano cheese. Let me make this simple. Help me out of this predicament, Jem."

"That is clear, thank you," the gestalt intelligence agreed. "I've been analyzing the data, and I think the only course of action is you'll have to exit your suit before you become incapable of escaping. Then plug your comm system into the wall from where the neuralyzer beam is emanating."

"There *is* a neuralyzer?"

"There is not. I'm using your word so you understand what I'm talking about."

"Jem, you're growing on me. I'm not warm to the idea of leaving my suit while I'm in the guts of a possibly hostile ship."

"I have a working hypothesis that the ship is trying to help you as much as you are trying to help it. I think you are in no danger."

"Then what was with that bit about not being able to escape the Gamera?" Trapper started the process to open the suit. He had no reason to believe he'd be safe in the strange environment, but he maintained complete trust in Jem, which was one thing that Jem warned all the humans about.

Trust but verify. Trapper had no choice, though. He wasn't completely on his own. He could have recalled the other squads, but he would save that. He wasn't sure what he would warn them about, but he couldn't let them run headfirst into a trap. "All Marines. We've run into an energy-sucking corridor that has rendered 2nd and 4th Squads inoperable. I don't know why my suit is still functional, but it is. Spread out and watch for the Marine in front. If they lose power, then back off and await further instruction. I'm exiting my suit to examine the corridor in an unpowered manner. I'll stay in touch. Don't blow anything up if you don't have to. If you have to ask, then you don't have to. Trapper out."

The major exited his suit and buttoned it back up. The first thing he noticed was that the temperature wasn't quite friendly to humans.

"Holy fuck, it's cold!" he exclaimed before gritting his teeth and working his way forward. A shiver ran through his body. The Marines were face-down, keeping Trapper from making contact through the face shields. Getting the dampener or whatever it was turned off was his primary objective. "I'm tingling, Jem, all over my body, and I don't think that's related to the cold."

"I need more information, Major Trapper. Press your comm unit against the wall."

Trapper looked for a spot where he could stand. The Marines' suits blocked most of the access. When he crawled across them, it felt colder than ice, like being in space, but with air. Trapper held the comm unit against the wall and moved it slowly, trying to find where Jem could pick up the transmissions. He started to shiver uncontrollably but forced himself to press the unit harder against the wall to keep it from shaking.

"Your discomfort is understandable, Major. Temperatures are nearly minus forty on your Celsius scale."

"No shit, Jem. I hate to mention this, but you need to pick up the pace. I'm not sure how much longer I can stay out here."

"I'm sorry, Major. I'm working as quickly as I can. A physical link with the data stream would be optimal, but I know that isn't possible in the current environment. Leave your portable comm unit here and return to your suit. Your biometrics suggest your life is waning and can be measured in minutes instead of years."

"You and Doctor 'Strange Bed' Fellows should talk about how similar your bedside manners are." Trapper fumbled with the comm unit. He tried to move the arm of a Marine's Gamera suit, but it was too heavy, and he could no longer feel his fingers. He thought it was Sergeant Bing, the Marine on point when they reached the corridor. The major started climbing over the suits to get back to his own. When his skin touched the suits, the cold burned. He left a chunk of flesh from his palm on Corporal Klipsch.

Trapper started to stumble. He fell onto his suit and wormed his way inside. The cold had permeated the interior, surrounding him with pain. He tried to tap his controls, but his fingers wouldn't work. "Power up." He croaked the command to his non-responsive suit.

The Zeen Worldship

"Our Interceptors were successful at destroying a Jemmin ship of the class you call Gatecrasher," Bob announced.

"What Gatecrasher?" Xi wondered, facing her Zeen escort and throwing her hands out in frustration.

"Zeen are satisfied with Terran efforts to protect *Zeen Home Three*. Symmetry."

"Did we lose any ships?" Xi asked before adding, "I need to talk to my people."

"We can patch your portable communication device through our systems to give you full-time access to whomever you wish to call," Bob said almost too eloquently.

"Bob! Your language is almost better than mine. I'm impressed." Xi slipped her comm into her hand and looked at it for a moment before keying it. "Major Bao to Colonel Jenkins, come in, please."

"Our technology is finally aligned with translating your barbaric tongue."

Xi chuckled. "Spot on, Bob."

"Good to hear from you, Major. Status report?"

"Zeen will assist as long as they aren't put at the front of any Terran formations. That's their only condition. Well, one more.

They want me to stay on board during the campaign, not just the next operation."

"Maybe we can deliver *Elvira* to you with her can, Monkey, and Wrench, just in case you need to drop to the planet.

"I like the way you think, Colonel." Xi relaxed before digging deeper. "I heard there was a Gatecrasher."

"They flew into the wrong staging ground. The Gatecrasher existed for less than two minutes in the NA2 system, but Jemmin did a shitload of damage during that time. Most of it can be fixed. Crews were already dispatched. Not a single civilian freighter was damaged in the attack, and I think we have a number of gems hidden within our additions to the fleet."

The colonel couldn't keep the pride out of his voice. The fleet was more than he hoped for, the response overwhelming. It seemed that he wasn't the only one who was fed up with human politics. People were willing to go to Jemmin space and risk their lives rather than listen to another feed from one of the propaganda stations. Action trumped words every time.

And now was the time to act.

"Congratulations on the freighters. Who did they send on that shithole mission?"

"I volunteered you, but they knew you weren't available, so the general sent me."

"That's fucked up. You can't volunteer someone who's not there to defend herself!" Xi Bao had a hard time not laughing at how turnabout had bitten Leeroy Jenkins on the ass. "How many did you get?"

"I think the last count was one hundred and seventeen. We only have a few super-haulers. Most are medium- to small-sized freighters that are a tad aged. Plus, we picked up three frigates and a cruiser who'd had enough of the bullshit spewing from New America."

"Sounds familiar, Colonel. Let me talk to my people to coordinate with your people about getting my rig over here. I feel naked without her."

"That's an image you don't need to share with me, Major," the colonel replied after snorting. "I'll see what I can do as soon as I get back to the *Mencken*."

"Where are you now?"

"*Blencathra*. Captain Van Dorn's destroyer. Good thing we didn't send a heavy to solicit for volunteers. I don't think we would have been as warmly received. But, all's well that ends well. Gotta run, Major. I have a shuttle to catch."

Xi closed her comm device and stuffed it back into a cargo pocket, securing the flap so it wouldn't fall out when flying up or down the worldship's transit corridor.

"The Terran fleet has lived up to its agreement in this first engagement. Zeen are happy to ally with Terrans. Symmetry. What is your status with the '*Keeper*?"

Xi shrugged. Bob didn't appear to understand the gesture.

"I'll call and find out." She removed her comm device and keyed it. "Major Xi Bao for Captain Podsednik, over."

She nodded at her Zeen escort and smiled as she waited. The walls of the corridor leading to the spherical room were nondescript, almost cave-like in their appearance. "What kind of art do the Zeen embrace?"

"I don't understand," Bob replied.

"Major, good to hear your voice," Podsy answered over the comm channel, interrupting the Zeen. "What can I do you out of?"

A typical TAC response to forestall any requests for assistance.

"In my official capacity as liaison to our allies, the Zeen," Xi began to let Podsy know it wasn't a social call, "we'd like to know the status of the *GateKeeper*. Have you made any progress in taking control?"

"There's the rub, Major," Podsy replied slowly. "We're in the middle of launching two platoons of Crimson Knights to support Major Trapper's Marines. I know your head is about to explode, but don't worry. Our *friend*," Podsy dodged saying "Jem" since he couldn't remember if the Zeen knew about the gestalt intelligence, "is in the process of accessing ship's systems because there is an energy dampening field that's playing hell with the Gamera armor. And, turns out the ship's internal temperature is barely warmer than outer space."

Xi started to pace. "Knowing our Marines, I suspect they found that out the hard way."

"Doctor Strange Bed is on the Crimson dropship to render aid."

"Of course, he is." Xi let off the switch and looked at Bob. "Anything else you need me to ask them?"

"Zeen are ready to render assistance in taking control of the *GateKeeper*."

Xi stopped pacing and stared at her escort. "Could you have told me earlier about this offer of assistance?" Xi didn't go so far as accusing the Zeen of using the humans as cannon fodder in ensuring the *'Keeper* was safe before stepping aboard, but she thought it.

"Zeen were happy with Terrans taking the lead, but with Jemmin arrival, the timeline is now condensed. Zeen believe we have hours at most before next Jemmin fleet arrives, and it will not be four ships. It will be hundreds."

Xi relaxed. Bob was correct. Jemmin's arrival changed the equation.

She cut to the chase. "Zeen believe more Jemmin are on the way and that we may only have hours before they arrive. Their offer is to speed up taking control and help us to get the hell out of here."

Podsy clicked his tongue over the open channel. "Thanks,

Major. I have some calls to make, but consider the offer accepted. Prepare to return to *Mencken*."

"Part of our agreement with the Zeen is that I stay onboard the worldship. Don't waste a shuttle on me, but if you can manage it before we haul ass, send *Elvira* in a can." Xi decided she needed to add an additional two cents. "The colonel offered."

"We'll consider it. Podsednik out." The channel went dead, and Xi secured the device.

"*Zeen Home Three* is sending multiple engineering hives."

"Thanks, Bob. We need all the help we can get. This galaxy is complex, and if we don't have the time to figure things out for ourselves, then it falls on the greater good to come up with the solutions."

Bob clicked and fidgeted. Xi wondered if he was communicating with the hive.

"Zeen are greater good?" he finally asked.

"For all humanity," Xi answered.

"Terran-Zeen Alliance. Symmetry."

"That, my friend, is how we all define symmetry. Multiple parts to a single whole." Xi started walking toward the central corridor but stopped when she realized she had nowhere to go. "Can we watch what's going on outside the ship?"

"There is a viewing sphere," Bob offered.

Xi motioned for Bob to lead the way. He didn't move. "Can we go there, please? I'm a visual creature and have a powerful need to see our tactical situation."

"Of course," Bob conceded. He sauntered past Xi on his way to the air lift.

8

FIXING THINGS

"Major Trapper." The voice was persistent. Disembodied, like in a dream. The major remembered falling into his suit, but it was cold. He started to shiver before he realized he was no longer chilled.

"Report," he ordered.

"You're back with us," Jem said softly. "The Crimson Knights are on their way and will reach you shortly. I've neutralized the dampening device and have gained access to some of the ship's systems, including life support. I've turned up the heat, so to speak."

Trapper tried to move and discovered he was both stiff and sore. He couldn't feel his fingers or his toes. "I feel like I've been a pugil-stick dummy. What's wrong with my hands?"

"That would be frostbite, but Doctor Fellows is with the Knights. He will be able to treat you."

"I guess I'll wait, then. What about my Marines?"

"You can talk to your Marines anytime you want. Their suits protected them despite having their systems locked up."

"Only me, then. That works." Trapper tried to blink his mind clear, but it remained fogged. He was happy that the sacrifice to get the unit functional had been his alone. He would always put his people at risk. That was their job. But freezing on an alien starship wasn't in the job description. They didn't train for that. "Power up."

The combat suit came to life, running through a series of system checks before delivering full control to their users.

"HUD," Trapper requested. The display came to life before his eyes, clearer than he expected. The suit started to pump chemicals into his system to relieve some of his symptoms and stop the physical damage done to his body. Waves of infrared heat washed over him. "Damn. I still feel like shit." He switched to the platoon channel. The heads-up display showed the 1st and 4th Squads bracketing his position. "Sergeant Wu, report."

"The corridor is secured. We've added a comm tap on the bulkhead where you placed your handheld. We're getting a full feed from the *Mencken* as they work to access 'Keeper control. They've uploaded a map to our suits. Check this shit out, Major."

Trapper's screen filled with maps that would have confused even the greatest urban sprawl in the history of humanity. "Is that the whole ship?"

"It's what fits on screen. If we zoom in, the Mencken has drawn a path to Central Control, the ship's brain center."

Trapper followed the route with his eyes, forgetting to blink until his vision clouded. "Distance to target?"

A number appeared on the display. Twenty-four kilometers.

"How fucking long would we have been wandering around this tin can trying to find that fucking place?" the major grumbled.

"Infinity and beyond, Major. It's good to have you back. The *Mencken* has shown us seven points of interest within the ship in addition to Central Control. When the Knights arrive, we'll split the units to cover all seven. If you're up to it, we'd be honored if you joined us at the primary objective."

The *Mencken*. Jem was relaying instructions through the ship to the platoon. "Sergeant Wu, I like your plan. I'll tag along for the ride if Doctor Feelsgood gives me a clean bill of health. Or at least confirmation that frostbite won't kill me or get worse while we do this thing."

"Doctor Feelsgood?" a new voice joined the channel.

"Awesome to have you here, Doc!" the major claimed.

"I see," Doctor Fellows replied. "Let's see what the suit pumped you full of. Okay. A little of this, a little of that. Some piss, some vinegar, and before you know it, you'll be right as rain."

"What language are you speaking?" The major crawled backward until the corridor ceiling was high enough that he could stand. He struggled to his feet before anchoring the suit to the deck. He unbuttoned the suit and climbed out the back, happy to feel a comfortable ambient temperature. He shivered unintentionally. Strange Bed watched him closely.

"Let me see your fingers," the doctor ordered. Trapper hesitantly displayed them. They were starting to turn black. "Put them in here."

The doctor held out a box.

Trapper looked from the box to the doctor and back to the box. "What's in it, Doc? Pain?"

"Healing. It stimulates the skin and restores the blood flow. It'll only take a few minutes if you do it sooner rather than later."

"Maybe some cookies," Trapper quipped before shoving both hands through the opening. A tingle made his skin itch. He resisted the temptation to pull his hands out. "I'm destroying the gom jabbar!"

"The what?" Doctor Fellows looked around to see if space sickness had gotten to any of the other Marines.

"Obviously, you're not well-read, but I'll let it go. Thanks for coming out here to fix me up, doc."

"It's my job, but this ship is magnificent. I've been to a lot of the galaxy's shitholes, Major, but this is not one of them. The 'Keeper is an exceptional find for the Terrans."

Trapper nodded. "Chalk one up for the good guys. This ship doesn't need a gate, just like the Zeen worldship. I have high hopes that we can figure it out."

Fellows gestured for the major to remove his hands. The fingers were no longer black, but bright red as new blood coursed through them. "Now, your feet."

Trapper grumped and groaned as he leaned against his suit to take off his boots and socks. His toes hadn't turned black, but they were white and waxy.

The doctor set his magic box on the deck and Trapper eased forward to stuff his toes inside. The tingle that went through him threw him off-balance. Fellows caught his hand to steady him.

"If they haven't told you yet, you have less than two hours to figure the ship out because Jemmin are coming, and with an armada that we won't be able to defeat."

Trapper didn't hesitate. He leaned over his shoulder. "Sergeant Wu, Sergeant Bing, take your squads to the control center double-time. You need to travel twenty-four klicks through the ship, and I'm giving you less than an hour to do it. I don't want to see the Crimson Knights holding down an objective that we were supposed to get to first."

"Aye, aye, sir!" Bing shouted. He issued the orders, and less than three seconds later, 4th Squad was on their way, heavy metal boots pounding the deck, with 1st Squad squeezing past the major to get through the bottlenecked corridor.

"I guess that answers your original question," Fellows stated, eyes on the box's indicator lights.

"I'm going, but I'll have to catch up," Major Trapper replied. "There's no doubt in my military mind that I need to be in the control center, and I will stay there as long as needed."

"You may want to talk to the *Mencken*."

"Damn it, Strange Bed! You're a creepy motherfucker on the best of days, and now your bullshit is spewing at the cyclic rate."

"My bullshit?" Doctor Fellows shook his head. "And you are one bullheaded asshole for a patient. I know a few others like you, and they seem to be the people in charge of this circus. Where would we be without such as you and me?"

"Fuck off. Now give me your comm device. Mine seems to be missing." Trapper held out his red and tingling hand, palm up. He crooked his fingers.

"You have a strange way to ask for a favor." Fellows produced the handheld device and held it forward with both hands, head bowed. "The device for which this loathsome being shall mightily fuck off."

Trapper took it, chuckling briefly before turning back to the task at hand. "Trapper to *Mencken,* requesting an update."

"Colonel Jenkins here. Glad to see you're back among the land of the living."

"No one is happier than me, Colonel. Two squads are en route to the primary objective of the control center. 2nd and 3rd Squads are en route to objectives two and three. Request Crimson Knights secure objectives four through seven. I've heard that we have no time to get this done."

"Understood. When you're back in your suit, the information will be on your HUD. I'll need you to take charge as soon as possible and coordinate. You're the senior officer over there, and I need you, Tim."

"Roger. Momentarily, it seems. Doctor Fellows confirms." The doctor nodded and pointed to the box, motioning for Major Trapper to take his bare feet out.

"One other thing, Major. The Zeen have docked a ship and are deploying a couple dozen scientists and engineers to aid in the takeover of the *Keeper*. The Marines and Knights have been notified. We don't need anyone killing a Zeen. Jem has confirmed that there are no living entities on board the ship, and most importantly, that the ship itself is not hostile. At one point in history, it welcomed all visitors. When it could no longer do that, it traveled beyond those who threatened its safety. It only came back because it believes humanity can restore what once was."

"It believes?" Trapper looked dumbly at his bare feet, the toes bright red. He had no time to waste, but his body was shaken by the prospect that a planet-sized ship was alive.

"Yes. Jem will have to explain. I don't get it, but I accept it. And you need to embrace that the ship is trying to help you, despite almost killing you earlier. That wasn't intentional."

"Hurt like hell, Colonel, but pain lets us know we're alive. At least the Originators have confidence in us. They clearly haven't seen us when we're between ops. Otherwise, the ship might not feel the same way."

"It's never a good idea to let anyone peek behind those curtains, Major. I'll leave you to it. We have a million things to do over here and no time to do them."

"Roger. Trapper out." He handed the comm device back to the doctor, looked at the man for a moment, and then leaned against his Gamera combat suit to put his socks and boots back on. "It's been real, and it's been fun, but it hasn't been real fun, doc. I got places to go and people to see."

"What about me?" Fellows wondered.

"If you go back the way you came, you might be able to find

a bot that will make you some clothes." Trapper climbed back into his suit and buttoned it up. He dropped and quickly crawled through the bottleneck before bouncing to his feet and accelerating away.

"Marines stopped maturing at the age of twelve!" Fellows yelled. His comm device crackled. "Hello?"

"Tell me something I don't know, Doc. Get yourself back to that big lounge. Someone will be along shortly to collect you," Trapper said.

Doctor Fellows started to laugh. He looked around, to find himself alone in the guts of a ship as big as a small planet, being harassed by a man who he wasn't sure was a friend while under instructions to meet with a robotic tailor. "Sometimes, my good doctor," Fellows said to himself, "one must embrace the absurdity of it all. Humanity's role in the universe is based on never taking anything too seriously. Least of all, their fellow humans."

He started retracing his steps, wondering what kind of clothes a million-year-old ship would recommend.

9

RUNNING BEFORE THE ENEMY

Podsy paced in his quarters. Every one of the ship's crew was doing their job, and he needed to confer with Jem to make sure he wasn't missing anything. As the ship's captain, he was relegated to following orders from the Fleet admiral. His ability to influence those decisions was minimal, especially at this point in time. Moving fleet assets, both civilian and military, required knowledge he did not have. It left him free to think about other things. "We're fixated on getting the hell out of Dodge. Maybe we could trap Jemmin and kill them right here instead of driving this ragtag bunch to the corners of the galaxy?"

"If Jemmin is not destroyed at their epicenter, this fleet will only be a ripple. When Jemmin issuing the orders are eliminated, this fleet will be rendered inoperative."

"Dammit!" Podsy unleashed his frustration in the privacy of the captain's quarters, where the others couldn't see. He had to present a calm and collected exterior when on the bridge. It made sense. The crew could never see him lose his cool. Morale was a fragile and fickle thing. He couldn't risk cracking it, let alone shattering it. With confidence, the crew could accomplish anything. If they lost faith, then they'd curl up and die, thinking their demise inevitable.

Hope was the greatest emotion he could give them. He always had to embrace the hope that they would survive to accomplish the mission out there, where they could see him. In here? He had to vent.

"Where will we go, Jem? When we run toward the enemy, where will that leave us?"

"We cannot go to the Nexus, and we cannot retreat closer to Earth. We must use the Zeen worldship's gate to evacuate the fleet."

"Have they agreed to that?"

"I do not have direct access to the Zeen," Jem explained. "Maybe it is time to explain my presence to them."

"I don't remember if we told them about you or not, but I don't think so. Otherwise, there would have been questions. Maybe we did, and they didn't believe us."

"The Vorr know."

"I expected." Podsy stopped pacing and threw his hands up. "None of that matters, Jem. Where the hell do we go, and what about the 'Keeper? If we can't get that ship flying, we can't leave. We can't let it fall back into Jemmin hands, or claws, or paws, or whatever the hell they have."

"Hands. I agree. The GateKeeper is the single greatest acquisition for all humanity. It must be protected at all costs. He who controls the GateKeeper controls movement throughout the galaxy. Nexus space, New America, New Australia—all of it is dependent upon the GateKeeper."

Podsy continued to stare at the device in which Jem resided. "But those gates were functioning before the 'Keeper came out of retirement."

"If the 'Keeper fell under Jemmin control, all the gates could be turned off except the ones they want, and then, only when they want."

"That's new. If that's the case, why do we have to run? Why can't we just shut down the Nexus gate?" Podsy didn't wait for an answer. He tapped his console. "Comm, get me Admiral Corbyn."

Zeen Home Three

"Look at all those ships," Major Xi Bao muttered, in awe at the resolution of the Zeen observation center. When she was jacked into *Elvira*, she sensed all the mech sensed, but even then, the imagery wasn't as immersive as the three-dimensional display in which she found herself. Bob showed her how to manipulate the projections, and soon, she was exploring the fleet, getting closeups of the many new ships that had joined. The cruiser was sleek. A newer design, probably newer than anything the TAC had, even with the additional two hundred ships from Solar space.

The Solarian fleet had been sequestered until their systems could integrate with those of the Terran flagships. They had been grossly out of position when the Gatecrasher arrived and could do nothing related to their stated goal of defending the Zeen worldship.

That situation was being rectified as Xi watched.

The kabuki dance of ship movements was dizzying. "Flight Control must be tearing their collective hair out."

"Why would they do that?" Xi's Zeen escort asked.

"It's a human expression, Bob. I mean the intricate movements required to keep hundreds of ships from running into each other when space is at a premium. It looks like no one is sitting still. You know that none of those ships can make a sharp turn, especially the freighters. They're lucky they can turn at all. Must be a few hundred million tons of cargo out there."

"Asymmetry?" Bob had turned inquisitive, asking questions instead of making statements. Xi hadn't noticed, but it became glaringly obvious with the latest question.

"I don't know. It might be genius if it helps us when we're out of range of any support base. Or it could be folly if they slow us down and make us more vulnerable. Time will tell. Talking about time, how are your engineers doing aboard the 'Keeper?"

Xi didn't know how they communicated with each other, but they did. Bob went silent and motionless for a few moments before answering, "They have almost reached the GateKeeper's Central Control."

"We are in a race against time, Major Bao. Zeen believe Jemmin are coming with a great fleet. The human Admiral Corbyn agrees this is neither the time nor the place for such a battle. No matter whether the Terran fleet is ready to move or not. Zeen Home Three will leave before Jemmin so they cannot track where Zeen Home Three has gone."

"I need to get back to my ship!" Xi started to run from the spherical room but stopped when a door closed before her.

"You cannot leave Zeen Home Three right now. The ship is locked down. The GateKeeper is the only ship that can facilitate the movement of the Terran fleet. It must be operational. Zeen engineers will make it so, and we will all leave together. If not, then Zeen Home Three will leave alone."

Xi wasn't surprised. TAC considered the survival of the worldship to be equal to the survival of the 'Keeper. Separating them if necessary would ensure at least one survived a massed Jemmin assault.

"I understand." Xi hung her head. She didn't like being taken out of the battle before the fight started. It wasn't in her nature to run away from anything.

But the die was cast, and her role as liaison to the Zeen gave her no choice.

"I've been promoted beyond the fun stuff."

"Dying in a ship destroyed by Jemmin is not fun," Bob countered.

"Okay, maybe it isn't, but from a hive perspective, are you willing to watch others die just so you can survive?" Xi crossed her arms as she focused entirely on her Zeen escort. She had nothing else to do. The ships maneuvered around the space in a way that made her dizzy.

"Zeen has sent the very best engineers. All of them. It will be a great loss to *Zeen Home Three* if they are left behind."

"I'll be damned. I guess you do get it. I thought the hive would be more insulated against individual loss. How much time to estimated Jemmin arrival?" Xi turned back to the perplexing three-dimensional image in which she was embedded. Fleet assets, both military and civilian, intermingled to the point of being indistinguishable.

"Fifty-seven of your minutes." Bob didn't display his emotions during the conversation, almost as if he were patiently explaining a science problem to a young pupil.

Humanity was the younger race. Maybe the Zeen were right. As long as one human remained alive, the fight would go on.

"But that fight would suck," Xi said out loud before apologizing. "I don't want to leave the Metal Legion behind. What can I do to influence the situation? Come on, Bob, work with me here. We have a saying that metal never dies. I don't want to be the only one to carry that forward."

"Zeen are aware of this saying. It is odd because metal never lived."

Xi laughed heartily, doubling over from the effort. Her eyes started to water as she gasped to catch her breath. When she could, she explained. "That's where you are very wrong. Put some Metalheads into an old mech and it comes to life. *Number of the Beast* raging over the loudspeakers. Oh, yeah. Humans are the heart and soul of the living mechs. Metal never dies, bitch."

"Symmetry," Bob conceded. "The human capability of fighting within the mechanized combat machines defies mathematical predictability."

"Symmetry, Bob. That is some serious fucking symmetry. *Elvira* hasn't made it over here yet, has she?"

Bob hesitated as he communed with the hive. "It was turned back because *Zeen Home Three* is locked down pending emergency gating."

"You're starting to piss me off, Bob. You're telling me my mech in a can was on its way, but now it's not? Fuck you guys. We aren't going anywhere. Who do I need to talk to? And open this fucking door, or I'm going to start breaking shit."

GateKeeper, Central Control

The last kilometer was slow going. Major Tim Trapper, Junior had to adjust and twist to get through normal-sized corridors. Maybe the Originators weren't giants.

He turned a corner and came to an abrupt stop. The Zeen contingent was hurrying ahead, their spindly legs and odd locomotion covering the distance quickly, but nowhere near what Trapper was able to manage in his combat suit.

But they filled the space before him, ignoring his presence as they headed for the spot marked on his HUD as Central Control.

"I'm one minute out. The Zeen are right in front of me. Sergeant Wu, report," Trapper requested.

"Roger on the Zeen. We'll roll out the red carpet, Major. This place is like something out of science fiction. We are transmitting everything to *Mencken*, *Sima Yi*, and anyone else who thinks they can help."

"The Zeen better have some answers, or we are fucked." Through the gaps in Zeen appendages, Trapper watched the oversized door leading to Central Control open. A Marine not in his combat suit stepped out to hold the door for the engineering team. They walked by without acknowledging his existence. When the major reached him, he stopped. "Think nothing of that, Private. They're here to save us from ourselves."

"Funny, Major. I thought they were here to save us from Jemmin."

Trapper ducked to step through the doorway and found a massive room with hundreds of stations. In an open area, the Marines had parked their Gamera-class combat suits, lined up as if they were in formation. The major stopped in perfect alignment with the others and unsealed it to climb out the back. He flexed his still-tingling fingers and toes.

"Good to have you back, Major," Sergeant Bing remarked.

"Freezing sucks. I don't recommend it."

Bing pointed toward a bank of systems and displays, but before they could take a step, a Zeen engineer commandeered the space and started actively engaging. "If we had been able to go over there, you would have been able to access a certain amount of information surrounding the gate launch bay."

The Zeen at the position looked up and made eye contact with its fellows. Two of them joined it in the area, and all three started tapping and gesturing madly.

"Is that a good sign?" Wu asked.

Trapper shrugged. "No clue. What we *can* do is make sure this area is secure. Spread your people out and give the Zeen all the room they need. Did you find a terminal the Zeen have not taken over where I might be able to access anything within the *'Keeper*?"

Bing took two steps and tapped a fingernail on the nearest terminal. It came to life. Trapper and the two sergeants looked at it but couldn't make heads or tails of the information on the screen. "We send it to *Mencken* and they tell us what it says. Who the hell over there reads Originator?"

Trapper knew the answer—Jem—but remained vague. "There are some ridiculously smart people in the Legion. Don't ever underestimate the Metalheads."

Bing nodded. "Wasn't my intent to disparage our sisters in crime."

"I'd say drop and give me infinity, but we got shit to do. Secure the room and let the Zeen take care of business. I need to coordinate with the *Mencken*."

The sergeants acknowledged the order and hurried away. When Trapper was alone, he used a P2P channel to contact Jem. "Trapper here. I'm at one of the stations in the *'Keeper's* Central Control. Hundreds of people could have worked in here at the same time, and they still would have had plenty of room."

"My analysis suggests they don't need anyone, despite having that many stations. At one point, the ship might have used a manual interface, but that is no longer necessary. I think you already knew that," Jem replied.

"Stating the obvious, Jem. What if they built this control center for us?"

There was a longer delay than usual with Jem's reply. "That is an interesting premise, Major Trapper. The Originators defy analysis in many cases. The question of whether they could see the future is in doubt since time has not been conquered, but the rise of a sub-species to a position of dominance within the universe is calculable. Humanity's rise might have been predicted. The humanoid shape is more common than not. I can see the variables—"

Trapper interrupted Jem's train of thought. "I'm sorry to harsh your buzz, but can you focus on helping us take over this damn ship?"

"My apologies, Major. I'll need you to conduct manual adjustments using the panel until such time as I can connect directly. This is nothing like the life support system, which is similar to our own." Jem started directing Trapper, describing the symbols and naming them to make it easier as they progressed.

Fifteen minutes later, Trapper wasn't sure they'd made any progress. They had to keep backtracking from dead ends to explore new paths through the system.

When Trapper looked up, he found the Marines looking tense, while the Zeen were doing the same thing he was, and actively gesturing above screens at stations throughout Central Control. Trapper tried not impacting the screen with his fingers. He adjusted the angle at which he approached a symbol to activate it. The result changed.

"Hang on, Jem. This system is three-dimensional. It's controlled not by tapping but by gesturing in the space above the screen." Trapper splayed his fingers and made a waving 'S.' The panel extended into a virtual space in front of him where he could see a thousand symbols in a ten by ten by ten matrix. "This complicates things."

Once Jem understood what had happened and could see the symbols, he started directing the major through a complex series of gestures, coming in from the side and slashing down through the symbol he wanted to activate. Down or up to activate, or at a forty-five-degree angle to open more options from a single symbol.

Trapper blinked to clear his vision, looking up to allow his eyes to adjust. He found a Zeen standing close, watching him. "Can I help you?"

"Show Zeen," it stated, stabbing one of its "fingers" at the virtual interface. It led Trapper back to the station it was working on. With a swish of his hand over the top, the interface appeared. The Zeen pushed Trapper out of the way and started interacting as if already a virtuoso and the keyboard had just appeared.

Another Zeen tapped him on the shoulder.

"Fine." The major hurried from one Zeen station to the next, activating their displays. When he made it back to his own, nearly ten minutes had passed. His comm device lay on a counter next to the station where he'd been working. It was blinking.

"Sorry, Jem. I had to give the Zeen a hand. You know what they say. Hands with fingers are better than hands without."

"I am not sure I have ever heard that expression before, but maybe I do not know the proper 'they' you reference. But that is irrelevant. May I encourage haste?"

"We're running out of time, aren't we?"

"I would prefer not to put you under such pressure, but since you asked, yes. We are almost out of time. Please activate the interface, and let's get back to where we were."

10

SOMEBODY MUST DO SOMETHING

H.L. Mencken **Conference Room**

Admiral Corbyn was on the screen. Ten other ship captains were muted and watching.

"These are my final orders until we can regroup. The mission is to eliminate Jemmin influence on humanity. Our analysis shows that we must go into Jemmin space to attack them where they least expect it, to cut the head off this snake. Then we need to do the same to the Vorr. I've broken the fleet into three separate task forces: a Jemmin primary called Task Force Sword, a Vorr primary called Task Force Spear, and a small reserve force called Task Force Bow, standing ready to go where needed. Repair and resupply will reside with Bow. They will maintain comm and supply lines with both Sword and Spear.

"General Pushkin, embarked on the *Mencken,* will command Sword, and Commodore Meng aboard *Sima Yi* will command Spear. I've transferred my flag to *Blencathra,* a destroyer, to direct the strategic engagement as part of Task Force Bow. Sword will travel with the Zeen, and Spear and Bow will move with the *Keeper*. I've transmitted the hull numbers of those ships assigned to each TF. Rally your forces and prepare to fall in behind the alien heavies. We will travel through their virtual gates to rally points Beta Four One and Zeta Seven. Questions?"

They had lots of questions, too many to ask. Time was a luxury they didn't have. Planning was critical for success, yet they didn't have any time for that either—only a loose plan with the largest human fleet ever assembled, preparing to go deeper into space than anyone had ever gone before.

Sounded like a pipe dream.

Or a story of legend.

The admiral wished them well in the Fleet's traditional way. "May the solar winds fill your sails now and forever. Corbyn out."

Pushkin scowled as he looked at the faces around the table. "Captain Podsednik, put the ship next to the Zeen worldship and keep us there until I say differently. We will protect it like it's the last steak in the chow hall. Bring the ships around to us and form up on the Zeen."

Podsy nodded and bolted from the room.

"Colonel Jenkins, Colonel Cao. I need you to be ready. We're taking the fight to the Jemmin homeworld."

"Do we have any information about what to expect?"

"Jem provided estimates, but we have no certainties. We won't be able to breathe their air, but that hasn't held us back. Plan for self-containment throughout the op we'll call 'Home Plate.'"

"Population numbers? Urban environment? Above ground? Underground? A contested descent?" Pushkin shook his head at all the questions. "We know just about zero. My guess is that they will be a lower population, high-technology society. They'll have their full arsenal of weapons at their command, and most of those will be invisible to us, at least initially. It'll be the hardest attack you'll ever make because your mechs will die even when they've done everything right."

Colonel Cao of the Solar Marines acknowledged the general's fears stoically. Jenkins tilted his head from side to side as if that would help him better internalize Pushkin's concerns.

Jenkins finally conceded that he would have to drop with less than ample planning time. "We'll make it work. When do you think we'll make it to Jemmin space?"

"And there's part of the friction of war, Colonel. We don't know where the Jemmin homeworld is, so it may take a few tries before we enter the right system."

Leeroy Jenkins wasn't as bothered by that as he was by not knowing what the Metal Legion would drop into or what its objective would be once there. "Will we need to drop?"

"If we're ready to make planetfall and don't need to, nothing has been lost, but if we need to and aren't ready?" Pushkin let the two colonels fill in the rest of it.

"Understood. We'll get our units packed and racked and ready to drop."

"Same," Colonel Cao said. "About my forty Marines on 'Keeper?"

Pushkin looked at the table, slowly shaking his head. "They'll be going with Task Force Spear. We have neither the time nor the assets to recover them from the 'Keeper."

Cao clenched his jaws until the muscles started to creak. He gave a curt nod. It wasn't the answer he'd expected or wanted.

The Mencken started to accelerate but within the lower range.

"Take your stations, gentlemen, and good luck," Pushkin told them as he stood. The colonels stood to attention and then hurried out. General Pushkin sat down and tapped the computer interface to bring up the tactical situation. The dots on the board looked like fireflies around a flower patch. "What a shitshow. I hope we do not lose anyone just trying to get into formation, but I am not going to hold my breath."

The assault carrier had already been fairly close to the worldship, on the back side of the Nexus gate. The other ships were trying to catch up. *Henry VIII* maneuvered behind the *Mencken,* while *Mencius* limped toward the formation of civilian ships that raced to catch up.

"Fucking stem bolts ship assigned to Spear. What in the hell am I supposed to do with an old beater filled with stem bolts?"

Zeen Home Three

Xi glared at the Zeen encircling her in the spherical room. Bob had already talked to them in their language without allowing the major the pleasure of knowing what they were saying. She had no idea if he was an advocate or telling them to be cool around the crazy human.

"I need my mech. You can call it an emotional support device if you want, but it needs to be on this ship."

"Zeen have contacted *Mencken*. Your combat machine is on its way," Bob explained.

Bob had been an advocate, then.

"Thanks, Bob. Let's go meet it." She turned to the crowd, remembering not to bow. She faced them eye to eye. "Thank you for your accommodation. I will continue to do my best for *Zeen Home Three*."

"Symmetry," one of the Zeen said in a rough, translated voice.

"Symmetry, my friends."

Bob led the way out. When they reached the transit shaft. Bob walked into the airflow without breaking stride. Xi rolled into it and assumed a sitting position like she was in a recliner. She carefully crossed her legs and laced her fingers behind her head. "I think you have something here with the pneumatic, frictionless, partless lift."

"I don't understand." Bob rotated slowly until he faced the major.

"An elevator with no moving parts. I can get behind something like this. Would the Zeen be willing to share this technology? We can be rich, Bob!"

"Rich was a name that I discounted. Too many non-applicable meanings."

"And Bob doesn't?" Xi countered.

"If a battle goes poorly and we are jettisoned to space, Bob seemed more correct than Rich."

"I'll be damned. Zeen have a sense of humor! Whodathunk that?" Xi threw her hands up and started to spin. She regained control. "On a serious note, I think this technology could revolutionize movement between decks of our bigger ships. How do you keep from crashing into each other?"

"Zeen look before leaping."

"Son of a bitch, Bob! You are on a roll. If our world wasn't going to end any minute now, I'd invite you to the next Metal Legion party. You'd be a big hit and have a great time."

Bob fixed Xi with a stare from his multi-faceted eyes. "Jemmin come. We must hurry."

"To the hangar bay to pick up *Elvira* and my people?"

"No." Bob tried to move into the central column of air to descend, but Xi grabbed a leg and struggled to hold him back.

"We're not leaving my people out there!"

·   ·   ·

H.L. Mencken

The emergency klaxons sounded. "Battle stations!" Podsy commanded from the captain's chair of the assault carrier. "All hands to battle stations. This is not a drill."

Podsy looked at the report from Jem as relayed from the Zeen to Major Trapper. It had two words. "Jemmin come." The message had been broadcast to the fleet, which was scattered while simultaneously being grouped too close together. The civilian ships were in the middle of finding their places within a protective fleet boundary, but they hadn't made it yet. The kabuki dance continued.

Freighter captains jumped on the broadcast channel, demanding instructions. No one identified themselves. They couldn't be allowed to decide for themselves. Chaos was imminent.

"Task Force Sword assigned ships, follow your orders and flight paths as already directed. Do not deviate. Do not speed up. Do not slow down. Terran heavies will take a position between you and the gate as long as you continue as instructed. If anyone runs for it, you risk killing yourself and anyone you *will* run into." Podsy looked at the comm officer. "Repeat that as often as it takes for the freighter jocks to get the word."

Pushkin signaled the bridge. Podsy checked his station. P2P. Another ass-chewing inbound. *Welcome to the big time,* Podsy thought. "Captain Podsednik," he answered as formally as he could make himself sound.

"Nice job, Skipper. Trying to change anything at this point would have killed us all. I'm going to move *Henry VIII* to assist *Mencius,* which is already in position because it can barely move under its own power. It's probably toast. I'm ordering minimal crew. Freighters need to be ready to pick up evacuees. Stay focused on the worldship, and get the rest of the fleet out of here. I'll cover our backs. *Henry VIII* will be the last one through —if it can make it."

"On it," Podsy said, but the general had already cut the link. At least his instinct to stay the course had been validated. He turned back to the tasks at hand, which was keeping the fearful from panicking. "Open a channel to the freighters."

"Open," Comm confirmed.

"I know you just got here. You've already seen one fight that was lopsided in our favor. The next one won't be. You'll see ships die at the speed of light. Don't let that detract you from your mission, which is to be ready to transit a gate that the Zeen worldship will create. I need all of you to carry out your orders. You've joined the battle for humanity. If we lose, no one will be safe no matter where they live or how far they fly into the void. People and ships are going to die. It's just how it is. Make your peace now, and every minute beyond this one will be gravy for the rest of your lives. Buckle up and get ready to fight. For our freight warriors, that means delivering goods and supplies when we need them so the warships can get back into the fight. Get your welders and metal plates ready because we're going to have ships that need to be fixed and no time to fix them before the next wave of missiles arrive.

"This is the moment when humanity stood up to Jemmin and gave them the finger. The last great act of defiance will be taking as many of those bastards with us as we can. Stay the course, people. Humanity is counting on you to get through this next gate, and then the next, and the next, until there are no more gates to cross. Then we'll come home. Prepare to gate on my mark."

Podsy drew a finger across his throat, and Comm closed the channel.

"Nicely done, Skipper," Commander Peter Wythe, the

tactical officer, said softly. He led the bridge in a round of clapping.

"Thanks. May we not die so my ego can glow under the bright lights of adulation."

Helm's head dropped. "New contact coming through the gate. It's Jemmin," he said softly, but everyone heard him as if he had bellowed the words.

Zeen Worldship

"Jemmin are here," Bob reported as they watched the hangar door open for a shuttle pushing an ungainly drop-canister through. The hangar door started closing as soon as the shuttle was through. "*Zeen Home Three* will gate now."

"I know," Xi confirmed, feeling a strange warmth within. Jemmin were crashing the party. Within her mind, she extrapolated the ship movements from the positions she had last seen them. Less than half the fleet would escape, and that included the hardest-won prize in the universe—the Originators' *Gate-Keeper*. "Any news from your engineers?"

Bob watched the shuttle move the drop-can into place on the deck and then unclamped to park next to it. Magnetic clamps locked both down. The shuttle side hatch opened and her crew stepped off: Penny, *Elvira's* Wrench, main mechanic, and Lu, the Monkey, the gopher who did the other jobs to keep the mech functioning. The shuttle's pilot stepped out after them, looking around for where to go. Bob opened the hatch, and Xi stuck her head out and yelled.

"Get over here; we're getting ready to gate! Double-time!"

The three started to run. Used to riding into combat, they were still fit and covered the ground quickly.

"Oh, no," Bob said.

"What'd you do, Lu?" Penny said, slapping the Monkey on his shoulder.

"There is a delay in the gate process," the insectoid explained. "We've received new coordinates from the *Gate-Keeper*. Come." Bob scrambled down a different corridor than they had taken the last time they left the ship's hangar.

Xi shrugged at her fellows, and together, the four humans hurried after the Zeen.

11

A NEW HOPE

GateKeeper Central Control

"A Jemmin cruiser is coming through the Nexus gate," Sergeant Wu announced to everyone in Central Control.

"Come on, Jem. We're out of fucking time," Major Trapper was starting to lose focus. The Zeen engineers had grown agitated and were communicating in their own language, which sounded like an odd buzz, growing in volume to the point that it was almost painful.

"I have not been able to access the system. I have failed," Jem apologized.

The buzz reached a crescendo and suddenly stopped.

"The system is unlocked," Jem declared. "Stand by."

"What does that mean? Jem? What's going on?" Silence was his only reply. Major Trapper looked from one Marine's face to another. "Get your suits on, boys and girls. We'll fight them any way we can."

The Marines were galvanized into action. They smoothly ran across the space and climbed into their suits using well-practiced motions.

"Major?" Sergeant Wu wondered after the two squads were

powered and secured.

"A few moments more," Trapper muttered as he watched his interface for clues to tell him what was going on.

"Central projection," Jem finally said.

A realistic image of the gate appeared, with a Jemmin cruiser nearly completely through. The gate flashed and a sheet of darkness cut across the opening, cleaning slicing the ship in half. The reactor lost containment and the explosion acted like a rocket, blasting the remains of the ship forward. The superstructure couldn't handle the acceleration and started to come apart.

Railgun fire from *Mencius* stitched the wreckage and sent it tumbling away from the fleet.

"Nice trick, Jem. Thanks for the visual. Does that mean what I think it means?"

"If you are thinking that the Originators' ship is powerful enough to turn gates on and off like turning lights on and off, you are correct. It also means we are one step closer to understanding the technology behind the gates."

"What does that mean for a layman like me?" Trapper gave the Marines the hand-signal directing them to stand by.

"It means that we might be able to redirect gates while deploying new gates. There are three completed gates inside the appropriately-named *GateKeeper* that are ready to be rolled into space. If we can activate them and link them to a gate we want to travel from, the Terran fleet's chances for success in Operation End of War have just greatly improved."

"That would be real nice, Jem. Don't tell me what our odds used to be. I'm glad to hear they're better. You had best brief Admiral Corbyn and the task force commanders."

Zeen Home Three

Bob stopped, stood motionless for a few moments, then

turned back to his human charges. "Jemmin have been stopped. Would you like lunch now?"

Xi furrowed her brow as she contemplated the Zeen's words. "How?" she managed to ask.

"Nexus gate has been rendered inoperable."

"I'm liking that!" Xi exclaimed, throwing her hand over her head so her crewmates could deliver high-fives. "The last thing I wanted was another trip through Nexus space. Too many battles in what used to be safe space, but then again, that's probably our fault since that's where the bullies hang out. Fuck those spunkmasters."

"Right in their oversized eyeballs," Penny added. She smacked Lu's smaller hand, and they hooted "Oorah" in unison.

"What are the next steps, Bob?" Xi asked, still smiling from the short celebration.

"Lunch?" the insectoid wondered.

"Of course, lunch. Metalheads are always hungry. But after that, what will the fleet do? I need to talk to my people, but I am sure they're still picking up the pieces. Is my comm device live to receive calls from the fleet?"

"Like Zeen in a hive, Major Bao has not been disconnected from her people. Your comm is funneled through our systems for maximum connectivity."

"I wouldn't want you to miss the chance to listen in," Xi shot back before thinking that they were listening anyway, no matter where she went on the ship.

"Only if Major Bao agrees. Zeen have many concerns."

The major's stomach growled a low roar. "I guess that settles it. Thank you, Bob. Lead on to lunch."

Xi's comm device buzzed before she could take a step.

Blencathra, TAC Fleet Command

"We've bought ourselves some time, nothing more," Admiral Corbyn clarified to Commodore Meng and General Pushkin. The captains of the other heavies watched with interest, fidgeting because they all had a million things to do now that they had extra time.

"Request support vessels assist in the repair of *Mencius*. I'm still picking up the pieces over here," Commodore Kyu-bin stared at the screen. An ugly bruise darkened one eye. His hair was messed up from continually running his hand over his head. Lights flickered in the background.

"Dispatch the necessary assets," the admiral told someone off-screen. He turned back and made eye contact with Kyu-bin. "On the way, Commodore. Hold down the fort until they arrive. That's your mission for now. Report back when you have an estimate of when you'll be able to rejoin the fleet."

The commodore saluted and signed off.

"What about the civvies, General?"

"They didn't run away. They stayed on assigned routes at designated speeds. I know they wanted to flee, but they didn't. The freighter jocks showed some mettle. I'll take that as a win."

"I think we can all call that a victory that isn't anywhere near as minor as it sounds. They did what they were told to do. At some point in time, we will need them to exercise their own initiative, but that time is not now. We are too many sardines in too small a can."

It wasn't a question and didn't invite discussion.

It was time for something Admiral Corbyn had held onto for as long as he could.

"Some of you already know this, so bear with me. For the others, this is not common knowledge, and there's no reason for it to go beyond this small group." He made sure everyone acknowledged his words. "And that goes for everyone else listening with you, who I expect are your senior staff." He took a deep breath. "For some time now, thanks to the efforts of Colonel Lee Jenkins and Major Xi Bao, we have had open communication with a Jem'un."

Someone gasped, which threw the admiral off his game. He pressed his lips together, the expression commanding the others to silence. "A long, long time ago, there were two races, Jemmin and Jem'un. After a bloody civil war, the Jem'un were virtually eliminated. What we have is a gestalt intelligence we call 'Jem.' It is the stored intelligence of the remaining Jem'un survivors, consolidated into a single entity. Jem has been able to help us stay one step ahead of Jemmin for the past few campaigns, including our victories over the One Mind, the Arh'kel, and of late, Jemmin. We have Jem to thank for closing the gate, but we also have our Zeen allies to thank for unlocking the '*Keeper*. We win as a team, even though it looks like the humans are blocking for our all-stars, who are in charge of scoring."

The reference was lost on many, but the sentiment was solid. Humanity was out of its league but trying to catch up.

"They need us every bit as much as we need them," Colonel Jenkins said. "I bet Jemmin have never had a door slammed in their face like that. I wonder what kind of conversations are happening over in Jemminville."

Admiral Corbyn smiled and closed his eyes for a moment. "I'm sure it's not pleasant. Jem, can you join us, please?"

"I am here, Admiral Corbyn, General Pushkin, Commodore Meng. Thank you for inviting me."

From a shoulder bag, Podsy removed the device within which Jem existed and set it on the table. Measuring five centimeters in diameter and approximately fifty centimeters long, one end of its ruby-red depths seemed somehow alive with flickering movement. The other end was dark, extending for most of its length. No light reflected from it, yet it shone. "This is Jem."

Captain Podsednik placed a comm relay and translation device next to the crystal. It blinked as Jem worked through it.

"What kind of time do we have before Jemmin figure out a way to get to this system?" the general asked.

"Jemmin do not have independent faster-than-light technology. I calculate they have a twenty-four percent chance to override the gate lockout within the next seven days. Within thirty days, there is a ninety percent chance that Jemmin will restore access from the Nexus side of the gate."

"Well, shit," Jenkins mumbled.

"I wouldn't put it quite that way," General Pushkin stated. His words, along with a look, issued a mild reproof to the colonel. Jenkins didn't care. He wasn't about to change. They had more important things to do than worry about protocol. They needed a plan that didn't rely on time.

Admiral Corbyn regained control of the meeting. "Assets?"

"Eighteen mechs combat-ready, cruiser grade and lighter. One hundred twenty drop-ready Marines. Two hundred thirty-one warships, and one hundred seventeen freighters with a total haul capacity of over a hundred million tons," Podsy reported, reading a document that had also been sent to the general. He knew the general wanted the numbers out for all to consider.

"Personnel count?" the admiral pressed.

Those numbers had not been consolidated. Information from the freighters was still coming in, but in such a haphazard way, it wouldn't readily integrate into the database. "A moment, Admiral." Podsy started typing furiously to write a quick program that would count the numbers from the disparate reports. "Looks like a shade over one hundred and four thousand, with ninety-five thousand being Fleet assets. Nine thousand civvies tagging along to protect."

"That is the point I wanted to make, Captain." The admiral gave Podsednik an approving look. "Ninety percent of our force to protect the other ten? No. They are coming forward with us. We'll do our best to keep them out of harm's way, but our combat power needs to be focused on offensive measures. We're taking the fight to the enemy. Every single asset can be committed to the battle. Don't forget that when tackling your plans, or heaven forbid, reacting to something that's spinning out of control."

The admiral looked at those watching remotely before directing the conversation down a darker path.

"I don't have an acceptable attrition rate. If we can do this without losing a single life, let's make it happen. But we all know that's not going to happen. We've already lost people and will lose more. Probably too many more. Who will return to Terran or Solar space? I don't know, but there must be at least one to tell humanity whether we've won the war or not. It's a low bar, but it's all I have. I know it's bad luck to send your final wishes to loved ones staying behind before we move out, but now's the time. You all know what you need to do. I'll be working with TFs Sword and Spear, along with the *Keeper* and the Zeen, to determine when we'll gate out. You'll know the date and time as soon as I do. Dismissed."

Corbyn didn't bother taking any questions. The orders had been issued. They had a month's worth of work to do and maybe a week in which to do it.

Jenkins and Colonel Cao stood up, but General Pushkin waved at them to keep their seats. Podsy had been reaching for Jem and stopped mid-motion.

"It's time we let the Zeen know about Jem," the general remarked.

"I think they already know," Podsy replied. "But we can confirm it for them."

Pushkin nodded. "Comm, get me Major Xi Bao and the Zeen."

12

ALL HANDS ON DECK

Zeen Home Three

"Major Bao," she answered, looking oddly at the comm device while her stomach protested the inevitable delay before being fed. It rolled with a new growl, demanding her attention. She tightened her abs and clenched her teeth. "Just deal with it!"

"General Pushkin here. Deal with what, Major?"

Xi's mouth fell open at the Russian-accented reply.

"My apologies, General. We have a minor internal rebellion ongoing since chow time has come and gone. Thanks for making sure my rig and can made it over. I also have one shuttle pilot in tow."

"Send the pilot back. We've got work to do. If you hadn't heard, the gate is locked out, but that is a temporary delay. Admiral Corbyn and I would like to talk to the Zeen about our mutual friend from the Brick."

"Understood. Stand by." Xi looked at Bob. "We'll need to have this conversation in the round room as soon as we send the shuttle back."

Bob started walking toward the hangar access hatch. They

hadn't covered much ground and only a minute passed before they shook hands and sent the shuttle pilot on her way. Bob moved toward the central shaft.

"You guys are going to love this. Follow my lead. It is the next best thing to driving a mech."

Bob ignored the humans following him as he maintained a steady pace deeper into the worldship. He stepped into the shaft leading to the hive core, slid smoothly into the middle flow, and headed downward.

Xi dove through the opening and executed a somersault, followed by going spread-eagle to stop herself in the descending stream. Penny and Lu stepped in and immediately started to rise.

"Get into the middle!" Xi shouted through cupped hands. The Monkey and the Wrench swam until they reached the central channel and started downward. They made their bodies into torpedoes to move faster, to catch up to the major, who was far ahead. She waved them off, but it was too late, as was her cry of "Noooo!"

Penny slammed headfirst into her before Lu clipped them both and they all started to spin and tumble.

"Dumbass!" Xi settled into the flow, rubbing her stomach and rib cage while Penny mumbled a steady stream of apologies. Lu recovered and slowed himself until he was even with the rest of the crew.

"This is pretty cool," Lu commented.

"I've asked about the technology for when this is all over. Can you imagine New America high-rises with air elevators? We'd never need another playground."

Penny and Lu chuckled.

Lu was the first to speak. "What do you think the Head Shed wants with the Zeen?"

"Discuss the timeline. Coordinate next steps. Figure out

where the hell we're going. We still don't know where Jemmin homeworld is." As Xi thought about it, Jem was the combined memories and personalities of four hundred ninety-two Jem'un. How could they not know where Jemmin called home if they had come from one race of beings? Every human in Terra knew where Sol was and vice versa. "The good news is that we won't have to wait long. Get ready to roll onto the landing."

Xi pulled past the others to show them how it was done. She didn't want to make an entrance like last time.

Bob exited smoothly, stepping onto the landing. Xi misjudged, but only by enough to flex her knees heavily before following Bob. She didn't look back when she heard the grunts as Penny and Lu crumpled onto the landing. They stood and brushed themselves off before limping after the major.

Xi walked to the middle of the sphere, while her people remained just inside the doorway. Bob stood nearby. "May I have comm piped into the room, please?" Xi asked.

Bob replied, "It is ready."

"General Pushkin, are you there? We're live with the hive's leadership," Xi announced.

"I am here, along with Admiral Corbyn. We wanted to make sure we kept no secrets from our allies. We have with us a gestalt intelligence, a combination of four hundred ninety-two separate personalities formerly known as the Jem'un."

"Zeen know," came the simple reply. Xi couldn't tell who spoke, but the words went unchallenged. "Jem'un were destroyed every bit as much as the Zeen, but Jem'un gave Zeen a new world and a new chance at life. Jem'un had no such chance. Asymmetry."

"Meet Jem," General Pushkin announced in a relaxed voice.

"Good morning. May I ask the status of your development of the gravity cannon based on Jem'un technology?"

"Holy crap, Jem!" Xi mumbled under her breath.

"Zeen gravity cannon is not functional." The translated voice sounded neutral.

"Ah. We suspected it would take time to rebuild your civilization to a standard by which the cannon's schematics would be replicable. I was incorrect in my assumption. I had hoped the gravity cannon would be operational to help us during our foray into Jemmin space."

"Zeen transmitting current engineering to Jem," one of the Zeen stated from within the sphere. Xi thought the voice had come from below her, but it was hard to tell. It bounced around the room, sounding like it came from everywhere. She wondered if such an arrangement would improve video game quality.

"I have received your transmission. It will take me some time to get through this. I am searching through all available data to narrow the possible location of the Jemmin homeworld. Can you provide any assistance?"

"Jemmin homeworld is not the original home. That was lost when Jemmin blew up their own sun. Arrogance cost them dearly."

"Can you transmit the coordinates of the original homeworld?"

"Done." The Zeen were fabulously cooperative. Xi started to grow suspicious.

"Do you know where Jemmin leaders are? How many are there? How many Jemmin exist in the galaxy?" she asked.

"No, but we know where they are not."

Cryptic, but better than nothing, Xi thought.

"They have a top-heavy leadership structure. Find the top, and the rest will disintegrate. They will follow their last orders for the rest of their lives."

Xi winced. "They seemed more independent than order-following drones. They fight like they have free will. And there was only one of them on a planet with millions of Arh'kel. I don't understand how they could be drones."

"Interesting information. Thank you," General Pushkin inserted as a warning to Xi. She put her hand over her mouth as a reminder that she was an observer in this meeting, not a participant.

"Thank you for helping us," Admiral Corbyn stated. "Zeen-Terran alliance. Symmetry. We estimate seven days before Jemmin have a realistic shot at breaking the lockout code and reactivating the gate."

"Symmetry. We must be gone in seven days' time. Zeen recommend Briallus Cluster, inner world seven four."

After a brief pause and some shuffling, Admiral Corbyn replied, "We don't know where that is."

"Coordinates transmitted," Zeen responded.

I guess that obviates rally points Beta Four One and Zeta Seven.

As if reading her mind, the admiral said the same thing. "We'll assign new rally points based on coordinates within the Briallus Cluster. We'll have the pleasure of escorting and protecting *Zeen Home Three* in exchange for sharing the Zeen FTL?" The admiral made the last question sound like a statement.

"Symmetry," the Zeen agreed. More than one voice had spoken. The hive agreed.

"What is the status of the *GateKeeper*?" Corbyn asked.

The Zeen delayed for a while before answering, and when they did, they didn't answer anything. "Working."

Mencken, **Bridge**

"You should probably get some sleep, Podsy," Colonel Jenkins said softly to the ship's beleaguered skipper. It had been five days since the gate had been shut down. Time was running out, and they were only halfway done repairing and rearming the combat fleet. The civilian ships had become a drain on resources, specifically fuel and parts for fusion reactors. They'd abandoned a dozen civilian freighters that couldn't be easily repaired and consolidated the crews on other civilian vessels, except for those who were useful on the TAC ships.

"Volunteers," as the leadership thought of them. They weren't sure what the engineers and useful hands thought of themselves.

Sometimes you weren't given a choice, which was how Captain Podsednik felt with the weight of the universe on his shoulders.

"I'll sleep tomorrow." He produced a stim from his pocket, but Jenkins caught his hand before he could inject it.

"Sleep today. Tomorrow is going to be a bum's rush, and then we'll be moving. When we make it to our new rally point, if we're secure, then we'll rest again. You've been there too many times," Lee cautioned. "You will never know when you won't get another chance to rest. When we encounter Jemmin, it's going to be a run-and-gun until we can hit them where it matters. After that, if we're still alive, we can sleep. Don't peak too early."

Podsy slipped the stim back into his pocket. "Tactical, you have the conn. Carry out the plan of the day. I'll be in my quarters for the next eight hours. Make sure no one bothers me."

"Aye, aye, Skipper." The tactical officer replied using the Marines' term. Podsy nodded. He liked it. Skipper of the boat. He shook hands with Colonel Jenkins and strode briskly off the bridge. "Captain off the bridge!"

GateKeeper

"Sir?" The voice sounded like it was coming from a thousand miles away through dense Arh'kel atmosphere. "Sir?' the voice insisted.

Major Tim Trapper, Junior, forced his eyes open. "I'm sure I've felt better, but I don't remember when," he grumbled.

Sergeant Rast from 2nd Squad loomed overhead. "Your watch, Major. I tried to talk you out of it, but you insisted."

"Did anyone see who was driving the dropship that hit me?" Trapper struggled to sit, then rubbed his face and head before standing.

"Don't go forty-eight hours before getting some sleep next time, sir!" The sergeant wasn't wrong.

"How long was I out?" The major swayed and blinked. The space had been converted into sleeping quarters for the platoon. Gamera combat suits filled the majority of the space, while tactical sleeping bags were organized in rows. Twenty Marines slept while Rast had the second to last watch. With the change of guard, nineteen slept.

Trapper wanted his people to get as much rest as possible before the fleet transitioned away from New America 2 space. And Marines, in their usual fashion, never slept unprotected. They always had a guard. In every clime and place, they were vigilant, so those they protected could sleep soundly, without worry. It was part of what made Marines special. They didn't do it for the adulation of the masses, but for their brothers in arms, the spirit of the Corps, and the higher ideal they aspired to.

And they got to fire the best weapons available and blow a lot of stuff up.

"Thanks, Rast. Hit the rack. I'll be banging the gong in a couple hours. And if you want my opinion, which you're going to get anyway, you need all the beauty sleep you can get."

"Tell me something I don't know, sir."

"Sleep fast, Sergeant." The major offered his hand, and the two shook.

Marines didn't salute uncovered, which meant anytime they were indoors. Saluting had gone out of fashion because space didn't offer the conditions of old, where Marines hit the beach, screamed their war cries, and headed inland to engage the enemy. The space versions were just as fierce, but behind the suits and spread far apart to limit the destruction caused by area weapons, nukes, plasma bolts, and railgun pellets accelerated to fantastic speeds. The amount of damage done in the modern combat environment would overwhelm lesser warriors, but Marines trained their whole lives for it, finding order within the chaos.

The Marines fought harder and better. It's what they did.

Trapper looked his platoon over. Men and women, some snoring, most not. Nothing more than small and soft bundles, vulnerable. He'd wake them in three hours, not two, and start with an hour of PT, physical conditioning to harden their bodies and get the blood pumping for what was to follow.

He walked the perimeter of their makeshift quarters, checking that the suits were powered down but ready for emergency occupation. He verified the rear hatch was secure. He continued until he stepped into the corridor and closed the main door behind him, then pulled out his comm and looked at it for a moment before making the call.

"Colonel Jenkins, Trapper." After a reasonable wait, Trapper repeated his request. The colonel finally answered.

"Colonel, I wanted to request that the Marines return to *Mencken*. You're going to need us when we hit J-Ville."

"Negative, Tim. The safest place to be will be on the 'Keeper until Jemmin break through our lines. I expect they'll try to take over the ship, which means we need a defensive force ready to repel boarders. Colonel Cao and the remaining Solar

Marines will be joining you, along with all the Marine drop-ships and their support crews. If we control the skies and have space superiority, we'll launch you to whatever planet needs your delicate touch. If we need the Marines in an offensive role, you'll be there, but we also want our combat force intact. I think it's going to be a mess out here, but that's just me. I think Admiral Corbyn has more faith in the fleet than I do."

Major Trapper's head started spinning through the possibil-ities—twenty Terran Marines and sixty Solar Marines to defend a ship the size of a small planet. "Repel boarders," Tim said slowly. "I can't visualize that since we've never gone head to head with Jemmin ground troops."

"One Jemmin and a thousand drones," Jenkins replied cryp-tically. "There's no way Jemmin will sacrifice themselves in hand-to-hand. They're just as soft and squishy as we are."

"Speak for yourself, Metalhead," the major quipped.

"I always do. Stay frosty, Tim. We'll be moving the fleet later today, and our first jump will be into Jemmin space. I don't think there will be much peace after that. Anything else?"

"Negative, sir. Thanks for your candor. We'll protect the 'Keeper as if it was our own daughter. Trapper out." He checked the time. Two hours and fifty-four minutes before raising the dead.

13

BEHIND ENEMY LINES

H.L. Mencken, **Ready Room**

Admiral Corbyn, Commodore Meng, and General Pushkin were the only ones in the video meeting.

"We're as ready as we'll ever be unless you can give me another month and a real shipyard for the capital repairs," Commodore Meng stated. He knew full well that they were out of time. "Task Force Spear is ready."

"Task Force Sword is green," General Pushkin declared without further commentary.

"And Task Force Bow is set. We'll follow Sword through the worldship's wormhole. I cannot emphasize enough that you *have to* keep those two ships alive and well. We will be a thousand light-years behind enemy lines. The worldship and the *'Keeper* are the only way to get back here."

Meng and Pushkin understood that only too well. It had complicated the general planning for the commitment of assets. They were going on the attack with a heavily defensive strategy. It reduced the amount of combat power they could project against an enemy stronghold.

"It would be nice to have bigger bombs, better bombs, but

we don't have any of that. There's no Bahamut in anyone's hold, waiting for the right time to be deployed. There are no extra Vipers. There are no extra mechs. This is all we have." Corbyn ran his fingers through his graying hair, looking old and tired. He sighed heavily before sitting up straight and clenching his teeth.

"Sounds like business as usual for the TAC," the general said easily, giving a one-shoulder shrug.

"The best time to plant a tree is twenty years ago," the commodore started. "The next best time is today. What do you say we plant a tree in Jemmin's ass to thank them for the last twenty years of their bullshit?"

Corbyn chuckled. "Gentlemen, End of War begins now. Execute. See you on the other side."

The other men nodded and signed off. General Pushkin stepped from the small ready room not far from *Mencken's* bridge. When he walked onto the bridge, Tactical announced his arrival. The crew rotated in their seats to watch him. Captain Podsednik and Colonel Jenkins stood.

The general locked eyes with Podsy. "Contact the Zeen for immediate gate to Rally Point Ignatius."

The captain tapped his comm. "Coordinate and execute, Jem."

"The Zeen are ready. You can begin moving the fleet. The gate will form momentarily five kilometers off the worldship's bow."

Jenkins snorted. "Where is the bow on a round ship?" The crew snickered, but the answer came almost immediately as a whirling vortex appeared and expanded.

"*Henry VIII* is aligning with the gate and accelerating," Helm reported. A stream of ships started to match the virtual gate's spin, leaving only two kilometers between them. If anything waited on the other side, it would be a short-lived expedition, which was why they were going to the Briallus Cluster. It was the closest point to a number of Jemmin planets, while also having the lowest risk that Jemmin would be there to contest the incursion into their space.

Twenty-seven warships transited before the freighters started heading through. The gap between ships had been reduced to a single kilometer, leaving no room for error. The Zeen had delivered tight parameters that the fleet had to follow since they could only hold the gate open for so long.

While next up to the gate, a mid-size freighter blew a thruster. The explosion sent minimal debris into space, but the ship stopped spinning with the gate and started to drift. The pilot tried to compensate, but it was too late. The freighter hit the side of the gate out of sync. The ship was twisted through the edge of the corona, pulled into the gate as a pile of contorted metal.

"Power through!" Podsy shouted on the command channel. "Ignore it and keep going. Push the debris out of the way on the other side and keep going. You hesitate, you kill everyone behind you!"

Podsy clenched his fists and snarled at the screen. "Fucking garbage scows."

"Easy," Jenkins cautioned. "One team, one fight. I'm sorry for that ship's crew and their families."

Captain Podsednik looked at his shoes before nodding, white-lipped.

"No mercy from our enemies. No mercy from the elements. May the gods have mercy on their souls, so the dead may watch over the rest of us, to give us peace," the general intoned.

The ship following the doomed freighter aligned and sailed through. The next one behind it spun carefully and maintained a smooth speed. Podsy relaxed.

"Bad equipment is a bane to the brave," he said. "And keep

pressing forward. We're heading to J-ville, Jemmin central. There may be a few wrecks between here and there, but when we show up on their doorstep, they'll get the angriest version of us they've ever seen."

Task Force Bow took its spot in line following the civilian freighters assigned to Sword, the destroyers going first, sandwiching the freighters between the warships. Bow was ill-equipped to fight off a determined Jemmin resistance but could add the right firepower at the right time to sway a battle in flux. *Blencathra* lined up behind the last of its civilian shipping. Sword's final warships slid in smoothly behind Bow, lining up a kilometer apart as directed. Time was running out.

"Accelerating," Helm announced as the *Mencken* headed for last place in the long parade. Ship after ship went through without further mishap.

The assault carrier matched the spin, where the image on screen appeared to be static. The ship eased forward at the pre-programmed speed and edged over the event horizon. The viewscreen blanked. An instant later, the screen slowly cleared. The ship bumped something before they could see what it was and where they were.

Besides the ship that had been destroyed inside the gate, the two behind it had run into the debris and were heavily damaged. Metal and broken ship sections littered the area.

"No damage," Helm reported, trying to anticipate the captain's question. "The fleet is formed up ten thousand kilometers to starboard."

In the distance, the even ranks looked more like a shipyard than a designated incursion. Beyond, a rotating gas giant exuded spiraling clouds.

"Always stop to smell the roses," Jenkins said softly. "That's not something you see every day."

Podsy nodded. "Rear projection." The screen shifted. The

Zeen worldship slipped through the gate. Waves shimmered from the physical disruption of space before dissipating when the Zeen closed the gate, killing the wormhole.

"Contacts?" General Pushkin asked.

"Nothing besides the friendlies. Board is clear," Tactical answered.

The general nodded. "I'll be in the op center," he said before strolling out. The op center was the conference room where he'd planted his flag as task force commander. It had the full communications suite, which was all he needed.

"May I join you?" Jenkins asked. The general waved at him to come. The colonel had significant concerns about the next phase of the operation.

GateKeeper

"That's it. Sword is on their way," Major Trapper said. Colonel Cao acknowledged the statement with a slight tip of his chin. They were watching the same screen.

The Zeen wouldn't open a second gate simultaneously. They weren't sure what would happen, but there was a higher than zero chance it would result in something cataclysmic. The only way to test it was to run two virtual gates. The Zeen were unwilling to risk *Zeen Home Three* as part of an experiment.

"Gate to Briallus Cluster is opening," the Zeen announced through their interpretation device.

The wormhole started as a pinpoint and expanded large enough to encompass the entire *GateKeeper*, a massive vessel. A sparkling circle, distinct yet vague, rotated evenly, sending waves outward as if a stone had dropped into the center of a pond. A series of cruisers and destroyers started moving toward the opening, matching rotation as they approached. The first slipped over without issue one kilometer apart, closer than the initial Sword warships. The task force operated on faith. They wouldn't know until they met up in phase three of Operation End of War whether they were successful in transiting the gates.

"Four ships at a time," the Zeen instructed.

Someone on the *Sima Yi* replied, "We didn't prepare for that. This will be a master cluster if we start rearranging ships now. How about an offset through assigned quadrants of the gate?"

"Asymmetry," the Zeen responded.

"Sending a visual of my intent." The voice was that of Commodore Meng.

After the quickly assembled graphic arrived and played in the projection area, the Zeen agreed. "Symmetry."

The fleet broke into four separate streams, each independent of the others, heading for a different quadrant of the colossal rent in normal space. They matched rotation and disappeared through the looking glass and into the void. It cut the transit time by two thirds and not three fourths because of the initial delay in rearranging the ships. *Sima Yi* accelerated toward the center of the opening, filling the space behind Task Force Spear. The *'Keeper* closed in behind the Republican-class dreadnought, almost too close.

A second screen appeared in the central projection area, showing the Nexus gate. It remained dormant.

The *'Keeper* entered the gate and exited the other side, like going from one room to the next. The fleet was reassembling on the other side. A pinpoint of light represented a gas giant at the extreme edge of normal vision. Beyond that, Rally Point Ignatius. It was two weeks' flying time if they needed to get there, but for now, Task Force Spear would settle for implementing phase one of the op plan.

"Colonel Cao, please respond." The commodore was calling. "Defense status."

The colonel held his device close to his mouth and started talking, rapid-fire delivering the details of an extensive plan hampered by the extreme distances within the great ship. The Originators had built the vessel with high-speed travel corridors. The Marines had locked out the six systems so they could fly in their suits down the tunnels without risk of running into a magnetically levitated train, a maglev.

The plan was simple: spread themselves thin for purposes of detection. Report and rally the troops to the hotspot. There was no predicting where a Jemmin craft would try to penetrate into the ship.

"What about *GateKeeper*'s defensive systems? Can it protect itself, or do we need to install some close-in weapons for point defense?"

"The Marines will handle it. There is an airlock near each of the posted coordinates. The Marines will use manual point defense to supplement the *'Keeper*'s limited systems. This ship's defense is mostly electronic or phased magnetics or some such technology that I've never heard of before. The Zeen tried to explain it. I'm not a fan of passive defense, Commodore."

"I would expect not. Marines tend to enjoy seeing things blow up. I am a fan of anything that keeps our ships from being on the wrong end of explosions. It might work better than you think."

"Unless the Originators never contemplated the level of violence modern species are willing to wreak upon each other."

Major Trapper glowered at the thought. The levels of damage that could be inflicted by a single Marine in a Gamera suit was staggering, let alone what a Jemmin cruiser could accomplish, or a Terran dreadnought.

"I fear we will find out all too soon what that looks like.

Make sure your dropships are fueled and ready. Be prepared to redeploy from defensive positions around the *'Keeper* to the dropship for tactical insertion planetside. More to follow. Be well, Colonel. Meng out."

Colonel Cao showed the screen on his device. A countdown clock had started running. Three hours and fifty-nine minutes remained.

"Time to gate?"

"Time to gate," Cao confirmed. "Have your people suited and ready in two hours for equipment checks. At three hours, we assume our position. And at four hours, we follow Sword into Jemmin space. This time, though, Major, we will have no reconnaissance. We're heading into a potentially hot zone completely blind."

Trapper wasn't dissuaded. "But we're bringing a lot of firepower with us, just in case the natives want to make a stink. Two hours to inspection. We'll meet you in space Queen 1147-4."

"Roger."

Trapper hurried away. They had broken the ship into five thousand frames nose to tail and twenty-six letters from port to starboard sections. The last number was the deck above the keel, if the ship had one. It was a rough system, but no one could find whatever the Originators had used, and the ship was too big for arbitrary designations. At least the grid system would get them close.

Colonel Cao stayed in the central control area with the relentless Zeen. They hadn't stood down from their stations since they'd arrived seven days earlier. Cao wondered if they ever slept.

He was happy to have them on board because they made it possible to do things the humans could not. It took Jem to crack the operating system after the Zeen had unlocked it, but Jem could only do so much. The efforts were burning Jem's life force. Over eighty-five percent of his power was gone, leaving him with reduced capacity, slowing his calculations and ability to multi-task. Jem's almost exclusive efforts had been to determine the location of Jemmin's home planet, something they strove to keep secret.

Jem had to break codes to view system data from recovered Jemmin wrecks. So much mismatched and convoluted information designed specifically to prevent someone from doing exactly what Jem was attempting. The difference was that Jem would succeed, with time and enough data.

Just not yet.

But Jem wasn't on board the *GateKeeper*. He was with Task Force Sword, leaving Colonel Cao with the Zeen to provide his insight. And they weren't talking.

He approached the closest Zeen to encourage information sharing. "What does a Vorr planet look like?"

The insectoid stopped what it was doing. "Water. Much water."

"Are their cities underwater? And what kind of fortifications do they have?"

"Unknown." The Zeen returned its focus to the workstation, ignoring further questions from the human. Cao had time to kill, so he found a quiet spot, sat cross-legged, and closed his eyes. He started reviewing the possibilities based on a sea-dwelling enemy. Water impact on weapons and movement. Sensor limitations. Objectives. Would they even need to go dirtside?

By categorizing the options, he could adopt the ones that applied more quickly. He had eighty Marines counting on him to get it right.

14

PHASE 1 COMPLETE. BEGIN PHASE 2

Zeen Home Three

Xi Bao completed her fourth circuit down and back up the airlift. Penny and Lu stepped out after the second trip.

"Bored, Major?" Lu called through cupped hands.

"Just a lot," Xi replied, but she smoothly slid across the wind and stepped lightly onto the landing that led to the quarters that had been allocated to the humans. Next door was a place to get food, but it wasn't quite what any of them would call a kitchen. They had taken to raiding *Elvira's* long-term food supply for the nutribars.

"What's going on?" Lu wanted to know. So did Penny and Xi.

The major removed her comm device and keyed it. "Colonel Leeroy Jenkins, Major Bao." It only sounded formal to the crew. No one called Lee Jenkins "Leeroy" to his face. Well, definitely not any of the junior ranks, except for one upstart.

"Major," came the terse reply.

She cut to the chase. "We're dying over here. What is going on, and how can we help?"

"We're wrapping up our preps so we can jump in an hour.

I'll need you in the Zeen control room or whatever the hell that place is. Be ready to engage, whether that's in your mech or as part of the Zeen crew. We've gone in blind before, but never blind and deaf. We'll be hitting the most likely candidate for the Jemmin homeworld. My orders are, be ready for anything."

"Pretty broad, Colonel." Xi wasn't complaining, but she wondered why he hadn't contacted her before this. She could have helped with the planning. She started to believe she'd been sidelined. "I feel left out."

"These are the preliminaries, Xi. The chance of this planet being the homeworld is thirteen-point-one percent, but it's the best. Jem has determined that there are thirty-one candidates. This could be a total goat rope, or we might be jumping into a hornet's nest. We won't know until we get there. We have eighteen total mechs, but thanks to you and *Zeen Home Three*, at least one will survive if the *Mencken* goes down. As long as there is one person left to pull the trigger and one vehicle left to fire at the enemy, we have a chance. You, Major Xi Bao, and your crew are our insurance policy. Who will take over the TAC if I go down with the *Mencken*? That's why you're over there instead of being here with the rest of us Metalheads. Live to keep the fight alive."

"Where in the fuck did the doom and gloom cloud come from? We're going to walk across the grave of Jemmin together. All of us. Trapper Junior, too, for his old man's sake. For all those we lost. The dark cloud over my head is filled with lightning. Jemmin can stand the fuck by because they've never seen us this pissed off!"

Xi started to stomp as she talked, until she caught Lu and Penny giving her odd glances. She waved them away.

"I've only seen you that pissed off when you haven't been fed. The Zeen chef not up to snuff?" Jenkins quipped.

"They're trying to feed us bug spit. We're eating *Elvira*'s emergency rations; you know, the ones you only eat in case of imminent death. We're thinking that Lu's sacrifice to feed me and Penny will be greatly appreciated. I'm going to miss him."

"Hey! No one is going to eat me." The Monkey raised his fists. The taller Penny put her palm against his forehead. He lashed out but couldn't reach her.

"I have no doubt you'll get into the fight, Major. Have patience, and look for the *right* opportunity." He emphasized the word "right" because he knew she would be looking for any opportunity to engage. A bored Major Bao was not a good thing.

"What about the *GateKeeper*?" Xi asked.

"What about it? It's with TF Spear."

"We have three gates we can deploy if I understood the briefing from Jem. We could leave one here as a rally point, giving us two endpoints behind enemy lines, one in Vorr space and one in Jemmin space."

"It's a rough game of tic-tac-toe, Major. Deploying these gates isn't as easy as dropping mines. I'm told the calibration process takes a full day, and that the end gate must already be in place."

Xi stopped fidgeting and closed her eyes. It was like a logic puzzle with too little information. "I'll keep thinking about it, Colonel. I'll drop a word if the answer comes to me. You *know* I won't be shy."

"That's what I expect from my XO. Pay attention, and remember, when the time is *right* and not before. I need your brain fully engaged on this one. I don't think it'll be resolved by chain guns and fifteen-kilogram mains. We launch in an hour. Be ready. Jenkins out."

Penny held out her hands. "What do you think he was trying to say? It sounded like a code or something."

Xi nodded and held her finger to her lips, looking conspiratorially left and right. She winked at her Monkey and Wrench before heading to the small kitchen to see if anything edible had appeared. She also needed time to think. Jenkins had been trying to tell her something, but she had no idea what it was.

H.L. Mencken, Task Force Sword

"Fusion reactor to one hundred percent. Bring weapons online," Captain Podsednik ordered.

"Battle stations are manned. Board shows green. Interior bulkheads are secured. Systems energized," Commander Wythe reported from Tactical.

Podsy re-checked the order Admiral Corbyn had transmitted two minutes earlier. It was three simple words: "Launch Phase Two."

"Very well." Podsy thought for a moment and pointed at the comm station. "Give me ship-wide." When the operator nodded, Captain Podsednik stood and clasped his hands behind his back. "We're a thousand light-years behind enemy lines. This is where we part company with our brothers and sisters of Task Force Spear. They're on the other side of this system, and they have their own mission, just like ours, but to Vorr space. We wish them Godspeed. For you, puff out your chests with pride and prepare for the ride of your life. We have up to thirty-one planets to visit in search of the Jemmin homeworld. When we find it, we're going to have a nice conversation with their ruling council or whoever is in charge. And then we're going to end this war. Metalheads, man your mechs. Warriors, prepare to fight. Helm, signal the Zeen. Open the gate to J-ville One."

Jenkins clapped Podsy on the shoulder. "I'll be in *Powerslave*, watching the show." The colonel ran from the bridge on his way to join the rest of the Metal Legion in their mechs inside their drop-cans. *Powerslave*, the colonel's command mech, was a walker, and it took up a lot of space. There were five more walkers and eleven additional mechs. It was the smallest force Jenkins had yet commanded as a TAC colonel.

He was ready and didn't consider it below his pay grade. It was a rally of the survivors, every able-bodied mech Jockey, Monkey, and Wrench was saddling up to head wherever they were needed. Jenkins ran through the mostly empty corridors. The holdup was transiting through the secured bulkheads. He had to open and close five separate hatches. He could feel the ship moving, which meant the fleet was already heading through the Zeen's wormhole. He sprinted through the final section, breathing heavily for his efforts, trying not to bounce off the walls with the ship's movements. He reached the launch deck and cycled his way through, then jogged to *Powerslave*, smiling as he looked at it. In the past week, the crew had worked on a couple of modifications to increase the power, while adding additional plating in the most vulnerable areas. He'd also had the mortars pulled. They were perfect against the Arh'kel but useless against a less concentrated enemy. He hoped the SRMs that had taken their place would be the right answer.

Jemmin had seen the mechs before, and there was no doubt they learned from each engagement. What had been vulnerable before would be targeted without mercy. Turning a weakness into a strength was Jenkins' legacy because if Jemmin were targeting the wrong spot, it gave the mechs more time to counterattack.

Humans learned, too. Jemmin were no longer invisible to Terran sensors. An extra few moments might be all the time they need to eliminate a threat. Cut off the head. One Jemmin ran the defenses for an entire planet. All they had to do was find Jemmin and kill it.

Jenkins climbed into *Powerslave* and took his seat. "Systems online," Hammer reported. "Welcome back, Colonel."

"It's good to be back. Slaving to *Mencken's* main screen. Sit back and watch. Be ready to deploy."

"You were right, sir. We're making this up as we go, aren't we?"

"The plan will be developed en route to the objective, which will be determined before the plan is developed but probably after we get dropped. We'll have a good ten minutes to come up with everything we need. Gives us eight minutes to drink coffee and read a book."

"I like your confidence, Colonel. It's my honor to serve with you."

"We'll drink a sparkly water to celebrate when this is all over," Jenkins said. As an alcoholic, he had to avoid strong drink, but his crew was aware and never pressed him.

"Pinch your butt cheeks together and be ready. Countdown to gate, thirty seconds." Jenkins dialed up a clock and set it on the screens.

Task Force Sword's combat power headed through first. Every single warship led the parade. Next through would be the civilian fleet, and last through would be the Zeen worldship. By the time the Zeen arrived, the task force had to have the area cleared, or at least subdued enough for an emergency egress.

The countdown reached zero, and the rotating ship crossed the event horizon to instantly materialize inside Jemmin space next to the planet designated Jemminville One, or J-Ville for short. When the screens cleared and sensor information started populating the system, the truth was clear. Jemmin were not happy with the intrusion.

H.L. Mencken, the Bridge

"Thirty degrees to port, fifteen degrees rise, accelerate to four gees," Podsy ordered.

The *Mencius* was directly ahead, shrouded in light and smoke from the amount of firepower it had sent downrange. Visual acquisition wasn't possible since the enemy was somewhere beyond. The Terran fleet was scattering to prevent damage from debris, and more importantly, bring more weapons to bear on the Jemmin warships.

A brownish-green planet rotated in the distance. With standard cloud cover, it looked unassuming.

When the *Mencken* cleared the congestion, three Jemmin cruisers appeared on the tactical board. They accelerated to forty gees as they maneuvered to counter the incoming missile barrage. *Mencius* was up to ten gees, holding steady with that acceleration to keep the crew functional. If the ship took any damage, they'd have to slow down so the crew could leave their acceleration couches. The *Mencken* didn't need the couches, not yet, but at battle stations, each crew member was only a step or two from safety.

"Fire a spread of Cloudy Sky to designated coordinates. Bracket those bastards." Podsy tapped the screen, and a small line appeared on the main screen to the left of the Jemmin cruisers.

"Roger to Cloudy Sky," Tactical confirmed. Two seconds later, a dozen big missiles jumped from their launch tubes and accelerated toward their target coordinates. Filled with mini-magnetic explosives, they created a space minefield.

The Jemmin cruisers seemed less than fully committed to the engagement because their defensive maneuvers took them farther and farther from the Terran fleet.

Over the general channel, Admiral Corbyn conducted the engagement by putting the chess pieces in play across the board. Cloudy Sky would have popped up on his board as another element to the strategy. An order came in from the admiral.

"Cut off Jemmin retreat. Jemmin cannot be allowed to escape."

"Kill them all," Podsy growled. "Ship-wide. Order everyone into their couches. Helm, maximum acceleration."

The blinking light that appeared on the board was the system's gate, and Jemmin were trying to get there.

Mencken groaned as the engines passed one hundred percent on their way to one hundred fifteen. Podsy flopped into his couch at the last moment, adjusting under the stress of increasing g-forces. He manipulated his pads to open a channel to the bridge. "Fleet orders are to make sure these cruisers don't escape, which confirms this isn't the homeworld. But it's a source of information. That's one target down. Maybe thirty to go. If any of those cruisers get through the gate, our job will get a whole lot harder."

The crew registered their acknowledgment, along with their disappointment that this wasn't the homeworld. Podsy dialed up a P2P. "Jem, are you tapped into ship's sensors?"

"I am, Captain Podsednik. This is not the homeworld. Sensors are showing minimal Jemmin presence on the planet."

"We'll probably go clean that up as soon as we finish the runners."

"Keep their bridge information systems intact for recovery if you can," Jem requested.

Podsy chuckled through clenched teeth as the special couch squeezed his extremities to keep the blood from pooling away from his brain. "We'll see what we can do, but don't count on it. The best cruiser kills are the ones with the most spectacular explosions."

"The information from the last cruiser through the NA2 gate was illuminating, but I did not have sufficient time to scan everything in the recovered database. I have the time now and will start working on it, in addition to adding new information into my calculations for a potential Jemmin homeworld."

"Thanks, Jem. Don't kill yourself doing this stuff. Save some for our retirement." Podsy was concerned. The fifty-centimeter ruby-colored crystal had been vibrant with light and warmth but was now mostly dark since the stress of the calculations was burning out the gestalt intelligence.

"One cruiser down," Tactical reported. Podsy turned his attention back to the battle. *Henry VIII* had powered around the extreme right flank and delivered a crushing blow, putting the cruiser between two barrages of railgun and missile fire. The ship came apart in four pieces as if dissected, each sparking and venting. Then the power plant lost containment, erupting in a white flash, momentarily blanking visuals. When the external ship's view returned, there was nothing left of the first Jemmin cruiser to die in Jemmin space.

Operation End of War was underway.

The second cruiser splattered explosions as it accelerated through the Cloudy Sky field. The mines sought the metallic object, clustering onto it.

The third Jemmin cruiser executed an extreme-gee turn that would have killed any humans aboard. The ship caught the front edge of the cloud, bouncing explosions off its hull as it accelerated toward the planet.

The second Jemmin cruiser broke through the cloud, but, as intended, the ship limped forward, accelerating at a mere fifteen gees. *Mencken* tried to match it but topped at fourteen.

Close enough for government work, Podsy thought, unable to speak aloud because of the tremendous forces on his body. He used his eyes to move his cursors and activate systems. Tactical acknowledged.

The main viewscreen showed its interpretation of a continuous stream of railgun bolts accelerated to one-tenth the speed of light racing across the void. *Mencken* vibrated slightly as its engines ran at maximum output. That created a small spiral effect for the railgun bolts, making them even more difficult to evade.

Ten missiles launched, followed by ten more. The engines fired, and the weapons screamed silently across the void in search of their target. As railgun bolts stabbed into the cruiser's aft end, its point defense systems came alive, sending an umbrella of projectiles to intercept the incoming.

Railgun bolts continued to stab into the Jemmin cruiser. It bucked and slowed another five gees. *Mencken* started to close the distance between the ships.

Could Jemmin make it to the gate if they didn't evade the incoming fire? Railguns heated up, triggering warning lights throughout the system. They would need to be shut down or face permanent damage. Podsy's eyes hovered over the cease-fire button.

The first salvo of missiles reached the engagement envelope, only to find a nearly impenetrable barrier of projectiles. Three, then five, then nine missiles were scrapped. One made it through the outer layer, but the close-in systems were relentless. Coil guns and PD missiles cleaned the board of the last missile.

The second salvo closed. *Mencken* continued to pour railgun fire into the cruiser.

A glance at the big board showed the third cruiser heading toward the gate on a long, circuitous route. *Henry VIII* was giving it all it could handle. Three Terran destroyers and the cruiser Colonel Jenkins had recruited were chasing it, using their maximum acceleration to try to keep up. Soon they'd be in front of the dreadnought's guns, silencing their attack.

Five more gees and the second Jemmin cruiser was down to walking speed in the relativity of space. Mencken was barreling down on it. The cruiser started to turn.

"Hit the brakes! Prepare point defense!" Podsy managed to yell. He tried to relax, but the effort to give warning had been instantly exhausting. The assault carrier pulled back roughly, jerking the crew, but the couches shielded them from any violence that would have been done to their bodies. In ten more seconds, they'd slow enough to exit the couches. "Launch Vipers!"

The Jemmin cruiser had decided it was time to fight back. Over one hundred missiles blasted from the damaged ship like a volcanic eruption. They spread out as they gained momentum, then they turned as one, with the singular purpose of destroying their tormentor.

With the relief of pressure, Pete Wythe jumped from his couch, and like a virtuoso, his hands flew across the tactical controls, sending twenty mid-range Interceptors on their way into the icy grip of space on a mission to help the *Mencken* to survive the engagement. Short-range missiles were spooled into the queue, and every coil gun and chain gun cycled to ensure they'd fire when needed.

Two dozen Vipers appeared on the main board, the last of the Terran space fighters under Commander Knighton's control. "Missile intercept duties, aye," she reported casually while the Vipers accelerated away from the *Mencken*. They stayed out of the line of fire, barely, to keep the travel distance to a minimum. There was no time to spare.

Tactical brought the ship's main railguns around, but Podsy had shut them down before they went critical. It would be another thirty seconds before they were cool enough to fire.

They only had twenty-eight seconds before the barrage arrived.

"Helm, remain nose-on, smallest available profile to the incoming," Podsy directed.

The second ten missiles bore down on the Jemmin cruiser.

Like the Terrans, they had redlined their close-in-weapon systems, and not all of them fired. The first salvo scrubbed only five missiles and their second destroyed another three, leaving the last two missiles to ram home.

The first hit it amidships, rocking the cruiser but failing to penetrate, leaving a five-meter-deep, hundred-meter-long gouge in the hull. The second missile hit toward the aft end, breaking through a bulkhead seam. Atmosphere vented, quickly freezing in the harshness of the void. The crater threatened to break the ship in half, but it continued fighting.

A second salvo fired, twenty more missiles to follow the first wave toward the *Mencken*.

Coil guns and chain guns started to hit max rpms, filling space with as much depleted uranium as possible. Short-range missiles followed the projectiles, heading for anything inbound. Targeting was a crapshoot. Automatic targeting jumped from one missile to another as the computer evaluated the highest-risk threats while discounting others. There was no doubt in Podsy's mind that all one hundred inbound missiles would hit if the *Mencken* took no action.

Maybe the luckiest ones in this war would be the ones who died first.

Podsednik didn't embrace that kind of luck. "Fire chaff and noisemakers port and starboard," Podsy said. "We need to cut down the numbers."

No one disputed that.

Podsy ground his teeth in frustration. The missiles were nearly one hundred percent effective against the inbound where Jemmin had gone for volume over quality, but that left over eighty missiles. The Vipers opened up, scratching the entire first rank of missiles. They adjusted and re-aimed, but the second rank started to juke—smart missiles, learning as they flew.

Only two bit it on the second attack, and all of a sudden,

they were past the Vipers. The fighters conducted max-gee turns to get behind the missiles, but they were already losing ground. They fired the rest of their small intercept missiles, hoping for a rear-angle kill.

Coil guns and chain guns did little damage at max distance. The squawkers convinced a few of the inbound missiles that they were more important than the assault carrier, drawing off the confused computerized targeting.

Sixty-four missiles remained. "Fire everything we have," Podsy said, certain they already were. "Target that cruiser with a full salvo of MRMs." There was no way Captain Podsednik was going to die without taking his attacker with him. "Fuck them right in their squishy alien heads."

It was a statement he'd remember later as not his most eloquent.

The Vipers' rear shots caught the inbound, blasting twenty more missiles and ruining their date with the *Mencken*.

Railgun fire crisscrossed the main screen, splashing much of the inbound wave. Tactical retargeted the point defense weapons on the remaining missiles, maintaining their cyclic rates of fire. The *Blencathra* and one other destroyer bore down on the missiles, but they'd already saved the day.

Scrapping one after another, the chain guns did what they could.

"Brace for impact!" Podsy dove for his couch. He couldn't afford another concussion. There was too much fight remaining in this war.

Many wouldn't consider a two percent success rate to be worthwhile, but those people weren't on the receiving end of the two Jemmin monsters that hit *Mencken*. The prow took a direct hit. Despite being the most heavily armored section of the ship, the hundred-kiloton explosion twisted and warped the metal, forcing the ship to start corkscrewing. It made it a quarter revolution before the second missile skipped off the mid-hull and exploded fifty meters away from the ship. *Mencken* bucked and screamed like a submarine getting hit by a depth charge.

But this was no submarine. Its back couldn't be broken by a shockwave. Even fifty meters was enough to dampen the effects. Without atmosphere, the shockwave was weakened. Still, one hundred kilotons was no firecracker.

The ship went through its own version of breakdancing before thruster control was restored and leveled the flight. Damage reports started coming in. "Take us out of the fight. Get me *Blencathra*."

"Captain Van Dorn."

"Thanks for the assist. You saved our bacon. I'm backing *Mencken* out, but if you need us, we'll strap ourselves in and charge forward." Podsy scanned the reports. The midship shellacking had taken many of the systems linking the fore and aft ends of the ship offline. He wasn't sure his ship hadn't been cut in half.

Although the front looked like a wreck, main sensors were still online, and the last missile salvo was on final approach toward the Jemmin cruiser. They accelerated while juking. Half the missiles penetrated the ship's depleted point defense weaponry. Slamming home in a rapid series, the explosions started small and grew with each successive impact. The third penetrated, the fourth deeper, and the last broke her back. The cruiser crumpled in on itself as if getting sucked into a black hole before blasting outward in a fantastic rainbow of burning elements.

"I think we're good on this one. *Henry* has his neck across the last one now. We'll move to the gate to intercept any reinforcements if they got the word out, but we don't think so," Van Dorn noted.

Admiral Corbyn broadcast on the open channel. "Continue with Phase Two in J-Ville One."

"Sorry, Jem," Podsy muttered before getting to work. "Get me comm with the rear section. We have to get this ship moving. We have some Metalheads to drop." Podsy switched to the Metal Legion channel. "Prepare to go planetside to root out any Jemmin who call that shithole home."

15

WE KNOW WHERE THEY'RE NOT

"Gate is active," the Zeen reported. Colonel Cao confirmed with the Task Force Commander, Commodore Meng, who ordered the fleet through. Just like Task Force Sword, Spear front-loaded their combat power, arriving nearly five AU from where Sword had entered the system. They were close enough to see what was going on without being caught in the battle, while still being within range if needed.

The initial plan had been to split the forces, taking on the Vorr simultaneously, but the admiral had scrapped that plan for two reasons. First, once the task forces were in two different systems, the admiral lost all command and control. The second reason was more basic: if the attack on Jemmin was unsuccessful, having the Vorr as an enemy would guarantee the elimination of the human race. But if the TAC didn't attack the Vorr, then a loss to Jemmin might yield a more active ally in fighting Jemmin. If they had time, the best option would be to foment more battles between the Vorr and Jemmin, letting the two heavyweights beat each other senseless before the fifty-kilo weakling stepped into the fight.

Splitting their meager forces wasn't worth the risk. Admiral Corbyn needed every weapon he could bring to bear.

Sima Yi led the way, a different strategy than that employed by General Pushkin and Admiral Corbyn. Commodore Meng had no reservations about being the first into a potential fight. He was followed by the heavy hitters in the group to bring the most firepower to bear as quickly as possible.

On the other side of the gate, *Sima Yi* found calm space and no contacts. Their arrival was timed to match the first messages from Sword, broadcast across the system. "Three cruisers and not homeworld." The message repeated for two minutes before switching to an in-progress report on the battle.

One cruiser down, then two, and finally all three. No Terran ship losses, but *Mencius* and *Mencken* had been damaged. That message was repeating when the *GateKeeper* crossed into J-Ville One space and closed the gate.

"Stand down from battle stations," the commodore ordered over the fleet-wide channel.

Despite the order, Trapper and Cao kept their Marines in position, scattered around the outer reaches of the *'Keeper*. It took fifty minutes for two of the Marines to find their place, even using the high-speed transit corridor. The ship pushed a mind-boggling one hundred kilometers in length and twenty kilometers across the beam. It was bigger than thirty Republican-class dreadnoughts.

It carried no weapons that the Marines could find.

The repeating message changed to announce the area around J-Ville One had been secured, and that Sword and Bow would perform in-place repairs while the landing force sought additional information. Wheels up and on to J-Ville Two in twenty-four hours.

"Sounds like it's time to run some drills," Trapper said.

Cao turned to him. "Make it happen for all eighty on board.

I need to find more information. I'll be into the computer system." He put his hand on Trapper's shoulder and pulled him close. "Pray for me."

Trapper backed up. "Colonel!" He started to laugh. "I knew you had a sense of humor buried deep inside."

The major nodded and headed for his combat suit. He climbed in, powered it up, and brought the HUD online, then looked at the overlay of where the Marines were. A good ten kilometers between each pair. Ten kilometers through the constricted corridors of a ship. The best he could manage was five minutes to rally an additional four Marines to a hot spot. What if he could get that down to four minutes?

"Listen up, Marines. It's party time. When I call out a coordinate, I'll need two teams to get there as quickly as possible. Your target is four minutes or less. It is okay if you break something, but don't blow a hole in the side of the ship. At the end of this, you're going to ask how we could have made this suck worse. Hold that thought. Stand by, first coordinates to follow..."

Trapper knew training was the only way to keep the Marines sane. Too much idle time would inevitably lead to bad things happening because Marines could never be trusted to do nothing. History was the harshest judge of those who creatively filled their downtime.

Zeen Home Three

"You're killing me!" Xi declared for the third time. "You have got to let me go dirtside with you. You *have to*."

"I'm pretty sure I don't, Major," Colonel Jenkins replied.

"I'm asking the Zeen if they'll let us serve a little detached duty." Xi waved at her Zeen escort. "Hey, Bob. I need to head down to the planet with the Metalheads. You okay with that?"

After a moment, Bob enunciated clearly, "Zeen need information from planet designated Jemminville One also. I will go with you."

"You hear that, Colonel? Zeen said it was okay."

"As long as Bob goes with you, that is." The colonel sounded skeptical.

"Nah. He didn't mean that. Hey, Bob! You're not coming with us. It could be dangerous down there."

"If Bob does not go, neither will Major Bao."

Xi jerked as if she'd been slapped. She opened her mouth, but no words came out.

"Fine. Dropships launch in thirty. Can you follow our trajectory in, or do we need to carry you?"

Bob stepped up. "Zeen will deliver Major Xi Bao to the target coordinates."

"I guess you shoot me the coordinates, and we'll meet you down there. What's our objective, Colonel?"

"There are three outposts that look to be occupied. We're sending six mechs to each to knock on the door and ask for a cup of flour and some eggs. You know, intel recce. The usual."

"Our usual means we'll get our teeth rammed down the backs of our throats. We'll meet you there, and thank you, Colonel. You won't regret this."

"I'm sure I will, but we're already past that. Kick the tires and light the fires, XO. We'll see you on the far side."

"By the way, the Zeen are sending my handler with us," Xi said coldly.

"Understood. Jenkins out." His reply was without emotion. He had already known.

"Come on, you slackers! We got a planet to invade," Xi shouted. The four jogged toward the hangar where *Elvira* and her drop-can waited. "We might need a tow into the upper atmosphere if you don't mind, unless you want to take the worldship in for a visit."

"Major Bao will be escorted for the duration," Bob clarified.

"What about us?" Penny asked.

Xi pushed her as they ran. "He meant *Elvira*, which includes Jock, Monkey, and Wrench. *Elvira* is nothing without us, and we're nothing without her. I guess it means Bob, too."

"Symmetry," the insectoid agreed.

"Symmetry, Bob. You'll see that in action when *Elvira* hits the deck. Three humans and one machine in perfect balance."

"Major," Lu started slowly, "are you still talking about us?"

"That cuts me to my very core," Xi joked. "When we have comm, get Chief Rimmer on the horn for an emergency resupply of chow. Not emergency rations, but real food. Pack it into *Powerslave* if he has to, but we have to eat. I think I've lost a couple kilos already, and I didn't have it to lose."

"Are the nutritional supplements provided by Zeen scientists insufficient?" Bob wondered.

"You deserve the truth, Bob. Zeen supplements for humans are the crappiest crap that ever crapped its way onto a chow tray. We can't eat it. Your scientists have failed you. Here's a thought. We could have some stuff sent over, and as a matter of fact, we can have it sent here while we're planetside. Your scientists can replicate what we like and is good for us. We can return triumphantly to a well-deserved feast."

"Zeen do not understand the human tendency to overeat."

"Neither do we, but that's just the way it is. Penny, tell Rimmer to take care of sending the very best samples over here. If I'm disappointed with the fare when I get back, I'll have his ass."

"Rump roast?" Lu offered. "Roasted Rimmer?"

Xi shook her head, feeling the best she'd felt since boarding *Zeen Home Three*. She wasn't a spacer. She needed solid ground beneath her feet. Penny and Lu seemed equally happy with the opportunity to get off the ship. She hoped Bob wouldn't get in the way, but they'd make do.

"Bob, are the Zeen sensors picking up anything from the planet? We gonna run up against a Poltergeist or one of their Spectres?"

Bob didn't answer right away. Xi took that as a good sign. Bob was coordinating with the hive. They reached the drop-can and crawled inside through the undersized hatch. They climbed into *Elvira* through the belly hatch since the ramp was blocked by the delivery vehicle's internal support system, the bracing that kept the container together during the violence of atmospheric entry and ground impact.

The crew climbed into their positions and got to work. Xi jacked into the system and let *Elvira* connect with her mind. "Bob? Anything on that planet we should know about?"

"Zeen can find no evidence. Zeen have calculated that Major Bao will be disappointed by not having an enemy to fight."

"Fuck, Bob! You can't drop that on me like that." Xi started running system checks. It had been a while since she'd synced with a mech, but she started to feel the systems as if they were part of her own being. Her breathing slowed with the warm embrace of the twenty meter and sixty-ton Scorpion-class mech, *Elvira 4.* "Penny, get hold of Rimmer because I feel a feed coming on."

Xi spooled up her communications. There was the right way to do things, going through official channels. And then there was the alternative.

"Major Bao to Captain Podsednik," she said softly over a P2P channel.

"Xi...may I call you that? You don't have to call me 'sir.' Unless you want to, of course."

"Don't forget you also literally carry a piece of me inside you, pudknocker. I need a favor," Xi countered.

"Call me names and ask for a favor in the same breath. I need to talk to Strange Bed because I suspect that means we're married. My mom told me I shouldn't settle, but here we are. If she were alive, she'd probably be pissed. Well, dearest, what do you need?" Podsy laughed as he spoke. It had been too long since he'd been able to banter with Xi Bao, his personal friend. Someone who had risked her life for him, including in the operating room, where she'd had all the time in the galaxy to think about it, and she still did it. He would do anything for her.

"I appreciate your good mood. Things must be going well over there. I'll cut to the chase. Zeen have no clue about human food. We're eating *Elvira's* emergency rations to keep from starving to death."

"It's that bad? You'd rather eat unflavored cardboard."

"It's worse than that, but I think the Zeen can replicate what we like if we send over samples. So, Podsy, can you send a variety of the good stuff over here for Zeen analysis? We've insisted on a feast for when we get back."

"That's relatively easy. I'll take care of it. In three months, probably not. We're going to run out of food fairly quickly. Do you know how much a hundred thousand people eat?"

Xi tried to do the calculations but always came back to the same answer. How much processing did it take to clean up after one hundred thousand people? Some recycling happened, but as they learned on Durgan's Folly, it wasn't anything you wanted to live on.

"I get you. Maybe the Zeen can help, or the *'Keeper*. Both ships were designed to be in space forever. They have to have the nutrition and sustenance questions answered." Xi had grown to trust alien technology for the things she didn't understand, but she relied on old-school human tech like her combat vehicle when she was knee-deep in the life and death struggle of close-quarters combat. Even though at one time she had been one of the premier systems hackers, her talents were her mind and her ability to consolidate available information, instantly turning it into something actionable.

Colonel Jenkins considered it a gift that he had encouraged her to use as often as possible.

When the time is right. Jenkins' words came back to her. She'd link up with *Powerslave* and ask him directly what he'd meant.

External views came online. Xi was surprised to find that two Zeen Interceptors were towing *Elvira's* drop-can out of the hangar bay and into space. She hadn't felt the movements or loss of gravity.

"Buckle in, people. Ride's going to get rough in about ten mikes." Xi leaned back in her Jock's seat, tightened her straps, and reveled in the feeling of being one with her ride. She tapped into her music archive. Ten minutes. She dialed up Led Zeppelin's *Carouselambra* and sent the Zep's crystal rhythms into the cabin at half-volume. The song would end about the time they hit the upper atmosphere. She selected the next one for the ride in—Black Sabbath's *Iron Man*.

Xi rocked to the rapid beat and lost herself in the music. Somewhere in the background, Bob was trying to say something.

16

THE PLANET FORMERLY KNOWN AS
J-VILLE ONE

The rockets fired, jerking *Powerslave* to slow the descent. They continued to fire for three seconds, crushing Jenkins and Hammer into their seats. The rockets cut out half a second before the can hit the deck. Explosive charges blasted the retainers, and the walls fell away. *Powerslave* stepped away from the vehicle, accelerating away from the landing site while sensors collected data from the area.

They learned that the structures were aged, but not vacant.

Jemmin. They had to be. Or slaves left behind. There was only one way to find out. He keyed the Legion-wide channel.

"Attention Metal Legion. New OpOrder. There are three settlements. They are designated Deltas One, Two, and Three. Major Bao will take *Fortune's Fury, Twilight's Fall, Godzilla, Fat Man,* and *Holy Diver* to Delta Three. Captain Koch will take *Web Spinner, Vainglorious Vulture, Hell's Hammer, Mr. Crowley*, and *Tolling Bell* to Delta Two. I'll take *Satan's Alley, Devastator, Kanban, War Pig,* and *Crazy Train* to Delta One. I hate to give the order of 'don't fire unless fired upon,' but consider that your rules of engagement for J-Ville One.

"We're here to collect information first. Personally, I don't care if Jemmin live or die, but if they're willing to talk to us, it could shorten our stay in Jemmin space. The less time we spend out here, the more of us go home. Do it right, collect the intel, then we recover to *Mencken* to do it all over again. Jenkins out."

His board lit up as each mech confirmed their status. All units showed green except for *Elvira,* which was executing her landing burn at that moment. "Take us out, Hammer. Delta One, 40kph until we can be sure everyone is keeping up."

The mech started to run. A tall humanoid model, it easily pounded across the mixed terrain. Hard-packed dirt in places, there was enough color to suggest that life had a firm foothold. The plants tended toward blue, based on the nutrients they pulled from the soil. The atmosphere was toxic to humans but not the flora. Or the inhabitants, suggesting they were Jemmin.

Jenkins updated the board with the reminder that no one was to leave their rigs without being in a self-contained environmental suit.

The P2P channel activated. "Major."

"Colonel," Xi replied. "Touch down, orders received, wilco. No blowing up the natives unless they shoot first, then it's weapons-free, I take it."

"Don't kill them all, but you're good about that. We wouldn't be here if it weren't for your restraint. Your battle with the Zeen on the ice cube was probably the greatest single effort ever. Gladiators and knights would be envious of what happened there, all to be declared 'not food.' I trust you, Xi. Let's keep our people alive. This planet isn't worth anyone dying."

"Are any of them?" Xi asked, but she knew the answer. "Of course, they are. All of them. We live for the pleasure to serve."

"You know that's bullshit."

"It is not!" Xi moved *Elvira* easily past fifty kilometers per hour as she linked up with the other five mechs of her tentatively designated 3rd Company. "We serve all humanity, and the Metalheads serve us."

"I'll give you that. Take care of business, Xi. See you on the other side."

The colonel cut the P2P link.

"1st Company, nice and steady. Target is fifteen klicks away. At ten, we'll separate two by two. *War Pig* with me. *Satan* and *Kanban* on the right flank, and *Devastator* and *Crazy Train* on the left. Rollers up front, walkers in the back. Max firepower to the front, but we are weapons tight until I give the order to change."

The mechs started to spread out. *War Pig* was a low-profile tracked mech, but it carried a heavy punch, with dual fifteens and a dozen LRM launchers. With quad fifties fore and aft and chain guns covering its flanks, it bristled like a porcupine. Its main vulnerability? It was the slug of the bunch, with a top speed of only fifty kph because of the extra armor it carried. *Powerslave* could go well over a hundred.

But the mechs could always split up if necessary. They were all capable of fighting solo, and even twenty kilometers apart, they retained interlocking fields of fire. 1st Company passed the ten-kilometer mark and the flanking mechs flared out to the sides, accelerating to remain equidistant from the target. The plan was to arrive at the same time.

Jenkins didn't have to issue the order to lock and load. They had done that before they left the *Mencken*. "Weapons tight. Defensive weapons engaged. Begin active scans." Jenkins watched the information feed into his command console. "Well, isn't this interesting?"

Elvira, J-Ville One, Target Delta Three

"How many kids you got, Bob?" Xi asked to pass the time.

"I do not have any. I am not the queen."

"Holy shit! You guys have a queen? How did we not know this?"

Bob cocked his head a little, his iridescent eyes sparkling red in *Elvira*'s interior lighting. "I don't know what you don't know."

"Neither do I, Bob. No matter. It's good to know you're one of the unwashed masses, just like us."

"It is a hive. Everyone is the masses except the queen."

"Is the queen on *Zeen Home Three*?"

"Of course. It is a hive."

Xi rubbed her chin. *Elvira* ran on autopilot, the automatic systems handling the complex task of keeping the six legs in sync. "Penny, I need you to load one HE and one AP into the mains." It was always good to have options. Xi checked her board to verify the positions of the other five vehicles. Unlike Colonel Jenkins, she had spread her mechs evenly across a wide front.

She put the two humanoids, *Godzilla*, a high-profile walker, and *Twilight's Fall*, a smaller weapons and systems platform, on the flanks. *Elvira* ran in the middle to set the pace, a smooth eighty kph. She had the fastest mechs of the bunch, and they were performing within normal operating parameters. They passed ten kilometers to target, and before they knew it, they were at five. All eyes were on the screens, watching for inbound missiles.

"Slow to fifty now and then twenty at two klicks out. Vegetation is getting thick. Pick your path, and keep your field of fire clear. Watch those scrubby trees for snipers."

The multiple paths heading toward the settlement soon filled with trees and terrain, funneling the approach into two navigable routes, passable without breaking stuff or blowing a hole through the budding blue forest. And then it became one.

"Spread out, front to rear. Be ready with your SRMs. I'll

take the lead with *Twilight* on my six and *Godzilla* behind him. Nobody shoots the mech in front of you. Leave yourselves a few hundred meters, front to rear. Batten down the hatches; we're going in."

Bob watched silently as Xi expertly guided her mech between the trees and other restrictions. Her eyes darted back and forth, even though the sensor data was fed directly to her brain. *Elvira* was at the top of her game.

The thud on the hull came as a complete surprise. Everyone held their breath as *Elvira* slowed to take stock of what happened. And then another. External cameras showed logs swinging from the trees to bounce off the hull and swing back, coming in again for a lighter tap before coming to a rest below the branch under which the log was tied. A creature stepped in front of *Elvira* with a bow and arrow. It took aim and fired. The arrow bounced off the cockpit window.

"Bob, can you tell me, is that a Jemmin?"

The insectoid unbuckled and stepped forward to look over Xi's shoulder. "I believe it is."

"I think that confirms this ain't the homeworld," she muttered before shouting to her crew. "I'm going out there. Halt the parade."

Lu passed the word, and the other mechs ground to a halt.

Penny put out a hand to stop the major. "Are you sure you want to do that? An arrow won't hurt *Elvira*, but it'll do a number on you in that environmental suit."

"This is where things get interesting, Penny. I don't want to go out there, but we need information. I doubt those Neanderthals will have it, but I have to ask. You heard the colonel's orders."

"I didn't."

"That's right. Point to point. Trust me. He said to make nice. Wouldn't be my first choice, but here we are. Report up the chain, but wait until I'm outside in case the colonel gets cold feet."

"I don't understand anything you are saying," Bob noted from the upper compartment. "Not since when we left the ship. I think the translation device must be broken."

"Just stay here and hang onto your butts. I'll be back as soon as I can."

Xi went to clap Penny on the shoulder, but she'd already snaked her way back into her hole. Lu gave the major a thumbs-up.

It took all of thirty seconds to get her environmental suit on. She took a deep breath and moved to the ramp, securing the hatch behind her to keep from flooding the interior with the toxic gas of a Jemmin planet.

She walked carefully out the back, head on a swivel as she looked for those who had been swinging the logs. She strolled carefully around *Elvira*'s legs, keeping them conveniently located between her and the woods, as well as the front path. When she made it close, she found that the friendly neighbor-hood archer was nowhere to be found. Overhead, the two Zeen space fighters circled lazily, like hawks waiting to pounce.

She held the translation device in front of her and started to yell, "Please stop shooting. We come in peace!"

"Is that the best you got, ma'am?" Lu wondered over the crew channel.

"At the moment, yes."

"Ten o'clock!" Lu shouted. Xi winced at the volume, but she was all eyes. The archer was back.

Xi held her hands up as if surrendering, not moving as the arrow was nocked and the string drawn back.

"I am Major Xi Bao from the Terran Armor Corps. I hope to talk with Jemmin."

The creature moved oddly. It wasn't humanoid, yet it had a

shape that suggested two arms and two legs, although it was mostly body, but a body that wasn't rigid. It flexed around the bow, the hands at the ends of the short arms holding the grip and the nocked arrow. A bulbous form sat atop the body without a neck. The creature did not appear to be wearing any clothing. The form was indistinct, without hair or body parts Xi could recognize.

"I mean you no harm. Please put the bow down." Xi tried to enunciate clearly to allow the translator to do its work. It emitted a language that the major had never heard before. Then it tried a second language and a third.

Xi put her arms down and waited. She watched Jemmin closely, looking for any sign that the words had registered or understanding that *Elvira* could kill it before it could let the arrow fly. The silence grew increasingly uncomfortable as they each waited on the other. Xi crossed her arms and started tapping her foot.

The creature aimed the arrow at the offending sound. Xi slowed until she stopped.

"We're going to have to do something at some point in time. The sooner we have a conversation, the sooner we can both get back to our business. There's a meal waiting for me out there, and I haven't had anything decent in ten days. So I'm ready to go. Speak now or forever hold your peace."

The creature eased the arrow forward and held the bow in one hand. Nothing moved where its face should have been, but the sound of a foreign tongue danced through the air. "What are you?" came the translation.

Now we're getting somewhere. Curiosity is good, Xi thought. "I am a human from the Terran Federation."

"Human," the voice uttered slowly. "Lesser race."

"Maybe at one point in time, but no more. Are you Jemmin?"

"Jemmin," the voice replied. "But not Jemmin."

"We were doing so well, too. Can you explain what you mean?" Xi requested.

"Jemmin a thousand years ago but abandoned."

"You have lived here all that time without any support? Why were Jemmin cruisers in orbit if they haven't stopped by in a thousand years? There's a gate, too."

"No Jemmin here. Just us."

"I'm sorry. No one should abandon their people. Do you know where they went? Where is the Jemmin homeworld? We want to talk to Jemmin." Xi stepped forward slowly so she could get a better look at who she was talking to.

The creature waved to the right and the left. From the corners of her eyes, she saw others emerge from the strange forest. Five newcomers joined the first and formed a half-circle around the major. Xi looked from alien to alien. They were mostly alike, loose skin on a large bulbous form, with small appendages for hands and feet.

"I am Major Xi Bao."

"Jemmin," one of the creatures said.

"Where did Jemmin go?" Xi reiterated.

One pointed toward the sky.

A bow and arrow. Log traps. These Jemmin had regressed to a point thousands of years earlier in human history. Xi felt sorry for them.

"Are you happy?" she asked.

"Explain," the one with the bow requested.

"In all the universe, we are asked what we do, who our family is, but no one ever asks if we're happy. I suspect you are, as long as Terran mechs don't show up on your doorstep."

"Life." The first one waved a hand as if the gesture meant something. The others became animated. "The joy of life is in living."

"Amen, sister. You don't know how many times I've asked for just one more breath. Life is pretty good, isn't it?"

"Not sister. Jemmin," the speaker clarified.

Xi chuckled. "Not food either, or so I've heard."

"Zeen," the speaker noted.

"What do you know about the Zeen?"

"Jem'un tried to destroy them but saved them in the end. Then Jemmin destroy Jem'un."

A voice broke through the comm relay attached to Xi's ear. "I have a clear shot, ma'am."

"No shooting," Xi whispered. "These aren't the Jemmin we're looking for. They know jack."

Elvira's rear ramp lowered.

"What are you doing? Stay inside!" Xi turned to find Bob walking slowly toward them.

The six Jemmin became agitated, but as the Zeen approached, they stopped and bowed, bending in the middle of the amorphous bodies. They straightened.

"Jemmin regards to Zeen."

Bob spoke in Jemmin's language, which threw Xi for a loop. She needed the translator to keep her up on the conversation.

"Zeen regards to Jemmin. When did Jemmin leave you here?"

The translator converted the answer from Jemmin time units to human standard. *Twelve hundred years.*

"Where did Jemmin go?"

"To Axiodocius. Through the Originators' gate."

Why didn't you answer me when I asked, ass? Xi thought.

"Zeen regards to Jemmin." Bob returned to the ship without further word or gesture.

Xi had more questions but decided to end on a positive note. It was Jemmin space. Humanity needed all the allies it could get. "Is there anything we can do for you?"

"Do not tell Jemmin about Jemmin."

"You have my word." Xi bowed slightly to the group of natives before copying Bob's goodbye. "Human regards to Jemmin."

The Jemmin bowed slightly to Xi. "Jemmin regards to human. Not food."

Xi waved and hurried to catch Bob before he closed the ramp. When the ramp was secured, the major turned on the insectoid. "You have some explaining to do, Bob."

17

RECOVER, REORGANIZE, AND REARM

"Recover to your dropships. Space lift will commence shortly," Jenkins ordered. They'd been dirtside for a grand total of seventy-four minutes. 1st and 2nd Companies never saw their objective before the *Elvira* crew delivered the information Xi had collected.

"Don't you leave without giving us our chow!" Xi called over the Legion-wide channel. Jenkins could see her in his mind's eye, Xi accelerating the Scorpion-class mech on a beeline toward him. He closed his eyes and counted to ten. When he checked his screen, it was exactly as he'd expected—*Elvira* redlined on an intercept course with *Powerslave*. The major's Zeen escorts raced ahead, then returned slowly before repeating the maneuver.

"It'd be nice if we all had our own personal Zeen over-watch," the colonel muttered.

"On my way, Colonel, for a personal exchange of informa-tion," Xi said smoothly and languidly. Jenkins started to laugh, and it turned into a full belly laugh. Hammer leaned out to see if the colonel was okay. The Jock shrugged and went back to what he was doing.

Mencken rolled into the upper atmosphere to extend the tether. 2nd Company was the first to recover. "Captain Koch, you have point. Take your people home."

"That's a roger, Colonel. *Kochtopussy* first on the tether pole." He wasn't going to be first. That was not how the Metal Legion did its business. He'd be last, but pole position was an honor. Being the first back to the ship meant the first one to chow and the rack. It wasn't an honor to be taken lightly.

Xi's company raced back to their drop-cans to prep for recovery while she diverted to meet the colonel. Colonel Jenkins would be the last one off the planet. That was a given. And she wasn't going back to the *Mencken*, so she could depart whenever she was ready.

Elvira ran up to *Powerslave*, turning to place the rear ramp closest to the Ettin-class walker. Xi strode out, wearing her environmental suit.

"Prepare to repel boarders!" the colonel called over the external speakers. Xi tried to give him the finger, but her gloves wouldn't cooperate. Penny and Lu followed her out. Behind them, Bob appeared.

The colonel lost his humor. "Hammer, transfer our food stocks to *Elvira*'s crew. Make the Zeen help carry, too. The major and I need privacy."

"Wilco," Hammer replied—Old Earth for "will comply." He headed below to put on his environmental suit and make the transfer within *Powerslave's* small airlock.

Two minutes later, Xi Bao stood in the upper cockpit and removed her helmet. "I don't know how people breathe in these things," she started. "Thanks for the chow. You're a lifesaver."

"My pleasure. I don't wish emergency rations on my worst enemies." Jenkins studied her features: cheeks sunken, dark circles under her eyes. He recoiled in shock. "Eat up. We'll send more as soon as we're back in orbit."

"Podsy is already on that. You know me. Always have a backup plan." Xi popped him on the shoulder. "I'll be fine. Jemmin. The ones here were abandoned by our enemy twelve hundred years ago. I think they weren't supposed to survive. They didn't seem to know anything about current Jemmin goings-on."

The colonel cocked his head and looked at a spot on the wall. "But Jemmin cruisers were in orbit."

"Here's my theory. Jemmin are waiting at every gate. I think they know we're coming, or at least suspect. But you know what that means?" Xi nodded with a grin.

The colonel shook his head. "I don't."

"Divide and conquer. We killed three cruisers and didn't lose anyone," Xi explained.

"We took damage, but I see your point. It allows us to mass our firepower against fewer targets. Still, they are depleting our ammunition before we get to the big show. Too many small encounters, and we won't have anything left if they throw multiple Gatecrashers at us."

"No one said it would be easy. If we go up against their major fleet, which, according to the Zeen, was coming for us at NA2, we'll be crushed. If we can stay one step ahead of them, we can avoid the sumo-wrestling altogether."

"I need to get this info to General Pushkin and Admiral Corbyn. Anything else you gleaned from Jemmin?"

"I'll send pictures. I can see why their bodies can handle fifty gees and beyond. They don't have anything to compress. Also, Zeen speak Jemmin."

"Don't tell me—"

"Sorry, Colonel. Bob helped himself out of *Elvira*. He can breathe their atmosphere, as you can see, as easily as he can breathe ours." They both looked out the small window to see Bob carrying the biggest crate while Penny and Lu carried smaller packages. "He spoke to them directly. They bowed to him."

Jenkins bit his lip as he tried to determine what that meant. "Maybe Zeen are a little different than what they told us?"

"I think there's a middle ground somewhere. Let me play this for you." Xi fumbled with the device in her pocket.

The device crackled since Xi had been recording from within her pocket, but she was recording the translator and not the original speech. "Jem'un tried to destroy them but saved them in the end. Then Jemmin destroyed Jem'un."

"That marries up with what Jem told us."

Xi touched her nose with her finger. "It also confirms Jem's implication about the Zeen. Jemmin respect the Zeen."

"Maybe that's only those who opposed Jemmin leadership. This is the group that was left behind."

"Back to we know what we know?"

"Square one. Business as usual, Major."

"Transfer complete," Hammer shouted from below.

"Time to get on our way. Zeen are going to tow us into orbit. It's like we have our own limousine service."

"Again, you mean. Seems to happen to you a lot," Jenkins chided.

Xi put her helmet on and waved. "A girl grows accustomed to the finer things in life. Hey, one last thing. What about your time-is-right comment?"

Jenkins turned serious. "You'll know when the time is right. Don't force it. Keep yourself alive, Xi. We have to make all this worthwhile so someone can tell the story of what we did and why."

She lunged forward and punched the colonel in the chest. "Don't talk like that! We're all going home. Those who survive may be carrying their fallen comrades, but we're going together." She collected herself, saluted with a wave, and headed out. "Colonel."

"Major." He watched her climb down the ladder and enter the airlock. "I want to believe we can all go home. I want to believe Alice is waiting for me, so I can sweep her off her feet and disappear to the beach. And you and all the Metal Legion. We've earned that, whether humanity knows or not. So it's on us to tell them. I hate fucking Jemmin and can't wait to stuff a missile into their shapeless faces."

The colonel ground his teeth and clenched his fists. He knew the major would help drag him out of the dark hole that threatened to consume him. He accessed the comm channel and blasted the next song in his metal playlist. Iron Maiden tore into the airwaves of J-Ville One with *Run to the Hills*.

GateKeeper, **Far Side of J-Ville One's System**

"The order is given," Colonel Cao stated officially. The Zeen listened, but they didn't acknowledge the process. The order to move came via *Zeen Home Three* from Admiral Corbyn by way of Commodore Meng on the *Sima Yi*. It was a convoluted chain of command, to say the least. The colonel sent a short message to the commodore for relay to the admiral requesting that he move his flag to *GateKeeper* and run the fleet from here.

"That makes more sense than anything I've seen so far," Major Trapper offered. He wondered why no one else had thought of it.

"I hope he takes us up on it. I feel like a parrot waiting here to repeat orders that the crew has already heard."

The Zeen prepared to open a gate not far from TF Sword and TF Bow to recombine the three groups. Commodore Meng had sorted the fleet into four separate lanes, assigning gate quadrants to minimize the transit time. The *'Keeper* activated its FTL engines, and ten kilometers in front of the massive ship, a whirling point appeared, quickly expanding into a fire-brimmed vortex large enough to swallow the entire fleet or one *GateKeeper*.

The ships matched rotation and accelerated forward four by four, then plunged headlong into the darkness of the wormhole. They could only tell if they made it once they were through. It was the ultimate leap of faith. Or discipline to follow orders unquestioningly.

The *'Keeper* was the last ship through. Once over the event horizon, the gate closed, leaving no trace that a fleet had ever been there.

"Comm is live," Trapper reported.

"*Mencken*, this is Cao. Please provide intel from the mission to the planet designated J-Ville One."

After a long pause, a familiar voice replied, "Pushkin here. Colonel, please join the conference with Admiral Corbyn and Commodore Meng. Bring Trapper with you."

"Give us two minutes, General." The colonel waved at Trapper to follow as he strode from Central Control. The senior Marines walked as quickly as some people ran, but they never ran when the troops could see. It had a detrimental effect on morale. The Marines needed to be in control at all times, or look like they were. Instilling confidence was as much their responsibility as executing an operation order.

They dodged into the small room they'd commandeered as an office. They had many problems, but finding space wasn't one of them.

Cao activated the portable video communicator. He and

Trapper stood. The Originators had no proclivity for chairs, but tables and workstations were human-friendly if one brought their own seat.

"Thanks for joining us," Admiral Corbyn said, tipping his chin toward the screen. "Your suggestion has merit, and my staff and I will transfer immediately to the *GateKeeper*. We'll leave a response force of twenty Solar Marines. Trapper will return to the *Mencken* with his people, and you'll put Marine companies on both *Henry VIII* and *Sima Yi*."

"This is a big ship, and one platoon isn't enough to protect it if it gets boarded," Colonel Cao protested.

The admiral hung his head. "Colonel, I fear that if the *Gate-Keeper* gets boarded, we will have already lost. I want my combat power forward, where we can deploy it. Playing defense isn't going to win this war. I count on the *GateKeeper* being able to protect itself. Twenty Marines is a reasonable investment if I'm wrong. I suspect one platoon is more than enough to hold Central Control against all comers."

"And destroy it if they can't?"

The admiral sighed and leaned back, away from the camera. "Prepare demolitions to be activated remotely. We can't let that ship fall back into Jemmin hands. If we lose this fight, we condemn the entire galaxy if Jemmin gain FTL technology, or worse, power over all the gates."

"Roger." Colonel Cao braced himself and saluted. Trapper came to attention and stood rigid, wondering what that was about since the colonel was uncovered. No saluting indoors. Maybe this was something different.

Admiral Corbyn returned the salute. "Carry out your orders, gentlemen."

The image faded.

"I guess that's that. With your permission, Colonel, I'll prepare my people for transfer to the *Mencken*."

Colonel Cao held out his hand, and the two men shook. "Go kick their asses."

"And take names, sir," Trapper replied before returning to his combat suit. He armored up. Once the system was online, he keyed his microphone. "Terran Marines. Recover to our original entry point. We're returning to *Mencken*. Sergeants, account for your people and gear. Rally time is thirty mikes, local time of nine forty-seven. Don't be late, or I'll have your asses."

The major was rewarded with a hearty round of oorahs. He set the timer on his suit and headed out. Now that he knew the ship better, he'd take a longer route but use the higher speed tunnels. Then the Marines would use their suits to fly across the void to the *Mencken* because Trapper hated waiting for a ride.

18

PREPARE FOR ROUND TWO

H.L. Mencken

"That is most interesting information from Major Bao, don't you think?" Jem asked.

"Jemmin bowing to Zeen," Podsy repeated. He leaned back against the couch in his quarters, waiting for the build-up to the next rush. The crew was finishing repairs on a few cracked breakers, accounting for the appearance of worse damage, but the *Mencken* had held up well to the attack. It still had a bent and broken nose, but the chief engineer said it gave the ship character without affecting its flight profile.

"I have cleaned up the audio and listened to the original Jemmin. The translator functioned properly. I did not hear any nuances in their speech."

"What about the Zeen? He spoke Jemmin."

"Unaccented," Jem confirmed. "I think we know less about the Zeen than we thought."

"I never thought we knew very much. The Zeen have FTL capability, but Jemmin do not? That is the greatest anomaly of all. I guess I'm not too surprised that the Zeen speak Jemmin.

It's how they learned to interact with another species. The biggest question is, how can we use that to our advantage?"

"That *is* a good question. I suspect they will be as well-suited to breaking into Jemmin systems as I am."

"And the *GateKeeper*?"

"Yes. I have placed trackers throughout the system, and I believe I am seeing all that the Zeen are doing. They are learning more and more about the ship and its capabilities, but operating the ship and understanding how it does what it does are two completely different things."

Podsy smiled and checked a maintenance report before replying, "Which means you haven't figured out the technology either."

"I am operating at diminished capacity, unfortunately."

"No disrespect intended, Jem. It's good if we don't have the tech to build and operate our own *'Keeper*. We're not ready for that yet. It'll be well beyond my lifetime before we are. So, what did the general and admiral think of what you shared with them?"

"Axiodocious provided additional context, enabling me to remove seven planets from the list of potential Jemmin home-worlds. We have a total of twenty-three remaining."

"I like our odds. We can't be dithering around out here too much."

"'Dither.' Interesting word, but I accept your premise. Stand by." Jem disappeared somewhere, giving Podsy time to get caught up on the admin and logistics of running a capital-grade warship. "The Zeen are able to directly access the gate and its information without activating it. Three Jemmin cruisers visited this system for three days, departing for one day before returning for three more days."

"Crap! When were they due to leave?"

"In one hour."

"General Quarters!" Podsy shouted at the comm system before grabbing his uniform blouse and running out.

Zeen Home Three

"Oh, God. I can't eat another bite," Xi said, leaning back with her stomach distended like a snake that had just swallowed a mouse. Penny looked like a stunned mullet, mouth hanging open, eyes vacant and staring. Lu casually took another small piece of something that looked like chicken.

"You need to pace yourselves." Lu finished his last piece and moved to box up the remainder, sealing it in the self-cooling container.

"How many days before we need a resupply?" Xi asked.

"Depends if you keep eating like you just did. A week, or if you eat like normal human beings, two. But the Zeen have the samples, right? Hopefully they'll be able to duplicate it, so they don't try to feed us any more fermented snot."

"Concur," Xi said sleepily, closing her eyes and letting her mind drift. Her comm buzzed. She groaned and fumbled with it until she could answer.

"We're scrambling for an imminent departure," Colonel Jenkins started. "Only fifty minutes, and this time we're going through the gate. Half of Task Force Spear will use the gate and the rest of the fleet will gate in to alternate points within the same system in order to catch any Jemmin between our three forces."

Xi blinked and tried to unscramble her brain. "Do we know what kind of force is on the other side of that gate?"

"We don't, but we're going. If we don't, Jem thinks there will be some kind of alarm that will go off because that's when the three cruisers are supposed to return. Instead of their own cruisers, they're going to get us."

"Surprise, motherfuckers," Xi agreed. She stood and smacked Penny in the back of the head. "Get in *Elvira* and wait for me."

"See you on the other side, Major." Jenkins signed off.

Xi tried to flex her abs, angry at herself for having eaten so much. She twisted and ignored the pain. Who knew when she'd get to eat next? Her anger evaporated. "I'm off to find Bob. Get your asses to *Elvira*."

The major tried to remain upright while walking briskly. She strode down the corridor and then to the airlift. She stepped in and torpedoed herself to race downward, then spread out to slow and drifted across the updraft to step easily onto the platform leading to what she'd taken to calling the roundhouse, the spherical room with the hive's leadership.

She found Bob inside. He blocked her from entering until they'd completed their conversation. Then he stepped aside. Xi glared at him, but she expected it was lost on him.

"We're going through the gate while also making an end run. What can we expect in Axiodocious?"

"Unknown."

"I think you know far more than you're letting on. When were you going to tell us that you speak Jemmin?"

"Zeen languages irrelevant to humans," Bob replied.

"Not so. Being able to operate behind enemy lines means we need to know all the assets available for the operation. Being able to speak Jemmin means we can spoof them!"

"Zeen do not understand 'spoof.'"

"Make believe that we're Jemmin. Get on the radio and tell them a made-up story to put them off-guard, give us the element of surprise. Cut our losses and increase theirs. All good things if we can get inside their heads. It starts with speaking the language."

"Symmetry."

"We're still going through the gate at the same time as running two flanking operations, aren't we?"

"Yes. But not at the same time. Gate, then *GateKeeper*, then *Zeen Home Three*."

"That's right. If we try two gates at the same time, the universe will explode, leaving only atoms behind, or something just as bad."

The Zeen didn't bother to answer.

"I'll be in my mech. Let me know when I'm launching, or it's safe to come out." Xi walked out, her measured stride thudding rhythmically as she left the roundhouse.

H.L. Mencken, the Bridge

"We're going with *Zeen Home Three*," Podsy muttered. The dreadnoughts lined up to race first through the gate. *Mencius* was the sacrificial lamb, with a big bite detailed to TF Spear for this engagement. *Sima Yi* lined up behind *Mencius*. Cruisers and destroyers followed, maintaining the now-standard one kilometer between the ships. The *GateKeeper* loomed over the area with its complement of warships and three-fourths of the civilian shipping. Because of how quickly the ships could transit the larger gate, the admiral had decided to separate the fleet to minimize the transit time.

Maybe at some point, they'd all go through the *'Keeper'*s gate together.

"General quarters," Podsy said in a normal tone. The klaxons sounded the order, and the lights flashed for emphasis. Those who weren't already on the job raced for their assigned workstations. The board started lighting up as departments reported staffed and ready.

Podsy took the reports in one ear while watching the fleet lined up before the system's physical gate. Task Force Sword lined up on *Zeen Home Three*, waiting for their turn to gate into a different location in the Axiodocious system. On the far side of the gate, the *'Keeper* waited. It would activate the physical gate and then shut it down before the Zeen would go.

Podsy tapped a button to display the countdown timer on the main screen. Three minutes until the gate opened. He estimated seven minutes until *Henry VIII* led the way through the Zeen gate, with *Mencken* close behind. So many moving parts.

The *'Keeper* would bring the remainder of the fleet at G-plus-eleven minutes. In many cases, the battle would already be over by then, with wreckage and debris scattered throughout the system.

Not this time, Podsy thought.

When the countdown reached zero, the gate opened. Instead of three Jemmin cruisers, the human fleet was on its way.

Mencius and *Sima Yi* accelerated simultaneously, like synchronized swimmers. They matched the gate's rotation on the radial between the circumference and center point. Accelerating through two gees, the *Mencius* was through, and moments later, the second dreadnought followed.

Podsy was not a fan of waiting, and time slowed to a crawl. According to the scientists, time was a constant at the pace humanity operated.

Perception was greater than reality. Podsy checked the ship's ready status and available weaponry. Then he took a quick stroll around the bridge, clapping his crew on their backs and making jokes. He could feel the tension in their shoulders. It was time to do something different.

"Listen up, people. We've been here before. Seems like only a couple days ago, we were doing this same thing." He let that linger. People nodded, but no one laughed. "Not so long ago, a Jock, a Monkey, and a Wrench landed on a shithole planet in the middle of nowhere. It had a minor bug problem that became the turning point in humanity's future. This gate may lead us to the last great battle humanity will ever fight or it may be three cruisers, dicking around. No matter what, we're going to hit it head-on, just like *Elvira* on Durgan's Folly. You will remember this for the rest of your lives. Make them the best memories you can. Do your jobs and show no mercy. God knows Jemmin will show us none. We're no more than cattle to them. This one's for you, Jemmin!"

Podsy gave his middle finger to the screen, and the bridge crew cheered and followed suit. Podsy's comm buzzed. General Pushkin.

Captain Podsednik took his seat and answered the comm while closely watching the timer as it counted down.

"I hope we have more than giving Jemmin a one-finger salute."

"We have a lot more, General. Just waving 'Hi,' that's all."

"Of course. Let's go kick some ass." The conversation was about nothing, but Podsy saw that the general felt the exact same way. Anything to kill a few seconds until showtime. The adrenaline was already surging throughout their bodies. Seasoned warriors both, they couldn't control it. They were on autopilot, slowing the world down so they could think and act faster.

The Zeen gate started to form, and Podsy forgot about the general. "Match rotation and accelerate," the captain ordered. Helm began the process. "Tactical, prepare to fire upon target acquisition. Point defense weapons hot."

Henry VIII led the way, disappearing over the event horizon before the assault cruiser entered.

The *Mencken* eased through. Podsy's heart raced during the two seconds the ship was blind to what was in front of them. As the view cleared and tactical information started to populate the screen, they realized that Axiodocious was the Jemmin version of the Nexus. Gates circled a massive ringed planet in orbit around a red dwarf. Ten gates on a two-dimensional plane separated by a few million kilometers.

The Zeen had opened a gate on a third dimension, outside the activity of the physical gates. Jemmin traffic dotted the area. Task Force Spear was fully engaged with twenty Jemmin cruisers and a bigger battleship-class vessel that was throwing salvo after salvo of missiles in the Terrans' direction.

"Into your couches!" Podsy ordered. "Maximum acceleration. Target the battleship. Fire when in range."

TF Sword rolled in behind the two heavyweights, starting to spread out as General Pushkin directed the pieces in a life-and-death chess match.

Mencius was taking a beating, brutalized by the combined throw weight of the Jemmin forces, furious at the intrusion into their territory and defending it with their lives.

Divide and conquer.

Podsy watched destroyers angle away from the task force, accelerating to their limits on intercept courses with the physical gates. *Can't let anyone get away to warn the others,* Podsy thought. He appreciated the tactic but lamented the loss of the firepower and limitation on enveloping actions.

"Forty seconds to range," Tactical announced through gritted teeth as the strain of gee forces pushed him tightly into his acceleration couch.

Podsy used eye control to access his panel to watch the fight in front of him.

Mencius had taken the brunt of it. Ever since the fight at NA2, the dreadnought had been living on borrowed time, but its crew continued to fight valiantly. Over two hundred short- and medium-range missiles filled the void, on their way from no fewer than five Jemmin ships with a single target in their sights.

Mencius countered with PD fire that lit up the darkness, exploding missiles at the cyclic rate. Some were so close together that they failed through a series of sympathetic detonations. And the *Mencius* cleared its decks of offensive firepower, sending every missile in its arsenal into space. They launched like there would be no tomorrow.

Because there was no hope of surviving the battle. The first of forty-eight missiles hammered into the already burning and battered hull. Then more landed. Atmosphere streamed from a dozen vents. The front half of the dreadnought went dark, a kilometer and a half of ship pushed lifelessly by the aft end. More missiles launched before the ship started to come apart. A few lifeboats launched seconds before a massive explosion ripped the sides from the crippled vessel. The front three hundred meters was the next to get torn away, separated in a series of small explosions. The fires were quickly extinguished by the lack of oxygen in space.

More Jemmin missiles slammed into *Mencius'* drifting hulk, blasting it into scrap metal. Finally, the dreadnought's fusion reactor went critical and punished what was left of the ship. No Jemmin were close enough for a final retribution. The dreadnought's death knell sounded in an empty void.

A missile barrage arced up and over the wreckage to follow *Mencius'* final salvo. Jemmin PD wiped the first salvo off the grid, but the second, programmed more tightly, twisting on approach, passed the first barrier and accelerated on final approach. PD weapons scrubbed dozens of inbound, but that was only half.

The rest slammed home on three targets, two cruisers and the battleship. The first cruiser received a lucky critical hit. The single missile penetrated the outer hull, wrenching deep through the ship's dense armor before exploding and sending molten metal into the interior. It cut into the reactor and sent it critical in the space of a millisecond. The Jemmin crew didn't have a chance to respond before the ship erupted in a single catastrophic explosion.

The second cruiser fared better, shrugging off the three hits when none of them penetrated into the interior.

The battleship received the bulk of the impacts. The missiles carved ugly caverns into the battleship's hull, but the depth of armor was something no Terran had ever seen before. A fifty-kiloton strike with a depleted uranium penetrator barely made the ship wobble. Atmosphere vented at a weak point amidships where one missile had cut deeply enough. The Jemmin battleship continued its murderous mission to eject the Terrans from Jemmin space.

A battleship, but not a Gatecrasher. It wasn't as big or as heavily armed, although it was armored to an extreme level, as if it were made to fly through a sun.

Maybe it was, but the rents in its skin suggested enough hits could break its back. The battleship begged for focused missiles to pound through the weakened areas like a siege of a medieval castle, hitting it again and again. "Target that vent," Podsy ordered. Tactical acknowledged, but not verbally. The gees were too great. It was eye-control only at that point.

Terran cruisers spread across the void to tackle the Jemmin cruisers, leaving the center ring to the heavyweights. *Sima Yi* did not disappoint. Commodore Meng attacked with no mercy as the cruisers tried to snipe the dreadnought. *Sima Yi* threw enough metal their way to keep them on the defensive. Cruisers launched grouped attacks, pummeling one Jemmin cruiser before moving on.

The battles with Jemmin over the past two years had prepared them for this moment. The combined horsepower of science, reverse-engineered technology, diligence, and study of the enemy put the Terran fleet on equal footing with Jemmin. It was no longer a one-sided fight, and the Terrans were putting the enemy on its heels.

Henry VIII launched its first salvo as it crossed into weapons range, throwing a full spread of long-range missiles into the void.

"Tactical!" Podsy grunted since the screen hadn't updated, leaving gaps in the picture, blinding him to potential threats. After a few tense moments, the screen cleared. Podsy didn't have the energy to ask what had happened. Pete Wythe was a professional. He wouldn't let it happen again if there was any way to prevent it.

A trio of Jemmin cruisers was trying to flank the new formation coming through the Zeen wormhole, but the *Blencathra* was already on it, taking five destroyers and three cruisers along for the attack. They cycled railguns before the enemy was in range in order to deny them space to maneuver. If Jemmin chose to fly through the enfilade, they'd take damage. If they avoided the area, they'd run into the Terran missile kill zone.

Either option was a win for the humans.

A quick check behind them showed civilian freighters still coming through the gate. *Zeen Home Three* had yet to join them. Podsy longed for interceptor support. It wasn't time to launch his meager squadron, but he wanted to let Commander Knighton know he had her in mind. He used his eyes and interface to tap out a quick message. **Your time will come soon. Prepare to launch against battleship counterattack**.

On your command, was the near-immediate reply. Podsy's initial problems with the commander were well in the past. Her Vipers had saved more lives than he could count. As he was promoted to increasingly responsible positions, individual details of politics or personal attitudes meant less and less. The only thing that mattered was how good they were in a fight. Commander Knighton wasn't just good. She was the best.

"Launching," Tactical reported the instant *Mencken* crossed into the range of the battleship. With a singular focus of all the firepower the assault carrier brought to the engagement, the first salvo left the tubes, immediately restocked by the autoloaders, ready for round two.

The battleship maneuvered on the only vector available to take it out of the Terran pincer. It banked hard, passing thirty gees as it redlined its engines, seeking more speed. *Sima Yi* lit up the exposed belly with its direct-fire weapons. Railgun bolts stitched into the heavy armor, shredding layer after layer. The plasma cannon launched swirling mass after swirling mass, splattering molten metal with each impact. These weren't death blows, only the initial jabs in a multi-round match.

The battleship was giving more than it was getting. Missiles launched at the cyclic rate, creating a stream of high-powered weapons searching for targets. They raced across the void at a hundred gees, defying an easy target to point defense systems.

Mencken's entire first salvo was sniped well before the missiles were a threat to the battleship. The second volley had a better chance for the simple reason that it was fired closer and the missiles had more fuel to maneuver, but the engagement envelope would shrink quickly as the battleship maneuvered away.

It found its course and jumped to fifty gees. *Mencken* had slowed its acceleration to ten gees as it looked for an optimal firing solution, as well as keeping the crew fresh.

"Cease fire!" Podsy called. Long-distance lobs would be a lesson in futility and a complete waste of a limited resource. Missiles were not easily replaced in Jemmin space.

From the front of the battleship, an orifice spun open, and power surged through the ship.

"Captain Podsednik," Jem interrupted.

"Sorry, Jem. I'm pretty busy." Podsy cut the link as he tried to guess where the battleship was headed next. In the distance, a massive wormhole opened. Behind the *Mencken*, *Zeen Home Three* tacked in the opposite direction of the combat ships of Task Force Sword, taking the freighters with it. Zeen Interceptors poured from hangar ports around the sphere.

The firepower of Task Force Bow slid through the gate. In less than thirty seconds, the complement of cruisers and destroyers were through. A couple of armed freighters slid in behind them as they accelerated toward the battle. The freighters started coming through in bundles of four and eight. As soon as they were through, they were being directed away from the battle, probably into the same area that the *'Keeper* was intended for. Admiral Corbyn would figure that out when he received the relayed order from Commodore Meng, right in the middle of the heavyweight bout.

The battleship discharged an energy-beam-turned-bolt that was unlike anything anyone had ever seen. It appeared as a distortion in space, traveling at one-tenth the speed of light. The cruiser had gotten too close and was unable to get away. The weapon enveloped the cruiser, crushing it like a cheap soda can and continuing on. Its energy dissipated with the distance, but two freighters had been too slow and ungainly to get out of its way. They were crushed by its immense power as well.

Podsy was in shock—three ships destroyed in the blink of an eye by a single weapon. He didn't think anything could stand before it, but they couldn't retreat. They were committed.

"Captain, I must speak with you," came Jem's insistent voice.

"Yes, Jem," Podsy said, unable to think what else he could do besides close the distance and fire until he was out of munitions.

"Jemmin have developed a gravity cannon. We cannot get in front of that ship, or we will be destroyed."

"How in the hell did Jemmin get the gravity cannon?"

"It has been a thousand years. They might have been able to develop it independently, which is beside the point of how we deal with it."

"By dumping everything that goes boom right on its head." Podsy thought about launching the Vipers to attack the battleship, but that would be throwing away good lives. They were better used for keeping the *Mencken* alive. "It looks like the battleship has a new target."

It continued its swing and zeroed in on *Zeen Home Three*. The maneuver brought it back into range.

"Firing everything we've got," Tactical shouted. Railguns sent projectiles streaking into the void on a line in front of the battleship. LRMs blasted into space, followed shortly by medium-range variants. One hundred and forty missiles left their tubes in less than three seconds. *Mencken* jerked by the backblasts before restoring its momentum. One hundred percent of the ship's weapons had fired.

Capacitors started to recharge. Auto-load systems thumped and clicked as they cycled new missiles into place, and through it all, the railguns continued to spew their deadly ire.

The battleship moved through the tungsten and depleted uranium bolts as if they were so much space dust. Bits of armor were torn off and flew away, adding to the wasteland of Terran and Jemmin metal already littering the Axiodocious Nexus.

"Jem, find us which gate leads to the Jemmin homeworld. Now that we know the *'Keeper* can interrogate the gates, let's ask some good questions. We just went from thirty options to nine." Podsy clicked off and turned his focus back to the fight.

19

PRAY WE SURVIVE THE FIGHT

H.L. Mencken

The battleship was in full defense mode as its main weapon spooled up for another shot. While building the energy, it kept up its relentless assault on the Terran fleet. Over one hundred missiles leapt from the launch tubes. "Battleship"—an apt name for a tool of war. More powerful than a Gatecrasher. Its weapons bristled from it like a porcupine in heat.

"Launch the Vipers. Missiles inbound," Podsy ordered as soon as he saw the Jemmin weapons ejected from their tubes. Seven seconds later, the Vipers appeared on the board and burned to an intercept point with the inbound volley.

"Anti-missiles away," Tactical called out as medium-range canister systems headed into space. They'd explode in front of the inbound weapons, sending a huge cloud of depleted uranium balls into the flight path. The combined momentum served to tear up the warheads' guidance systems and penetrate the engines, damage that would keep the missile from completing its task.

But Jemmin anti-ship missiles had hardened warheads and

tougher casings. These were all Tactical had left to fill the first line of defense. Tactical hoped to get in a lucky shot—penetrate a seam, or bounce a missile off-course. Maybe even make them burn extra fuel to avoid the impacts altogether.

It was the only option of an increasingly complex layered defense.

Sima Yi had also fired its first round of antimissile weapons, while also fighting off two Jemmin cruisers coming in with flank shots.

"Tactical, get that second strike on the battlewagon underway, and then the third as soon as it's ready," Podsy said evenly. "Clear the tubes."

The preference was to wait and adjust after seeing how the enemy countered the attack. Podsy wasn't seeing a whole lot of time left in the engagement. He had sworn to defend *Zeen Home Three*. The battleship was going to get a clear shot. No amount of Zeen Interceptors could disrupt the gravity cannon once fired. It wasn't like shooting down a missile. They had to stop the shot before it happened.

"Maximum acceleration toward the battleship," Podsy ordered loudly enough that everyone would hear.

"Max burn, aye," Helm replied.

Podsy checked the board. Of the original twenty Jemmin cruisers, only eight remained. Of the original two hundred and thirty-one Terran and Solar warships, thirty-seven were listed as off the grid. The Terrans continued to fight, and would until the count was zero. The human fleet had the greater combined throw weight by far, and they weren't giving in.

Half a dozen ship-sized missiles launched from *Zeen Home Three* and accelerated quickly through one hundred to two hundred gees. Zeen Interceptors filled the void. All weapons focused on the Jemmin battleship.

Coil guns and chain guns spun up, sending a message to the inbound missiles. Railguns cleared and cycled. Short-range interceptor missiles raced downrange, carrying enough punch to blow the offending Jemmin weapons out of the sky.

"Launch countermeasures," Podsy ordered.

"Already gone," Tactical replied. On the board, they were hard to see, buried beneath an avalanche of projectiles—noise-makers trying to convince the inbound that they were a bigger threat.

As the engines struggled past one hundred fifteen percent power, the couches embraced the crew more and more tightly. The g-forces kept them from speaking. The first battery of LRMs succeeded in killing only two of the battleship's missile salvo, leaving a target-rich environment for a squadron of hungry Viper pilots. They turned toward the inbound and fired their chain guns while lobbing their slower missiles in front of the wave.

The penetrating power of the heavy rounds cut into the missiles with devastating effect, sweeping a series of Jemmin weapons from the board. The small defensive missiles found success tearing into the armored warheads, realizing a fifty percent kill rate. The pilots whooped in celebration while sending another volley of both slugs and missiles, but they were playing catch-up, the wave had already passed. Forty-one missiles bore down on the *Mencken* as it accelerated toward them.

Podsy watched in helpless frustration. They needed to continue on the current acceleration curve for twenty-four more seconds if they were to intercept the battleship. The Jemmin missiles would be here in twelve. *Mencken's* first wave was arriving now, getting splashed across the board. Only one missile from the first salvo made it through, to explode with no visible effect on the grossly armored hull of the Jemmin battle-ship. The flying fortress continued on its course to target its gravity cannon on *Zeen Home Three*.

Coil guns and chain guns fired until they were glowing red, even with space to cool them. Tactical maintained fire at the cyclic rate, well beyond design standards.

All or nothing. Sometimes it only *seemed* like the alternative was nothing, but in this case, it was. The weapons would be no good on a dead ship. There was nothing to save them for.

The *Mencken* belched a final round of SRMs.

Four Jemmin missiles deviated toward the noisemakers. Coil guns scrubbed sixteen more. Missiles took out nine. Viper fire killed eight from behind. And that was all the assault carrier could do to protect itself.

The remaining five missiles bored relentlessly into the *Mencken*.

Three hit the misshapen and battered front end of the assault carrier. They exploded, tearing the massive armored plate off the ship. Its previous damage saved the *Mencken*. The armor separated from the hull without sending the lethal shock-waves, without allowing the blast to penetrate. The last two missiles skipped off the reinforced hull plating of the acceler-ating ship and detonated close to both port and starboard flanks.

Two titanic explosions rocked the ship, shaking it to its very keel. Teeth rattled even though the crew was already clenching them to weather the high gees. Tactical's station cracked in half with a great cry of anguish.

The ship screamed in protest while plowing ahead at maximum acceleration. Podsy used his eyes to key in **Damage Report**. The reports came in automatically from ship systems. Bent and broken but not destroyed, except the impact armor that had covered the ship's bow section. Without it, even a small asteroid strike would be catastrophic.

The Zeen missiles continued, unperturbed by defensive fire from the battleship. The missiles accelerated to nearly five hundred gees.

Previously, the Zeen had lived and died using only Interceptors. They'd lost a worldship, but as the Zeen had said, there were different hives, and they never talked.

Why hadn't Xi told him about it? She couldn't have known, Podsy thought. Otherwise, she would have. *How many other secrets did the Zeen have?*

None of that mattered as the seconds counted down.

Ten seconds before the *Mencken* would ram prow-first into the beast. Then, a spark of hope.

The battleship recognized the Zeen threat. It diverted the entirety of its combat power into destroying them. The engines spiked on infrared as the main weapon powered while defensive systems cycled.

And the Zeen missiles continued unerringly.

"Abort!" Podsy screamed with every fiber of his being. Systems responded, driving the ship on the shortest path to escape the suicide run.

Defensive missiles exploded near the inbound Zeen weapons, to no effect. They continued to increase speed. Bearing down with destructive speed comparable to that of a ten-kiloton nuke, two of the missiles jerked to a ballistic trajectory alone, slowing with the loss of propulsion.

Then another dropped back. The final three continued their death sprint. A gap in defensive fire allowed the missiles to plunge into the bow of the great Jemmin warship. The first one disappeared into the gravity cannon's maw. The second hit the rounded, ram-like prow. The last jinked to the side and back to slam into the hull plating, hitting a spot that had already seen impacts from multiple Terran strikes.

The *Mencken* groaned as thrusters blasted full and engines drove it away from its former suicide track.

Podsy wondered what had happened since the Zeen missiles had not exploded. Time seemed to stop as impact was imminent. He tried to say, "I'm sorry," but the words couldn't get past his teeth. Podsy closed his eyes.

When he opened them, alarms sounded, insistent on attention. *Mencken* had missed the battleship, blown clear by three world-rending explosions, driving the crew past their human ability to stay aware under the gee forces. The engines were offline, and the ship was slowing. With the bridge bathed in red light, Podsy leaned forward until he could climb from the acceleration couch.

"Damage reports! Injuries?" Podsy shouted to get the bridge crew's attention. People crawled from their couches, wincing at the pain of blood returning to tortured limbs. In less than a minute, the crew was back on their game. The klaxons stopped. One by one, damage lights disappeared from the internal grid. The main lights returned as the engines restarted after the emergency shutdown to prevent overload.

Injury reports started coming in. Impact injuries from debris thrown through spaces, but no deaths. Captain Podsednik sighed in relief, but the battle wasn't over.

"Tactical, bring us up and get our weapons back online. Helm! Find our Vipers."

The main screen lit up with the tactical display. The Viper squadron protectively circled *H.L. Mencken*, keeping it safe from all comers during the time it couldn't protect itself. Destroyer squadrons hunting in packs were giving it to the final four Jemmin cruisers. Each was venting atmosphere and leaving trails of debris, being denied entry to gate after gate.

The '*Keeper* had shut them all down. Missiles pounded the

cruisers from all directions. One by one, they died in the cold of the Axiodocious Nexus.

Admiral Corbyn's voice came over the general broadcast, standing the fleet down for recovery and repairs. A few lifebuoys floated among the wreckage, with freighters already working the area to recover them. The admiral also wanted to reassure the survivors.

"We have lost a total of forty-nine warships and two freighters, but we know which gate will take us to the Jemmin homeworld. When next we go, it's to cut the head off the snake. Get something to eat, get some rest, fix your ships, and then we'll leave. The Zeen estimate that we had best be gone in five days or less. Make the most of your time, people. Task Force leaders and key ship captains will convene on board the 'Keeper tomorrow at thirteen hundred hours. Corbyn out."

The message repeated twice more.

Podsy's P2P buzzed—General Pushkin with a simple request. "Come see me right fucking now."

"Commander Wythe, the bridge is yours. I'll be in the Task Force Command Center."

Pete raised one eyebrow knowingly. Podsy smirked.

"Congratulations on surviving the Podsednik Kamikaze. I'm off to receive assurances that it was the right thing to do, and I should endeavor to do at least one in every battle from here to the end of the war," Podsy mumbled as he passed. The commander snickered before assuming the task of overseeing the ship's repairs.

Podsy hurried to his quarters to pick up Jem before heading deeper into the ship to meet the general.

Zeen Home Three

The battle had lasted a grand total of thirteen minutes. In

that time, the human fleet had lost a quarter of its combat power, including one of three Republican-class dreadnoughts, and expended an untold amount of ordnance.

Xi was still shocked at the maneuver the *Mencken* had pulled. And last but not least were the missiles the Zeen had sent downrange. She rounded on Bob.

"When were you going to tell us that you had those things?"

"Now," Bob ventured. "That was the first firing. Initial data suggests we put the program on hold to examine why three of the missiles did not reach the target."

"Three hits, and any one of them by themselves would have destroyed that ship. You have a missile that can destroy something like a Gatecrasher? Sumbitch, Bob. What else aren't you telling us?"

"Nothing." Bob didn't sound confident.

"Neither one of us believes that. You're a lousy liar, Bob. Let me show you how it's done." Xi shook her head and brushed a finger through her short hair. She assumed a welcoming pose, arms to the side and hands out. "I love your Zeen food, Bob. Is there any way we can get more?"

"Yes. I can have it sent up."

"Don't send anything. That was a lie. I was showing you how to do it, but that's not right. Don't lie. You're better off. I don't like Zeen food. I don't like what you did with the samples we gave you for replication. No matter how you're programming your systems, it still churns out bug snot. We'll get stocks from the fleet before we gate next. Don't worry about feeding us."

"Oh." Bob sounded cold and displeased, something new for him and the translator.

"Since the cat is out of the bag, tell me, what were those things?"

"Zeen have never seen a Jemmin battleship before, and the

gravity cannon is alarming. It is a weapon that could unbalance any fight."

"My question was about your missiles, but the one after that was about the battleship and the master blaster space-warper. If you insist on calling it the gravity cannon, we can go with that."

"The missiles are experimental."

"You already said that," Xi scolded. "When did you develop them, and how many more do you have? Scratch that first part. I don't care when you made them. The only thing that matters is how many more you have."

"Zeen have six more, but they are not available because of the poor performance of the trial launch."

"Poor performance? They saved the life of *Zeen Home Three*!" Xi didn't understand the alien brain and was sometimes exasperated by Zeen logic.

"Emergency. Different."

"So they're not available, but they really are. Six. We can make a difference with that many, Bob." Xi walked back and forth with her hands clasped behind her back. "I need to call *Mencken* and rip Podsy a new asshole for that dumbass attempt to ram the Jemmin battlewagon."

"Catalyst in decision-making process to use missiles. Alternative was to gate away before gravity wave hit."

"You can gate that quickly?" Xi saw the gating process as somewhat laborious and time-consuming, requiring matching alignment and speed.

"Yes, but it may have damaged Zeen human cargo."

Xi stopped and recoiled at the claim. "What human cargo? Who else is on board?"

"Major Bao and her crew, of course," Bob replied, sounding hurt.

"Call us self-loading cargo. We are just passengers. That's a completely different take, Bob. So *Zeen Home Three* was never in danger? Damn. I hadn't considered that. Thanks for testing your missiles on our behalf. I need to talk to my ship, and thanks, Bob. But please, no more secrets. Help us. The gods know we need it. If my math is right, we took a big punch in the mouth during this fight, and lost ships and people we can't replace."

"Symmetry." Bob walked away, leaving Xi in peace in the spherical room where the entire battle had taken place in three dimensions around her. The Terran and Solar fleets were reconsolidating, repairing, and rearming.

Xi looked at her comm device, wondering who to call first. Chain of command. "CO, this is the XO." She liked her title and her ranking officer. It was the way of the TAC to keep the chain informed. She had deviated from that in the past, but Leeroy was on the Task Force flagship. He had direct access to everything, including the right people, and he could buffer the message from Xi, reshaping it to make it more palatable.

"Major. Serendipity smiles upon you. We have a few questions, needless to say."

"I hope I have answers. Let me tell you what I know." Xi took a deep breath and waited to see if the colonel had a different approach. Silence meant consent. "Zeen considered three strikes out of six to be a near-total failure. They have six of those missiles left. They were never in danger. I guess they are capable of gating within a few seconds, which was their primary plan until they launched their super-secret, extra special prototype missiles to save Captain Podsednik from himself."

"We've already had that conversation with the good captain, but I am not convinced he was wrong. Our orders were to protect the Zeen worldship at all costs. Maybe Podsy was the only one who understood what that meant. No one knew they weren't in danger, so we had to go with what we knew. There will be no tribunals second-guessing the split-second decisions of those of us in combat. We answer to each other, period."

Xi nodded to herself. "A welcome change. I can face a thousand Arh'kel, but waiting in the hallway to be called on the carpet was always a freighter-load of bullshit."

The colonel returned to the task at hand. "I'm here with General Pushkin, and we have Admiral Corbyn and Commodore Meng on the line. Can you tell us more about the missiles and anything else you've learned that might help our battle plan?"

Xi stood slack-jawed. She had thought she was only talking to the colonel. The shocking part was, Admiral Corbyn had sat in on one of her tribunals. She shook her fists in frustration. "Gentlemen," she started, "Zeen are hesitant to use the next six because they think there should be a one hundred percent success rate. Regardless, as long as it's an emergency, they will use them. The bad news is, I have no idea what constitutes an emergency, but the trigger was *Mencken's* imminent destruction. Zeen were not willing to let that sacrifice happen. Maybe it's because Jem is on board. I don't know, but I wouldn't include that weapon in a battle plan since we don't know if our request would rise to the level of an emergency."

Admiral Corbyn cleared his throat before taking over the conversation. "For the record, I did not enjoy those tribunals either. But they don't matter anymore. We have a far different challenge now. Major Bao, your role as liaison to the Zeen has paid huge dividends for this fleet. I think the reason they saved the *Mencken* is that your friends are on board. They don't want a sad or angry Xi Bao on their ship. When you were in prison, did you ever contemplate that you might become the savior of the human race?"

Xi's heart skipped two beats before it started again. She grew momentarily lightheaded.

"If there was anyone who exemplifies the Zeen saying of 'not food,' it's you, Major," the admiral continued. That made Xi feel better. It was the highest compliment the Zeen paid. It was binary. Either you were, or you weren't. Xi had convinced the Zeen that the whole human race was not food. "We counted two hundred and forty Zeen Interceptors. Is that all of them?"

"I don't know," Xi replied. "I haven't seen the majority of the ship. What assets have we found on the 'Keeper? Major Trapper should be exploring his ass off."

"We recalled most of the Marines for tactical deployments. We feel the GateKeeper can protect itself because we are convinced that no one will seek to destroy it. They want it for themselves. The Zeen have been forthcoming with what they are finding onboard, like the ability to interrogate the existing gates for travel data. That was how we've determined which one leads to the Jemmin homeworld."

Xi smiled darkly. "When are we going?"

"In just under five days. We'll transmit the countdown to Elvira, as well as load her up with everything we know, including your favorite: logistics reports." Admiral Corbyn chuckled with the last, an inside joke among the senior leaders.

"As sexy as doing performance appraisals," Colonel Jenkins added.

Xi groaned before answering, "Next steps, Admiral?"

"Get yourselves ready. We still don't know if we need a land force, but better to be ready and not needed. Put your game face on, Major. This is the big one."

"We hope," Xi agreed. "If nothing else, let me go brief my crew. No need for chow or weapons resupply. We are topped off at present."

General Pushkin entered the conversation. "That is good because there will be no more weapons resupplies. All munitions have been distributed. There is nothing left to give or get."

"Back to work, everyone. We have a lot to do and no time to do it."

"Business as usual," Commodore Meng suggested. The others agreed before signing off.

"Time to talk to Bob and the bowling ball boys," she said, referencing the spherical room and its apparent ruling council.

20

SETTING THE STAGE

GateKeeper

Admiral Corbyn leaned back. Colonel Cao had briefed him on available amenities, encouraging the fleet staff to bring their own chairs. It wouldn't do to keep the admiral standing or sitting on the floor.

The chair was the only thing keeping him upright. The weight of the losses, combined with the impending battle, bore down on him. He hadn't slept more than a couple hours each day in the previous week. His eyes were sunken with dark circles, his hair unkempt, even as short as it was.

"Maybe a tribunal would be better than this," he muttered to his counterpart, a man they'd kept secret. He was in a wheelchair, unable to walk, and there weren't facilities for the disabled onboard fleet combat ships. But General Moon wasn't just anyone. He was a leader of the TAC who had fought and made a difference for the Metal Legion. His injuries had left him a shell of his former self. Depression had kept him from stepping up earlier, but Admiral Corbyn had always believed and had dragged the general along with him on this foray into the deepest pits of the void.

Onboard the 'Keeper, the general had come around. The latest battle had brought tears to his eyes for the valor of those who fought, in addition to the pain of horrific losses.

"A tribunal is necessary to make sure we're still doing the right things. That the front-line leaders understand the intent behind the orders. We don't need to second-guess combat decisions, only understand what went into making them. Then we adjust our training. When it became a political weapon is when it lost its power and alienated the Metal Legion."

"Talking politics sucks the life out of me," Admiral Corbyn admitted. "How about discussing keeping this fleet alive? Is there any chance of winning this next fight?"

"Just between us? Yes, but it'll take everything we have. There's no hope of going after the Vorr. In the end, our people will fight and die for the sole purpose of changing masters who won't be pleased with us for cutting them out of the Zeen-Terran-Vorr alliance."

"I have an idea about that, but it's meaningless until we defeat Jemmin."

General Moon rubbed the scruffy growth on his face. He had never had a beard, but he'd let himself go since the accident took his legs. The medical facilities hadn't been made available for TAC wounded, which drove the general deeper into depression. He almost gave up, but Corbyn talked him into coming along. Moon was glad he had.

"Are we that angry with Jemmin?"

"They fucked with humanity and were caught. They are unrepentant, which means that once they considered us a threat, they would eliminate us, which is exactly what they were trying to do with the Arh'kel. Breeding those fuckers in the Solar System? Yeah, we're that pissed."

"I remember something about revenge and digging two graves, but we're going to dig a hell of a lot more than that. As we see in the Ax Nexus, we'll fill the void with the skeletons of the once-proud Jemmin fleet. Fuck you very much. I like the Zeen ship-killer missiles, for what it's worth."

"A pleasant surprise for us all. I didn't want to lose the *Mencken*, or General Pushkin or Jem or any of them. The worst part is, I don't think it would have accomplished anything. I think the battleship would have shrugged it off. It was ballsy, though. Gotta give the kid that."

"Zealot?" General Moon wondered.

"I don't think so. His record suggests he is data-driven. He calculated the odds of what it would take to save the worldship, and that was his best chance, consequences be damned."

"We need that ship, because, well, you know, have you seen the logistics on there?" The general laughed.

"Do you want to tell Podsednik that he's facing a board of inquiry, or should I?" Corbyn smiled broadly and clapped his friend on the shoulder. Admirals and generals had no one to joke with. They were the faces for all who served. They saw the chance to let their hair down for only the briefest of moments, and they took it. "Help me dig through these and decide what we need to do with the freighters that have been emptied."

The general's expression soured. "You and I both know what's going to happen to them."

"I do. The question is, will it happen with the crew onboard or remotely?"

"Depends on whether the ship can handle remote control. If Jemmin get their digital mitts inside them, our problems will multiply."

Admiral Corbyn hung his head for a while before looking up. "It never gets any easier, does it?"

General Moon didn't have to answer. They turned to the grim work of building primary and secondary battle plans for the attack on the Jemmin homeworld.

. . .

Terran Assault Carrier *Mencken*

Jenkins took Podsy's hand and shook it firmly and for longer than usual. "You've made me proud," the colonel said.

Podsy didn't know what to say to that. He frowned as Colonel Jenkins let go and turned to head to the drop deck. "Go kick their asses, Lee."

"You, too, Stanley. No fear."

"The name's Andrew," Podsy corrected.

Lee was taken aback. "When did you change it?" He waved and walked out.

Commander Wythe chuckled. "Stanley Podsednik? Damn. Your parents didn't like you much."

"It's not Stanley." Podsy watched the tension melt from the bridge crew. Smiles replaced fear and worry. Colonel Jenkins, leadership genius. "Business as usual, people. Get me Chief Rimmer."

"Rimmer," came the answer after Comm connected them.

"Chief, I need this to be the best drop you've ever made. Is everything ready down there?"

"Are we sure we're dropping?" Rimmer asked.

"No, but better to be ready. I think we have to send them no matter what, so they don't bust up your deck. You know how Metalheads are when they don't get to blow up the enemy."

"Don't I," the chief agreed. "Gotta keep your eyes on 'em at all times."

"Be great today, Chief. Don't make me come down there and ram my metal leg up your ass."

"Sometimes I miss the contentious old Podsednik, but that ain't today, Captain."

Podsy nodded to Comm, who cut the link. "Fleet-wide

signal coming from the *GateKeeper*," Comm reported before transferring it to the ship-wide broadcast.

"Admiral Corbyn here with someone you might know to share a few words before we head out. General Moon, they're all yours."

Podsy instantly felt remorse at having no idea that the general had come with the fleet. It made sense. He'd spent his entire career preparing for this moment. Podsy wondered if they gave him legs.

"Good morning from the *GateKeeper*. There's nothing I can tell you that you don't already know. When we fight, we fight to win. The objective is to decapitate Jemmin leadership. Based on everything we've seen, that is what it will take to render their remaining forces less hostile. Our combat power is set. We have what we have. But so do they. Since we control this Nexus, they won't be getting any reinforcements either. It'll be as fair a fight as we're going to see this deep into Jemmin space. No human has ever been as far as we're going. Revel in being the first and then knuckle down. Do your jobs. It's as simple as that."

The general hesitated before finishing his thought.

"Some of you may wonder why I'm here. I wouldn't have missed this for the world. I don't have much fight left in me, and a wheelchair is no way for a soldier to travel, but we fight with what we have in ways that we're capable. Thank you for coming with me."

Admiral Corbyn picked up the broadcast. "T minus fifteen. Confirm your formations and travel through the gates. One last check of your weapons systems. See you on the other side."

"Metal never dies," Podsy said under his breath before switching to his outside voice. "Now's the time to go if you need to."

"Go?" a junior engineer asked from one of the side stations.

"One last check of your weapons systems means to hit the

head, as in, visit the bathroom. The last thing you want when we're knee-deep in the shit is to have to stop and take a leak."

"Oh!" the engineer exclaimed, embarrassment reddening her face. Podsy was surprised she hadn't heard the expression before.

"Tactical!" Podsy pointed to the main screen. The tactical display appeared, with the fleet properly color-coded by task force. The ships were arrayed neatly beside the heavies. By the 'Keeper, the freighters were in four neat columns behind eighty combat vessels, also in four columns.

In formation next to the Zeen worldship, forty warships were aligned in a single column, "asshole to bellybutton," as the military might say since they were tightly packed one behind the other. Only twenty freighters traveled with the Zeen. Single file was too limiting and took too long.

Seventy-four additional warships remained between the two task forces. Bow was ready to reinforce wherever the 'Keeper told them to go before the gates closed.

With the data from the gate close at hand, the Zeen and the 'Keeper had calculated what they thought was the optimal gate location. The 'Keeper was going first to bring the most combat power in the least amount of time. Then the worldship would gate in.

That was where the admiral and general expected the plan to start falling apart, but they'd both be in the Jemmin home system and could adjust as needed.

Status of the mechs and the Marines appeared on the big board. Colonel Jenkins' *Powerslave* finally showed green. Major Trapper with twenty Marines in the advanced Gamera suits were deployed on the Marine dropship piloted by Lieutenant Smiling Wolf. The Marine dropship showed green well before the Metal Legion's drop-cans.

Competition was fierce on the drop deck. The first can was

in the chute, ready to launch. All they needed was to skip into the planet's upper atmosphere, and the Chief would cycle the cans like dropping depth charges. The Marine dropship would make its own way to the surface. Simple, until recovery time. The chief even had two resupply cans ready to go. He also had six empties because there were no supplies to fill them with.

Podsy looked at the report, a blank expression on his face. Two cans for eighteen mechs. That was barely enough for four. Podsy thought about keying up the colonel and reminding him that a supply drop would be negligible, but he knew the Metalheads had already been told to shepherd their ammo.

He shook his head and focused on the screen, but fond were the memories of being the Wrench and Monkey in *Elvira* with Xi Bao at the helm. Those were easier days. Fly by the seat of your pants and solve problems on the go—the ultimate chess match. Many thought of mech combat as two heavyweights slugging it out, but it was far more than that. The heavyweights would argue that theirs was a chess match, too. Anyone who'd been in a fight would argue that better tactics would usually win the day.

And Podsednik and Xi Bao were still standing.

"General Quarters," Podsy ordered. Klaxons sounded for the obligatory length of time, with the appropriate red flashing lights. The ship returned to normal lighting. He watched his board light up as departments reported in.

Tactical's job was to report combat status. Podsy already knew the answers, but let the commander make his report. "Bulkheads sealed, ship is at General Quarters and ready for combat."

"Very well," the captain answered. "Follow the plan until we need to deviate. Then we'll make a better plan."

The *GateKeeper* spun up its gate, expanding it to a size that could swallow a small moon. The ships accelerated as one, four by four, rotating in alignment with the wormhole's radial axis. *Sima Yi* was first through with three cruisers, followed by four more, missile platforms and destroyers. Lots of destroyers of all different classes, with wildly varying armaments. They raced through the gate with barely five hundred meters between them. Then came the freighters in a choreographed dance that boggled the mind. As the last ships passed the 'Keeper, the massive beast accelerated through its own wormhole, closing the door on its way out.

The Zeen immediately activated their gate drive, and the wormhole opened, spread, and stabilized. "Go," General Pushkin ordered, and the reorganized Task Force Sword moved as one. The *Mencken* has been moved to the back of the combat ship line, right before the freighters. Podsy's maneuver had scared the leadership enough that they'd decided to keep the assault carrier out of the first push. Despite the combat power, they needed *Mencken* to deliver the mechs, the Marines, and the Interceptors.

21

JEMMIN HOME WORLD

Mencken

"Tactical, where are my screens?" Captain Podsednik asked. They had been in the system for ten seconds, and they still had no information. "Give me visual, for fuck's sake!"

The tactical feed gave way to the external video. "Hard to port!" Helm said at the same time as the captain. The destroyer in front had started to slow. At slower speed, thrusters helped drive tighter turns. The *Mencken* jerked out of line, narrowly missing the ship in front of it. With scrap hull plates from a former Jemmin cruiser welded to the front to provide some impact protection, the *Mencken* was better than it had been but not as good as the original.

Podsednik didn't want to test it.

"Heavy jamming throughout the system. All channels are impacted," Tactical reported.

"Stick to the plan in case of comm loss, so why are those ships slowing down?" Podsy muttered. Numerous views appeared on the side screens. A group of Jemmin cruisers maneuvered in front of the emerging task force and blasted the first cruiser. Not everyone in line responded in the same way, leading the ninth and tenth ships to collide. Both streamed atmosphere as they found their way into the fight.

Podsy took an expanded look at the star system. A single K1V-class star shone brightly in the distance. Four planets were spaced out, with the first closest to the star and the third and fourth in orbits near each other but at the far reaches of the heliosphere. The second planet looked to be in the right orbit to support life. There was no other data because it was all visual.

As the Terrans were able to fan out, they brought their array of weapons to bear. Missiles fired after visual target acquisition might have had little chance, except that they were danger-close to Jemmin. Beam weapons tore into Task Force Sword. The *Belvoir* was sliced from stem to stern. Her own missiles blew up in their launch tubes, ripping the outer shell away from the hull. The destroyer explosively decompressed across the entire ship. Not a single escape pod launched.

The two destroyers next to *Belvoir* maneuvered away, seeking safety. One exposed her belly to Jemmin, who ravaged the ship with beam and projectile weapons. The *Underhill* lost her entire port side before limping away on thrusters only until she completely lost main power. Four escape boats launched before the ship went completely dark.

The *Runnymede* achieved maximum acceleration before the engines were blasted by a Jemmin beam weapon. Right up the tailpipe turned the fusion reactor in a hundred-kiloton explosion, the ship expanding into a blinding white shower of debris.

It was Sword's poor luck to enter where Jemmin had cruisers positioned. The system's physical gate stood not far from the second planet, where the preponderance of the Jemmin ships were stationed. Visual was inconclusive with the count, but the two Gatecrashers stood out. So did the six battleships and a smattering of sparkling lights that signaled too many Jemmin cruisers.

But the ships didn't die in vain. They drew the incoming so the rest of the fleet could take aim and fire. Over a thousand missiles sped into the void on a collision course with Jemmin. The cruisers accelerated through one hundred gees.

"I have a shot," Tactical declared.

"Hold fire." Podsy watched the cloud of missiles rain into the Jemmin ships. Point defenses were useless under the onslaught. Missile after missile struck home. He winced at the waste after the missiles exploded uselessly against the remnants of the three destroyed ships.

Task Force Sword fanned out as they increased the distance from the gate. After the loss of the Jemmin cruisers, partial external systems returned. Comm was still down, but sensors showed the near space. The task force got itself under control, even though General Pushkin was unable to send instructions.

Prior planning and all that. In the absence of new orders, follow the old ones.

The *Mencken* assumed a position to the side of the forming-up destroyers and cruisers.

"Three of ours for three of theirs," Tactical noted.

"And at the cost of over a thousand missiles." Podsy shook his head. "The chess match is underway. Be frugal, Tactical, up until we can't be. Eight heavyweights. We can't waste hundreds of extra missiles on cruisers. We have to kill them with just enough."

"An injured Jemmin is a dangerous Jemmin," Commander Wythe remarked.

Podsy knew about the six Zeen ship-killers. He wondered at what point the Zeen would consider it an emergency and launch the missiles at Jemmin. The aft view showed that the gate had closed following the worldship's transit.

That was when Jemmin's fleet took note. Four battleships detached themselves from their defensive posture near the physical gate. A few cruiser squadrons arrayed themselves around the heavies. Moments later, they were on their way as an intact battlegroup.

"Prepare to engage Jemmin. Hold fire. No long-range shots. Prepare to launch the Viper squadron."

Tactical confirmed the order. Podsy checked how the ships were spread near him, memorizing the image. He figured they would lose sensors with the approach of the Jemmin fleet.

"Comm, any luck breaking through the jamming?"

"Not *yet*," the comm officer replied, emphasizing "yet" to make sure the captain knew he was working on it.

"Engineering reports all systems nominal," the junior engineer announced.

"Status?" General Pushkin requested.

Podsy hopped on the P2P link. "Green across the board. We've taken our position on the far right flank of the formation. We're down a cruiser and two destroyers. Others appear to have taken some damage, but their status is unknown, although they've taken their positions within the task force."

"What I'm seeing from our sensor scans of the second planet is that there is significant industrial output, along with a massive communication array. The jamming is coming from there, relayed by Jemmin ships throughout the system."

"The head shed?" Podsy wondered.

"At least connected with it. If we're to win this fight, we need to coordinate our attacks. Prepare for an end run, Skipper."

"We can't tell the others what we're doing. We might have to go it alone."

"Viper escorts all the way. I think we'll have a few destroyers joining us. Make it happen. I'll let Colonel Jenkins know he is a go." The general signed off.

"Give me ship-wide." Comm confirmed by holding one hand over his ear and pointing at the captain. "Into your couches, people. We're going to make a high-speed run to the second planet, the place we believe is the Jemmin homeworld. We're going to drop off the Metal Legion and then hightail it out of there. No matter what happens, we need to deliver those cans. The rest of the fleet is counting on us. Put on your game faces. It's showtime."

Podsy entered his couch and positioned the screen in front of his face. He took note of the new array as Mencken smoothly accelerated on a looping course far away from the incoming, using the system's gravity wells to assist their efforts in getting to the homeworld more quickly.

"First humans ever to step foot on Jemmin home. I wonder if they contemplated that when they started manipulating species to do their bidding," Tactical said, doing the same thing as Podsy—memorizing everything he saw before the sensor view was lost. "A destroyer squadron has detached itself and is joining us. Seven ships."

Which of those destroyers was part of this arrangement? Podsy thought, marveling at the foresight to build such a contingency into the plan. He hadn't known, but the admiral and generals didn't have time to tell everything to everyone. What mattered was that those who needed to know were speeding up to join the *Mencken* in assaulting the planet.

Podsy touched the screen for a comm link to Colonel Jenkins. "Colonel, we have to hit and run. You won't have fire support for more than a couple minutes, and probably none after you're on the ground, when you'll need it the most. We won't even be able to detail the Vipers to you. They'd splash down in no time when they bingo on fuel. I'm sorry, but we're hanging your asses out there."

"Get us to the planet, Skipper. We'll do the rest. Cry havoc and loose the dogs of war or something like that. I understand. You have nothing to apologize for, but thanks for checking in. You take care of my home. I have a room and some meager possessions to come back to."

"We all do, Colonel, with a big roger on 'meager.' If TAC wanted us to have nice things, they would have issued us nice things."

"Amen to that. I'm going to eat a few snacks and then take a nap. Call me when we're there." The colonel clicked off before Podsy could reply.

The screens started to flicker as the jamming intensified.

Look at this, Tactical sent in a message to the captain.

Podsy watched the external view from the aft camera. Two Zeen Interceptors were towing a drop-can. Forty additional Interceptors flew in a tight formation to protect the can.

Major Xi Bao, reporting for duty, Podsy thought. He activated his screen with his eye movements and sent the image to Colonel Jenkins before getting back to watching for Jemmin threats to materialize. With the technology and information from the captured Poltergeist, the mechs and fleet shipping were able to see Jemmin. No surprises, but Podsy never trusted technology unless he could double-check the information.

Still, he expected something to come at them out of nowhere. In the last system, it had been the battleship.

This was the Jemmin home system. Their best toys would be here, wouldn't they?

Now that they were executing the third phase of the operation, Podsy wanted someone to talk to, but the acceleration prevented conversations.

The destroyers kept adjusting course to stay with the assault carrier. The *Mencken's* wide swing was adding critical minutes to the overall flight profile, but it kept the ship out of reach of the battleship squadron on its way to engage *Zeen Home Three*. The remaining warships scattered to improve their angles and increase the odds of their attacks finding their targets. The numbers were even, but the throw weight favored Jemmin.

I'd call this an emergency, Podsy thought, the pain of imminent loss bearing down on him heavier than the g-forces pressing him tightly into his acceleration couch. He wondered how many Terran ships would be sacrificed before the Zeen would engage? Or would they gate away, leaving the Terrans to their fate? But there was a different piece in the game. The Zeen were providing a robust escort for Major Bao.

They wouldn't leave their people behind. Speculation was the best anyone could do because their communication throughout the system was jammed. The *'Keeper's* task force was doing something. They had to be, but every ship besides the *'Keeper* was beyond visual range.

The *Mencken* continued through the curve, reducing acceleration to maintain a steady speed on an arc toward the Jemmin homeworld.

Why isn't anyone coming to intercept us? Tactical sent to the captain.

I expect they believe planetary defenses will be sufficient, Podsy typed back. **Make ready to deploy the noisemakers and chaff dispensers. Low tech versus high tech.**

"Sensors still jammed," Tactical reported after the g-forces had reduced enough for him to speak clearly.

Podsy climbed from his couch but waved for the others to remain. He switched the views on the main screen. Aft video showed numerous explosions and missile arcs. They were no longer able to see individual ships, so they couldn't tell who was getting the better of it, but a massive space battle was underway. Side views showed the '*Keeper* moving at an angle away from the star system's rotational plane. Jemmin heavies were chasing. Podsy could only assume the smaller Jemmin and Terran/Solar ships were equally engaged in either following or running. As the planet approached, they lost the visual.

"Chief, prepare to deploy the cans," Podsy transmitted to the drop deck. "Helm, get ready to hit the brakes to launch speed and then slingshot us around the planet. Maybe we can get back in time to help someone."

The Zeen Interceptors raced ahead and started blasting the skies in front of the *Mencken*.

"What are they shooting at?" Podsy wondered.

Tactical stood from his couch and accessed his panel. Sensors were offline, but he was able to get a better look with an expanded visual. "Sir, it's a minefield."

The ship jerked when it hit the upper atmosphere, then bounced and ground its way downward. The Jemmin plates welded to the bow started to glow from the friction and heat. The Zeen pulled away and remained exo-atmospheric while still flying the same route, clearing mines along the way.

"Target is the comm array. Drop coordinates entered," the underutilized Ground Control Officer reported.

Podsy watched the viewscreen until the time was right, then keyed the comm. "Execute the drop."

One second later, the first can raced down the chute and toward Jemmin home. The hangar door opened, and the Marine dropship followed the cans down.

22

WHERE NO HUMAN HAS TROD

Watching her external view, Xi started to vibrate in anticipation. The Zeen had dropped her in the midst of the other drop-cans on their way to the ground. She had yet to get comm and had no idea of the plan, but she was headed dirtside to the most important target humanity had ever tackled.

If only she knew what that target was. A massive array dominated the auburn and puce landscape. Sufficient urban sprawl suggested they were in the right place.

Bob stayed in his seat, uncomfortably strapped in because Zeen didn't fit in human-shaped chairs. But he remained silent, taking the drop in stride.

"Welcome to J-Ville Central," she told her crew. The drop-ships ahead of her activated their retro-rockets, slowing their descent and easing their impact with the ground. "Oh, shit. Hang on!"

Elvira descended directly toward the roof of a small building. The rockets fired, but the can still hit hard. Xi felt the pull from the heavier-than-Earth-normal gravity before the sides popped open, freeing the mech beneath the Jemmin sky.

"Woohoo!" Xi cheered as she trundled the Scorpion-class

mech out of the can. Sensors were nothing but white noise. "Looks like we're all visual, boys and girls. Let's see if we can find *Powerslave* and get some orders."

She stopped and swayed the cockpit—the vehicle's head—left and right, looking for a way ahead. The can had half-crashed through a flat roof. She peeked over the ledge—a twenty-meter drop. No problem. She slid over the edge and hooked the middle legs, then pushed forward and slid down the side of the building until the back legs hooked. *Elvira* stretched her front legs until they touched the ground. Xi moved them forward before releasing the back legs. She pushed off with the middle legs to gain forward momentum. *Elvira* lurched across the ground until all six legs were on the level and settled into a smooth six-legged gait.

The humanoid walkers were easy to spot on the outskirts of the once-great city. Age and decay had started to set in, or maybe Jemmin plans to take over the galaxy had been a budget drain. Xi wondered where they got their resources. Did they have someone like Thucydides who owned banks filled with credits?

Elvira made a beeline toward the Ettin-class walker. As she closed, she confirmed it was Jenkins' ride, *Powerslave*.

"Atmosphere outside?" Xi asked.

Penny checked the externals. "Looks like you'll be fine with portable O2 and goggles. The air is shit but breathable."

"Hook me up." Xi unlinked from the mech and climbed out of her seat. "Stay here!" She stabbed a finger into Bob's chest. She continued toward the airlock, grabbing her safety gear when she passed the Monkey, and strapped both the mask and goggles over her face before cycling the airlock and running out. When she hit the ground, she realized that hers were the first human feet to ever touch Jemmin soil. She snarled, "You shouldn't have fucked with us."

Jenkins exited as she arrived. "Quick and dirty," she requested.

"We take out this array, which is responsible for jamming the whole system, then we find whoever is running this circus." Jenkins made to get back inside, but Xi stopped him.

"This doesn't look like the center of a galactic empire." Xi pointed back toward the city.

"Intel says it is." Jenkins shrugged. "Let's go blow some shit up."

"I can get behind that order." Xi waved because they didn't salute in the combat zone. "Colonel."

They climbed back into their vehicles, but they missed their chance. *Kochtopussy* had already fired the first shot, and 2nd Company was having an unmolested field day against the defenseless target. A series of MRMs fired at short range to increase the explosive power because of unused fuel started a cascade of destruction on the hundred square kilometers of hardware facing skyward.

The mechs kept up the barrage until Colonel Jenkins broadcast to all units to cease fire. "Major Bao, take your company, find out what powered that thing, and destroy it." The jamming was gone. Sensors started to paint pictures of the nearby landscape and fill the databanks with information.

Two kilometers away from the city, the power feed to the apparatus appeared as a tunnel. Major Bao sent the packet to *Godzilla* to check it out.

"Wasn't that way too easy, Colonel?" Xi asked while simultaneously sending coordinates to the five mechs under her command and moving her unit into the smoking debris.

"That was the easiest op I've ever run, and it feels wrong. All kinds of wrong. 1st and 2nd Companies, spread out and get me some information. Find me a Jemmin to talk to so I can learn what the hell is going on."

The mechs were aggressive in their initial moves toward the city, but no one wanted to get caught in a crossfire. They became more tentative quickly, moving into a diamond formation for maximum three-hundred-and-sixty-degree defense.

"Maybe they've never had to defend their homeworld before. With the fleet guarding the one gate, maybe they've grown soft over the millennia."

"I'd like to think that was it," Jenkins replied.

The neural link shocked Major Bao with the identification of inbound bogeys. "Belay my last. Poltergeists inbound. Looks like twenty of them."

"Get me a firing solution on where they came from!" Jenkins requested. Hammer complied with an initial calculation, but the target area was too broad. At least the Metal Legion could see them, an upgrade thanks to capturing one.

It didn't make them any easier to bring down. Eighteen aging mechs versus twenty Poltergeists. "Trapper, where are you?" Colonel Jenkins requested.

"Circling above you. Give us some target coordinates, like where Jemmin leadership might be, and we'll take care of business."

"I don't know where that is. Yet! Can you provide a tactical assist with these Poltergeists?"

"HE up," Xi reported. "On the way." Two fifteen-kilogram loads headed into the path of a Jemmin Poltergeist moving at one-hundred-fifty kph, ten meters above the ground. The vehicles were freelancing since they usually operated alone, no more than one or two on a planet because a single Poltergeist controlled a vast fleet of drones. Which begged the question, where were they?

"We'll try to find a good snipers' nest," Trapper replied quickly before signing off.

Jenkins didn't have time to see where the Marines were

going. He had more immediate issues, like a thousand inbound Jemmin missiles. "Holy. Fuck." Jenkins calculated the trajectories and made an instant decision. "Get into the city, flank speed."

His walker became a runner, accelerating quickly to over one-hundred-twenty kilometers per hour.

Xi looked at her information. She could make it to the city in time, but the rest of her company was too far away. She bolted after them, refusing to save herself.

"You're right, Major, the power feed for the jammer is a tunnel," *Godzilla* reported. The mech was another Ettin-class walker. If he could fit, everyone else was golden. "Going in."

"Everyone into the tunnel right now!" Xi accelerated. Her engines hit one hundred ten percent and heated to the redline as she pushed her rig. The ride grew rough even though the ground was smooth. *Fat Man* rolled in, then *Holy Diver*. *Twilight's Fall. Fortune's Fury* was barely keeping pace in front of *Elvira*. "Come on, *Fury*, pick up the pace."

"Actuators two and three are out. Shit. Just lost four," the Jock reported. "We're jumping."

Abandoning ship.

Xi did not have time to pick them up. The missiles wouldn't hit her people if they could find shelter. "Dig in. We'll come back for you," she ordered.

Elvira vaulted the stalled mech and raced into the tunnel. "HE up. Safeties off." She aimed at the tunnel entrance and fired. The heavy shell exploded in the roof, sending a fireball out the tunnel entrance. The release loosened the shallow roof and it came down, opening a new entrance on a steep angle overhead.

"Keep moving!" The other mechs continued downward. *Elvira* scrambled backward. Explosions rained overhead like hail on a tin roof, filling the tunnel with dust, debris, and a hellacious amount of noise. Xi's fears that a missile or three would chase them underground didn't materialize. It was worse than that. Under the relentless battering, the entire roof caved in, bringing hundreds of tons of auburn-colored rock and dirt down on their heads.

H.L. Mencken

The Zeen Interceptors cleared a path through the minefield for the *Mencken* to return to space before they swooped back to the planet. Podsednik's plan to use J-Ville Home's gravity to swing back toward *Zeen Home Three* wasn't viable because of the minefield around the planet. The *Mencken* and her destroyer escort remained on course toward the general area of Task Force Spear.

"Sensors are online. Comm is live!" the comm officer shouted through the clenched teeth of a full-gee burn.

Tactical populated the board with the first sweep and updated it with successive scans. It was as bad as they feared. The number of ships facing off was staggering. TAC had brought over two hundred ships into Jemmin space. The Jemmin were countering with nearly as many, but their heavies far outweighed humanity's capital-grade ships. The *GateKeeper* was as big as the combined size and weight of either the Jemmin or TAC fleets. Its willingness to fight was unknown. As an asset to be protected, it was held back from the battle.

It held a position half an AU from the gate at forty-five degrees high from the system's second planet. The remainder of Task Force Spear's warships arrayed themselves between the *'Keeper* and Jemmin. The freighters remained behind the monstrous ship from eons past that was still the most technologically advanced vessel in the known galaxy.

General Pushkin frantically made call after call to get information from Task Force Sword, but they were a long way off. It would be a full minute before the *Mencken* received the response. The tactical board was sparse with details from the distant task force.

Before them, missiles clouded the void, each force venting their spleens upon the other, trying to win the day. Two battle-ships and two Gatecrashers accelerated toward Spear, bringing over a hundred cruisers with them. The Gatecrashers weren't designed for a head-to-head contest. They were meant to fire backward at enemies hiding behind a recently transited gate. They powered forward regardless because they carried enough firepower to deliver a death blow to any human ship. Soon enough, the ships would pass each other, and woe be to those who didn't maneuver quickly enough out of the Gatecrasher's deadly backblast area.

Antimissile protective fire came to life from both fleets, sending missiles and projectiles into the void like a spider-webbed shield through which too many offensive weapons passed. The tidal wave refused to be stopped.

Podsy closed his eyes amid the fury of the final protective firing as Jemmin missiles were scrubbed from the board, but not quickly enough, and not in great enough numbers. When he opened his eyes again, it was like getting stabbed in the gut by a trident. Twenty-four TAC warships were off the grid. Another seventeen had been critically damaged.

Only eleven Jemmin cruisers succumbed to the inbound weapons. A two-for-one trade meant the imminent death of the Terran fleet, but there was nothing more dangerous than a wounded animal.

Terran and Solar cruisers and destroyers accelerated, turning themselves into weapons as much as their missiles and railguns. They each picked a different target.

For all humanity, they launched everything they had left.

Missiles cycled through fire and reload until the racks were empty. It didn't take long, but the firepower from the remaining fifty-six ships filled the sky like a wet blanket being dropped on a fire. Podsy leaned close. Where was the *Sima Yi*?

He found it emerging from the far side of the *'Keeper*. Why was it staying so close to the Originators' ship? Why hadn't they received any orders from Admiral Corbyn? He couldn't wait any longer.

He typed a quick message using his eyes. **Task Force Spear, this is Mencken group. Successful insertion of Metal Legion to planet's surface. No chance to rejoin Sword. Will join Spear. ETA 2 mins 30 secs**. He broadcast the message to both Commodore Meng on the *Sima Yi* and Admiral Corbyn on the *'Keeper*.

"Peel off. Remain available for Legion recovery," Admiral Corbyn ordered in a dark voice.

If we don't win this fight, they'll come after the Mencken. Better to fight now with a battlegroup than be isolated for later, Podsy replied. **ETA 2:10**.

A broadcast reached the *Mencken,* ordering an attack into the rear of the Jemmin fleet advancing on the *'Keeper*.

In the absence of other information, Podsy directed the *Mencken* to turn hard back toward the planet and skip past the Jemmin fleet to get a better attack angle from behind them. The *Mencken* started its high gee turn, pausing any further communication as the crew pressed close to unconsciousness.

In the distance, the physical gate came to life. The remainder of the TAC fleet left behind at the Axiodocious Nexus began their transit, turning once their screens cleared and Corbyn's broadcast hit their receivers. Ship after ship raced through until all seventy-four were bearing down on the Jemmin fleet, attacking directly into the Gatecrasher's kill zone.

Half the Jemmin fleet started high-gee turns to engage the new force, but only one battleship did the same. The remaining three heavies bore relentlessly toward the *'Keeper,* with the Gate-crashers slowing to best engage the inbounds running up behind them.

The TAC cruisers and destroyers weren't done. They had one more trick up their sleeves. Clouds of material ejected from airlocks and cargo decks reflected sensor scans as if they were the ships they had come from. The smaller ships of Task Force Spear turned hard off their collision courses, suffering mightily from the withering Jemmin fire. Six more Terran ships went down, then fourteen, leaving half the original number that had entered the system.

The Jemmin cruisers impacted the clouds of chaff that weren't chaff but explosives that upon impact with a ship fired a liquified titanium core to penetrate a ship's hull and wreak havoc on its insides. It was the least expensive and least tech-demanding weapon in the improvised arsenal of the Terran Armored Corps. Cruisers tried to shrug off the explosions, but they were too much. One ship died under the micro-assault, then a second and a third.

Sima Yi launched an impressive array of weaponry, from LRMs to special high-yield nukes, the entirety of the launch directed toward the lead battleship. Where the fast-attack warships intertwined, they cleared the way for the heavy-weights to square off.

The Jemmin battleship powered ahead as the remaining cruisers peeled away in pursuit of their prey. The battlewagon had a larger target in mind. It opened its bow door and started energizing the gravity cannon. *Sima Yi's* missiles were sniped from the cold of space one after another, as if the battleship had all the time in the world.

When nine missiles broke through the outer barrier, close-in-weapons systems went ballistic, shredding the cosmos with a hundred coil guns firing a combined twenty thousand projectiles a second. The heavy missiles barrel-rolled and corkscrewed, twisting and turning on final approach. The battleship's engines and thrusters struggled to turn the great beast, moving the gravity cannon out of the line of fire.

Six missiles died under the barrage before the exposed flank bared itself to the final three missiles impacting the ship at ninety degrees, the optimal angle for maximum penetration. Pounding through the heavy armor, something lesser missiles could not do, the two long-range missiles and a high-yield nuke entered. Milliseconds later, a blinding flash erupted from an expanding split. Secondary explosions rocked the heavy from stem to stern. The ship bulged and rocked. Its fusion reactor lost containment and went critical. The back half of the battlewagon disappeared within a mini-supernova.

Sima Yi slowed to stay near the *'Keeper*, but the big ship had started to move.

Forward, directly at the remaining three battleships and two Gatecrashers.

23

FIGHT OR DIE

Henry VIII

Commodore Sosunova exhaled heavily through clenched teeth. On *Henry VIII's* screen, a tactical pause allowed the two fleets to take a breather, assess, and regroup for the inevitable next round.

Task Force Sword had fought the incoming cruisers to a deadlock, both fleets veering away to lick their wounds, while the four battleships maneuvered to get the best shots while staying a long way from the Zeen worldship, as if they knew it could destroy them if it chose.

Two battlewagons had already fired their gravity cannons. The good news was that the power dissipated over a long range. The bad news was that quite a few ships had died in the blasts to discover the extent of their range.

Task Force Sword had fared better than Spear, their kill ratio one to one-point-five, but with the twenty-seven Jemmin casualties came eighteen TAC losses. That left only twenty-one smaller ships, *Henry VIII*, and the Zeen worldship, along with twenty freighters hiding as far from the battle as possible.

Two hundred Zeen Interceptors crisscrossed in front of the worldship as if that were sufficient deterrent to hold Jemmin off.

It wasn't that. Jemmin were biding their time, lurking, watching, and positioning. The battleships moved in a strange choreography. The remaining TAC warships stayed as far away from the gravity cannon lines of fire as possible. Move. Counter-move. No rest.

Zeen Home Three remained unmoving, as the dominant piece on the board to which all other ships deferred. *Henry VIII* stayed in front, but to the side of the worldship, just in case they declared an emergency and fired their ship-killers. Sosunova didn't want to be on the receiving end of one of those.

"Damage report," Comm said. The commodore checked the list, to find repairs proceeding faster than normal. No one wanted to be nursing a broken ship when they were killed. They wanted to go out with some spunk. The last high-speed pass by a Jemmin cruiser group had been painful, costing the dreadnought a number of its launch systems. Many of those were already restored, increasing *Henry*'s combat readiness from fifty-two percent to eighty-five—a much better way to fight a battleship or four.

The tactical view didn't change. Numbers were even between the two forces, with an edge to Zeen Interceptors on one side, but the massive weapons of the four battleships created overwhelming superiority on the Jemmin side.

Except for the Zeen. With Major Xi Bao off the ship, they'd lost access to the Zeen, who didn't reply to calls for information or requests for help. A squadron had escorted the major to the planet and had not returned. The remaining Interceptors stayed close as if knowing something the humans did not.

Which was most likely the case, but the stubborn humans still wanted to know what they didn't know. It was the way of humanity.

"Clear the decks and return to battle stations," the commodore ordered. She'd been watching the battlewagons and thought she'd detected a pattern. She wanted to test her theory. "Helm, prepare to accelerate to flank speed."

Powerslave

Jenkins was the last mech into the shelter of the buildings. The Jemmin missiles fell short without exploding since they refused to enter the airspace above the buildings.

"Looks like they don't accept collateral damage of their city, which tells me there's something here they don't want to lose. Spread out and find what that is. If it's Jemmin, snag me one. I want to talk to them. And keep your eyes peeled for the Poltergeists. They're still out there."

A series of "rogers" crossed his board as the five other mechs of 1st Company, *Satan's Alley, Devastator, Kanban, War Pig, and Crazy Train,* headed into the city, carefully, maintaining oversight of each other. Never a mech alone, but two by two, bracketing the lone stranger, with Jenkins bringing up the rear. The Ettin-class could see over most of the buildings, giving him the opportunity to hold back but still be within visual range of the company.

"This place looks rundown," *War Pig* reported. "Seeing no activity. No sign of life. Nothing on near-range IR."

With communications restored, the company's sensor outputs were linked in real-time to *Powerslave*. Jenkins was already seeing the information, but the report told everyone what the others had seen.

"Major Bao?" Jenkins repeated his call twice before expanding his search. "Anyone from 3rd Company? Anyone at all?"

A weak handheld comm signal popped up. "Slash here.

Fury is down. Poltergeists are consolidated over the antenna farm. XO took the company underground. Oh, shit. They see me. Surrendering."

"Keep the comm open!" Jenkins shouted, but the channel was already dead. "Slash, are you there?"

Hammer leaned close to the ladder leading to the colonel's station on the *Powerslave*. "Has anyone ever been taken prisoner by Jemmin?"

Jenkins shook his head. "We've never done anything like this before. We're on the Jemmin homeworld. If I were them, I'd be a bit pissed off about it, just like when we ran into those cockbags on the moon."

Hammer returned to his position and angled the mech through a narrow gap between two buildings. He loved driving the massive walker. It made him feel like a *kaiju* of old.

"Trapper here, on a hill two klicks beyond the array. Poltergeists are consolidating around the collapsed tunnel entrance."

"What about Slash?"

"Too much dust. No visual. Stand by."

Jenkins looked at his comm system. He knew the fog of war was present in every op, but he hated it all the same whenever it raised its ugly head. End of War had more unknowns than anything he'd ever been involved with before. It was like humanity closed its eyes and hurled themselves into the void, accepting whatever fate had in store.

"Colonel Jenkins, Captain Koch," the 2nd Company commander called. *Kochtopussy* was pulling a dual mission. He was the field repair mech, but he also led a combat team. With eighteen, now seventeen total vehicles, everyone was pulling more than their own weight. But with twenty Poltergeists waiting, there would be no damage to be repaired; there would only be complete destruction. Jenkins was still trying to convince himself that someone would walk away from this mission if they could only find the Jemmin head shed. The leadership team, where the Metalheads could cut the marionette strings.

"Jenkins, go."

"We have power spikes five klicks north of our position. We're going to investigate, adopting a half-moon formation. Nothing else to report." Half-moon, an arc of five mechs, with one behind. It was a good formation for a logistics guy like Koch to take, defensive with max firepower forward. "Speed is twenty kph."

"I copy fifteen minutes to target. Stay within city boundaries. At least for now, it's keeping the Poltergeists away. 1st Company is headed toward the center of J-Ville. The high-rises beckon. Keep your eyes out for drones. Twenty Poltergeists can control about a hundred thousand of those things. We could be buried before we know it."

Unlike in modern movies, the high-rises in J-Ville Home weren't magnificently soaring pieces of art. They were pedestrian, no more than twenty stories high. Blocky and unremarkable. Earth had sexier buildings, even in some of the low-rent districts.

Intel said this is it. I can't believe we've been fighting the B-Team all these years and they've been kicking our asses. Something isn't right, Jenkins thought, reiterating his and Xi's earlier impression. He thought briefly about his XO and smiled. "Of course, you went underground."

"Inbound," Trapper reported. Jenkins' display lit up like a Christmas tree.

"1st and 2nd Companies, prepare to light 'em up. Spread out; don't give 'em easy targets."

"It's the Zeen," Trapper clarified.

Forty-two Interceptors screamed through the sky on their way to intercept the Poltergeists. The Jemmin ships scattered like cockroaches when the light was turned on. The Interceptors fired. Jemmin fired anti-aircraft missiles in wave after wave. The Zeen started to weave through the sky in a deadly game of cat and mouse. The Interceptors continued to fire as the Poltergeists headed for open ground before turning skyward, accelerating to three hundred kph. The first ones to go vertical were sniped from the sky before they reached a thousand meters in altitude.

The Zeen bore down relentlessly. The Jemmin defensive fire was withering, filling the sky with death. Five Zeen Interceptors fell victim to the first wave and three to the second, but the Zeen still had numerical superiority and more.

Speed was on their side as they slashed through the air of the Jemmin homeworld, adding insult to injury when, with a boost of three thousand kph at launch, missiles raced toward their prey. The Poltergeists demonstrated extreme aerobatics as they twisted and jerked to avoid the smart missiles, but they couldn't avoid the rain of railgun projectiles accelerated to hypervelocity. The distance between the forces evaporated before the Interceptors split, heading over the city before turning around and racing back toward the enemy.

The Poltergeists hesitated, waiting to fire until the Zeen were no longer over the city.

"Interesting," Jenkins muttered as he watched the battle unfold.

The Zeen slowed to a near-stall and launched a mass attack on the maneuvering Poltergeists. Jemmin were used to taking the offensive. Only two vehicles had run, while the others stayed to fight. The remaining Poltergeists were stymied by the low attack, using the city as the backstop for any defensive fire. By the time the vehicles turned to flee, it was too late.

Smoking craters and flaming wreckage falling from the sky marked the demise of the first eighteen Poltergeists.

The last thirty-four Zeen Interceptors accelerated to top

speed and quickly closed on the running Jemmin, whose end came quickly. The Zeen went vertical and flew toward space.

"Go pick up Slash and his crew," Jenkins ordered. "The way is clear, and while you're there, see what happened to Major Bao."

"On our way, Colonel," Trapper replied.

The *GateKeeper*

Admiral Corbyn strolled around Central Control. The Zeen ignored him, and he ignored them. It wasn't hostile. It was what the Zeen preferred. They executed his orders without question, at least as far as he knew. The battle hadn't been lost, nor had it been won. The *Mencken* had joined the *'Keeper*, adding a destroyer squadron, too.

Corbyn wondered where the Zeen Interceptors escorting *Mencken* had gone. He wanted every asset available to respond if called. General Moon waited patiently nearby, watching the admiral.

"Our hands have been dealt, eh, Sunny?" The admiral used the nickname that only he called General Moon.

"Our hand was dealt long before now, Admiral," the general replied. "Like leaves blown before the storm, the best we can do is keep from dashing to the ground, but that is where we will all be in the end."

"Simpler than that. Our ships versus Jemmin. The Zeen have shut down the gate, so we have a respite in order to win this fight. That is the hand we are currently playing, but I agree. The game continues, and if Jemmin forces in the Ax Nexus are able to open this gate, then we'll play a new hand, but we will only have two cards to their fifty-two. If they come, they will bring every ship available to them. We are down by fifty percent, with no reinforcements."

"It is not optimal, but a strike this deep into enemy territory!" General Moon made a fist and shook it in front of him. "The sheer human audacity!"

The admiral's head snapped back to the three-dimensional tactical screen. He waved for the general to follow as he moved closer.

"They're coming," Corbyn stated while pointing.

The Jemmin battleship kicked its approach toward the 'Keeper into high gear. The second battlewagon began a hard turn away from the smaller ships to align its gravity cannon on the 'Keeper.

Jemmin cruisers dispersed and attacked in a massive dogfight. Task Force Spear cruisers and destroyers paired off to fight the more heavily armed and armored Jemmin cruisers. The battlefield of space took shape with the ebbs and flows of acceleration and maneuver as if mountains and valleys offered protection from the weapons that filled the sky.

Ever-present in the middle of the screen was a battleship followed closely by one of the Gatecrashers. The second Gatecrasher had come to a near-full stop and begun launching waves of missiles at targets behind it. The TAC warships quickly learned that the safest place to be was at knife-fight range with Jemmin.

The ships danced in intricate maneuvers of life and death. A misstep, missed point defense, and fusion reactor containment loss ended the crew's suffering.

TAC counterfire struck almost as quickly as it left the launch tubes, barrels, and rails. It was no longer a chess match, but fighters standing toe to toe, seeing who would fall first. Jemmin ships were built better to withstand such an onslaught, but the dogged determination of the TAC fleet gave them the edge.

For the moment.

Double volleys of overlapping fire caught Jemmin in a place they didn't want to be. Impacts cut into the armor, followed by hull-penetrating attacks. Jemmin cruisers started to die faster than TAC fleet ships.

Neither would get reinforcements. Neither would get a resupply. The last one able to fire would be the side that won.

The first to run out of ammunition was a destroyer called *Krakowiak*. It was left standing side by side with a cruiser that punished it for not being able to fire back. The Terran captain turned his ship toward Jemmin, but he only glanced off the side and drifted away with the loss of his engines. The Jemmin beam weapon lanced out at point-blank range and ripped *Krakowiak* in half. A small puff of atmosphere announced the ship's demise. There were no primary or secondary explosions. The reactor didn't lose containment, but the ship was dead all the same.

Loch Morlich and *Magog* teamed up to avenge their brother. Two salvos of missiles cut across the void, followed by a steady stream of coil and railgun fire. The Jemmin powered the beam for a second shot, but it didn't survive long enough to take it.

This scene played out again and again. As the *Puckeridge* launched its last salvo of missiles, it turned nose-on with the enemy and accelerated at flank speed on a collision course with the nearest cruiser. Defensive fire shredded the front of the destroyer, but the engines redlined on their way to going critical, driving the dying hulk into a Jemmin cruiser, exploding as the ship came apart with the impact. Both ships arced in a spectacular rainbow explosion.

Sima Yi moved between the battleship and the 'Keeper. As the Republican-class dreadnought came about, she launched a full spread of missiles. The battleship responded in kind with a full salvo. Hundreds of missiles rocketed into the void, missing each other as they passed. In space battles, there were no arcs like the Metal Legion was used to seeing dirtside. The missiles flew straight at their targets to maximize fuel economy until the final burn to defeat point defense systems.

Sima Yi activated her defensive systems first, reaching as far out as possible with a spread of antimissiles. The coil guns prepared to fire, while railguns streamed as many depleted uranium rounds as possible into the paths of the incoming missiles. The tactical board sparkled as the weaponry from both sides scrubbed incoming. The chain guns activated, and the last-ditch defense was twin-barreled fifty-caliber machine guns. With a range of over two kilometers, the old-school heavy machineguns represented the final protective fire.

One hundred forty, to ninety, to thirty, to fifteen. The coil guns focused on ten of the final incoming, scraping seven from the sky. Eight remaining targets were too many, so the series of twin fifties worked on just four, finishing them all off, but the explosions wiped two of the machine gun emplacements off the dreadnought's side. The final four rammed into the *Sima Yi*. Three breached amidships and the last creased the bow, exploding while still trapped in the heavy armor. That one did little damage besides splattering the armor and leaving an ugly gash.

The other three tore through the armor and the second hull before getting trapped within bulkhead-protected interior spaces. The explosions fountained volcanically from their entry points, destroying anything and everything within those spaces.

Sima Yi twisted and rocked from the violence of the three explosions, but she kept her keel beneath her and powered through. Terran dreadnoughts were tough beasts, but she was injured. Another strike into the massive holes through to the exposed interior might break her back. Commodore Meng turned the ship, moving the damaged side out of the line of fire, and launched another salvo.

Warning lights lit up the bridge from the damage and from the danger-low on ammunition. Even the mighty *Sima Yi* was running out of firepower, but until then, she'd fight.

She fired a second salvo, only twenty missiles, shepherding her scarce resources until she had the highest chance of hitting the enemy.

The Jemmin battleship opened her bow doors and exposed the beating heart of the gravity cannon, a swirling vortex of reds and yellow as the weapon powered up.

The inbound missiles from the two salvos were redirected toward the open maw to kill the weapon before it could unleash its fury on the *Sima Yi*. The battleship's counterbattery systems unleashed on the incoming with an intensity that crushed the *Sima Yi's* spirit. The close-in-weapons systems didn't need to fire because both incoming waves were sniped from the void well before becoming a threat to the gravity cannon.

Admiral Corbyn and General Moon watched, faces frozen in a warrior's stare as the gravity cannon fired its deadly wave at the exposed flank of the dreadnought. Being close enough that the weapon delivered a full-power strike, the meter-thick armor rolled like paper in a light breeze, bulkheads buckled, and the ship started to collapse in on itself. Missiles still in launch tubes detonated, sparking brief fires from venting atmosphere. The bow and stern twisted inward as the ship bent 'round. Lights flickered and were gone. Plumes of gases marked hull breaches as if the ship had been unzipped.

With one final buckle, the *Sima Yi* went cold, its life and the lives of those it carried ended.

Admiral Corbyn sighed while his eyes glistened with the catastrophic loss. He couldn't see *Henry VIII* on the board; there was too much action in between. Two battleships approached the *'Keeper*.

A light freighter, barely ten thousand tons, raced around the Originators' ship and headed for the battleship.

"This is what we've come to," the admiral said as he keyed his mic and took over direct command of the remnants of Task Force Spear and Task Force Bow. "Execute Queen to King Two. I say again, execute Queen to King Two."

24

STAB IN THE HEART

Elvira

"COME ON!" Xi roared, making her crew wince as she worked *Elvira*'s legs back and forth to start digging herself out. A Scorpion-class mech had the ability to dig through dirt, but the hundreds of tons of rock made finding a seam difficult. She alternated the legs, trying to find a weakness in the surrounding materials. The right rear leg started rotating, making a hole.

There was little resistance. Xi pushed the entire mech toward that quadrant, trying to force a way through into the open, where she could get the legs beneath her and start moving again. Then the leg stopped. "Hydraulics are out!" Xi shouted.

Lu jumped out of his seat. "Gimme two," he shouted back and dove headfirst into the opening of the leg chute. "Duct tape!"

Penny delivered the remnants of a roll to his outstretched hand. Lu mumbled a thank you and began wrapping the split line. He crawled farther in and pulled an ever-present spanner from a slot in his overalls. "Bleeding the line...and we're back up."

Penny dragged him backward out of the opening as Xi started working the leg again.

With a screech and a groan, *Elvira* started to move. The front legs pushed backward. The left-side middle and back legs pushed sideways. Rocks pummeled the top of the mech as *Elvira* gave them space to fall, then they were through the hole and down. "Hang on!" Xi yelled, but Lu was already airborne, floating free as the ship dropped, landing tail-first, sending Lu straight into the airlock hatch. Wrapping his arms around his head saved his life, but the crack of his forearm impacting the mechanism suggested he hadn't escaped without injury.

She groaned until *Elvira* tipped forward, landing on her legs and stabilizing. Lu tumbled to the deck with a grunt. Penny jumped from her seat and ran to her diminutive crewmate. "Oh!" she exclaimed when she saw the arm.

Lu tried to look, but Penny stopped him. "Stay still. I better get a splint on that." She opened the emergency medical kit under her seat. A quick look didn't show her what she wanted. She dumped the contents on the deck and spread it around. "No splint."

"Hang on," Xi shouted back. The chain guns started to fire. Adjusted and fired again. Xi moved from her chair to the wall behind her, opened a case, pulled something out, and tossed it to Penny. She was back in her seat and firing before her Monkey could take another breath.

"What are you shooting at?" Penny called while carefully wrapping the pneumatic splint around Lu's arm.

"Drones. Not many, but they need to die because I'm pissed."

Penny didn't bother replying. She didn't want to see more of the major's ire. Penny sorted the mess she'd left on the deck and found a pain pill to stick between Lu's lips. "I'd like to give you light duty, but there won't be any of that. Back on the job, Wrench."

"We can fuck off when the job's done. Until then, get back to work. I rank you."

"Two privates arguing about their date of rank. I could use some help, people. Port chain gun is glitching."

"On it," Penny shouted, even though it was Lu's specialty, falling under Wrench duties. Xi had run *Elvira* with a single crewman before, Podsy filling both Monkey and Wrench duties.

The major keyed her microphone to the company-wide channel. "Major Bao to 3rd Company, report."

"Nice entrance, *Elvira!*" *Godzilla* replied. The rattle of additional chain guns filled the chamber *Elvira* had fallen into. "Take my three o'clock, *Diver*."

Holy Diver was a small humanoid with a crew of two. Its railguns were the main weapons, but it had dual racks of short-range missiles mounted over its shoulders. Quad fifties bristled from its thighs for close-in protection. Other than that, it was fast and maneuverable.

The fifties barked, and soon, Xi called a ceasefire.

"Report."

"*Godzilla*, standing tall!" her Jock Meathead remarked.

"*Holy Diver*, down and dirty."

"*Twilight's Fall*, wondering what the fuck I'm doing underground." The Jock's nickname was Sungod, and he preferred the outdoors, being more claustrophobic than your average Jock.

"*Fat Man*, blubberingly here." A tracked mech, *Fat Man* was a heavyweight with a plasma cannon and coil guns mounted on each of the corners.

"Okay, you whiny bastards. We have to find a way out of here, but only after we've dug through the underground for a little while. The power to jam an entire star system has to come from somewhere impressive. That means it might make a nice display when it blows up."

"Not with me down here, Major," Sungod shot back.

"We'll get you back topside, so calm your tits. Focus on your job, which is to keep Jemmin off us long enough to figure out if there is anything worthwhile down here. I don't expect we can talk to anyone until we can get a repeater into a spot where it can see the sky. Marking up the map. Tunnels are designated Alpha One through Delta Four. We're going to hit the two biggest tunnels. The others look barely tall enough to fit the beverage cart from the country club. *Fat Man,* you and *Diver* have Alpha Two. I'll take Charlie One. *Godzilla,* hold this chamber for our return. Sungod, you're with me. Sucks to be you. Let's go, people."

Fat Man's tracks dug into the dust from the roof cave-in until the mech climbed into the clear tunnel and continued downward on a gentle rocky slope. He shot a comm amplifier into the wall as he passed through the opening. A comm check showed he remained five by five with the company commander.

"Launching a drone," *Fat Man* stated. The small quad-copter flew away, giving the mech an advanced view of what was hiding around the corners and in the dark nooks ahead. No sense in running headlong into danger.

At least, not any more than the usual headlong jump into a viper's nest.

Xi tapped into *Fat Man's* drone feed to watch the walls for anything that would warn her, but for now, it looked exactly like it was supposed to be—a big tunnel filled with bundles of heavy cables to carry power from down below to the array above. She wondered why Jemmin weren't using power transmission technologies. Cables seemed so twenty-first-century human.

Another sign that things weren't what they seemed.

Xi kept her thoughts to herself, but they darkened her mind.

The remnants of the Metal Legion numbered seventeen mechs total. There were four Marine dropships, only one of which belonged to the TAC. Xi knew the fleet was getting pummeled. They needed to find the Jemmin leadership and cut the head off the snake hoping it wasn't a hydra.

"Pick up the pace, *Fat Man*. We aren't getting paid to lollygag our way through love tunnels."

"As you wish, Major. When it comes to the naked race, I always win." *Fat Man* fired up the output and kicked the mech into high gear. The treads roared with the additional power.

"That doesn't sound as impressive as you think it does," the major added amidst the snorts and chortles from her company's Jocks.

"On the flip side," Sungod said softly.

"Hold the fort. We'll be back." Xi clicked off and concentrated on driving, although matching the top speed of a pig like *Fat Man* took almost no effort. It gave her too much time to think about wasting precious resources on a mostly dead planet.

What if we can't get off this planet because there's no one left to pick us up? she wondered.

Henry VIII

"Belay my last!" Commodore Sosunova shouted from her acceleration couch. The dreadnought slowed into a tight turn before accelerating back toward *Zeen Home Three*.

She replayed the message. *Sima Yi* was down, leaving *Henry* and *Mencken* as the only remaining TAC heavies. General Pushkin's order to protect the Zeen had come through loud and clear. Either the Zeen or the *'Keeper* had to survive long enough for the remnants of the task forces to escape Jemmin space. As long as some humans survived, they could continue the fight.

They wouldn't make it if they were isolated in the Jemmin system.

"Task Force Sword, pull back to Rally Point Zeta," Sosunova ordered. She gritted her teeth through the final gees of deceleration before climbing out of her couch, then stood and stretched. Her intent was to race parallel to the battleships as they were swapping positions to take advantage of a blind spot to rapid-fire before escaping on a perpendicular route. She hoped to cause significant damage to two of the battlewagons while limiting the impact on her own ship. She gave it less than a fifty-fifty chance of working as intended, but she was out of options. The best defense is a good offense—something she had thought apropos, especially when captaining a Republican-class dreadnought.

The fifteen remaining ships of Task Force Sword gathered before *Zeen Home Three*. Half of the survivors were scored and burnt from being on the wrong end of Jemmin weaponry. The freighter fleet remained intact at a distance behind the worldship.

The Jemmin must have decided it was time to end that convenience. Ten cruisers broke off and headed into the void, perpendicular to Sword. They traveled outside the human firing envelope, not that the fleet would expend missiles at anything other than point-blank range to maximize the lethality of what was left. On the other flank, another ten cruisers headed out, leaving six cruisers and three battleships behind.

They had less than ten minutes before the attack, which had to be the final attack. Humanity was running on fumes.

The commodore signaled Comm to broadcast her message to the entire fleet. Sword would hear the message right away. Task Forces Spear and Bow would hear it in a minute or two. By that time, Sword's maneuvers would be underway, and maybe the final battle joined.

Ten minutes. It wasn't a whole lot of time.

"Task Force Sword, I salute you!" Commodore Sosunova started, speaking confidently. "Every able ship besides *Henry VIII* is to reposition to Rally Point Freighter. Clear the space on this side so the heavyweights can slug it out. Our mission is to protect the Zeen worldship. This means protecting our freighters, too. We'll surround the worldship with human resolve, standing toe to toe against our mutual enemies. Know that the line was drawn here. Only one side will fly away from this battle. Feel the roots of the Terran Armor Corps. Embrace the strength of the metal around you because metal never dies. Shout *Lok'tar Ogar* and run to war. All hands, battle stations. Prepare to fight. Sosunova out."

The crew hadn't left battle stations. They hadn't been engaged that long, despite the horrific losses already suffered. Space combat didn't last long. Death blows could come from any strike. A successful penetration through a ship's armor was quick and final.

The destroyers and cruisers hurried away. Some streaked across space, others limped, but they all left. The dreadnought stood alone between the three battleships and *Zeen Home Three*.

The Jemmin heavies spread out, angling thirty degrees from the center battlewagon. Simultaneously, all three opened their bow ports.

"Equal number of missiles at each. Target those openings. Fire."

Tactical quickly allocated the spread before sending the missiles downrange. Thirty-five LRMs for each target. The battleships surged forward, closing the range with the worldship.

"Railguns, fire. Angle fifteen degrees to starboard and accelerate." The commodore was trying to get between two of the battleships to deliver a final broadside with the last of her arsenal. She counted on the Zeen to protect themselves from the third.

But the Zeen had had enough. Two hundred Interceptors erupted from the worldship, and the final six ship-killers launched into the void and accelerated at a rate that put their previous launch to shame. They came out of the worldship as if launched from a railgun and accelerated from there.

Across the void they streaked.

"Get us out of here!" the commodore shouted. Helm responded by banking up and away from the battleships. The ship groaned from yet another max-gee burn.

Two missiles targeted each battleship. Defensive fire filled the void. From railguns to coil guns to chain guns to small beam weapons to antimissile missiles, the battleships had learned somehow from the previous engagement that the Zeen ship-sized missiles would kill them with a single impact. *Henry VIII* got her legs beneath her and escaped the worst of the back-splash. The battleships seemed to have forgotten about the dreadnought as they focused every molecule of their ships on destroying the inbound missiles.

But the inbound Terran missiles drew fire away from the Zeen weapons. Spread across all, there wasn't enough for any. The ship-killers lapped *Henry VIII's* missiles as they continued to accelerate. Jemmin defensive fire couldn't keep up as the missiles hit a point where they were only a streak across the darkness. The first missiles hit the battleship farthest from *Henry VIII*.

The next hit the middle battleship. The final battlewagon managed to snipe one of the missiles before its partner disappeared into the gravity cannon's well. As in the Nexus, nothing seemed to happen at first, then the impact of the strike screamed its fury to anyone with sensors to see.

Two missiles obliterated the first battleship. No secondary explosions, just a single expanding supernova where a Jemmin battlewagon used to be. The next one fared only slightly better. *Henry VIII* was closer than she wanted to be, earning a full buffeting for her failure to attain a satisfactory standoff distance.

The last battleship started to accelerate toward the Zeen worldship, but that lasted all of two seconds. The explosion within the ship blew the sides up like a balloon, but they didn't pop. The ship lost power and floated on a ballistic trajectory, but thirty missiles had survived the massed fire and continued their relatively slow approach. One by one, they entered the gaping maw and exploded within until the thirteenth, lucky number thirteen, hit something critical. The first explosion blew a crater out of the armored side of the ship. A series of explosions rippled to the stern, where the power plant lost containment and turned the back half of the Jemmin battleship into molten slag. The ship started to spin on its journey as space debris. Knocked off-course, it was no longer a threat to anyone.

Zeen Interceptors engaged the cruisers while Task Force Sword sat back, watching for opportunities to deliver blows through gaps in coverage or when the opportunity presented better odds for a successful strike. They launched two missiles here or there, keeping the railgun fire to a minimum since it would affect friend or foe equally.

Two cruisers down, then six. Ten Interceptors down, then thirty. The battle continued fiercely.

The dreadnought arced up and over the worldship on its way to engage Jemmin. The rest of the Task Force Sword warships saw the charge for what it was.

The momentum had changed, and it was time to sweep Jemmin from the sky.

"Attack at will," Sosunova broadcast. Two cruisers and twelve destroyers headed in one direction to mass fire on the surviving cruisers. With the Zeen Interceptors stinging the cruisers repeatedly, they weren't able to withstand the onslaught. Sword attacked Jemmin, cleaning up the battlefield and clearing the board before them.

The fleet rounded on the second arm of the Jemmin pincer, to find that the Zeen had already taken care of business, but with heavy losses. Seventy-five Interceptors had been scrapped, but the survivors regrouped with those on the other side of the freighters and returned to the worldship without so much as a flyby.

"Stand down from battle stations. Remain in place for repair and recovery." Sosunova took a deep breath, closed her eyes, and reveled in breathing slowly. Her heart still raced. She willed it to slow. "Give me a P2P with Admiral Corbyn."

When Comm confirmed the channel was live, she transmitted her message.

"Jemmin fleet destroyed. Remaining assets are *Henry VIII*, two cruisers, and twelve destroyers. Zeen losses top one hundred Interceptors. Freighter fleet and *Zeen Home Three* are intact. Ammunition is danger-low. Intent is to join Task Force Spear."

She drew a finger across her throat, and Comm cut the signal.

"Continue with repairs and reload. Tactical, get me a count of how much ordnance we have left."

"Already have it," the tactical officer remarked. "But you're not going to like it."

25

LOOKING FOR THE WAY

"Are you seeing this, Major?" *Fat Man's* Jock asked.

"It's hard to miss," Xi replied. The drone had flown out of the tunnel and into a complex that looked more Jemmin than anything they'd run across so far on the planet. "I'm starting to form a hypothesis. Slow it down, Fatso. I'm parallel to you, and it looks like I'm coming up on the same chamber. I want to put a Mark One eyeball on it."

Fat Man's Jock Fatso was reed-thin; a strong wind would blow him over. He liked his callsign for that reason.

"Dialing it back. That's a roger." *Fat Man* slowed to a stop. *Holy Diver* stopped behind a turn in the tunnel, keeping his distance in case it was a trap.

"Stay here, Sungod." Xi trundled forward, tiptoeing as much as a sixty-ton mech was capable of. *Twilight's Fall* halted mid-stride, balancing easily.

"I'm looking forward to having a little more room," Sungod noted.

"Aren't we all? Now, shut your piehole. I have some thinking to do." Xi eased forward to a point where the tunnel lost its rough edges and became a well-manicured path to an enormous chamber, so large it was impossible to see the far side. The tunnel opened on a small rise above a fantastic city of glass and tube design, gleaming metals scintillating. Xi captured imagery of it all, hesitating to use sensors, although anyone looking would readily see *Elvira*. Still, she didn't need to ring the doorbell and let Jemmin know the Metalheads had arrived. "Get up here, Sungod, and provide overwatch. You too, Fatso. I think I see your tunnel mouth up the road a ways. Show me your face, *Fat Man*."

The crawler eased to the entrance and poked his nose out.

"Eyes on, Fatso. Hold position. *Godzilla*, get on your hands and knees and get down here. I doubt we're going out the way we came in. We need your firepower."

"Roger. Engaging crouch-crawly mode," Meathead replied.

"Make yourselves comfortable, people, and collect all the data you can, but passively. No active scans."

"I bet they know what 'passively' means," Lu offered with a slight slur. "It's like you're being demeaning on purpose. You know, talking down to them."

Lu started to laugh.

"How many of those things did you give him?" Xi growled at Penny.

"Just one, but look at him! He can't hold his liquor, that's all."

Xi shook her head while adjusting *Elvira's* optics to take in everything within visual range. Fully half of the area looked like a science experiment. "Lu, Penny, take a look at this. What do you think it is?"

"Organic power generation?" Penny offered. Lu mumbled something incoherent before his chin dropped to his chest.

"You have your moments, Penny. Did you set his broken bone?"

"Do I look like a sadist?" she replied.

"Do you want me to answer that?" Xi took one final look at the chamber before keying a P2P link with Fatso. "Keep an eye out and sound the alarm if anything happens. I'll be out of the chair for a minute."

She joined Penny in *Elvira's* main compartment. "He's going to think you're hitting the can."

"Not a bad idea, but taking responsibility for what Fatso thinks is an added burden I don't want. Hold him." Penny wrapped her arms around Lu from behind, pinning him to the seat. Xi adjusted her grip on Lu's bicep, keeping the arm in place. Lu groaned at the added pressure on his injured limb.

Xi removed the splint before balancing against the console, one foot braced against Lu's upper arm while she took hold of his wrist. "On three." Xi never bothered to count. She pulled the wrist toward her until the bones passed each other and settled back into place.

Lu tried to come out of the chair like a man possessed, unleashing an ear-splitting scream. With eyes wide and unfocused, his mouth remained open while Xi quickly put the splint back in place, tightening it around the injury. She carefully cut two slits in the Wrench's coveralls as an ad hoc sling, and despite the gasps, pushed Lu's arm through to hold it stable.

"There you go. Right as rain," Xi told her. Lu stared in shock.

The major wasn't sure what else to say.

"Do your best." Major Bao slapped Penny on the shoulder. "Thanks for your help. I have no idea when we're getting out of here. It could be a while before he gets real medical treatment. We can't let anything fester. And there won't be any resupply, so take it easy with the ammo. Congratulations, you've just been promoted to Monkey."

"Thanks, I think. But he can't do the Wrench work."

Xi laughed and smiled. "You misunderstand me. You have

both jobs now, so as I told Lu, do your best." Xi hit the small head for a quick relief before returning to her seat.

The chamber looked the same. Her board showed no imminent messages. She activated her neural link, reconnecting with *Elvira*. The scraping in the tunnel behind them suggested *Godzilla* had made record time.

"Time to see what Jemmin are up to. *Godzilla,* on my six. Then *Twilight. Fat Man,* provide overwatch and bring up the rear. *Holy Diver*, get yourself past Fatso and follow us in."

H.L. Mencken

Podsy stood with his feet spread. Queen to King Two—protect the *'Keeper*. Helm maneuvered the *Mencken* into position a thousand kilometers in front of the Originators' ship. He watched the freighter as it continued its slow acceleration toward the lead battleship.

"Is this what we're reduced to? Kamikaze runs by baby freighters?" To support Podsy's premise, a lifeboat launched off the freighter as the ship soldiered on. "Who is that? At least we can memorialize his name for whatever that's worth. He's got some jumbo coconut balls, that's for sure."

"Terran registration. It's the *John Wayne*, sir, captained by one Serenity Monk."

"*She* has some jumbo coconut balls." Podsy corrected himself. They watched in fascination as the ship dodged incoming, but the battleship made no concerted effort to destroy the freighter. No need. The ship's engines spiked and went offline, leaving the freighter on a ballistic trajectory, ignored as nothing more than space junk.

Podsy shook his head and turned his attention to the rest of the fleet. The TAC warships had consolidated into a single task force. Thirty-two remained. The nine that had accompanied the

Mencken to the planet were the only undamaged ships left in the fleet.

Comm waved to get the captain's attention. "Message coming in from *Henry VIII*."

"On screen," Podsy ordered.

"Audio only," Comm replied. The bridge went silent.

"Jemmin fleet destroyed. Remaining assets are Henry VIII, *two cruisers, and twelve destroyers.* Zeen *losses top one hundred Interceptors. Freighter fleet and* Zeen Home Three *are intact. Ammunition is danger-low. Intent is to join Task Force Spear."*

A cheer rose from the bridge crew. "What do you say we finish this and go get our people off the planet?" Podsy said softly. The crew turned back to their stations, pecking away with renewed vigor, bringing ship's systems online and racking the reserves into place. Every weapon they had left was loaded.

Mencken's magazines were empty.

Podsy looked at the backs of heads as people went about their tasks. He stood tall and started to think out loud. "It's the fifteenth round, and we're bloodied and bruised. We never signed up to take such a beating. Some of us signed up to get out of jail." He chuckled as he thought about his history and that of his closest friends. "But here we are anyway. This is no time to throw in the towel. Whoever is still standing at the final bell gets to hoist the trophy. The award is nothing less than the survival of humanity."

Pete Wythe threw his hands up. "I respect you, Captain, but sometimes you speak in tongues. Bells and rounds? Towels and trophies? Can you translate for people who aren't career Metalheads?"

"I feel you, Commander. We had too much time to kill traveling between shithole worlds, and we watched a lot of old-timey vids." Podsy strolled toward the tactical station, his expression serious. "We are the only ones who can win this war.

Terra and Sol don't know we're out here. This battle is about us fighting for ourselves. If we win, there's a big prize to be had."

"Aren't there other Jemmin fleets out there?" the commander asked.

"Probably a shitload of them," Podsy agreed. "But our bet is that if we can take control of J-Ville Central, we can defang the Jemmin ships. As long as we have the worldship and the *'Keeper*, we can do what we need to do to keep humanity safe."

Podsy held up a hand to stop Tactical from continuing. The next word coming out of his mouth was going to be "Vorr." That was a fight for a different day.

Captain Podsednik turned back to the main screen. "Get your game faces on, people. It's showtime."

The battleship and two Gatecrashers started accelerating as the cruisers maneuvered to get better firing angles. Jemmin had verified that their tactics of throwing their weight at one target at a time had proven successful with the death of *Sima Yi*. There was no reason to change it. The Jemmin heavies were coming for the *Mencken*.

Powerslave

"*Kochtopussy*, report." Jenkins scratched his head and rubbed his eyes. There was nothing showing on his screen. Everything looked dead.

"We're closing on the heat source, but it's not looking mechanical," Captain Koch replied.

Jenkins waited for the rest of the report.

"It's a geothermal heat vent, but it passes through a structure that seems designed for it."

"Geothermal power. That makes sense. Is there a way down?"

There was a delay before he answered. "Say again, Colonel.

I thought I heard you ask if I wanted to crawl down an active volcano's throat so I can take a swim in the lava."

"'Geothermal' doesn't mean an active volcano. It means it's hot enough for a significant temp change. Technology from centuries ago. Heat exchange to generate power. I expect it'll get hot, but you won't be taking any lava baths. I think you'll be surprised at what you find down there. We need to know."

Another delay. "Launching a drone," Koch finally remarked. "Sending the feed."

Jenkins watched the view of the drone descending a shaft carved through the planet's bedrock. The heat ticked up, but nothing that indicated molten rock waited at the bottom. Two kilometers down, the shaft widened and brightened. Tunnels led in all directions from a mechanical structure mounted over the shaft that continued downward.

"I see what you mean," Captain Koch admitted. The drone stopped to hover over a retaining fence surrounding the heat vent. Temperatures dropped significantly to what humans could tolerate. "The mechanism looks Jemmin, as far as what I've seen close up of Jemmin engineering."

The drone registered movement and angled a camera toward it. A creature, squarish body with short hands and legs and a bump where a neck and head could have been, approached—a Jemmin.

It was standing in a floating vehicle and seemed curious about the drone. It adjusted its heading.

"Kill it," Jenkins ordered. "Kill that Jemmin before he can sound the alarm."

"This isn't an armed drone. It's an inspection drone."

"Fly it into him and blow it up! Hurry."

The drone's nose dipped, and it raced forward on a collision course with the unsuspecting Jemmin. It tried to turn its vehicle, but the Jemmin was too slow. The drone impacted the body and bounced off. The hover vehicle slowed. The drone rebounded and charged in a second time. The view turned to white noise as the drone self-destructed.

"That could have gone better," Koch muttered.

"I guess you're climbing down that shaft," Jenkins suggested.

"Fine. We'll figure it out." Koch signed off.

"What do you think, Hammer?" the colonel asked. He missed having Xi to bounce ideas off. He wondered what her take on it would be.

"I think *Powerslave* dominates the small and pathetic Jemmin. Rawrr!"

Jenkins leaned to the side so he could look through the hatch at Hammer. "Are you okay down there?"

"Sorry, sir. It's not often we get to do the *kaiju* thing through a city without fighting for our lives. This is the mech life I dreamed about!"

Jenkins checked the board before looking out his viewport. Since there was no resistance, 1st Company was making great time on its way through the city. They had seen no signs of life.

"You're impressing a dead city, Hammer. Sorry to burst your bubble."

"You can't burst my bubble. Look at me loom over the small and insignificant! Hahaha." Jenkins didn't try to see Hammer's face to assess if his Jock was joking or maniacal. He decided it didn't matter as long as he was ready to fight if and when required. Jenkins had adopted minimal standards regarding behavior the second he took charge of the Metal Legion.

They were a bunch of misfits, but they weren't suicidal. They were fighters, like Xi. Once they entered battle, they didn't run. They took their lumps while giving the enemy all they had. At the end of the day, some would be lost, but not because they cowered in fear. They died like Metalheads—in their mechs, firing until they couldn't fire anymore. They wanted to live as much as they wanted to win.

Jenkins checked the positions of the other mechs. They continued forward in the half-moon formation while *Powerslave* wove back and forth, closing on the right flank before meandering back toward the left. The view remained the same. Empty streets. Empty buildings. Nothing growing. No wildlife. It was like something out of an incomplete video game.

As the buildings grew in height, *Powerslave* lost its dominance. "Stay center mass, Hammer," Jenkins directed in his command voice. The Ettin-class walker assumed a regular stride down a wide street, equidistant between the two flanks. The lead mech, *War Pig*, rolled forward a kilometer ahead on the same street. "Stop here and give me a look inside those windows."

Powerslave came to a smooth halt and leaned close to a bank of floor-to-ceiling windows in a building that rose two more stories above the viewport.

Jenkins leaned close and adjusted the setting to filter out the reflection. The interior of the room came into sharp focus. It looked like a typical human conference room. There was a table with chairs neatly arrayed around it. A buffet stood by the wall, empty of everything except a square, nondescript vase. "That is creepy as fuck," Jenkins muttered. "It's like they copied it from the 1950s back on Earth."

"Then there would have been ashtrays," Hammer offered, having come down from his *kaiju* high. "Or pictures on the wall or something."

"Parallels. Don't tell me humans are descended from Jemmin."

"Is bad taste genetic?" Hammer shrugged. "Or was that more social engineering courtesy from our overlords when we never knew we were being manipulated?"

"That's more like it. Lots of changes in the twentieth century."

Jenkins nodded. "By leaps and bounds, almost as if by magic. Take us into the city, Hammer. I know exactly what we'll find, and after that, we will need to locate the real prize."

26

REVELATION

H.L. Mencken

"Fire ten LRMs," Podsy ordered. The micro-salvo launched and raced across the void, already maneuvering and corkscrewing to defeat the battleship's defensive fire.

"Why hasn't he launched yet?" Tactical asked.

"Because when he hits us, it's going to be with everything he has. Like a cat, he's playing with his food before he eats it. Let's see if we can give him a sour stomach. Ahead slow." Captain Podsednik stood next to his acceleration couch, ready to jump in at a moment's notice. Tactical was the only other member of the bridge crew not in their couch.

Tactical fired random patterns, three here and four there, staggering the launches but timing their arrival so they would make their final approaches at the same time. The battleship destroyed the first three missiles shortly after launch. The next ones were sniped. Having so few missiles allowed the Jemmin heavy to concentrate fire. The missiles never had a chance.

The bow doors started to open. Podsy and Tactical jumped into the couches. "Max acceleration! Launch everything we have at that opening." But the battleship had gotten close enough that it was picking off the missiles within a second of them leaving the launch tubes. Sixty missiles gone in two seconds. The only missiles remaining were antimissile types, too small a warhead to do any damage to the battleship. "Railguns."

"Railguns! Eat this," Tactical shouted from his couch as the gees started to increase. The battleship launched a full salvo. The last of the missiles jumped into the void, seeking the Jemmin inbound. Coil guns and chain guns cycled. The railgun continued to send a stream of hypervelocity projectiles into the heavy battleship's armor.

In front of the Jemmin battlewagon, the freighter's engine flared to life, it maneuvered into the maw, too close for defensive fire to hit. The engines redlined, went critical, and exploded, sending a full load of stem bolts as high-speed projectiles right down the throat of the gravity cannon.

"Hard to starboard, and keep up the defensive fire." The maneuver exposed *Mencken's* flank to the inbound, and too many missiles made it through the meager shield the assault carrier was able to deploy. Strike after strike from the smaller missiles impacted, as if the battleship was indeed toying with the humans.

"Outer hull is holding," the engineering station reported in her small voice.

"Any breaches?" Podsy asked. He searched his display for the information, but damage reports were scant.

"No breaches, but the railguns are gone, and half our slug-throwers."

"He's going to neuter us and then make us watch as they do whatever they want with the '*Keeper*,'" Tactical posited.

Podsy did not think he was wrong. The battleship jerked and bucked as if it were being yanked about by a god's hand. A blinding light erupted from the gravity cannon. Podsy winced before closing his eyes and trying to take his imminent death with a modicum of courage. Tactical shouted expletives. Shrapnel peppered *Mencken*'s hull. Podsy opened his eyes to find the battleship listed on the tactical screen as dead.

"Woohoo!" Podsy cheered through gritted teeth. "Back us to three gees and bring us around. Put us back on station in front of the '*Keeper*."

When the ship slowed enough for him to stand, Podsy did just that, then flexed and stretched. "What happened?" He turned to Commander Wythe.

"*John Wayne* took out the bad guy…with stem bolts."

"She'll live in infamy." Podsy looked for more information. He'd lost track of the fight between the cruisers and the rest of the task force. "Launch the Vipers. Commander Knighton, Yellowhammer, now's the time for your magic. Looks like our fleet is taking a beating."

"On the way," the commander replied.

Two Gatecrashers continued toward the '*Keeper*. The battle on the flanks was reduced to individual dogfights. Jemmin beams slashed across the void as TAC ships sought refuge until they could counterattack. Nine Jemmin cruisers versus eleven human ships. It would have been a fair fight if the task force vessels had a full load of weapons. They were running on empty in all ways, maneuvering to make sure each shot had the potential of being a kill shot.

Even at the risk of their own lives.

A call came over the P2P. "Captain Podsednik, Lieutenant Styles."

"Styles? Where the fuck are you?" Podsy blurted.

"I've been working on something. Look for it passing you to starboard."

One of the larger freighters appeared from behind the *'Keeper* and belched a mass of cargo into space. A ship-sized section came to life. The engine fired, and the missile they'd deemed "world-killer" accelerated across the void.

"You are my new favorite human being, Styles." Podsy turned back to the tactical screen. "Head in around the battleship, using the hulk as cover to fire once we clear the other side to distract Jemmin from their own missile. Maybe give it a better chance of striking home."

Mencken accelerated. Podsy fell into his couch.

Suddenly, death didn't seem imminent. The Vipers raced across space, using the ship, the only terrain nearby, as tactical cover.

Select your battlefield and fight the fight that is worth winning. Podsy clenched his jaw and reviewed ammunition stores. He had to come up with a plan that would help them win, and he had to do it soon.

Elvira

"Drop down a level, Fatso. There's no one around, just robots doing automated tasks. Looks busy, but no adult supervision, if you know what I mean. You need to be closer in case we have to haul ass because we aren't going out the way we came in."

Fat Man started rolling. "I don't see an exit sign, Major. Am I missing something?"

"Hold where you are. We're going to take a closer look at the tank farm. Make sure no one sneaks up on us."

Xi moved *Elvira* forward through a meandering space of manufacturing and processing equipment. Raw materials were brought in through a tunnel at the far end and separated and processed until they ended at a distribution system between the equipment and the tanks. What Xi had thought was a city was a massive production facility. That was what made Xi's hair stand on end.

Maybe she'd watched too many movies, but the facility was giving her the creeps.

When she could go no farther, she called to Penny, "Get your suit on. We're going outside."

"I will go," Bob offered. She had forgotten he was there since he'd remained silent, possibly at her request.

Godzilla loomed over the area. Meathead moved his mech through the facility until he found a machine that was bigger than it. He put his back against it and watched for movement. He set his external audio pickup to sensitive, but there was too much ambient sound. A high-pressure water pump whined throughout the space, along with the incessant noise of machinery. No clicks or bangs, but the constant movement of materials through a system. Bots whirled everywhere, oblivious to the invasion as they checked fittings, made repairs, and kept the system running.

Twilight's Fall stayed close to *Elvira,* while *Holy Diver* went the other way, deeper into the facility.

"Stay frosty. We're going outside," she told her company.

She checked Lu to make sure he was breathing before squeezing into the airlock behind Penny. They checked each other's gear quickly while the system cycled. The outside hatch popped, and they stepped out. Having already stood face-to-face with Jemmin, Xi knew the tanks and systems were made by and for them. Controls were in places easily accessible if your arms were no longer than a wrist with a hand. Head height was eye-level for Xi, but she was one of the shortest humans in the TAC.

Bob followed quietly, spending more time looking at things that held no meaning for the major.

They went to a second tank, and then a third. Xi started to run, a scowl darkening her face. At the fifth row of a near-infinite number of tanks, she stopped. "It's Boba-fucking-Fett!" she shouted.

Penny looked at her sideways while trying to keep her eyes on the tank. "You know this guy?"

She shook her head angrily. "Clones. The Jemmin are clones. Explains everything. All we need to do is find the ones running this place, and they'll take us to the ones giving the orders. Those are the Jemmin we want to talk to."

"The major is correct," Bob remarked.

She stormed back toward *Elvira*.

"Boss? What are we going to do?"

"We're going to send a message to Jemmin." Xi stomped her feet as she walked.

Penny jogged to keep up. "But boss, we don't know the way out!" The outer hatch cycled.

Xi turned to Penny. "We can't let this stand. Maybe we'll set them back a hundred years or forever. I'm willing to risk it because this is an abomination. It tells me that Jemmin are looking at the sunset of their existence. They are still plenty lethal, but what if our real target is the Vorr? Look at us! Eighteen mechs to invade an empire. No. We're going to kill the next ten generations of Jemmin because they aren't generations at all. They're a dying race on life support."

She fixed Bob with a steely glare.

"Did you know about this?"

"It was one of many options to explain Jemmin, but no. This is a crime against nature consistent with Jemmin ego. I will conduct calculations, but I expect not to be proven wrong."

"Care to share?"

"After."

Xi opened the inner hatch, removing the environmental suit within a couple of seconds and strapping it on the rack.

"And we're going to do this right." She accessed her playlist and activated the external speakers. She pressed the button, and Megadeth started to jam *Symphony of Destruction*. She keyed her company channel. "Listen up, Metalheads. We're going to lay waste to these tanks. They need to be destroyed. Save your missiles and let your guns sing along with the song of the day. Fatso, watch the back door and let us know when the parents arrive."

"HE up!" Penny reported, starting to get into the spirit of the inevitable.

"On my mark," Xi told the company. "Fire."

The fifteen-kilogram cannons roared, sending the heavy projectiles deep into the tank farm. They hit and exploded, blasting two craters, with a ripple of destruction spreading outward. Five mechs fired their chain guns. The impacts vaporized liquids and shattered tank after tank. Gory contents slid to the ground, rushing with the water of a thousand tanks.

Fat Man fired its plasma cannon, digging a trench where a line of tanks used to be. Vapor and mist filled the cavern from the violence of the energy attack. The mech started spooling up for a second shot.

Xi cycled her coil guns and chain guns before dropping a couple more high-explosive rounds from *Elvira's* mains. The sound of gunfire and explosions filled the huge chamber.

"Fatso, what's the count?"

"Stand by," Fatso replied. The tracked mech belched a stream of plasma that wiped out a grid square. "There we go. Destruction is complete."

"I don't think this machinery is serving any purpose either," Xi announced as *Symphony* ended. A three-and-a-half-minute cacophony to total annihilation. She smiled to herself. "Move to the tunnel designated Escape Alpha."

She transmitted the rally point to her company and stepped out. She clicked a P2P channel to Sungod. "Feeling a little less claustrophobic?"

"Blowing shit up takes one's mind off such things. Yes, but I see we're heading into another tunnel. I'm not feeling so good about that."

"You have to be the only Metalhead in the universe who is comfortable in a box, but uncomfortable when that box is in a tight package. How in the hell do you ever survive a drop?" Xi snap-fired into the machinery as they passed, shooting the mechanisms that looked hardest to replace. The others did the same. Some would call it vandalism. Xi called it tactical targeting.

"With my eyes closed, ma'am." Sungod blew a breath out and into his audio pickup. "How many more drops are we going to make?"

Xi mused before answering. There weren't plans for any more. If this was J-Ville Central, they'd finish the war right here. "Maybe none, maybe a hundred. You ever contemplate a move into a different line of work?" Xi was first to reach the designated tunnel. It looked like a superhighway, with walls that seemed to flow with a rippling breeze that disappeared into the distance.

"Why would I want to do something else? Nothing like driving a mech, but why do we have to keep going underground?"

"Because that's where the bad guys hide. The exterminators gotta root 'em out at the source. Get a hold of this corridor. It's like walking in a park on a warm afternoon."

Xi took *Elvira* in. She activated her scanners, trading stealth for information. Plus, if Jemmin hadn't heard them blowing up their cloning facility, a few active scans wouldn't alert them either.

"Why are there no defenses down here?" Sungod pressed. "Jemmin are pretty smart and foresee everything. How could they not contemplate an enemy finding their homeworld?"

"They have great fleets, but we had something they didn't know about—the *GateKeeper*. We blocked the fleet that was coming to NA2. We leapfrogged them and trapped them in the Illumination League Nexus, then we isolated the Ax Nexus. And then we made it here. The fleet defending their home-world was the scraps of what remained, and it was more than equal to the fleet we brought. I wonder how they're doing up there?"

Elvira never minded a healthy stroll in the park, but this was taking too long. The thoroughfare seemed to go on forever.

"All mechs, flank speed. I feel like this is the *Road to Nowhere*." She started playing Ozzy's music.

"Or the *Highway to Hell*. Plasma cannon charged," Fatso reported.

Xi's instruments started to spike. "Energy source ahead that's off the charts." The walls started to ripple in the colors of a thundercloud. Lightning arced across the tunnel. "I think they know we're here."

Powerslave

"Look for a tunnel entrance, anything that leads under-ground," Colonel Jenkins ordered. "*Devastator*, what are you doing? Stop climbing that building. It's like watching a bunch of baby pandas!"

"Just trying to get a better look," *Devastator* replied easily. Without a credible threat, the mechs had gone off-script and were freelancing their movements. They scoured the area, but even active scans proved fruitless. The Metalheads were denied their prize.

"Looks like we're joining *Kochtopussy* in doing it the hard way. Fast as you can, rally at the heat vent."

The mechs took off in an uncontrolled sprint. *War Pig* was the slowest and started falling behind. It was also the mech that probably couldn't make the climb, even with a cable assist.

"*War Pig,* you stay topside and be our comm relay."

"I thought you'd never ask. The answer is yes!"

"*War Pig,* check your O2 supply. I believe it's been polluted with nitrous oxide," Jenkins countered. "Bounding overwatch. First up, *Satan* and *Kanban,* then *Devastator* and *Crazy Train.* *Powerslave* into the rocking chair, and *War Pig* bringing up the rear. Two by two. Execute."

Jenkins clicked over to a point to point channel with Captain Koch. "What are you seeing down there?"

"Not there yet. This sucks ginormous moose balls, since you asked," Koch replied.

The fight to save humanity had relaxed the Metal Legion's professional barriers. Still, they had it where it counted. In a fight, there were no better.

"ETA?"

"One minute for *Kochtopussy* touchdown. Then, *Web Spinner, Vainglorious Vulture, Hell's Hammer, Mr. Crowley,* and *Tolling Bell,* carrying the red lantern. Should have all in place in five."

"1st Company will be right behind you. Set up a defensive perimeter and wait for us."

"Roger. We'll set up a few surprises, just in case Jemmin grow a backbone." Koch waited for a moment. "Do you get it? A backbone!"

The captain started laughing.

"If you see any Jemmin, you know what to do. Keep that

attitude, Skipper. The hairy stuff is coming. I feel it in my bones."

"'Hairy Bones.' That's better than Leeroy Jenkins. I think you should change your name. Touchdown. Gotta go, Hairy. Too much to do, and not enough brain to do it all and chitchat. Koch out."

The screen was clear. It looked like smooth sailing.

27

DESCENT INTO MADNESS

H.L. Mencken

The assault carrier rounded the battleship and turned toward the Gatecrasher. "What are we going to fire at him?" Tactical asked.

The railguns were offline. Half the point defense systems had been scrubbed from the hull. And the ship's entire missile inventory could be counted using just one person's fingers and toes.

"The power of our personalities?" Podsy said. A dozen Vipers rolled in behind the Mencken, staying in the big ship's shadow while it maneuvered toward the Gatecrasher. The Jemmin world-killer that Styles had resurrected disappeared into the sensor shadow on the opposite side of the battleship. It reappeared a few moments later, homing unerringly.

The Gatecrasher never fired. The ship-sized missile continued its approach, not deviating, not leaving any doubt about where it was headed. But a Jemmin ship was incapable of firing on a Jemmin weapon.

Lieutenant Styles. The Legion's programming genius had done it again.

The world-killer rammed into the Gatecrasher's bow, the outer layer peeling away after it had done its duty. The inner missile penetrated through bulkhead after bulkhead until it reached the ship's core, where the fifty-megaton warhead exploded within the enclosed space. The massive ship cracked along its seams, splitting into a hundred different sections that accelerated outward with the expanding fireball.

The Jemmin cruisers had decimated the TAC fleet and paid the ultimate price. The last destroyer sent its reactor into over-load as it crashed into the last enemy cruiser. A Pyrrhic victory, but the battlefield was clear.

Knighton brought her Vipers back to the *Mencken* after wreaking what havoc they could behind enemy lines. Seven Vipers rolled away from the littered space and a newly expanding cloud of debris. She waited patiently until the right target presented itself. When the sky cleared, the second Gate-crasher was slowing. In the distance, the tactical screen showed the remnants of Task Force Sword sweeping wide to avoid coming into the Gatecrasher's cone of fire.

General Pushkin activated a P2P channel with Podsy. "Get comm with Jemmin."

"I'm sorry, what?" Shock froze Podsy in place.

"Follow my orders, Captain," the general reiterated in a cold voice.

"Comm. Get me the Jemmin vessel."

"By saying what?" Comm wondered.

"Request a meeting to discuss terms. If humanity and Jemmin wish to cede J-Ville home to the Zeen, then we can keep fighting since none of us are walking away from this next fight. I think Jemmin hate the Zeen more than they want to throw down with us," Podsy suggested, guessing at the general's intent. "Once you have them, patch them through to General Pushkin."

Much to Comm's surprise, Jemmin answered on the first call.

"Shimmering North Star. Why are you calling Jemmin?" came the terse reply.

Comm patched it through but kept the audio playing.

"General Pushkin here. You have no future in this star system. May the stars guide you to a better place."

Flowery language of Jemmin. Podsy wondered where he had learned the diplo-speak.

"You surrender now. Leave the *GateKeeper*. All others will be allowed to leave."

"I'm sorry," General Pushkin said softly, sounding as sincere as he could. "That's not going to work for us, so we'll have to destroy you and with you, destroy any hope Jemmin has of surviving this day. The Zeen will stand on the Jemmin homeworld. That will be the legacy of Shimmering North Star."

"Your presumptions are incorrect and do you dishonor."

"I had to try," Pushkin conceded. "Prepare to be boarded."

Podsy asked his bridge crew, "Boarded by whom? We don't have anyone left."

"Jemmin will consider this." The link went dead.

"Send a message to TF Sword. Do not attack the Gatecrasher."

"Sent," Comm confirmed.

Mencken slowed but didn't come to a complete stop in case the ship needed to reengage quickly.

"Recover the Vipers. Rearm and prepare for relaunch," Podsy ordered. Knighton accelerated, bringing the other six ships with her as they made a high-speed return to the hangar deck.

"There's nothing left to reload, Captain," Tactical remarked. Podsy turned to him and nodded.

"*Mencken* looks like she's had better days," Knighton reported.

"She has, just like all of us, but something tells me the best is yet to come," Podsy replied.

"I look forward to seeing that."

"I look forward to seeing you too," Podsy added and signed off. Tactical raised an eyebrow. Podsy caught the look. "Can you remember the day we weren't at war, Pete?"

"Before the Arh'kel attack on New Australia?" the commander asked. "Not really. You were there, weren't you." It wasn't a question.

"I hated the Arh'kel with every fiber of my being." Podsy strolled around the bridge, helping his people from their couches, but no one spoke because the captain wasn't finished. "And then I learned to hate Jemmin. And Solarians. And those Fleet bastards, too." Podsy chuckled but didn't make eye contact with anyone. Half the bridge crew had come over from Fleet. "But that kind of anger doesn't keep you warm inside. It burns you up. I just want to do my job and fight those who need to be fought just until they're done fighting.

"That Jemmin out there has had enough, too. The fact that he talked to us suggests our Metalheads on the surface are making progress. If he was under the thumb of centralized control, he wouldn't have talked to us. We're winning, Pete. And I want this over with, and yeah, you guessed it—I want to sail into the sunset with a Viper pilot. I'm not happy about that either, believe you me."

The bridge crew started clapping. "I knew it!" the young engineer exclaimed. Podsy gave her an incredulous look.

"How? Even *I* didn't know it."

"Women know," she declared and turned back to her workstation.

Podsy clumped to the captain's chair. His cyborg legs could

go for as long as he needed, but he was starting to get tired, and his hips were sore. One too many trips into the couch. He pulled a stim from his pocket and injected it before he could change his mind.

He tapped his console. "Chief Rimmer, find me some more bullets to throw at the enemy. I don't care if you have to strap Acme rockets to the backs of coyotes. Give me something."

"Naught plus naught equals naught, Captain. But we aren't at zero yet. How much time do I have?"

"Ten minutes. Ten days? Sooner rather than later. Jemmin is considering our request that he surrender the Gatecrasher to us. I'm thinking he'll tell us no, but at least we have a few moments to get our feet under us. Work your magic, Chief, and I'll stop giving you shit."

"No, you won't. Rimmer out."

"He'll do it," Tactical suggested before giving Podsy a thumbs-up.

Comm turned to the captain. "Admiral Corbyn requests a meeting with you, the general, and Commodore Sosunova.

"I'll be in the Task Force operations room."

Elvira

The lightning grew more intense, but it wasn't a high-voltage display. It made Xi's skin crawl as if ants were all over her body, but it didn't short out any systems. She continued driving *Elvira* forward, despite the difficulty in seeing the way ahead. Sensors were blinded by the electro-magnetic storm outside the mech.

Xi had had enough. She cycled through her systems until she found the grappling cable and winch. She fired one end into the floor and then sent the other end into the wall. The lightning arced along the cable and into the ground. The air in front of *Elvira* cleared as more and more lightning found its way along the cable.

The other mechs followed suit until the lighting storm was finished. Xi retracted the grapple hooks on both ends of the cable and reeled it in. With a deep breath, she nudged *Elvira* into an easy canter before an all-out gallop. The tunnel wasn't getting any shorter. There hadn't been any side tunnels, only the main tunnel that seemed to stretch to infinity. According to the mech's instruments, they'd already gone forty kilometers.

"This is some serious bullshit," Bob blurted.

"Holy crap. Bob. You're learning to talk like me."

"I can only be humble before the master." Bob bowed his insectoid head. "My estimate is that there are twelve Jemmin remaining. Those you found on the planet deemed J-Ville One were clones, but ones with anomalies in their development."

"Anomalies?"

"There are always anomalies. Organic replication is a complex process, but it appears that Jemmin have somewhat perfected it." Bob spoke once again with unusual eloquence. He never ceased to amaze her.

"But they couldn't build a gravity cannon or FTL. I'm not a fan of Jemmin. Those were monsters in that chamber. A race that would do such a thing are monsters."

"Race. Yes. There are twelve of them."

"You said that, but it doesn't make any sense. They've conquered most of the known galaxy, manipulated humanity, and developed the Arh'kel as a biological weapon. Maybe the Finjou and the Berk, too. You're telling me that only twelve Jemmin accomplished all that?"

"A single Jemmin clone can actively manage the defense of an entire planet from its Poltergeist. Each Jemmin can manage a thousand direct connections, and those thousand can manage a thousand, and so on. I extrapolated my estimate based on

Jemmin reach throughout the galaxy. I don't believe a non-clone Jemmin has been off this planet in fifteen thousand years, but that's just a guess."

"Just a guess? Bob!" Xi shook her head and continued her sprint down the tunnel. "Do you know where these twelve are?"

"Follow the power," Bob advised.

A clunk signaled an equipment failure. The front right leg seized mid-stride, threatening to topple the Scorpion-class mech. Xi raised the other legs to skid on her belly. "Get out there and fix that attenuator!" Xi shouted at Penny.

"Tools are already in my hand," she stated as she bounded through the rig, opening a panel and disappearing into the leg. Xi raised the rig on five legs and ambulated forward at half-speed. The short delay gave *Fat Man* a chance to catch up. Xi blasted the sensors on full.

"Bob, what else did your analysis tell you?" Xi looked for power sources. The sensors only returned signals from directly ahead. Xi's neural link told her the front leg was back online. She raised it to keep from tripping herself before dropping it into sync with the other five legs, and soon she had the rig back over one hundred kph.

"Zeen fear that *Zeen Home Three* might be the last remaining hive."

"That's another revelation you don't just drop on someone, Bob."

"But you asked." Bob sat still while Penny climbed out of the hatch, securing it behind her. She hurried back to her position to do the thousand tasks usually split between two people. Lu remained out cold. Penny checked on him as she passed.

"Are you sure they are on this planet?"

"Most precious Jemmin resource is the original genetic material. They are here. I am positive."

"Now, that's something I can embrace. I wasn't having a

good feeling about it. Hang on." Xi opened the company-wide channel. "Heads up. Sensors show a chamber ahead, looks to be similar in size to the one we just left. Let's see what we can fuck up. Lock and load, people."

She didn't need to issue the last order because she knew they were ready to fire. *Fat Man's* capacitors were charged and ready to send a full load of plasma downrange. She liked to say it, and thought it fired up the troops. She liked to hear it when Jenkins made the call. Xi briefly wondered how he was doing. She clicked over to the Legion-wide channel. "Major Bao here. Anyone out there? I have some information that will knock your socks off."

She repeated her call twice before abandoning the effort. She would tell them when she got back topside. She started daydreaming about twelve Jemmin in near-comas getting harvested for their genetic material, being kept alive by clones and bots.

The beam weapon lit up the tunnel like a strobe and cleanly separated the leg that Penny had just repaired. *Elvira* spun in a full circle before coming to rest at a forty-five-degree angle against the wall. From behind her, Foetype's cover of *Who Let the Dogs Out* played at max volume. A plasma beam blinded her sensors as it passed far too close for Xi's comfort.

28

A FINAL SOLUTION

GateKeeper

Admiral Corbyn shook General Moon's hand. "The courage of our convictions, good allies, and a little luck."

"The power of good people. No one will ever know the quality of the souls who died today," the general said sadly. "Their tales end here, but not the story of humanity. Their duty and loyalty bought that for those who still ply the void. A Gatecrasher is out there, contemplating what to do. We wait, nursing our wounds while looking at empty missile racks. Everything we have isn't enough to put a dent in that thing, but he doesn't seem to know that.

"*Zeen Home Three* has joined us, along with the entirety of the freighter fleet. We die so they can live. That is what the military has been doing since time immemorial. It's what we signed up for. Pain and hardship. Trials and tribulations. We have this last fight, and the gods willing, Shimmering North Star will pack it in. If that happens, we'll move the fleet to J-Ville Home and support the ground operation there. If the Gatecrasher decides to fight, we'll converge all assets on the bow of that thing and deliver the final protective fire. We'll shoot everything we have, and then we'll ram it with what we have left. I, for one, don't want to be taken captive by Jemmin.

"The Crimson Knights will protect the *'Keeper*. Repel boarders, should it come to that. Report your resources, and let's take a look at what we have."

"*Mencken* reports twenty mid-range missiles with conventional yields in the ten kiloton range and seven Vipers. Railguns and point defense systems have been destroyed."

"*Henry VIII* reports two cruisers and twelve destroyers that are bingo on missiles. Railguns can operate at full capacity. Chain, coil, and defensive systems are intact." Commodore Sosunova reported for the Zeen as well. "*Zeen Home Three* launched their remaining ship-killers. They have fewer than one hundred Interceptors intact."

"*GateKeeper* weapons are unknown," the admiral added. "Looks like the space fighters are our greatest asset. Twenty total missiles. And railguns. We can work with that."

The admiral looked defeated, but General Moon was all smiles.

"Fear is the mind-killer, ladies and gentlemen. We have the advantage. Never before has Jemmin stopped an attack after a call for surrender. Everything is unprecedented from this point forward. Hell, everything from the second we appeared in J-Ville Central has been unprecedented. No matter what happens from here, I'm proud of you all. The Metal Legion. The Tactical Armor Corps. The Terran and Solar Fleets. Our motivational speeches suck! But you know what we mean. We're all tired, but once more, when the call comes, we know you'll be there, standing tall. The metal in the Metal Legion. For all humanity, we fight."

Admiral Corbyn nodded and cut the link.

Podsy looked at General Pushkin. "I seemed to have missed the part where they told us what the plan was."

The general started to laugh. "I think our plan is to damage his fists with our faces. It may not be the best plan, but it's all we have."

"We'll do our best, General." Podsy excused himself and headed to the drop deck. When he arrived, he found Chief Rimmer surrounded by deck apes, a job Podsy had been relegated to once upon a long time ago. The Chief was elbow-deep in the guts of an old piece of hangar equipment. "Impress me, Chief."

"Your Loftiness," the chief replied.

Podsy wanted to pound the man. He settled for something less physical. "Jam it in your ass, Chief."

The chief pulled his arms out and faced the captain. "What you are looking at is a modified spin-shredder." He swept one arm dramatically from front to rear.

"Your lips were moving, but nothing intelligible came out. You're going to have to explain a little better for the dumbasses from the bridge."

The deckhands snickered and moved aside.

"I've modified the size to fit in a launch tube. This thing is useful danger-close only because it's not very aerodynamic. Once launched, it'll start spinning. That kicks off these baby rockets, which spins it even faster. That kicks these arms out, and it turns into a massive drill bit. Once inside, the remaining fuel ignites." The chief looked far too proud of himself.

"This thing will bounce off that armor!" Podsy stated.

"Depleted uranium tips. We have all that coil gun ammo we can't use because the last attack scraped our coil guns."

"Those rockets come from spare drop-cans?"

"From the resupply cans." The chief looked less confident.

"If we don't win this fight, those cans will go to waste. Well done, Chief. Now, make a few more of the Rimmer Spinners. Keep making them until you run out of parts, and then make one more. You know what they say: 'Quantity has a quality all its own.'"

Podsy offered his hand, and the two shook. Never friends, sometimes enemies, but always united in a single goal: to win.

The captain strode briskly through the corridors of his ship. It had taken a pounding, but it was still operational. He would love to get a full refit because he'd loved the look of it when it still smelled of new paint from the last refit. Oh, well. Warships went to war, and war was a hard place.

In his cabin, Podsy picked up Jem. "You deserve to be on the bridge."

"I appreciate your sentiment, and I am honored to join you."

Podsy carried Jem like a scepter as he walked the short distance from the captain's quarters to the bridge. The door slid aside as he approached, and he stepped through without hesitation. The crew was hard at work. Pete Wythe stopped what he was doing to make the announcement. "Captain on the bridge."

Podsy nodded at him. "As you were," he said out of habit. They were doing what needed to be done to take the ship into a fight. No cheers and no tears. Professionals doing their jobs. He walked from position to position, calling each by their first name, letting them know he appreciated what they did. Then he returned to the captain's chair, with Jem held prominently in one hand.

"A message from the Zeen," Comm called.

They all waited. It wasn't common for the Zeen to communicate with the humans, which meant they had not contacted the humans from *Zeen Home Three* since Major Bao joined them.

"Stand by." The channel closed.

"You have got to be shitting me," Podsy intoned. "I guess that's supposed to mean something?"

Comm shrugged and shook his head.

"Get me Admiral Corbyn," Podsy asked. The main screen lit up as the visual link connected. The admiral answered quickly.

The Zeen had transmitted the message to him, too.

"Do you have any insight into what that means?" Corbyn asked before Captain Podsednik could ask the same question.

Podsy shook his head and chuckled. "I was hoping you'd be able to answer that. The Zeen on the *'Keeper* can't explain?"

"Tight-lipped as always. They seem to be learning more secrets of the *'Keeper* with each passing hour, which makes me suspect the two events are connected." Admiral Corbyn pursed his lips and looked off-screen before turning back. "I think this ship does a lot more than build and install gates. A lot more. We've hijacked your man Styles. He's over here right now."

"Roger on Styles. We need to give him a commendation for his work with the world-killer. It bought us time and possibly new life."

General Moon wheeled himself into the picture. "Those are the things we'll take care of when this is over, Captain. I have a folder filled with notes. The actions of Commodore Meng and the *Sima Yi*. The freighter *John Wayne* and her captain, Serenity Monk. So many selfless acts of valor. We'll memorialize them all when the time is right."

"Roger," Podsy agreed. "Keep your eye on Styles, or he'll be streaming dead-body porn to every screen on your ship. Podsednik out."

The admiral gave a thumbs-up before his image faded.

"What do we do now?" Tactical asked.

Podsy sat down heavily, realizing he was still carrying Jem like a scepter. He placed the Jem'un in the space next to him. "We wait."

. . .

Powerslave

The climb down the shaft was nowhere near as bad as Jenkins had thought it would be. Thanks to a cable pulley and the beast called *War Pig* anchoring the effort, the mechs dropped without issue into the four-way intersection wrapped around the Jemmin power production equipment.

Koch had found the Jemmin who'd spotted the drone. The explosion had delivered its death blow, which alleviated some concerns while raising others. Did Jemmin know where the Metalheads were?

"I thought I heard a call from Major Bao, but when I tried to reply, there was nothing but static."

"You can bet she's down here somewhere, rooting around inside their guts. She has an innate talent for wreaking havoc when she's underground," Jenkins replied, feeling an over-whelming sense of relief. He hadn't realized until the report just how much he missed having his XO within comm's reach. "Any intel?"

"Nothing besides machinery sounds in all four directions," Koch replied over the P2P.

"Split your company down Tunnels C and D. I'll take A and B." Jenkins transmitted the map overlay. He chose Tunnel A for himself because that led in the direction of the array and where Xi had gone underground.

Koch issued his orders. "*Mr. Crowley*, you take *Hell's Hammer* and *Tolling Bell* with you. *Spinner* and *Vulture*, come with me. Let's see where these tunnels lead. Emplace comm repeaters as necessary to boost signals back through this inter-section, which is designated Rally Point Blake's Seven."

The map on Jenkins' screen updated as 2nd Company's assets deployed.

"*Devastator, Crazy Train,* and *Kanban*. Take Bravo Tunnel. *Satan* and his *Powerslave* will be exploring Alpha. Maintain comm. Report often. I think you'll find that Jemmin don't live on the surface of this planet, they live down here. We're not here to take prisoners. We're here to find the ones issuing the orders throughout the entirety of Jemmin-controlled space. That is your primary objective. And if you run across 3rd Company, welcome them back into the fold."

Powerslave was a huge walker, but Alpha Tunnel was large enough to accommodate him as he strolled forward. Hammer crouched the rig so he could run without bouncing off the ceiling. The tunnel was big, but running an Ettin required the great outdoors.

Hammer accelerated to a meager thirty kilometers-per-hour as the mech collected data with both passive and active sensors. It was ten kilometers before a side tunnel appeared. It was even bigger than the one they were in.

"Deploy a signal booster," Jenkins ordered. Hammer shot one into the ceiling, avoiding the string of cables that lined both walls. "Send a drone ahead, and let's see what's up there."

Jenkins would have preferred to send multiple drones and keep them in front of him at all times, but they were one of his limited assets. With only two left, he didn't want to peak before they were critical. He hoped he would know when that time came. He suspected it would be soon.

He keyed a P2P link. "Major Bao? Are you out there?"

He was on his second attempt when the link came to life. "Leeroy! Love to chat, but we're in a firefight. Read this while we get Jemmin sorted." Xi killed the link before Jenkins could reply. A data packet had come through to the colonel's terminal.

Jenkins sent a series of ranging pulses, hoping that Xi received them so the intervening tunnels could be mapped before he opened the packet.

"Well, now. That's different," he mumbled as he kept reading.

. . .

Elvira

Fatso's plasma attack destroyed an emplacement embedded in the tunnel wall. For good measure, the five mechs poured fire indiscriminately down the corridor.

"Cease fire," Xi called. She maneuvered off the wall and regained her balance, then started forward again much more slowly.

The ranging signal came through, and she told her system to deal with it. She'd look at the map later. For now, she wanted to review the defensive system to see if they were getting close. If Jemmin didn't protect the clone tanks, what was important enough to rate the beam weapon?

She could only come up with one answer. They were getting close to the last living Jemmin.

"Heads up," she started. "I'm sure that's not the last we'll see of those. Who has drones? We need one to scout ahead. We can't be feeling out the route ahead. This isn't bad foreplay."

"I thought that was good foreplay," Sungod offered. "Maybe I've been doing it wrong. Damn, Major! You're making me rethink my life choices."

"It's a gift. Thanks for that, Fatso." A drone appeared on her board and raced ahead. She tapped the feed into her terminal and watched the stream while moving forward at a sluggish twenty-five kph. The other mechs fell in behind her.

"Maybe I can take point for a while?" Sungod offered on behalf of his mech, *Twilight's Fall*.

Xi wanted to lead the charge, but her mech was missing a leg. "Do it, but leave me a clear line of fire."

"Consider it done, Major," Sungod confirmed. *Twilight's Fall* was a cruiser-grade roller with independent suspension and drives for each of its oversized wheels. The tunnel floor was a superhighway for a mech like the *Fall*. It raced ahead, traveling almost as quickly as the drone.

"Rein it back in, you big husky," Xi ordered. Sungod eased off the throttle and started to build distance between his mech and Fatso's drone. "Hold at the next intersection, standard self-protection mode."

Xi had to order self-protection mode to keep *Fall* from stepping into the intersection. She liked her people to be aggressive, except when they were in J-Ville Central and Jemmin had just deployed a capital-grade beam weapon. "Stay frosty. Expect that we'll start penetrating increasingly violent defensive layers. Don't hang your asses out in the wind."

"No ass. Aye, aye, ma'am," Sungod replied. "Hang on."

The drone cleared the corner and quickly rotated to deliver a three hundred sixty-degree view. A flash signaled the end of the drone and the feed.

"A Poltergeist," Xi announced. She ran the feed back and looked into the distance. "Make that two Poltergeists, and would you look at that? They appear to be waiting for us. Form up two by two. Shorties like me in front. Tall in the rear. Fatso center mass."

Xi steeled her nerves and headed forward, happy she'd held Sungod back. *Twilight's Fall* wouldn't have lasted more than two seconds on the receiving end of a Poltergeist ambush.

"What's the plan, Major?"

"We're going to fight 'em," Xi replied matter-of-factly. Before they reached the corner, the Poltergeist hovered into the intersection and turned.

H.L. Mencken

The comm channel opened.

"Jemmin Skywagon Seven is standing down," Shimmering North Star reported before closing the channel. The _Mencken's_ bridge crew breathed a collective sigh of relief.

Admiral Corbyn broadcast a message to the fleet. "Jemmin have stood down. Colonel Cao and his Crimson Knights will board the vessel to defang the beast, as it were. Good job, people. Mencken, get back to the planet and check on your Metalheads."

"On our way, Admiral," Podsy said. He pointed at Helm, who immediately kicked the big ship into gear, accelerating smoothly but not quickly enough to force the crew into their couches.

"ETA, one hour," Helm reported.

Captain Podsednik tapped his panel and activated a P2P link. "Commander Knighton, please meet me in Ready Room One for a debrief."

He walked out without making eye contact with his crew. He continued down the corridor, walking faster and faster as the hangar bay seemed farther and farther away. But he made it, palms sweaty. The Ready Room door opened, and the commander stepped out. Podsy took another two steps and stopped. He stared but didn't know what to say. She carried her helmet in one hand. She tossed her head to shake her hair out, but it remained matted and stuck to her head. Podsy carefully uncoiled the mass until some of it straightened. He made a face.

"That bad?"

"I don't think I made it any better."

"Are you going to do that for the other six pilots?" she asked.

Podsy's face sank. "Twelve Vipers leave and seven return. I'm sorry, Yellowhammer."

She shrugged. "They died well. We never know when the magic missile has our name on it, but when it does, let it be while we're clearing the magazines on target. Back to the issue at hand. Just me, then?"

Podsy tried to play it cool but failed. "Yeah. Just you. We're on our way to the planet to see how Colonel Jenkins and his people are doing. I hope they have good news. I'm ready to go home."

"Just me, then?" she pressed.

Podsy felt smaller and smaller. He turned to walk away. "Yeah. Only you."

"As long as you can commit to that, count me in. Come here, Captain."

Podsy sauntered back to her, his confidence building with each step. At the last minute, she thrust out her hand. He looked at it oddly before she pulled it back and stuck it out again. Finally, he took it to shake. She pulled him to her. He stumbled and fell. She caught him behind the neck and held him steady as she leaned in...

. . .

GateKeeper

Colonel Cao raced off, on his way to the bay, where a shuttle waited. It wasn't their normal dropship, but the Marine and his twenty Crimson Knights were supposed to be going in unopposed.

Unlike the Terran Marines, the Knights didn't operate in textbook military fashion, using a pyramidal command and control structure. There were twenty individual operators and the colonel watching it all. He could adjust on the fly, but the Knights had latitude.

Which meant preparation and mission orders were key to make sure each Knight was given the tools he or she needed to make the best decisions that supported the operation's objectives.

The colonel had neither time nor sufficient intel regarding the Gatecrasher to formulate a plan.

It took thirty minutes to rally the Knights since many were thirty kilometers or more away on the massive *'Keeper*. While they gathered and prepared to board, Colonel Cao worked on the plan. He stayed in constant contact with Lieutenant Styles, who provided what information he could glean using the *'Keeper*'s sensor systems. He built a rudimentary map of the Jemmin ship's interior, highlighting points of interest.

Dismantling the weapons systems to prevent a change of mind was one of the critical objectives. The Knights had no explosives, so they had to improvise and build ad hoc booby traps. They carried comm boosters and repeaters that they could use as detonators once harmonic vibration sequences were determined. Cooking off a missile in a storage area would have a devastating effect.

If they were able to determine the harmonics and Jemmin didn't dismantle the systems while the humans weren't watching. Cao started to think a Crimson Knight presence on board the Gatecrasher was going to be important until the mission on the planet was finished.

Colonel Cao started to transmit the orders to each suit, using the designators the Knights preferred—impersonal and anonymous. The Knights never documented who was what number, and they renumbered after each operation.

Cao looked at his board. He had numbers one through twenty that he could assign. "One through Ten will secure the aft end of the ship, seizing and controlling all weapons launch facilities. Eleven and Twelve will accompany me to the bridge, which is located in the very center of the ship. Numbers Thirteen and Fourteen will find and secure a defensible bivouac area close to resupply and capable of adjusting the atmospheric conditions so we can get out of our suits. Fifteen and Sixteen will position themselves in support of One through Ten. Seventeen through Twenty will investigate and report these designated nodes."

The colonel added the additional points to their HUDs. He checked the map. It was spartan, to say the least. "Jemmin have surrendered. Do not fire unless fired upon. If there is any resistance, I will reevaluate and issue new orders. In the absence of a change to orders, continue on your individual assignments and complete the mission."

The final Knights ran into the bay and took their places on the shuttle. Colonel Cao was the last to board. The deck ramp closed, and the shuttle headed out.

"What is the command word for recovery?"

"Reporting words: arrival on target is Gemini, target secure is Cygnus, retrograde from target is Mercury. Command signal for weapons hot is Dragon, weapons tight is Glynnis, recover to the bivouac site is Bivvy Prime, and recover to the shuttle is Retro Sax. Questions?"

The shuttle made short work of the trip between the

'*Keeper* and the Gatecrasher. It maneuvered to a designated access hatch. The shuttle depressurized and opened the back hatch. Colonel Cao was the first out, flying in his combat suit across the void and into the open hatch. The Knights silently followed him in. The space was big enough to accommodate all twenty-one suits.

Colonel Cao stopped the entries at ten. "Eleven through twenty, wait for the second round," the colonel ordered. He remained skeptical of Jemmin duplicity since if they wanted to destroy humanity, all Jemmin had to do was unleash the firepower of their warship. The TAC Fleet had no weapons to defend against it. That nagged at the back of the colonel's mind, leading him to distrust Jemmin more, not less.

After the last of the first group entered, the hatch automatically cycled. The colonel and Knights One through Ten waited in tense silence while the inner hatch cycled. It opened and Cao rushed through, his standard-issue high-capacity rifle at the ready. No one waited for them, not even a bot. With a hatchet motion, Cao directed the Knights down the wide corridor ahead. According to the map that Styles had provided, it ran from bow to stern as a major transit route. The Knights raced past, boots clumping as they ran ahead.

ETA four minutes. The corridor was perfectly straight, allowing Cao to maintain a visual on them while the second group cycled through the airlock. The readings on Cao's suit suggested the air was toxic to humans.

Once the second group accessed the interior of the Gatecrasher, Colonel Cao moved toward the bridge. The two Knights he designated to go with him joined him without comment or further direction. The others split off and went their own way when they passed a side corridor that led to their objective. Once moving toward the interior, Cao found that there were no steps, only ramps that led between decks. Everything was arranged to make moving loads easy.

The corridors and ramps were clean, without cabling to catch on anything passing through. A single rail down the middle of the walls and ceiling traveled parallel to the floor as if the logistics and movement system within the ship stayed in touch with the rails to keep from hitting the walls. They passed small bots at regular intervals. The boxy devices ignored the Knights.

The colonel's HUD lit up as Knight One fired his weapon and then switched it to full-auto and kept up a stream of fire. Knights Two and Three opened up briefly, then all three weapons fell silent. The colonel stopped, holding an armored fist in the air as the hand and arm signal to the two Knights behind him to halt. He pulled the information on those firing into the center of his display. Pulse never went above one hundred and was already rapidly dropping to the mid-sixties. An image appeared as part of One's report. It looked like a small train car, but it had filled the corridor. "Supply cube destroyed. Continuing," One stated.

Colonel Cao didn't have to tell the others to be on the lookout for transit cubes moving throughout the ship. He gave the hand signal to keep moving. Down two ramps and across a kilometer of the ship before they reached the area designated as the bridge.

Now we see, he thought.

Inside the space, there was a single workstation. Numerous systems were tied into a central hub, where the squarish body of a Jemmin was plugged in.

"On behalf of the Tactical Armored Corps, Terra, and Sol, I am Colonel Cao and here to take over your ship." There was no response to indicate Jemmin had heard him. The creature seemed oblivious to the presence of the humans. He wanted to yank him out of the couchlike chair, but the interfaces seemed to be far more than an external connection, as if Jemmin was a permanent part of the ship.

The colonel activated his P2P link with Admiral Corbyn. "Do not advise physically removing Jemmin from the ship." He included an image to support his recommendation.

The admiral had been waiting for the report and immediately replied, "Confirm. Plant comm device on the equipment located at ten o'clock."

Cao removed the unit Styles had thrust into his hand before he raced out of Central Control. He looked at it briefly before activating the magnetic coupler and sticking it on a tall piece of equipment behind Jemmin. He lightly tapped the button with his armored finger, and a green light appeared. It flashed for a short while before turning solid green.

"Device active," he reported in case they didn't see it on their end.

The Jemmin spasmed and bucked. His body jerked violently like a doll tossed about by an angry child. Cao stepped back. The Jemmin's wild gyrations lessened, eventually stopping entirely. The creature deflated and sank into the seat.

"We have taken control of the ship. Secure the launch systems and access missile storage," Corbyn said. "Begin the immediate transfer of armaments to the *Mencken*."

The colonel's HUD updated with a detailed map of the Gatecrasher.

A list of requested missiles appeared too, with locations designated. He transmitted the new request to his team, shaking his head at the changes. They could have told him what they intended. He looked at the two Knights accompanying him. "Assist One through Ten in acquiring the missiles. I'll move the shuttle to an aft access port."

The two Knights clumped off the bridge. The colonel made

a quick transit to record the equipment and the setup. He returned to Jemmin and used his active sensors to verify if the creature was still alive.

It was not. The forced disconnection from the ship had killed it. The colonel had no problem killing Jemmin, except that it had surrendered, the first one ever. He considered the prisoner to be in his charge, and he hadn't protected it. *Did they know it would die when it was disconnected?* he wondered. A dark cloud settled over him. The Terrans weren't like that. As much as they hated Jemmin, they operated with a code of honor.

The colonel knew the truth as soon as he asked the right question. It hadn't been the humans.

It was the Zeen.

Elvira

"FIRE!" Xi shouted as she sent two fifteen-kilogram AP rounds two hundred meters ahead into the Poltergeist. A plasma beam scorched *Elvira's* topside as it followed the Scorpion's mains into the side of the massive battle tank. Missiles shrieked from the Poltergeist, but the mechs had already fired up the coil guns, filling the tunnel with projectiles and creating a nearly impenetrable barrier. Two missiles snaked through the barrage and hit the upper glacis of *Twilight's Fall*. The violence of the explosions threw the roller backward. Unspent fuel contributed to the carnage, delivering secondary explosions that filled the tunnel with a thousand-degree fire.

Elvira's automated systems flushed foam over the hull, just like the other mechs, except *Fall*. The initial impacts had left it incapable of protecting itself. Xi jumped *Elvira* sideways to drop her mech onto *Fall* and share her firefighting foam.

"AP up!" Penny called.

"Fire!" Xi said, sending two more shells into the side of the Poltergeist. The hovertank blasted backward with the latest impacts. It crashed to the floor and slid into the tunnel wall.

Xi cycled the autoloader for another two rounds. That second Poltergeist worried her. *Fat Man's* plasma main was still charging. She targeted two MRMs on the spot where the first Jemmin tank had been. Warnings flashed through her neural link. She turned the safeties off and sent the missiles off their rack as soon as the second tank appeared around the corner.

It continued through the intersection. The rest of her company fired, but too late. The MRMs hit at the same time as the two fifteen kg shells. The Poltergeist was thrown backward and wedged against the far corner of the four-way intersection. The Jemmin cleared its weapons racks before the rest of the 3rd Company's incoming rammed home.

The missiles shrieked into the tunnel. Coil and chain guns cycled but not quickly enough. A short-range missile hit *Elvira* right on her nose, just below the cockpit screen. *Holy Diver* and *Fat Man* took the brunt of the missiles. The extra hundred meters to *Godzilla* bringing up the rear was enough time for the barrage to have more impact. The inbounds exploded over the shorter mechs, pounding them from above in addition to the direct hits on their hulls.

Holy Diver reeled from the blows, staggering as its railguns bent and warped. SRM racks over the small humanoid mech's shoulders were shredded and dangled from their destroyed mounts. *Diver* froze in place as its systems went offline. *Fat Man* shrugged off the impacts and fired the plasma cannon. If there was any doubt the Jemmin tank had survived Xi's attack, there was no doubt that it didn't survive Fatso's strike.

Xi launched one of her final precious drones to look ahead. "Penny, I've got alarms in the section below the cockpit. Check and see what's going on down there."

The Monkey/Wrench jumped up and disappeared through a hatch into one of *Elvira*'s crawlspaces.

"Sungod, report," Xi ordered, holding her breath as she waited.

"Cracks, report." Xi's feed with *Holy Diver* had been cut, which could have been the neural link getting knocked offline. She moved *Elvira* forward after the drone confirmed that the intersection before them was clear. "I'm going out there," Xi said, not waiting for acknowledgment.

She threw on her environmental suit and impatiently cycled through the airlock. When the rear hatch opened, she was hit by a heatwave that almost threw her back into the ship. She waited for her systems to equalize before pressing forward. One of the missiles had penetrated the inner compartment before exploding. One look through confirmed that no one had survived.

"*Twilight's Fall* is down," she told the company while running to *Holy Diver*.

The damage there was more than cosmetic but not catastrophic. Xi was able to cycle through the small airlock and get into the mech and found the crew working with a sense of urgency to bring the systems back online.

The Jock cheered and gave Xi a thumbs-up. After he jacked back in, he spoke softly. "You miss me, my good girl?"

Xi didn't think he was talking to her. She never questioned Jocks' relationships with the machines wrapped around them. The Wrench ripped a part out of an access port and stuffed a replacement into place. The power surged through the mechanical systems and the ship came back to life, flexing its legs and arms.

"Carry on," Xi told them and climbed out. She walked back to her mech. Debris littered the ground. Some of it was from *Elvira*, but most was from *Twilight's Fall* and *Holy Diver*. Xi stopped before entering *Elvira*. She had a bad feeling none of them would get off the planet. Her losses had been too great, the impact to her combat power too excessive. *Diver* was back in the game but had lost its punch. It had become little more than an armored personnel carrier.

She boarded and resynced with her mech. She checked the drone feed before moving into the intersection and sending maximum power to her sensors.

Bob sat quietly

"Fatso, at my nine o'clock. Meathead at my six, and Cracks, you're tail-end Charlie," Xi ordered. The sensor feed was clear. A glowing hub of energy radiated from straight ahead. "I'd say don't be in a hurry to your own funeral, but let's not give them time to set up. Flank speed for four kilometers, then we'll be cautious. Move out."

Xi kicked the Poltergeist wreckage with *Elvira's* remaining foreleg before powering through.

30

PRIMARY OBJECTIVE

Powerslave

"That looks like a mech company engaged with the enemy," Jenkins remarked to himself as the board lit up with the power of energy weapons and heat of explosions. He grimaced at the brief and extreme action. Temperatures spiked above twenty-five hundred degrees Celsius before settling down. Plasma and beam weapons were the only sources of such intensity.

"Major Bao?" he ventured, but there was no answer. "3rd Company?"

Hammer kept his head down and drove *Powerslave* onward, coaxing a little more speed from the big beast.

Jenkins shook his head. "Slow us down, Hammer. Whatever the major just encountered isn't something we want to dive headlong into. ETA?"

The number was on the board, but Hammer slowed, and it changed. "Nine minutes."

"*Satan*, take the lead to clear your line of fire." Hammer moved to the side of the tunnel, hugging the wall to let the cruiser-grade roller take the lead. It accelerated forward. The environment made it easy for mechs with wheels to travel. They rarely got to travel over such accommodating terrain. Jenkins let him have his legs. There weren't any intersections for the next six kilometers.

They settled into a smooth pace of sixty kph. Jenkins sat back and watched his screen, looking for anything from ahead that would indicate Xi and her company had come through the engagement.

"Major Bao," he tried once more when his patience ran out.

"On our way to primary objective," she replied. "Down to four rigs, three nominally combat capable."

"Casualties?" Jenkins pressed.

"Sungod and his crew. No idea what happened to Slash before we escaped underground."

"Trapper made the recovery of *Fortune Fury's* crew. The Zeen took care of the Poltergeists, clearing the way for our operation into the city, which is just a façade, as you already figured out."

"Jemmin live underground. Knowing that makes it easy to understand why the Arh'kel claimed the caverns as their own. We rooted out the rock-biters, and we'll root out Jemmin."

While they talked, Xi transmitted the mapping information from the sounding signal the colonel had sent earlier. "I am only ten kilometers away. Slow down, and I'll catch up."

"How many are you bringing?"

"Me and *Satan*."

Xi grunted. "We could probably use a little more ass. The Jemmin are becoming less and less agreeable."

"Copy that. Stand by." Jenkins switched over to the Legion-wide channel. "1st and 2nd Companies. New orders. Return to Rally Point Blake's Seven. Captain Koch, leave two units at the Rally Point and bring the remaining mechs at best possible speed. Route and location should be updated on your displays."

Captain Koch verified receipt of the order, followed by the

four mechs of Jenkins' company. The blips on Jenkins' screen updated in real-time, thanks to the repeaters and signal boosters embedded in the walls. They stopped and turned around, accelerating back the way they'd come.

Jenkins' map updated with the information his two companies had gathered. Extensive tunnels, but they had not come across any chambers. The Jemmin had to use the hoverplatforms to move the extensive distances. Robots must take care of the majority of the maintenance. Combined with Xi's information regarding the clones, the picture came into sharper focus.

3rd Company continued to move away from Jenkins but at a slower pace. *Powerslave* and *Satan's Alley* were gaining, but not quickly enough.

"Slow it down, Xi. Don't go in there without backup."

"From what I've seen, the more time we give them, the worse it will be for us. These last two Poltergeists weren't completely set up for a proper ambush; otherwise, things could have been a lot worse for us. You know we can't stand toe to toe with a Poltergeist. We need to strike fast."

"*Satan's Alley*, *Powerslave*. Flank speed to 3rd Company's position. Give it all you've got. We'll be behind you all the way. Don't worry if we fall back. We can't maintain your speed."

"That's a roger," *Satan's* Jock replied. The mech increased speed beyond one twenty, redlining at one-hundred-ten percent reactor power. It topped out at one-hundred-twenty-five kph. Powerslave instantly fell back. At eighty-five kph, the walker threatened to hit the ceiling with each stride. Hammer backed it to eighty-three, relieving some of the pressure. "ETA six minutes forty seconds."

Jenkins keyed his mic. "My ETA is eight and change."

Xi continued her drive into the depths of the Jemmin homeworld. *Fat Man* led the parade, with *Elvira*, *Godzilla*, and *Holy Diver* in tow.

"Please?" Jenkins pleaded.

H.L. Mencken

Podsy stood with his legs spread and hands clasped behind his back. He held his head high as he watched the main viewscreen. The assault carrier powered downward into a lower orbit. The planet's surface came into sharp contrast, with dull colors and little relief. Browns and reds, with oases of a greenish-blue. Each planet had its own character: the way the clouds formed, the way the mountains stood out if it had them, the cold of the poles. J-Ville Central seemed to be mostly a dead rock with little surface water.

"Packet coming from the surface, from Colonel Jenkins."

With the arrival of the *Mencken* into orbit and comm relays throughout the tunnels and *War Pig* on the surface, contact had been re-established.

"Open it, and let's see what they've found."

Jenkins had added a few notes to Xi's concise report. Podsy read in silence. When he finished, he closed his eyes for a moment. "Send that to Admiral Corbyn, please, exactly as it is."

Jem remained in the captain's chair. The device that allowed Jem to speak aloud was wrapped neatly around the base. Podsy sat next to him. "What do you think, Jem?"

The gestalt intelligence sparkled along the remaining live end. "I think that was the answer I was missing in my analysis. This makes the next phase of the operation even more critical."

"Where Xi Bao executes all twelve for their crimes against the universe, and humanity in particular?"

"I almost feel sorry for the final Jemmin survivors. I think they've earned their place on the wrong end of the good major's ire. But no, I'm talking about the impending war with the Vorr."

Podsy hung his head. "Shit, Jem. You can't think we're in

any shape to go to war with the Vorr." It wasn't a question. Podsy stood and started to pace. They were a little too far from the *'Keeper, Henry VIII*, and the Gatecrasher for instantaneous communication. "We'll be in my quarters."

Captain Podsednik took Jem and headed out. He almost ran Lieutenant Commander Knighton over since he wasn't watching where he was going. He was singularly focused on what Jem had called the next phase. He had thought that went out the window with the near annihilation of the TAC fleet.

The commander stopped him in his tracks. "Teresa," he exclaimed. She raised one eyebrow. "Commander, I mean."

"Captain." She waited.

"I'll be in my quarters," Podsy told the bridge crew. Every single eye watched as the hatch to the bridge closed, with the commander turning to follow the captain.

He hurried to his quarters. Teresa entered without hesitation. She closed with him, but he glanced at Jem. She stopped.

"Have you seen the latest from Colonel Jenkins?"

She shook her head, expression changing to all business. Podsy accessed his terminal and brought up the report. "Care for something to drink?"

"Are we on or off-duty?" she asked.

"I'm afraid we're still on." He looked at his small galley, opening the refrigerator for added support. He was a confirmed bachelor, and his stock showed it. "How about some Tang?"

She mumbled a response while reading the report. He mixed two glasses and brought them to the desk. Teresa was in his chair, so he leaned against the desk.

"That's some bullshit right there. We've been fighting the B-Team this whole time? And then they're telling us that there is no A-Team. Makes me feel like humanity might not be the best choice to lead the other races."

"Humanity is the only choice. I'm not sure who can be

trusted to enforce the peace and allow self-determination. Definitely not Jemmin or the Vorr, or the Zeen, for that matter. If we don't take charge, someone else will subjugate us, but they'll probably be less subtle than Jemmin have been."

"I agree with that determination, Captain Podsednik," Jem interjected. "Humanity must assume its role in the universe as the leader of freedom."

"If we must," Teresa conceded and smiled. Her hair remained matted, and sweat had stained the collar of her flight suit. She sipped her Tang. "If we end Jemmin, we'll have to face the Vorr. I've been out there." She waved indiscriminately around the room. "We're in no shape to fight any more battles, not now, and not for a long time."

"That's my concern, and why I wanted some time to think and talk to the generals and the admiral. I don't think we're going to have any choice. How can we take on an empire with five ships, all five of which have limited offensive capability? The only one with any punch is the captured Gatecrasher, assuming we can make it work for us."

Podsy started to pace, mumbling to himself as he started to detail the variables, listing the pros and cons of each.

Teresa helped herself to a short stroll around the captain's quarters, noting his private head with a regular shower. "I have my best thoughts in the shower," she said as she pulled Podsy's old work coveralls from his closet and headed for the bathroom, closing the door softly behind her.

"You should bounce your ideas off her," Jem recommended. "She is the best tactician you have available. The fact that she has survived numerous battles with technologically superior enemies should confirm my assessment."

"I've always had to count on myself, but then Lee Jenkins and Xi Bao appeared. Talk about believing we could accomplish what we did! How arrogant was humanity back then? But they were right. Not only that we had to try, but that we could win."

"I don't think you'll have to be alone anymore, Captain Podsednik. As I've learned after being liberated by the Metal Legion, you have to plan for the future, but you have to live for today. I'll leave you alone since I have some calculations to make, based on the new information regarding Jemmin."

The translation device went silent.

Podsy slid a chair next to the bathroom door. He cracked it and spoke while not looking. "When you're out there fighting greater numbers of the enemy, what gives you the edge?"

"Don't be where they're shooting," she replied easily.

"How do you do that?" Podsy wondered.

"By knowing what their target is. They rarely came after us because they were focused on attacking the assault carrier or a dreadnought or some other ship that was a greater threat. We used the distraction to our advantage." The water stopped. "What the hell? Where's the towel?"

Podsy saw it lying on the bed. He picked it up and did a quick sniff check. It was mostly dry.

He stuffed it through the small crack and reached in as far as he could. She pulled it from his hand. He closed the door and started pacing across his quarters that suddenly seemed too small.

"What is the Vorr's goal? How can we catch them going after a prize while not looking at us?" He stared at the floor as he walked. Teresa stood there in his too-big coveralls with her arms crossed. He blew out a breath. "Thank the gods you didn't come out naked. We've got shit to do."

"I like your priorities, Captain. I think I'll give you a shot at being the future ex-Mister Knighton."

Podsy tried to parse the words but failed. He settled for shaking his head. "I'll commit to being seen in public with you."

"As long as we don't get ourselves killed. I think the first thing to focus on is Jemmin. They still have fleets of ships out there."

"We can't do anything about that until we learn what the Metalheads discover when they find Jemmin."

Elvira

"HE up!" Penny called. Xi took careful aim at an obstruction two kilometers ahead. The rounds wouldn't rise too far before falling back to the target. Gravity made everyone pay its price.

"On the way," she stated coldly and sent the heavy weapons into the tunnel. The close quarters exacerbated the muzzle blasts, washing flame and light smoke over the mech slightly in front and to the side. "Sorry about that, Fatso."

"Heavy metal and fire, Major!" Fatso replied as he sent a plasma beam down the tunnel. It dropped more quickly and skipped off the tunnel floor.

Xi's mains hit home, blasting the hastily constructed barricade.

"Who is building this crap?" she grumbled. Fat Man's plasma hit the obstruction from the bottom, missing the armored front and taking the barricade in its softer interior. The beam blasted it apart, scorching the tunnel as it burned the wreckage at plasma temps. "Nice shot, Fatso, now pick up the pace."

"If I may," Bob interrupted. "Your strategy is correct in limiting Jemmin's reaction time."

Bob kept his place, strapped into a cockpit seat. Xi waited, but the Zeen had shared what he wished to share.

"What will we find in there?" Xi asked, leaning aside to show him the sensor picture—a huge chamber ahead with numerous tunnels leading in and out. It glowed with the flow of energy.

"You will find what you seek," Bob replied.

"Peace for humanity?"

"Jemmin. If Jemmin means peace, then yes."

"The end of Jemmin means peace," Xi suggested. She moved back into her seat and focused on what the input through the neural implant was telling her. "The atmosphere is changing outside, and it looks bad. Everyone get your suits on."

The mech company slowed as the crews geared up. Penny put her suit on quickly before trying to get Lu into his. Xi started forward again before she finished.

"Fatso, hit that intersection again."

"Fire the cannon!" *Fat Man's* jock cried out. The plasma discharged and headed down the corridor. Less than a kilometer, it splashed through the debris and into the oversized chamber.

Elvira surged forward to enter the chamber on the heels of the plasma strike. The embers still glowed as she stepped on them on her way past. Once inside, she took aim with her twin fifteens.

A Jemmin appeared and walked to a spot in front of *Elvira*. It stood there patiently.

Her mind was torn between talking to Jemmin and destroying the facility as she had done with the clone tanks. Her coil guns started spinning, ready to send a thousand rounds a minute downrange. She let off and howled in anger.

"I'm going out there. Come on, Bob. They'll love seeing you in their sacred chamber."

"It would be my honor as the first Zeen to stand here. Zeen-Human Alliance. Symmetry."

"Something like that." She got out of her chair and stopped.

"Why can't I just blow it away? It's only a Jemmin clone. It's food, right?"

"That is why humanity must be in charge," Bob offered.

"They've wronged us enough that justice would be served if we killed them all, just like we did to the clones."

"The clones are bio-engineered products. They weren't fully functioning Jemmin. Not even partially functioning."

"I had no problem with the clones, and I assume these guys are more. I doubt the real Jemmin are standing guard duty in front of a Scorpion." Xi took one last look to make sure it was still there. A second Jemmin had joined it.

Xi headed through the airlock and outside. Bob was close behind. The Jemmin showed no response when the Zeen appeared. Xi strode purposely toward them, a richly burning fire behind her eyes.

"You must not fire your weapons in here," Jemmin said.

"Makes me want to fire them that much more," Xi shot back. "How about you surrender yourselves and the living Jemmin, and we'll call it a day?"

"Please don't think I'm here to negotiate. I was sent to warn you about destroying certain equipment in this chamber."

Xi removed her hand comm device. "Fatso, pick a target where you're not going to splash me and take aim."

Fat Man moved beside *Elvira* and aimed its plasma cannon at forty-five degrees into the chamber. "If you need the equipment to survive, surrender." *Godzilla* loomed over the two shorter mechs, deploying its missile launchers by aiming over Xi's head.

Xi couldn't tell what Jemmin was thinking. Bob started speaking. Xi moved the translator closer to her ear.

"You will do as the human demands. Do the math. You have lost because you underestimated the will of your *lesser* races." Bob moved closer. "We have come to take what is ours."

"What are you here to take, Bob?" Xi asked, stepping closer to the insectoid. She was unarmed because in all her diplomatic trials, the lack of fear was a negotiating tool. She dialed up her P2P. "Penny, aim the chain guns at these two Jemmin in case we need to splatter them."

Elvira's weapons whirred in response.

Bob turned on Xi and took a quick step.

"Not food," she said softly. "Symmetry."

Bob pulled back. "We are here to take back our standing in the universe. *Respect* is what we are here for. Jemmin tried to kill our race."

Xi smiled. "Zeen have humanity's respect, Bob. Have you never heard that the victor writes the history? I see Jemmin kneeling before us, their lives in our hands as they surrender. That is the history we're going to write. Jemmin will be a black mark over a long period, but then comes a new age, the age of the Zeen-Human alliance. Jemmin's respect is irrelevant."

Bob appeared to relax, deflating. "Symmetry."

Xi strolled past the two Jemmin, clapping one on the shoulder. "Stand over there and wait for further instructions." Xi waved in the general direction of the wall. "Come on, *Fat Man.* Follow me into the treasure room."

Bob ignored Jemmin as he followed Xi into the chamber.

The howl of a mech running at high speed echoed down the tunnel. 1st Company had arrived.

31

CLEANING OUT THE RAT'S NEST

H.L. Mencken

"Live feed coming from the surface," Comm reported. *Elvira's* external video showed Xi and a Zeen talking to two Jemmin.

"What are they saying?" Podsy wondered.

"There is no sound at present. Major Bao has her transmitter muted."

Captain Podsednik bit his lip. *Of course, you do.*

When the major waved for *Fat Man* to follow, her audio clicked over. "We are entering the chamber of J-Ville Central. I believe we'll find the last surviving Jemmin in here, and the equipment they use to transfer their orders to Jemmin scattered throughout the galaxy. This is the place where Jemmin hatched their plan a millennium ago to interfere in the development of the human race. And this is the place where the humans are going to end their interference. Thank you for the technology, but we've had quite enough. Time to unplug you."

The Zeen called Bob started to talk to the major. She muted her microphone.

"Come on!" Podsy blurted. Commander Knighton put her hand on his arm. She was still in his coveralls. The bridge crew had the decency not to stare, but Podsy caught their approving glances.

"Where are the other ships in the fleet?" Podsy asked.

"*Henry VIII*, the Gatecrasher, and the *'Keeper* are holding station at one AU from here. *Zeen Home Three* has assumed a high orbit."

"Comm, transmit the live feed to Admiral Corbyn and get me *Zeen Home Three*."

Comm confirmed both orders. "No answer from *Zeen Home Three*."

"Get me Major Bao."

The link clicked through.

"I'm a bit busy," the major replied.

"*Zeen Home Three* has just entered orbit," Podsy reported.

"Bob?" The image on the screen showed Xi stop and tap the Zeen. His answer didn't come through Xi's audio.

"We're good," she announced before they continued walking.

Podsy scrubbed his forehead, hoping the headache that had just appeared would go away.

"They're going to go dirtside," Teresa said matter-of-factly.

Podsy nodded and gave up trying to make the headache go away. He reached into his pocket for another stim. Teresa stopped him. "How many have you had?"

He couldn't remember the last time he'd slept. "Probably too many." He put it back in his pocket. "I'm going to see General Pushkin."

When he turned, he found the general standing there, watching.

In his heavy Russian accent, the general said, "I think you now know what it's like to be us, the command staff. We issue the orders, and what happens after that is what will be. Did we communicate our priorities, making sure the mission parameters were clear? Does everyone know what the objective is? How the Metal Legion achieves those objectives might not be how we would do it, but that is something you have to let go, or you will drive yourself insane. Major Bao will end this war if you let her. I'll be in my quarters catching up on sleep." The general sauntered away, nodding to the bridge crew as he made eye contact with them.

Captain Podsednik looked at his chair. He'd left Jem in his quarters. He touched Teresa on the shoulder. "Can you get Jem and bring him back here?"

"Captain's quarters are voice-activated for access," she said softly.

He looked away. "You're good," he whispered.

She walked away, giving him a healthy dose of side-eye as she passed.

Podsy turned back to the viewscreen. "Get me Colonel Jenkins."

Powerslave

"My ETA is under a minute," Jenkins relayed to the *Mencken*. "Standby."

The colonel didn't have time to keep them apprised. He wasn't a control freak, but this was it. This was J-Ville Central. This was where the command to destroy him and his people had originated, but he had to let Major Bao follow her instincts.

The walker jogged up to the mechs filling the tunnel and stood in line behind them. "I'm going out," Jenkins announced. He threw his environmental suit on and wrapped a pistol belt around his waist. He quickly descended the ladder and cycled through the small airlock.

He hit the smooth tunnel floor and broke into a run.

Hammer notified the rest of the units that the colonel was on the ground and in transit.

Jenkins noted the two Jemmin standing near the wall with *Elvira's* coil guns trained on them. It increased his already monumental respect for Xi Bao. No wonder the Zeen had designated her as their liaison—not the colonel, but Xi Bao. A good leader helps those he's in charge of. Their success was to be celebrated. He searched inside himself to find a little envy, but he was just proud of her and her singular focus on winning the fight for the Metal Legion, That meant all humanity would win, too.

He slowed to a walk, taking in the equipment as he went. He had no idea what the purpose was and accepted that it was advanced far beyond anything he could understand. There were no manual interfaces. In this chamber, two kilometers from wall to wall, energy surged and flowed. The place radiated with power. And it was completely controlled by Jemmin.

The original Jemmin.

Lee caught sight of Xi and Bob ahead. They examined equipment as they headed in a straight line toward the center. It took time to get there, but no one was shooting. Jenkins hurried to catch them.

"Major," he called when he was close enough.

She nodded. "Colonel. Let me introduce Bob." She pointed with her hand.

"Good afternoon, Bob," Jenkins offered, not expecting the insectoid to respond.

"It's afternoon? Shit." Xi hung her head for a moment to collect her thoughts but continued her march to the middle.

A Jemmin appeared but stepped aside. They walked past without acknowledging it.

"I think that's their way of saying they surrender," Xi

remarked. "It also means we need to figure out how to take control away from them."

"Zeen will help," Bob said.

Xi pursed her lips and turned her head. "We've got other things to do, together with our Zeen partners. I was thinking someone more like Jem."

"I'm not sure that's our decision," Jenkins replied, knowing his feed was being relayed into orbit for everyone to hear.

"Then get permission, because it's the only answer that makes sense," Xi shot back.

Jenkins knew she was right. "We'll take care of that in a little bit," Jenkins conceded. "Pretty impressive evil doctor lair, don't you think?"

"It is," Xi agreed, holding up her hand for a high-five.

The final equipment towered over the rest, creating a protected area within the circle. A walkway along each of the cardinal directions provided access. Inside, four Jemmin attended the twelve.

The original Jemmin were pale shadows of their clones, secured within beds that contained a half-moon of gleaming metal wrapped over the bumps that represented their heads, situated on top of their squarish bodies.

Xi approached one of the attendant Jemmin. "How can we talk with them?" she demanded.

"You speak. They will hear and understand."

Xi rotated in a slow circle. She had contemplated this moment but hadn't thought about what to say. She took a few breaths and let the words flow. "Jemmin's influence over this universe is finished. Humanity's time has come. We thank you for the technology you shared that enabled us to get here. But it's not just us. It is every race Jemmin has manipulated. We have sacrificed enough. Surrender control of your systems to us. The alternative is we turn this chamber into a slag heap. Do you want to be the ones who are responsible for Jemmin being erased from history?"

A voice came out of nowhere. "History is never kind to the ones who misjudged their foes."

"More power in friendships than making enemies." Xi turned to Bob. "Symmetry."

"Symmetry," Bob agreed.

"The disagreement between Jemmin and Jem'un was the stone that started the avalanche that has crushed the Jemmin empire. It was inevitable; the only question was when. Zeen development of a faster-than-light drive and the reappearance of the Originators were both unexpected but hastened the time-line. We surrender to humanity."

"Podsy, send Jem down here most ricky-tick. If Jem agrees, of course."

"Zeen will come, too," Bob stated.

"Deliver Jem to Trapper and his people so they can bring him down here. They can hang out and keep an eye on things, if you know what I mean."

"Five by five, Major," Podsy replied. "Jem has agreed and is on his way via a personal delivery by Commander Knighton."

"I hope she lets him have more room than she gave me." Xi looked around, momentarily lost. She turned to the Jemmin attendants. "Is there a shorter route down here than the one we took?"

"No."

"Fine." Xi thought for a moment. "As part of your surrender, stand down the Jemmin fleet in any operation that is not directed specifically against the Vorr. We will absorb Jemmin ships into the TAC soonest. Thank you for your cooperation."

"We have one request," Jemmin said. "We would like to see our star one more time. Feel its warmth on our skin."

"We'll see what we can do once Jem confirms it's safe to move you." Xi looked at Lee. "What do we do now?"

"A shower. Sleep. Maybe some hot chow?"

Xi laughed. "There is nothing more soldier than what you just said. That's what I want, too. What do you say we make that happen for our people?"

"Bullseye, Major."

32

A NEW MISSION

H.L. Mencken

Chief Rimmer shouted commands at the crew as drop-can after drop-can came aboard. They unbuttoned the mechs from the tether and moved them into separate areas based on the severity of repairs needed.

When *Elvira* came aboard, the deckhands cheered and clapped. Xi exited, with Lu between her and Penny. Attendants from Sickbay rushed to them with a stretcher, taking responsibility for Lu's medical care.

"Welcome back, Major. Where's Bob?" Captain Podsednik asked, powering through the crowd to hug his former boss.

"He stayed on the planet. Trapper's keeping an eye on him and the other Zeen. Hot chow for my people?" she asked.

"I passed a bunch of Metalheads in the corridor on their way to the chow hall. The best we have available is out and waiting."

"That's what I wanted to hear. I'll stop by and see how they're doing before I hit my quarters for a shower. And then I think we have some planning to do."

"Sleep for all hands, Major. That's Admiral Corbyn's

orders. We're standing down for the next eight hours while the Gatecrasher stands watch."

Xi crossed her arms and gave Podsy the hairy eyeball. "If I must," she conceded. "Colonel Jenkins is the last one up. What's on the schedule for us after this?"

"Making major didn't make you smart, did it?" Podsy quipped. "Sleep. After eight hours of downtime, we'll tell you what happened up here, and you tell us what happened down there. We'll compare notes and look at the way ahead."

"We have a Gatecrasher working for us? How bad of shape is it in?"

"Intact one hundred percent. You made that possible. Now, off with you." Podsy shooed her away, ignoring her other questions as he made his way to Chief Rimmer.

Xi surrendered the field of battle to her friend the ship's captain and power-walked to the dining facility. She caught up with Penny.

"You know what they have?" she asked.

Xi threw her hands up. "The same thing they always have?" she guessed.

She didn't press it. They arrived to the smell of something burnt. The cacophony of loud conversations pressed outward, making Xi and Penny feel like they had to wade through them to get into the short serving line.

Penny stepped aside for the major to go first. "Don't you dare. Get your ass up there." She pointed. The Wrench shrugged and grabbed a tray. She followed her in. Something that looked like meat sat in a boiler tray. Rehydrated egg product. Rehydrated green stuff that could have been broccoli, spinach, or fungus. It didn't matter. The cooks had put out the ketchup and hot sauce dispensers.

The two hurried through the line, then sat with a group that quieted when they put their trays down. Xi nodded and started to eat, swirling the food items together. "I didn't put enough hot sauce on it," she complained.

Penny smiled. "We beat Jemmin, and you're bitching about tasteless food."

"We have standards to maintain, no matter who's in charge of the galaxy. Get with the program, Penny."

She returned to eating while Xi looked around. Those holding animated conversations were intermixed with those who hung their heads, either exhausted or reeling from the inevitable losses. Xi hadn't heard. She leaned toward the crewman next to her.

"How many ships did we lose?"

He grimaced. "You haven't heard? We lost all the Fleet ships except for *Henry VIII* and *Mencken*. We only have seven Vipers left. I think we lost only three or four freighters. Zeen and the *'Keeper* were untouched, and now we have ourselves a Gatecrasher."

"All of them?" Xi's chest tightened, and she couldn't breathe. She closed her eyes and fought back the tears. She knew too many people she'd never see again. "*Sima Yi?*"

"Blaze of glory, fighting a Jemmin battleship by herself. They bought us time."

Xi relaxed. "I'm sure that's most of the stories. It's good to hear they died well."

"They all did, ma'am."

Xi picked up her tray and headed for the scullery to drop it off on her way out. She was no longer hungry. That shower sounded even better. She reached her quarters without having to talk to anyone. She pulled off her coveralls and left them on the floor, then jumped into her small shower and let the sonic waves hit her, clearing the tears away as they fell.

· · ·

Mencken, Operations Center Recovery of the Metal Legion plus twelve hours

General Pushkin shook the hands of his senior commanders, Colonel Jenkins, and Major Bao.

Podsy stood until the general sat. The four looked at each other for a moment before the hard business of planning the next operation began.

"The Vorr." General Pushkin let the word hang in the air.

"We have every Jemmin ship available to us," Xi started.

"That will be true as soon as the array is rebuilt. Someone did a number on it. They'll be starting from scratch. The Zeen have offered to replace it, remaining in a high orbit to relay transmissions until it's ready."

Jenkins leaned in. "Do we trust the Zeen that much?"

"We have little choice, but putting Jem in the hot seat in J-Ville Central is going to pay dividends. Jem will be a buffer between the Zeen and us."

"Do we trust Jem?"

Podsy spoke up. "With every fiber of my being. He was giving his life to help us. I'm not sure I can give any higher testimonial. I just hope he has enough horsepower left in his crystal lattice to do what needs to be done without further degradation."

The general accepted the input before continuing. "The Vorr," he repeated, more ominously this time.

Xi chuckled before biting her lip.

"Aren't we running on empty, General?"

"That's why we are here. Thanks to Captain Podsednik and Lieutenant Styles, we have a plan that is completely outrageous." The general deferred, and Podsy went into a brief review of the plan the admiral had approved.

General Pushkin tapped the console before him, and

Admiral Corbyn and General Moon appeared. They linked Commodore Sosunova in.

"We are ready, Admiral,"

"Move *Henry VIII* into proximity with *Zeen Home Three*. Bring the Gatecrasher into formation with the *Mencken*. Prepare to transit to Nexus space through the *'Keeper*'s gate. We depart in thirty minutes. Questions?"

"Is there a role for the Metal Legion?" Jenkins asked.

"We don't have time to engage in knife fights. This next battle will be fought in space. We could use the major's expertise in the cyber realm, so if she's willing to plug in and keep an eye on Styles, I'd appreciate it. On a side note, Colonel, we're all the Metal Legion. As long as one of us lives, we all live. Metal never dies."

"Never," the colonel repeated.

After the link was terminated, Xi leaned on the table and stared at the general. "Can I help you?" The general wasn't amused.

"We've come full circle, General. As a nobody back on Durgan's Folly, I was relegated to watching over Styles. How many lifetimes later, and I'm doing the same thing."

"I don't have Ben Akinouye's gift for the right philosophy for all events, but I'll give it a shot. Water will always find the lowest point, but stars will forever remain in the sky."

The general stood, prompting the others to stand. He strolled out as if he didn't have a care in the world.

Xi looked at Lee. They both turned to Podsy.

"What the fuck was that supposed to mean?" Xi asked.

Podsy shrugged. Jenkins looked at her. "Maybe when you're a general, you'll figure it out. When that happens, tell me what it means."

"I'll be on the bridge," Podsy said on his way out.

"Hey!" Xi stopped him. "What's this I hear about you and a certain fleet commander?"

"Nonsensical rumors. You can't trust whoever spews such drivel."

Xi nodded. Podsy took a step. "Jem told me."

"Crap." He looked into the corridor conspiratorially. "Don't tell anyone."

"Why not?" Xi asked. "And who the hell would I tell?" She looked at Jenkins, and he pulled an imaginary zipper across his lips. "I'm surrounded by teenagers."

"Who wanted to gossip about who likes who?" Podsy shot back.

"Fair enough." Xi wedged past him and waved one hand dismissively over her shoulder. "I'll be on the bridge," she said in her best Podsy imitation.

GateKeeper

Admiral Corbyn stood in Central Control and watched Styles work. They'd acquired a barstool with a back, on which the lieutenant had sat for nearly every minute of the previous three days. The admiral was worried, but the engagement was too critical to split up among lesser programmers.

"Just a little while longer, Lieutenant," the admiral said, trying to be encouraging, but he doubted Styles heard him. In the center of the room, the three-dimensional tactical grid showed the three ships in a line, with the 'Keeper bringing up the rear. The gate formed to take them to the Illumination League Nexus to begin the execution of End of War Phase Three, which had been dead until they realized the full capabilities of the 'Keeper. The Gatecrasher was the catalyst to make everything viable.

"Accelerating, matching rotation and speed," Helm

reported. The *Mencken* slipped across the event horizon, through the wormhole, and into Nexus space.

When the sensors cleared, the screen populated by two massive fleets, Jemmin on one side and the Vorr on the other. Wreckage filled the nearby area as a monument to more than one battle fought between titans. *Mencken* sailed between the two fleets on its way to the gate leading to the Vorr home system.

Unlike Jemmin, the Vorr were latecomers to the gate system. They weren't able to hide behind a series of gates like their enemy Jemmin.

The Jemmin fleet accelerated at maximum speed in the opposite direction.

Mencken slowed as the Gatecrasher caught up and started to pass. The Vorr fleet started to move. The Gatecrasher sent a barrage of long-range missiles in the direction of the lead ship.

The gate opened, and the Gatecrasher slipped through. The *Mencken* followed closely behind.

The 'Keeper opened its own gate and disappeared through.

The Gatecrasher was firing full salvos of its entire range of weapons. As soon as *Mencken* appeared, a missile hit it on the front quarter. "Fire!" Podsy called, but the screens had not yet cleared. When they did, they found themselves in the middle of a firestorm.

Tactical launched the full complement of weapons that had been borrowed from the Gatecrasher and jury-rigged to launch from *Mencken's* tubes.

"Full reverse," Podsy ordered, wincing with each new hit.

The 'Keeper appeared nearby for a grand total of ten seconds. The gate opened, and the *Mencken* backed through. The Gatecrasher executed a full reverse, matched the spin just like the *Mencken* had, and disappeared back through the gate. The gate closed, reopening as the Vorr fleet lined up to follow their enemies back to the Nexus to provide a double pincer to end the upstart humans who appeared to be allied with Jemmin as well as destroy the Jemmin fleet that had been holding station in the Nexus.

Mencken crossed into New America 2 space behind the Gatecrasher. They cruised quietly ahead, slowing on a ballistic trajectory.

The gate closed behind them.

Podsy stared intently at the screen.

"*GateKeeper* off starboard," Tactical reported before adding, "The board is clear."

"Damage report," Podsy called.

The reports started to come in. Hull breaches and atmospheric containment lost. Twenty-four casualties. No injuries.

"May they be the last," the captain stated. "Damage control to all stations."

"Already dispatched," Comm noted.

Colonel Jenkins stepped up. "When can we go back and check on the freighters?"

"Soon." Podsy held up one finger as he received additional reports. "Twenty-two casualties, not twenty-four. Two trapped and not vented to space. Where were we? Back to J-Ville Central. We need to give the Vorr fleet enough time to get through the gate before we show back up. We need to check the Nexus first, and then go back to collect our freighters and friends."

The engineering officer looked confused. Major Bao sat next to her, jacked into a secondary station. The young woman tapped Xi on the shoulder. "What happened? Where are the Vorr if they followed us?"

Podsy stepped in and Xi deferred, getting back to her terminal for a final check before logging out.

"It was the double switch. The *GateKeeper* can travel any distance, so while everyone was sleeping, they shot a billion light-years into the Gamma Quadrant and dropped off a one-way gate. After we went through the Nexus gate, Styles reprogrammed it to send the next ships through to the Gamma Quadrant. Same thing for the gate from the Vorr system back to the Nexus. After we went through, it was redirected."

"The Vorr fleets were sent where they can't get back to us?"

"Not in a hundred lifetimes," Podsy replied.

"What if they didn't follow?"

"Then we'll use the Jemmin warships to hunt them down and destroy them. They've lost the support of their homeworld and probably half their warships. We've defanged the beast. I hope that makes them more likely to come to the negotiating table."

The young engineer looked relieved. "Can we go home now?"

"Soon. We're out of this fight. We have nothing left in the magazines besides Chief Rimmer's spinners, and I'm not sure we ever want to use those. There's just as much a chance we'd drill a hole in ourselves. No disrespect to the chief. We gave him nothing to work with, and he came up with something."

Podsy strolled across the bridge, hands clasped behind his back.

Jenkins grabbed him. "Nicely done, Skipper. Do you need anything else from us?"

Xi joined them. "I'm out, boss. More chow, and hopefully, it's edible this time. And then maybe a day or two of rack time. Tell me when it's time to show up and collect my back pay."

"Don't forget, we're rebels. Your pay stopped as soon as we ran from NA1."

"Easy come, easy go. Maybe we can set up a resort on J-Ville? There's a whole city that no one lives in," Xi suggested. "For sale cheap."

Commander Knighton entered the bridge in her flight suit. She stopped at the door, saw the crowd, and left.

"Tactical, you have the conn," Podsy announced.

"Go get 'em, tiger," Pete Wythe said softly. Podsy couldn't help but smile.

Leeroy Jenkins and Xi Bao joined Podsy for the short walk down the corridor. They stopped outside the door.

"Aren't you going to invite us in?" Xi asked, biting her lip.

"Well, um, no. I think I have company."

"Exchanging room keys already? You crazy kids." Xi waved with one hand and took Lee's arm with the other, guiding him away. "You know we have to go back, don't you? Alice is waiting. Everyone should have someone waiting for them."

"Do you?" Jenkins asked before slapping a hand over his mouth. "Never mind. Last we saw, Alice was in a world of hurt. Yes. I'd like to go back and find out what happened to her."

"You mean, *find her*. She can tell you what happened."

"And that. Sleep well, Xi."

The colonel walked away with his head bowed. Xi watched him go. She didn't have anyone to lose, but she understood the colonel's pain. If she made it back home, she would get a dog. And if she deployed again, for whatever reason, the dog would go with her.

33

END OF WAR

"All hands to battle stations," Podsy said sadly. After the board showed green, Admiral Corbyn was fed to all screens.

"It's time to go home. All the way home, to Terra and Sol. We will face whatever waits for us, but first, we'll transmit the report of what we have done, the names of those who died for our victories, and the message that the universe is a safer place because of the Metal Legion and those who followed them into the void."

Mencken's main screen showed a shiny second gate in the J-Ville Central system. It would lead directly to the second gate that the *GateKeeper* was deploying to New America 1 at that moment. As soon as it was active, it would come to life. *Mencken* and the Gatecrasher were lined up to go.

The gate shimmered and went dark, the stars behind it replaced by the nothing of the wormhole.

"Match rotation and accelerate," Podsy ordered. Colonel Jenkins and Major Bao stood at ease in their dress uniforms. Podsy wore his as well, along with the rest of the bridge crew. Commander Knighton was also on the bridge. They'd already decided they would not launch the Vipers to defend the ship if the Terrans attacked. Although the commander had transferred to TAC, the only dress uniform she had was her old Fleet uniform with her rank of lieutenant commander. Podsy smiled and took her hand. He wore a TAC uniform with his ground captain's rank. None of the bridge crew cared.

None of the ranks, awards, or decorations on the uniforms meant a thing. Actions were all that mattered. The crew could wear shorts and t-shirts, and everyone would give the others the respect they'd earned.

That being said, everyone wanted to look their best for the mug shots after being taken into custody as traitors. A subtle joke, but they didn't have any gas left in the tank.

Mencken crossed the event horizon. The screens went dark for a few nerve-wracking moments. When they came back, the *Mencken* started broadcasting the admiral's message across the full spectrum of channels.

"This is Commodore Xin Feng of the Terran Eighth Fleet," came the audio-only message.

Jenkins groaned, and his shoulders sagged.

"President Durgan welcomes you home. Proceed at best possible speed to orbit above the capitol."

"What?" Xi exclaimed. "Durgan is alive?"

"Helm, you heard the commodore. Best possible speed without making us get into our acceleration couches."

Commodore Feng appeared on a visual stream. "Durgan foiled an assassination attempt, reappeared on the night before the election, and won with overwhelming numbers. All charges against the TAC have been dropped. After reading the executive summary of your adventure, let me be the first to welcome you home."

"I'm getting a dog," Xi said matter-of-factly.

Jenkins hung his head. Podsy stepped up. "Commodore. Is there any word about Alice, our liaison from Sol?"

"She's in the capital city as ambassador from Sol to Terra. She's pining for some Metalhead, or so I've heard."

Xi looked at Lee. "You guys should get a dog, too."

The End

Metal Legion would not have been possible without you, those good people who are still reading. If you enjoyed this final installment of the Metal Legion, I hope you leave a review. Thanks for reading, but this isn't the end for books by Craig Martelle. It may be the last CH Gideon title, but I'm still me. I think I'll publish in my own name only from now in. Continue reading to the end, where I have a few extra author notes and the listing of my other books by series.

SUPERDREADNOUGHT 1

Have you read Superdreadnought 1, also from CH Gideon?

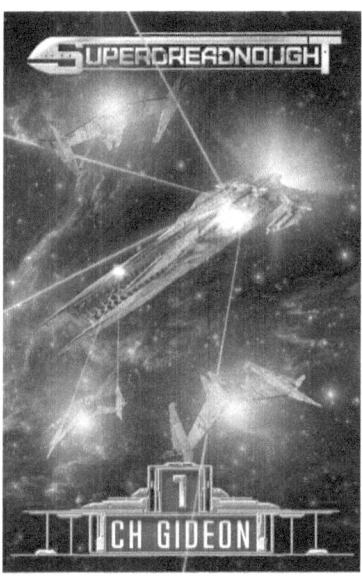

Alone and unafraid. Sometimes you prevent war by hunting down your enemies.

Integrated with a superdreadnought, the artificial intelligence known as Reynolds takes his ship across the universe in search of the elusive Kurtherians. He comes to a revelation. He's better in the company of living creatures.

He needs a crew. He needs information. And he needs to continue his search and destroy mission.

Needing a crew and getting a crew are two completely different things. Reynolds is out of his element as he tries to reach out and make friends. Through it all, he has his vessel, the superdreadnought, the most powerful warship in the galaxy.

Or so he believes.

Thank you so much for your continued support for the Metal Legion! We wouldn't be here and telling these stories if it weren't for you.

Commodore Sosunova shouted Lok'tar Ogar (means For the

Horde from World of Warcraft) as a rallying cry. I put this in there thanks to the suggestion by Joe Homer.

I wrote this book after heart surgery. I wasn't sure how it was going to turn out. The language might be a shade different from the previous Metal Legion volumes, but that's because I wrote this one in entirety. Caleb was unable to continue writing, and we have a contract for the audio, so it had to be written because you deserve closure. This is the last Metal Legion and the last book in this complex universe. Look for the books on audio from Dreamscape if you haven't already been listening to them.

This is my way of convalescing. A little storytelling to get the heart racing. Not necessarily a good thing, but we kept the pace nice and even. I had to add a little love, too. I served over twenty years in the Marine Corps and there was nothing like returning home to your loved ones after a long deployment. Or making new friends along the way. It's what makes any fight worthwhile. Marines don't just fight, they fight for something.

I hope you found their cause worthwhile. Damn the torpedoes, full speed ahead!

The weather in Fairbanks turned ridiculously cold. That kept me in the house even more while recovering from surgery. I wanted to go out, burn some calories but that wasn't happening when temps hovered between minus twenty and minus forty.

I also managed a quick trip to Las Vegas where I wrote the last fifteen thousand words of the story. It wasn't my home office, but it worked. I wrote ten of those fifteen on airplanes. The flights are at times that are conducive to my writing, as in, they aren't red-eyes. So I'm alert with my brain at full speed. Thank goodness. I needed to get this book done before this weekend as I'm attending the Alaska Comicon as one of the primary sponsors. I'll have most of my Metal Legion paperbacks on display, along with a wealth of other treasures. I'll take pictures and share them on Facebook. I'll try to get some shots with cosplayers.

But I just spent four days in Vegas and took a grand total of three pictures. I try to live in the moment and often forget to take a happy snap. Memories are better than pictures, always, but you can't see my memories and there are some great things to share, so I'll get more pictures. More than three, at least.

Closing this chapter. It was a great ride. Who doesn't love big honking mechs?

Until next time, peace, fellow humans.

BOOKS BY CRAIG MARTELLE

Craig Martelle's other books (listed by series)

Terry Henry Walton Chronicles (co-written with Michael Anderle) – a post-apocalyptic paranormal adventure

Gateway to the Universe (co-written with Justin Sloan & Michael Anderle) – this book transitions the characters from the Terry Henry Walton Chronicles to The Bad Company

The Bad Company (co-written with Michael Anderle) – a military science fiction space opera

Judge, Jury, & Executioner (also available in audio) – a space opera adventure legal thriller

Shadow Vanguard – a Tom Dublin series

Superdreadnought (co-written with Tim Marquitz)– an AI military space opera

Metal Legion (co-written with Caleb Wachter) (coming in audio) – a military space opera

The Free Trader – a young adult science fiction action adventure

Cygnus Space Opera (also available in audio) – A young adult space opera (set in the Free Trader universe)

Darklanding (co-written with Scott Moon) (also available in audio) – a space western

Mystically Engineered (co-written with Valerie Emerson) – Mystics, dragons, & spaceships

End Times Alaska (also available in audio) – a Permuted Press publication – a post-apocalyptic survivalist adventure

Nightwalker (a Frank Roderus series) with Craig Martelle – A post-apocalyptic western adventure

End Days (co-written with E.E. Isherwood) (coming in audio) – a post-apocalyptic adventure

Successful Indie Author – a non-fiction series to help self-published authors

Metamorphosis Alpha – stories from the world's first science fiction RPG

The Expanding Universe – science fiction anthologies

Monster Case Files (co-written with Kathryn Hearst) – A Warner twins mystery adventure

Rick Banik (also available in audio) – Spy & terrorism action adventure

Published exclusively by Craig Martelle, Inc

The Dragon's Call by Angelique Anderson & Craig A. Price, Jr. – an epic fantasy quest

For a complete list of Craig's books, stop by his website – https://craigmartelle.com